"I want you. I d

Her lower lip trembled
kind of woman who can do light and easy."

Gareth's joy was immediately obscured by suspicion. He was vulnerable when it came to Gracie. And a vulnerable man was a weak man.

"I have no business getting close to you...until I regain my memory. I have this gigantic void that scares me to death. I want to know but I'm afraid of what I'll find out."

"How is enjoying sex with me a threat?"

"You have everything, Gareth. Pretty intimidating for a woman who has nothing."

"You've held your own with me every step of the way. And I want to believe you came to my mountain without the intent to do wrong."

"You *want* to believe it, but you're not willing to make that last leap. And you can't bear the idea that I'll play you for a fool and cause you to betray your family."

For Gareth, the moment was lost. Gracie was right. Was she that good an actress?

Dear Reader,

What's better than a brooding alpha male with a touch of vulnerability? How about two families of them? I'm delighted to be introducing you to THE MEN OF WOLFF MOUNTAIN, my new series for Mills & Boon® Desire™. In this first book, you'll meet Gareth, the oldest Wolff son. But you'll catch a glimpse of some of his siblings and cousins, as well.

The extended Wolff family suffered a terrible tragedy many years ago. How each of the children dealt with that blow and moved on has defined who they are as adults. A man who learns to guard his heart from further hurt can be a challenge for a heroine who needs to know if he can fall in love.

The Wolff enclave includes a fabulous castlelike edifice on a remote mountaintop in the Blue Ridge Mountains. Acres of woods surround the wealthy family, providing the utmost privacy and seclusion.

I invite you to come with me as we meet this interesting clan one by one. They are strong, handsome and not easily won over. It will take special women to breach the walls and persuade these cynical men to take a chance on happiness.

Thanks for making the journey to Wolff Mountain.

Happy reading!

Janice Maynard

INTO HIS
PRIVATE DOMAIN

BY
JANICE MAYNARD

Published in Great Britain 2012
by Mills & Boon, an imprint of Harlequin (UK) Limited,
Eton House, 18-24 Paradise Road, Richmond, Surrey TW9 1SR

© Janice Maynard 2012

ISBN: 978 0 263 89210 9
ebook ISBN: 978 1 408 97778 1

51-0812

Janice Maynard came to writing early in life. When her short story *The Princess and the Robbers* won a red ribbon in her third-grade school arts fair, Janice was hooked. She holds a BA from Emory and Henry College and an MA from East Tennessee State University. In 2002 Janice left a fifteen-year career as an elementary teacher to pursue writing full-time. Her first love is creating sexy, character-driven, contemporary romance. She has written for Kensington and NAL, and now is so very happy to also be part of the Harlequin family —a lifelong dream, by the way!

Janice and her husband live in beautiful east Tennessee in the shadow of the Great Smoky Mountains. She loves to travel and enjoys using those experiences as settings for books.

Hearing from readers is one of the best perks of the job! Visit her website at janicemaynard.com or e-mail her at JESM13@aol.com. And of course, don't forget Facebook (http://www.facebook.com/JaniceMaynardReaderPage). Find her on Twitter at twitter.com/JaniceMaynard and visit all the men of Wolff mountain at wolffmountain.com.

For my siblings: Scotty, Kathy and Patti...
I love you all!

One

Gareth stepped out of the shower and stared at himself in the mirror. The frigid water had done little to dampen his restlessness. Still nude, he began to shave, his toes curling reflexively against the cool stone floor beneath his bare feet.

When his chin was smooth, he grimaced at his reflection. His thick, wavy black hair almost touched his shoulders. He had always worn it longer than current fashion dictated, but now it had grown so much it was getting in his way when he worked.

He reached into a drawer and drew out a thin leather cord. When he ruthlessly pulled back the damp shanks of hair, they made no more than a stubby ponytail, but at least it was out of his eyes.

A sudden loud knocking at the front door made him groan. Neither of his brothers nor his father would bother to announce their presence. And Uncle Vincent and his cousins sympathized with Gareth's grumpiness too much to bother him. Deliveries always went to the main house. So who in the hell could it be?

He'd had his fill of being the brunt of tabloid stories over the years. Later, the communal nature of military life had given him a deep appreciation for solitude. With the exception of family, Gareth had little desire to interact with humanity if he could avoid it.

When a man had money, everyone with access to him had an angle to play. And Gareth was tired of the game. He grabbed a pair of jeans and thrust them on sans underwear. The single item of clothing would have to suffice. He wasn't in a mood to get dressed just yet. Maybe his dishabille would scare away whoever was demonstrating the temerity to bother a surly Wolff.

He strode through the house, cursing suddenly as the leather thong broke and his hair tumbled free. What in the devil did it matter? Whoever stood on his porch was going to get short shrift from him.

He flung open the door and stared at the diminutive redhead with the wildly corkscrewing, chin-length curls. His stomach plummeted to his feet, but his libido perked up. He inhaled sharply and ground out a few terse words. "Who are you and what do you want?"

The woman caught her breath and backed up half a step. Gareth framed himself in the doorway, bracing his long-fingered hands against the lintel. His barefoot stance deliberately bore no semblance of welcome.

The woman dragged her gaze from Gareth's chest with an effort that might have flattered him in other circumstances. She looked him straight in the eye, speaking slowly but distinctly as if she feared he was a wild animal in need of soothing. "I need to talk to you."

Gareth glared at his undeniably sexy intruder. "You're trespassing."

She was fair-skinned, slender and had a spine so straight a man could use it as a plumb line…or maybe trace his tongue from one end of it to the other until the woman cried out in—

He sucked in a ragged breath and shoveled his hands through his hair, his heart thumping in his chest. He couldn't afford to let down his guard for a second. Even if fire-lit curls and delicate cheekbones were his own personal Achilles' heel. His sex swelled with no more than a whiff of her subtle perfume to give him encouragement.

How long had it been since he'd had a woman? Weeks? Months? He clamped down on the yearning that gripped his body like a fever. "What do you want?"

Her eyelids fluttered nervously over irises that were the clear blue of the sky above. Her small chin was stubborn, her posture defiant. As she wiped her damp brow with her hand, she smiled winningly. "Could we go inside and sit down for a few minutes? I'd love something to drink, and I promise not to take too much of your time."

Gareth tensed, and rage flashed through him with the ferocity of the furious torrents that arose in these mountains during thunderstorms and decimated the low ground far below. A user. Like all the rest.

He ignored her outstretched hand, crowding her, relying on his size and temper to bully her. "Get the hell off my land."

The slight woman stumbled backward, her eyes huge, her face paper-white.

He pressed his advantage. "Go on," he snarled. "You're not wanted here."

She opened her mouth, perhaps to protest, but in that instant, one foot slid off the edge of the porch into thin air. She tumbled backward in graceful slow motion, her hip and head striking his steps with audible, dreadful thuds before her small body settled into an ungainly heap on the unforgiving ground.

Mary, Mother of God. He was at her side in the slice of a second, his hands shaking and his brain mush. He was an animal, no better than the coyotes who roamed the hills at night.

She was unconscious. Gently he stroked his palms down her extremities, searching for breaks. Growing up with male brothers and cousins, he had seen his fair share of broken limbs over the years, but he might be sick if he found a sharp bone protruding through her silky, fine-textured skin.

He heaved a sigh of relief when he found none. But the purplish bruise blooming near her temple and the blood trickling down her leg galvanized him into action.

He scooped her negligible weight into his arms and carried her into the house and to his room, his private sanctuary. He deposited her carefully on the unmade bed and went for ice and medical supplies.

The fact that she was still unconscious began to worry him even more than the deep cut on her leg. He grabbed for the phone and dialed his brother Jacob. "I need you. It's an emergency. Bring your bag."

Ten minutes later, his sibling joined him at the bedside. Both men looked down at the woman who was dwarfed by the bed's size and masculinity. Her red-gold hair glowed against the somber gray and navy of the cashmere blankets.

Jacob examined her rapidly from head to toe, his mien serious, his medical training as automatic as it was thorough. "I'll have to stitch the leg. The knot on her head is bad, but not life-threatening. Pupils seem okay." He frowned. "Is she a friend of yours?"

Gareth snorted, his gaze never leaving her face. "Hardly. She was here for all of two minutes when she fell. Said she wanted to talk to me about something. I'm guessing she could be a reporter."

Jacob's brow creased. "What happened?"

Gareth leaned forward and brushed the hair from her face. "I tried to scare her off and it worked."

Jacob sighed. "That hermit act you put on is going to bite you in the ass someday. Maybe today. Damn it, Gareth. She could sue the family to hell and back. What were you thinking?"

Gareth winced when Jacob stuck a needle in the woman's leg, deadening the small area around her cut. She never moved.

"I wanted her gone," he muttered, irritated, brooding as he battled inward demons. He hoped this female was as innocent as the first pristine snows that fell in late autumn.

But she could just as easily be a viper in their midst.

Jacob finished the last stitch and covered the wound with a neat bandage. He checked his patient's pulse, gave her another shot in the arm for pain and frowned. "We'd better check for ID. Did she have anything with her?"

Gareth nodded. "It's on the chair over there." While Jacob rifled in the woman's long-handled tote, Gareth stared down at the intruder. She looked like an angel in his bed.

Jacob held up a billfold and sheet of paper, a troubled frown on his face. "Take a look at this photo. And her name is Gracie Darlington."

"Unless the ID is a fake."

"Don't jump to conclusions. You wear paranoia like a hair shirt, but this might be nothing sinister at all."

"And pigs could fly. Don't expect me to be gullible just because she's cute and cuddly. I've been down that road."

"Your ex-fiancée was overly ambitious. And cuddly wasn't in her vocabulary. It happened a long time ago, Gareth. Let it go."

"Not until I know the truth."

Jacob shook his head in disgust as he broke an ammonia caplet beneath Gracie's nose.

She moved restlessly and moaned as reality returned.

Gareth took her small hand in his. "Wake up."

She opened her eyes, blinking against the light. Her lips trembled. "There are two of you?" Her brow creased in confusion.

Jacob's chuckle was dry. "As long as you don't see four, I think we're okay. You probably have a concussion. You need to rest and drink plenty of fluids. I'll be nearby if you get worse. In the meantime, don't make any sudden moves."

His attempt at humor didn't register on Gracie's face. Her nose wrinkled in discomfort. "Where am I?"

Jacob patted her arm. "You're in my brother's bedroom. But don't worry. Gareth doesn't bite. And I'm Jacob, by the way." He glanced at Gareth. "Keep ice packs on her leg and the side of her head. I'm leaving a mild painkiller that should give her some relief as the shot wears off. I'll check back in the morning unless anything changes. Bring her to the clinic and I'll x-ray her to make sure I haven't missed something."

Gareth didn't bother to see his sibling out.

He sat down on the edge of the bed and winced inwardly when Gracie, damaged as she was, made the effort to move away from him. The simple exertion drained what little color she had left in her face, and she shuddered, leaned past him and emptied the contents of her stomach onto the floor.

Then she burst into tears.

Gareth was momentarily frozen with indecision. He'd never in his life felt such an urgent, desperate need to comfort anyone. Gracie might be a lying, cheating witch. And even worse, a woman who could cause untold trouble for his family.

But he was helpless in the face of her heartfelt misery. No one could fake such distress.

He went to the bathroom for a damp washcloth, handed it to her and proceeded to clean up the mess on the floor in silence. By the time he was done, her sobs had subsided into hiccupping, ragged sighs. Her eyes were closed, her body still as death. Probably because every little movement sent pain shooting through her skull.

Gareth had been thrown from a horse when he was twelve, and the resulting head injury had left him weak as a babe.

He knew how she felt.

He didn't risk sitting down again. Instead he went to the windows and opened both of them, letting the fresh spring breezes cleanse the room. He pulled the curtains together to dim the light, wanting to make her as comfortable as possible.

Afterward, he stood by the bed and stared down at her, wondering how a day that had begun so normally had rapidly skidded off track. He cleared his throat and gently pulled the bedding to cover her slight frame, tucking it to her chin. "We need to talk. But I'll wait until you've had a chance to rest. It's almost dinnertime. I'll fix something simple that won't aggravate your stomach, and I'll bring it in when it's ready." He hesitated, waiting for a reply.

Gracie tried to gather her composure, sure that any minute now she would get a handle on her scattered wits. This all seemed like such an odd dream. The glowering man tending to her with patent reluctance was huge.

His face was remarkable, wholly masculine, but striking rather than handsome. He had a crooked nose, a jaw carved from granite and cheekbones that drew attention to his deep-set, black-as-midnight eyes—eyes so dark, his pupils were indiscernible.

Equally dark hair framed his face aggressively, suggesting wildness and a lack of concern for polite conventions. The strands were thick and vibrant, and Gracie wanted to bury her hands in them and drag his head down to see if the tousled layers were as soft as they looked.

His broad, bare chest was golden-tan, its sleekly muscled beauty marred by three small scars over his rib cage. She frowned, her fingers itching to trace each imperfection. She refused to acknowledge that she was gob-smacked by his sheer magnificence. He left the room finally, closing the door behind him, and eventually, she dozed, rousing now and again to the awareness of pain and frightening loneliness. Shadows cast the room into near darkness by the time her host returned.

He carried a tray which he set on a wooden chest at the foot of the bed. She feared the sudden onslaught of bright light from the fixture overhead, but instead, he turned on a small antique table lamp with a cream silk shade. The diffused glow was bearable.

He stood beside her. "You need to sit up and eat something."

Questions clogged her throat. The smell wafting from a handmade earthenware container made her stomach growl loudly. He didn't comment, but helped her into a seated position. His manner was matter-of-fact. Everywhere his skin touched hers, she burned.

His expression was hard to read. When she was ready, he placed the tray across her lap. She sucked in a breath as she moved her leg beneath the covers. She hadn't even realized until that moment that she had injured more than her head.

He answered her unspoken question. "Jacob put six or seven stitches in your shin. You hit some sharp gravel when you…" His voice trailed off, and she saw discomfiture on his face. He pulled up a straight-back chair and watched her eat. If she hadn't been starving, his intense scrutiny would have made her nervous. But it must have been hours since she'd had any food, and she was hungry.

He, or someone, had prepared chicken soup, which required far more effort than simply opening a can. Large chunks of white meat mingled with carrots and celery in a fragrant broth. She tore off a hunk of the still-warm wheat bread and consumed it with unladylike haste.

Neither she nor her companion spoke a word until she had cleaned her plate, or in this case, her bowl.

Removing the trappings of the decidedly fine dinner, Gareth—was that his name?—sat back down and folded his arms across his chest.

He was dressed casually in old faded jeans and bare feet. But he had buttoned his top half into a rich burgundy poet's shirt made of an unusual handwoven fabric. Some men might have appeared ridiculous in such garb. On him, the shirt looked perfectly natural, enhancing his air of confidence and male superiority.

She struggled to conquer panic, postponing the moment of truth. "I need to go to the bathroom." It galled her that she required his help to stand up. Her injured leg threatened to crumple beneath her, but after a moment, she was able to shuffle to the facilities.

The bathroom was enormous, with a stone-lined, glass-enclosed shower. She caught a sudden mental picture of the mysterious male's huge body—nude—glistening beneath the spray of water and soap.

Her knees went weak. Despite her distress, she was stingingly aware of her host's blatant sexuality. She took care of necessities, washed up, and then made the mistake of glancing into the mirror. The image confused her. Good Lord. She was so white her freckles stood out in relief, and her hair was a bird's nest.

She rummaged without guilt through his drawers until she found a comb. But when she tried to run it through the worst of the tangles, she scraped against her injured skull and cried out at the pain.

He was beside her in an instant, not even making a pretense of knocking. "What is it?" he demanded, his gaze fierce. "Are you sick again?" In an instant he saw what she was trying to do. "Forget your hair," he muttered, scooping her into his arms and carrying her back to bed.

When she was settled, ice packs back in place, he handed her two pain pills and insisted she wash them down with milk. She felt like a child being soothed by a parent, but everything about her reaction to this strange man was entirely adult. He headed for the door. "Don't go," she blurted out, blushing as if he could see her inner turmoil. "I don't want to be alone."

He returned to the chair, swinging it around to straddle the seat, and folded his arms across the back. His expression was guarded. "You're perfectly safe," he said, his low voice rumbling across her shattered nerves with a tactile stroke. "Jacob says you'll recover rapidly."

Any bit of softness she sensed in him moments before had been replaced with almost palpable hostility and suspicion. What in the heck did he have to fear from her?

She picked at the edge of the blanket. "Does your brother live with you?"

He frowned. "Jacob has a house on the property. Why did you come here?"

Her tiny surge of energy abated rapidly, leaving her weak and sick again. She slid down in the bed and turned her head away from him toward the open window. "I don't know," she said dully.

"Look at me."

She did so reluctantly, feeling embarrassed and disoriented. He frowned. "You're not making sense."

She bit her lower lip, feeling the hot sting of tears behind her eyes. "You seem angry. Is it because of me?"

If she hadn't been watching him so closely, she might have missed it. For the flicker of a second, alarm flashed in his eyes and his white-knuckled fingers gripped the back of the chair. But as quickly as it appeared, the expression went away.

He shrugged. "Not at all. You'll be on your way soon enough."

He was lying. She knew it with a certainty that filled her chest with indignation. Her presence in his house was a problem. A big one. She threw back the covers, panicked and agitated. "I'll go."

His frown blackened as he straightened the bedding. "Don't be ridiculous. You're in no shape to go anywhere tonight. Stay in my bed. But tomorrow, you're history."

The pain in her head bested her. That and a heart-pounding

sense of foreboding. She clenched the edge of the sheet in her hands, fighting hysteria. "Please," she whispered.

"Please what?" Now his expression was confused.

"Please tell me who I am."

Two

Gareth narrowed his eyes, trying to disguise his shock. Here it was. The ploy. The act. Part one of whatever scam she was running. She couldn't be for real...*could she?*

He kept his expression bland. "Amnesia? Really? We're going to do the daytime soap opera thing?" He shrugged. "Okay. I'll play along. I'm Gareth. Your name is Gracie Darlington. You're from Savannah. Jacob and I checked your driver's license."

He watched her bottom lip quiver until she bit down on it... hard. She made an almost palpable effort to gather herself. A gifted actress could do as much. But the look of sheer terror in her painfully transparent gaze would be hard to manufacture. She sucked in a ragged breath. "How did I get here? Do I have a car outside?"

He shook his head. "As near as I can tell, you hiked up the mountain. Which is no small feat, by the way. There are no cleared trails at the bottom. Your arms and legs are all scratched."

"Do I have a cell phone?"

He cocked his head, studying her face. "I'll check." The only item she'd had with her when she arrived was the pink carry-all Jacob had examined earlier. Gareth rummaged in it without remorse and, in a zippered pocket, found a Droid phone. He turned it on and handed it to her, tossing the tote on the bed beside Gracie. Fortunately the battery seemed to be fully charged. Gracie pulled up the contact screen.

"Well, at least you remember how to do that." His thick sarcasm made her wince, but she didn't look at him. Instead she studied the list of names as if she were cramming for a test. Focused. Intent.

When she finally looked up, her beautiful eyes were shiny with tears. "None of these names mean a thing to me," she whispered. One drop spilled over. "I don't understand. Why can't I remember?"

He took the phone from her, squashing a reluctant sympathy. Gareth Wolff was no pushover. Not anymore. "You whacked your head when you fell off my porch. Jacob's a doctor. He says you'll be fine." But Jacob had left before the whole amnesia thing came to light. Damn it.

Gareth scrolled through the contact list himself, not sure what he was looking for. But then it hit him. There was an "I.C.E." entry. In case of emergency. Edward Darlington…and the word *Daddy*.

He hit the call key and waited. A man on the other end answered. Gareth spoke calmly. "This is Gareth Wolff. Your daughter took a fall and has been injured. She's been checked out by a doctor, and she's going to be fine. But she's suffering a temporary memory loss. It would be helpful if you could reassure her. I'll put her on the line."

Without waiting for an answer, Gareth handed the phone to Gracie.

She eased up into a half-sitting position, resting her back against the headboard. "Hello?"

Gareth sat down beside her, close enough to hear that the

voice on the other end was amused. Close enough to catch snatches of conversation.

"Hot damn, my little Gracie. I didn't think you had it in you. Faking an accident on Wolff property? Pretending to have amnesia? Good Lord, you've got him right where we want him. The whole family will be terrified we'll sue. Phenomenal idea. Nothing like going after what you want whole hog. Brilliant, my girl. Sheer brilliance."

Gracie interrupted the man's euphoria. "Father…I don't feel well at all. Can you please come pick me up and take me home?"

Darlington chortled. "He's standing in the room with you, isn't he? And you've got to play this out. Splendid. I'll do my part. Sorry, Gracie. I'm headed for Europe in half an hour. Won't be back for a week. And the house is a wreck. I told the contractor to go ahead with the remodel since we were both planning to be out of town. You'd have to stay in a hotel if you came back."

"This isn't funny," she muttered. "I'm serious. I can't stay here. They don't want me. I'm a stranger."

"Dredge up their guilt," he insisted. "They owe it to you to be hospitable. Flirt with Gareth a little. Play on his sympathies. Damsel in distress and all that. Get him to agree to our proposal. We'll talk next week. I've gotta run."

"No, wait," she said desperately. "At least tell me if I have a husband or a boyfriend. Anyone who's missing me."

Her father's cackle of a laugh was so loud she had to hold the phone away from her ear. "Of course not. Lay it on thick. I'm loving this. Wish I could see his face. So long now."

The line went dead. Gracie stared down at the phone, her composure in shreds. What kind of father did she have? Who could be so callous? So blasé about her injuries? Embarrassment and humiliation washed over her in waves, adding to her feeling of abandonment.

She laid the phone aside and managed a weak grimace. "How much of that did you hear?"

Gareth stood up and crossed to the window, his back to her. "Enough," he said, disgusted with himself and with her. If he had any sense, he would boot her off the property ASAP.

Gracie's voice wobbled. "He can't come pick me up right now, because he's on his way out of the country for a week. But if you'll make travel arrangements for me, I'm sure he'll reimburse you."

Gareth Wolff turned to stare at her with a mixture of suspicion and pity. "He thinks you're faking amnesia."

Her cheeks flamed. "The whole conversation was confusing. I came to see you for a reason. But I don't know what that is. Though he seems to."

"And you really don't have a clue?"

She shook her head. "I'm sorry. I'll leave as soon as I can."

"You're not going anywhere at the moment." Gareth's jaw was clenched. "If you really do have memory loss, then I have to let Jacob know. The Wolff family doesn't make a habit of throwing the injured out on the street. And believe me, Gracie, we're not going to give you or your unbelievably unconcerned father any ammunition for a lawsuit."

"We're not going to sue you," she said quietly. Depression depleted her last reserve of spunk. "I don't believe in frivolous lawsuits."

"How do you know?" he shot back. "Maybe the woman you can't remember would do just that."

Gracie slid back down into the bed, her skull filled with pounding hammers. "Please leave me alone."

Gareth shook his head, his demeanor more drill sergeant than nurse. "Sorry, Gracie." His tone didn't sound sorry at all. "If we're playing the amnesia game, I have no choice but to let Jacob know. I'll drive you over there."

The thought of standing up was dreadful. "Can't he come back here? It's not that late, is it?"

"It's not a question of being late. Jacob has a fully outfitted clinic at his place. He'll be able to scan your head and x-ray your leg."

"I'm sure that's not necessary. All I want to do is rest. Tomorrow you can get rid of me."

Gareth strode to the door. "You're in Wolff territory now. And in no position to call the shots." He paused and glanced back at her, his expression grim. "I'll grab my keys and shoes. Don't move."

Gracie closed her eyes, breathing deeply, half convinced she was in the midst of a dark and disturbing nightmare. Surely she would wake up soon, and all of this would be a surreal fantasy. *Gareth Wolff.* She whispered the name aloud, searching for meaning. Why had she come to see him? What did her father want? And how did she get from Georgia to Virginia? Did she have luggage somewhere? A hotel room? A vehicle? Maybe even a laptop? Her tote held nothing but the phone, snacks and some tissues.

She froze, her brow furrowed in discomfort. How could she know what a laptop was and not even remember her own name?

Gareth strode back into the room, his feet shod in worn leather boots. Everything about the room she inhabited made Gracie feel at a disadvantage—the expensive bedding, the masculine decor, the large scale furniture…the total lack of anything familiar.

But something about those scarred boots eased the constriction in her chest. They struck her as normal. Human.

Gareth approached the bed, his face closed. "I've spoken to Jacob. He's expecting us. Let's go."

Gracie screeched in shock when he gathered her up, blankets and all, in his strong arms.

He froze. "Did I hurt you? Sorry." The gruff apology was instantaneous.

She shook her head, trembling as they traversed a wide hallway. "You startled me. That's all." Not for anything would she admit that being in his arms was exciting and comforting at the same time. His scent and the beat of his heart beneath her cheek aroused her and gave her the illusory sensation of security.

The earlier fleeting impressions she'd formed of wealth and privilege increased tenfold as they passed through the house. Gleaming hardwood floors. Western-themed rugs. Intricate chandeliers of elk horn shedding warm yellow light.

But Gareth walked too quickly for her to carry out any deeper inspection. In minutes they were out the front door and stepping into the scented cool of a late spring evening.

And how did she know it was spring? The little blips of instinctual information that popped into her head gave hope that her memories were simply tucked away in hiding. Not permanently gone…merely obscured by her injury.

Gareth carried her carefully, but impersonally. It wasn't his fault if her hormones and heartbeat went haywire. He smelled of wood smoke and shampoo, a pleasing mélange of masculine odors. Despite his flashes of animosity, she felt safe in his embrace. He might not want her in his home, but he posed no threat to her well-being…at least not physically. The unseen dangers might prove to be more hazardous.

She *liked* being held by Gareth Wolff. What did that say about her?

Of course, her instinctive response could be attributed to something akin to Stockholm syndrome—the bonding between kidnapper and victim. Not that Gareth had done anything wrong. Quite the contrary. But at the moment, he was the only reality in her spinning world. He and his brother Jacob.

Most likely, her affinity for the surly Wolff brother was nothing more than an atavistic urge to seek protection from the unknown.

Gareth's Jeep was parked outside a large garage at the rear of the house. The building, roomy enough to house a fleet of vehicles, had been designed to blend into the landscape, much like the house. A cedar shake roof and rustic, carefully hewn logs seemed to match the edge in her host's personality. Gareth's home was enormous and clearly expensive, but it suited his gruff demeanor.

Once he had tucked her into the passenger seat, he loped around the side of the vehicle and slid behind the wheel. Thick fog blanketed their surroundings. Gracie peered into the darkness, shivering slightly, not from the temperature, but from the feeling of being so isolated. She'd seen horror movies that rolled the opening sequence in a similarly creepy fashion.

She clenched her fist in the blanket and pulled it closer to her chest. "Where are we?"

Gareth shot her a quick glance. "Wolff Mountain."

She cleared her throat. "I hope that's not as sinister as it sounds."

His quick snort of laughter ended as quickly as it began. She had a hunch he didn't want to show any signs of softening toward her.

He wrenched the wheel to avoid a tiny rabbit that scampered in front of them. "This is my home. I grew up here with my two brothers and three cousins. I'm sure all of this will come back to you," he snarled. "My family has no secrets."

She wanted to ask for more details, more explanations, anything to fill in the blanks. But her innocent question had clearly hit a nerve. She lapsed into silence, using her free hand to grip the door of the vehicle as Gareth sent them hurtling around the side of the mountain.

The trip was mercifully brief. Without warning, another house loomed out of the eerie fog. This one was more modern than Gareth's, all steel and glass. Almost antiseptic in design. Though in all fairness she wasn't getting a first look at it in the best of situations.

Jacob met them at the door and ushered them inside, his eyes sharp with concern as Gareth set her on her feet. "Any change?"

The terse question was aimed more at Gareth than Gracie, so she kept her silence.

Gareth tossed his keys onto a black lacquer credenza. "She doesn't remember details of her life. But functional knowledge appears to be unaffected. She knows how to use her phone, but the names are a mystery…or so she says."

Gracie flushed. She was embarrassed and exhausted. The last thing she needed was Gareth's mockery.

Jacob waved a hand toward a living room that looked like something out of a designer's catalog. "Make yourself comfortable, bro. The game's on channel fifty-two. Beer's in the fridge."

Gareth frowned. "I should come with you."

Jacob put a hand on his shoulder. "Not appropriate, Gareth. Trust me. She's in good hands."

He turned to Gracie, his smile gentle. "Let's get you checked out, little lady. I promise not to torture you too badly."

Unlike Gareth, Jacob trusted her to walk on her own. She abandoned her cocoon of blankets in the foyer and followed him down a hallway to the back of the house. Everything was in black and white—walls, flooring, artwork… A highly sophisticated color scheme, but oddly cold and sterile.

When she stepped through a door into the clinic proper, all became clear. Jacob Wolff had designed his house to mirror his professional domain.

Gracie's curiosity as she surveyed the state-of-the-art facility had nothing to do with her amnesia. She had never seen such equipment and facilities outside of a hospital. Even with her memory loss, she was sure of that.

As Jacob positioned the CT scanner, she cocked her head. "I may not remember much, but isn't this setup a little unusual?"

His quick glance reminded her of Gareth. "I have a number of high profile patients who want to be able to get medical attention away from the eyes of the paparazzi."

She gaped. "Like movie stars?"

He shrugged, adjusting a dial. "Politicians, movie stars… Fortune 500 CEOs."

Something must have shown on her face, because his expression grew fierce. "Having wealth doesn't make a person's right to privacy any less important. I'm fortunate enough to have the means to give them anonymity and quality medical care."

She held up her hands. "I didn't say a word."

"You were thinking it." He motioned to the machine. "Have a seat. There's nothing to be afraid of. You won't be closed in."

She sat gingerly on the narrow bench and tensed as he slid rubber wedges on either side of her head, immobilizing her skull in a semicircle of metal. The camera thingy rotated around her upper body in several quick passes, and it was all over.

Jacob waved her into a chair. "Now I'll show you the inside of your head. Hopefully we won't see anything too alarming."

She sat down gingerly. "As long as you find a brain…that's all I ask."

He chuckled, but didn't speak as he brought up the 3-D images on the screen. Gracie waited, her heart pumping madly. Jacob examined the results with the occasional unintelligible murmur.

Gracie lost patience. "Well?"

He pushed back his chair and turned to face her. "I don't see anything alarming…no fractures…nothing to require further medical attention. You have swelling, of course, as a result of the blow to your head, but even that is in the normal range."

She bit her lip, disappointment roiling in her stomach. If there was nothing to substantiate her amnesia, Gareth would think, more than ever, that she was liar.

Jacob seemed to read her thoughts. "Absence of fractures doesn't discount your current situation. All jokes aside, temporary amnesia is more common than you might think. And we have every reason to think it will resolve itself naturally."

"But when?" she cried, springing to her feet. "How can I go to sleep tonight and not know who the hell I am?"

Jacob leaned back and linked his hands behind his head. "You do know who you are," he said gently. "You're Gracie Darlington. It may take a little while for your brain to accept that as fact. But it will happen. I promise."

Gracie stewed inwardly as he finished his exam. As expected, the X-ray of her leg showed no sign of any damage other than the bad cut.

After a quick check of temp, blood pressure and a few other markers, Jacob patted her shoulder. "You'll live," he teased.

They walked back through the house and found Gareth sprawled on an ivory leather sofa. The thick, onyx carpet underfoot was a sea of inky, lush luxury.

Gareth bounded to his feet. "Sit here," he commanded Gracie. "I want to talk to my brother."

Despite the fact that they lowered their voices, Gracie heard every word.

Gareth grilled her doctor. "Well…could you tell if the amnesia is for real?"

Jacob muttered a curse. "This isn't an exact science, Gareth. All her symptoms fit the profile. But I can't give you any hard-and-fast answers. My medical opinion is yes, she's very likely telling us the truth. That's the good news. The bad news is that amnesia is a tricky bastard. It might be tomorrow morning or next week before she gets it all back." He paused and grimaced. "It could be several months. We have no way of knowing."

"Bloody hell."

Gareth's heartfelt disgust lodged like a thorn in Gracie's heart.

Jacob walked back into the living room, giving Gracie a gentle smile. "Take her home and put her to bed," he said to his brother. "Things always look better in the morning."

Three

Put her to bed. Gareth tensed inwardly as images teased his brain. Him. Gracie. Tumbling with abandon between the sheets on his comfortable king-size mattress. He'd never brought a woman into his bedroom on Wolff Mountain. Whenever his physical needs overrode his phenomenal control, he sought out one of a handful of women who were as much loners as he was. Mature women who weren't interested in relationships.

But the last such encounter had been ages ago. And the Wolff was hungry. Put a red hood on Gracie, and she'd be in big trouble. Or maybe she was in trouble already. Taking advantage of a damsel in distress wasn't his style, but then again, he had never felt such a visceral and instantaneous response to a woman.

He wanted her desperately, and they had only met. At some anonymous bar in a big city he could have invited her back to his room. But this was Wolff Mountain, and different rules applied. Though he was a reluctant host, he had no business lusting after her.

She stood up, her expression half defiance, half vulnerability. "Couldn't I stay here, Jacob? You know…in case anything happens."

"No way." Gareth blurted it out, uncensored.

Jacob and Gracie stared at him.

He shrugged, refusing to admit he had a proprietary interest in the redhead. "Jacob's a soft touch." He directed his remarks to Gracie. "I want you where I can keep an eye on you."

Jacob frowned at his brother. "Gareth's bark is worse than his bite, Gracie. He'll take good care of you. But don't worry. I'll be around in the morning to see how you're doing." He put an arm around her shoulders and squeezed. "Try not to worry. Everything will be fine. I'd stake my license on it."

Gareth ushered Gracie back out to the Jeep, this time letting her walk on her own. He'd liked holding her too damn much. It was best to keep his distance.

The short ride back was silent. Temperatures had dropped, and out of the corner of his eye, he saw Gracie pull the blankets to her chin. When they arrived at the house, he realized that he was actually going to have to be hospitable. And since she swayed on her feet from exhaustion, he shouldn't waste any time.

He motioned for her to follow him. At the insistence of his architect brother Kieran, Gareth had agreed to a five-bedroom home. The square footage had seemed like a useless expenditure during construction…and now, four of the bedrooms sat unoccupied. But at least for tonight, Gracie would have a place to lay her head.

He showed her the suite that would be hers…for a *very* short time, he promised himself. Too long, and his iron control might snap. "The bathroom is through that door." Even now his hands trembled with the need to touch her.

He eyed her clothing. She was still wearing the simple cotton blouse and jeans she'd had on when she arrived. "I'll find something for you to sleep in. Tomorrow we'll work on getting you some clothes."

When he returned two minutes later with one of his old T-shirts, Gracie was still in the same spot, her expression stark, haunted. Unwillingly his heart contracted. If she was telling the truth about her amnesia, she must be scared as hell. But sweet and courageous, and so damned appealing in her determination not to break down. The reluctant admiration he felt had to be squashed.

When he brushed her arm, she jumped, as if she had been a million miles away. He offered the substitute sleepwear. "Sorry I can't do better. You'll find toiletries in the drawers and on the counter. I let my cousin do the decorating, and she promised me that no bathroom was complete without all sorts of smelly soaps and doodads. Help yourself."

Gracie took the shirt and held it, white-knuckled. "Will you be in your bedroom?"

God help him. He knew she meant nothing by her artless question, but it shook him. "Yeah. As soon as I lock up and turn out the lights." He paused, feeling uncustomarily conflicted, since he rarely second-guessed himself. "Remember...I'm just around the corner. Maybe if you leave a light on, things won't seem so strange."

She nodded her head slowly. "Okay."

Something about her posture was heartbreaking. She was doing nothing to deliberately manipulate his sympathies, but the bravery in her narrow shoulders set so straight and the uplifted tilt of her chin touched him in a way he hadn't thought possible.

He hardened his heart. "Good night, Gracie."

She heard the door shut quietly behind him and felt tears burn her eyes. It took great effort, but she held them at bay by virtue of biting down on her bottom lip and swallowing hard.

She refused to let Gareth see her exhibit weakness. He was a hard, suspicious man, despite his physical appeal.

Even so, she wanted him. And the wanting scared her. She felt like the heroine of a dark, Gothic novel, left all alone with the brooding lord of a sprawling, mysterious house.

A glance at the clock sent her stumbling into the bathroom. No wonder she was so wiped out. It was late. Everything would look better in the morning. Darkness invariably bred bogeymen and unseen monsters. Her lack of memory fueled the fires of apprehension.

Gareth had told the truth about the facilities and accoutrements. The floor was inlaid with cream-colored marble veined in gold. An enormous mirror ran the entire length of one wall, showing Gracie reflection after reflection of a strange woman with unkempt hair and no makeup.

Jacob had covered her stitches with a waterproof bandage. Doggedly she stripped off her clothing and climbed into the enormous polished granite enclosure that boasted three showerheads and a steam valve. The hot water pelted her back and rained over her arms and legs. She bowed her head, braced her hands against the wall and cried.

When the tears finally ran out, she picked up a fluffy sponge and squirted it with herbal soap from a fancy bottle inscribed in French. The aroma was heavenly.

Twenty minutes later she forced herself to get out and dry off. Gareth's T-shirt hung to her knees, half exposing one of her shoulders. The woman in the mirror appeared waifish and very much alone.

She took a few minutes to wash out her undies and hang them on a brass towel rod to dry before returning to the bedroom. In her absence, Gareth had left several items on the bedside table. A pair of thick woolen socks, a tumbler of water with two pain pills and a copy of *Newsweek*. She wasn't sure if the latter was for entertainment or edification.

She put on the socks, and for the first time all day, felt a glimmer of humor at how ridiculous she looked. Even with no memory, she knew that a man like Gareth had his pick of women. He might be surly and prickly, but he exuded a potent masculinity that any female from eighteen to eighty would have to be blind not to notice.

Though her accommodations were worthy of the finest resort, sleep didn't come easily. She tossed and turned, even when the medication dulled the ache in her leg and her head. Every time she closed her eyes, she remembered waking up in Gareth's bed and seeing two strange men staring down at her with varying degrees of suspicion.

Why had she come to Wolff Mountain? What did she hope to accomplish? Was her father involved in something dishonest? The questions tumbled in her brain faster and faster, erasing any hope of slumber.

Finally, when the crystal clock on the bedside table read two-thirty, Gracie climbed out of bed and tiptoed to the door. It wouldn't hurt to explore the house. She'd seen very little of it so far. Maybe there was something out there that would jog her memory.

And besides, she was hungry. With her heart beating like a runaway train, she eased open the door to the hall.

Gareth knew the moment she left her room. He'd always been a light sleeper, at least as an adult, and even the faint whisper of Gracie's soft footsteps was enough to wake him. His frequent insomnia was the penance he paid for defying his father's wishes and enlisting in the military. A five-year stint in the army had taught Gareth that deep sleep could be fatal. It served him right for giving his father such grief.

Gareth crept down the hallway, following the muffled trail of sounds. He found his houseguest in the kitchen. At first, her mission was prosaic. She poured a glass of milk and consumed it with a chunk of cheddar cheese and a slice of bread.

When she was finished, she carefully washed her glass and saucer and placed them back in the cabinet. Gareth grinned. Did she think she was erasing any record of her nocturnal wanderings?

His amusement faded when she approached the laptop on the built-in desk. All important files were password protected, but a knowledgeable hacker could cause mischief even still. Gracie sat in the swivel chair, tucked her feet on the rungs and began to hit keys with a sure touch.

He worked his way around the adjoining room until he was able to approach her from behind. Her head was bent. She was focused intently on the computer screen.

Gareth's temper surged. He stepped into the room, girded for battle. "What in the hell do you think you're doing?" he demanded.

Her gasp was audible. She whirled to face him, guilt etched on her face. "I couldn't sleep."

"So you decided to poke your nose into my business…is that it?" He glanced down at the laptop and his jaw dropped. Hell. He hated being wrong.

She shrugged, her expression wry. "Apparently I remember how to play Solitaire."

"So I see."

She cocked her head and frowned. "Why would I be poking into your business? Do you think that's the kind of woman I am?"

He refused to apologize for well-founded suspicion. "I don't *know* what kind of woman you are. Therein lies the problem."

She shut down the game and stood up. "I'll go back to my room," she said, every syllable drenched in offended dignity.

"Oh, for Pete's sake," he muttered. "Do whatever you want." She wore his T-shirt like a centerfold model striking a pose, but he was a hundred percent certain her seductive invitation was unintentional.

As he turned to leave, running from temptation if the truth were told, she stopped him with a beseeching look. "Please tell me about your family…this place. Maybe something you say will trigger a memory."

"That's a convenient excuse." He still wasn't convinced that Gracie wasn't a reporter looking for a story. His family had suffered terribly at the hands of the press, the Wolff tragedy and grief offered up for public consumption without remorse. Never again.

Dark smudges beneath her eyes emphasized her pallor. "Please," she said quietly. "Anything. Tell me anything. I've combed my cell phone and I did a Google search on myself and my father. But I didn't find out much except that we own a gallery."

In spite of himself, compassion surfaced. "You're on top of a mountain in the Blue Ridge. My family moved here in the eighties. My uncle and my father live in a huge house at the very peak. My siblings and cousins and I are in varying stages of building homes here as well."

She frowned. "You all live here together? Like a commune?"

"Not a commune," he grated. "It's over a thousand acres. We're hardly in each other's pockets."

"So, more like the Kennedys at Hyannis Port."

"I suppose. But none of us are in politics, thank God."

"You're wealthy."

He narrowed his eyes. "You could say that." It was damned hard to carry on a conversation when he kept getting distracted by the way her nipples pressed against the soft knit fabric. All he had to do was reach for her arm and pull her against him. The knowledge dried his mouth. He didn't think she would stop him. Though not any more vain than the next man, he had seen interest in her unguarded gaze earlier in the day.

But he was an honorable man. Damn it.

She frowned. "If I hiked through the woods, how did I know which house was yours?"

"You had an aerial photograph in your bag." He shrugged. "My place is circled in black marker."

Now, every last shred of color leached from her face. "So all we know for sure is that I was trespassing and that I wanted something from you."

"That's it in a nutshell. And based on the conversation you had with your father, he knows why you came and thinks you're faking amnesia to get what you want."

Her lips twisted. "Maybe I don't want to remember. It sounds like I'm not a very nice person." She paused. "Why didn't I simply drive up the road?"

"It's private. You wouldn't have gotten past the guard gate without an appointment."

"Hence my ill-advised hike."

"Apparently."

"I'm sorry," she said simply.

"For what?"

"For whatever I was going to do. I wish I could remember."

"When you came to my door, you said you needed to talk to me about something."

"And then what happened?"

He felt his neck redden. "I may have been a trifle unwelcoming."

Her mouth fell open, and a flicker of emotion akin to fear flashed in her eyes. "You *pushed* me off your porch?"

"Oh, for God's sake. No. Of course not. All I did was tell you to leave. Forcefully. You backed away from me, and…"

"I fell."

"Yes." He was uncomfortably aware that the family lawyer would be hyperventilating by now if he were here to track the conversation. Gareth had pretty much incriminated himself.

He rubbed a hand over the back of his neck. "It was an accident. And you were breaking the law. So don't go getting any ideas about draining us dry. We have a legal team that would chew you to pieces."

"Why do you need a legal team?"

This conversation had gone on long enough. "Go to bed, Gracie. Get some sleep. Maybe when you wake up, all will be clear."

She hesitated, looking at him with need that went beyond simple survival. He wondered if she understood the feminine invitation she was unwittingly telegraphing. Deliberate or not, every bit of testosterone in him responded with a *hell, yeah*.

Groaning inwardly, he turned his back on her and left the room.

When Gracie woke up, the sun was high in the sky, the clock said it was noon and nothing was any clearer than it had been the night before. She leaped from the bed and then staggered when the pounding in her skull threatened to send her to her knees.

A hand to the wall and several long breaths finally steadied her. This time, the woman in mirror looked more familiar. She brushed her teeth, put on her clean undies and her not-so-clean clothes and went in search of food. The house was quiet, too quiet. In the kitchen she found a note scrawled in bold masculine handwriting. *Plenty of food in the fridge. Help yourself. I'm working. Will check on you midafternoon.*

She crumpled the paper and tossed it in the trash. Working? What did that mean? A sandwich and a banana later, the front doorbell rang. Gracie waited a few seconds to see if Gareth would appear. But when the bell rang a second time, she walked quickly toward the front of the house, grimacing when she saw her reflection in a mirror. She was hardly fit for company.

The woman who stood on the porch was a surprise. She gave

Gracie a blinding smile and muscled her way through the door, forcing a befuddled Gracie to step back.

"I'm Annalise," she said, holding out a hand after she dropped an armload of packages on the nearest chair. "Jacob had your height and weight, so we guessed at sizes. I've got all the basics, I hope. Enough to see you through at least a week. After that, we'll see."

"Well, I…"

Annalise was already pulling things out of packages. "My favorite boutique in Charlottesville couriered over everything I asked for. The manager there is really sweet."

Gracie quivered with alarm. She had no clue about her own finances. What if she couldn't afford all this? And heaven knew how much the delivery charges were. "Um, Annalise…" she said as she tried to slow down the mini tornado. "I really only need one change of clothing. I do appreciate all the trouble you've gone to, but I can't stay long. And until I begin to remember things, I don't know if I can repay you."

Annalise sat cross-legged on the rug and began removing price tags. "Don't be silly," she said happily. "Gareth is paying for all of this. It's the least he can do after you hurt yourself so badly."

An arrested look came over her face and she hopped back to her feet. "Speaking of which, Jacob wanted me to take a look at your head. He's only a phone call away if we need him."

Before Gracie could move or protest, Annalise was sifting through Gracie's curls, her fingers delicate as they parted the hair and brushed over the knot near her temple.

"Hmm," she said. "The swelling's not terrible, but you've got a nasty bruise." She fluffed Gracie's curls back into place and returned to her task of sorting through the new clothes. "That small bag over there has antibiotic ointment and more water-proof bandages. Jacob says you can take off the current dressing on your leg after you shower today and replace it."

"Annalise?"

She looked up with a winsome smile. "What?"

"Who are you?"

The beautiful woman with the waterfall of raven-black hair smacked her head and groaned. "Shoot. I'm always getting ahead of myself. I'm Gareth and Jacob's cousin, Annalise Wolff. The baby of the crew. Which is no picnic, let me tell you. Especially since I'm the only girl."

"You live here, too?"

"Well, not yet. But sometime soon. I'm only here for a quick visit with my dad and Uncle Vic. It was a good thing, though. Can you imagine a man trying to supply a woman with a new wardrobe? Lord knows what they would have chosen."

Gracie bent and picked up an item that still had a price tag attached. "A swimsuit? Really? Not entirely necessary, is it?"

The tall slender woman's eyes widened. "Gareth hasn't showed you yet?"

"Showed me what?"

"The indoor pool."

"Um, no. I haven't exactly been offered the guided tour. He doesn't want me here, you know."

"But you *are* here," Annalise said with a grin. "And it's about time someone bearded the grizzly old bear in his den. Gareth is a wonderful man, but he's let the past trip him up. His hermit ways aren't healthy."

"What about the past?"

Suddenly the other woman looked abashed. "It's not my place to say. I babble too much. Gareth can tell you what he wants you to know. C'mon," she said brightly. "Let's go to your room and try on all this booty."

Gracie participated more out of curiosity than from any urgent desire to play dress-up. Annalise fascinated her. She could be a runway model or a movie star. Gracie envied her the boundless confidence that radiated from her in almost physical waves.

What was Gracie's personality like? Here on the mountain, she felt wary, anxious and confused. But amnesia would probably have that effect on anyone. Maybe in *real* life Gracie was as self-possessed as Annalise. On the other hand, Gracie had a hunch that being wealthy and beautiful was the key. For someone like Annalise, the world was ready for the taking.

Gracie drew the line at modeling the wildly lavish lingerie. Petal-soft silk, handmade lace, confections of mauve, blush-pink and palest cream. It was the stuff of fantasy. But apparently Gracie was fairly modest when it came to exposing herself, even to another female.

At long last, Annalise glanced at her watch and screeched. "Lord have mercy. I'm going to miss my flight if I don't get crackin'. Daddy always wants me to use the private jet, but it's so damn pretentious. And do you have any idea how hard it is for a man to see the real you when he finds out about the seven-figure portfolio?"

"I can only imagine." Gracie's tone was wry. Annalise's artless comments weren't boastful. Her stream of consciousness conversation wasn't as practiced as that.

At the front door, Gracie put a hand on her benefactor's slim arm. "Thank you," she said simply. "I won't see you again, but I'm very grateful."

Annalise grabbed her in an enthusiastic embrace and kissed her cheek. "Never say never. Remember…don't let Gareth bully you. And as for the shopping spree…the pleasure was all mine."

Four

With Annalise gone, the oppressive quiet settled over the house again. Gracie wanted to explore, but the possibility of being caught snooping deterred her. Instead she escaped outdoors, relishing the spring sunshine. It was a perfect day…the sky robin's-egg-blue dotted with cotton-ball clouds, the sun warm but mild.

Her fingers itched for a paintbrush, wanting to capture the simplicity and lushness of burgeoning life. She stopped short, caught up in a memory…

I'm competent, Daddy, technically proficient, but I don't think I have that spark to take me to the next level. That's why I want so badly to be the gallery manager. I would be good at it, you know I would…

The snippet of conversation faded, and she clenched her fists in frustration. So she was an artist? But maybe not a very good one…and if that was true, what was the connection with her trip to Wolff Mountain?

Nothing. Nothing else materialized, no matter how hard she tried. And without something more concrete to go on, Gareth wasn't likely to be appeased by her efforts.

With a hiccupped breath, she fought back a sob. Patience. She would have patience if it killed her. She walked down the driveway, away from the copse of trees sheltering the house, and glanced upward. What she saw drew a gasp of admiration. The house at the top of the mountain defied description. It was part palace, part fortress, an amalgam of Cinderella's castle and George Vanderbilt's sprawling mansion in Asheville, North Carolina.

She stopped dead, this time seeing a vision of herself during a visit to the Biltmore House. The clarity of the memory sent a surge of hope rushing through her veins. She'd been wearing a red sundress. And she was laughing, happy. Someone stood beside her. Who was it?

Her head ached from the effort to concentrate. Moments later, the scene in her brain shimmered and faded. Tears of frustration wet her cheeks. The knowledge was so close, so damn close.

She took a deep breath and turned around to stare at Gareth's house. Yesterday she had stood on that porch. Had conversed with him. Why?

What had happened right before she fell? Was her mission in coming here sinister or innocent or somewhere in between?

No answers came her way. As hard as she tried, the earliest memory she was able to conjure up was waking in Gareth's bed. Now, in the light of day, feeling a hundred times better than she had twenty-four hours before, the knowledge that Gareth had cared for her in the moments after her accident gave her an odd feeling in the pit of her stomach.

She was sexually attracted to him. That much was clear. Even though she knew his Good Samaritan efforts were performed grudgingly. Despite his attitude, she had to be grateful that he hadn't called the police to cart her off the property.

She had trespassed. Knowingly. And in doing so, had paid a hefty price. A brain that was tabula rasa...the clean slate. Even if Gareth found her at all appealing, he would never act on that connection. Because she had broken the rules of polite society. She had invaded his privacy.

With a sigh, she headed back toward the house. Gareth was working. Where? Why? The man was a freaking millionaire. Joint heir to what appeared to be a sizable fortune. By all rights, he should be cruising on the Riviera. Playing the roulette wheel in Monte Carlo.

The image of taciturn Gareth Wolff as a jet-set playboy didn't quite come into focus. Some rich men enjoyed spreading their wealth around, flaunting their abundance. She had a hunch that the fiercely private Gareth would just as soon not be around people at all.

She wandered back toward the garage, stopping to stand on tiptoe and peer in the windows. Every pane of glass was spotless. She saw the Jeep, along with four other vehicles—a vintage Harley-Davidson motorcycle, a classic black Mercedes sedan, a steel-gray delivery van, and a small electric car.

The odd assortment intrigued her. Nothing about Gareth Wolff was easy to pin down.

She walked around the rear of the garage, and there, at the back of a large clearing, stood a third building. The exterior was fashioned to match the house and the garage. But this structure was smaller. A stone chimney, similar to the three on top of Gareth's house, emitted a curl of smoke. Feeling more like Goldilocks than she cared to admit, Gracie gave into the temptation to explore.

Instead of a traditional front door, the side of the building closest to Gracie was bisected by double garage doors, one of which was ajar. Feeling like the interloper she was, Gracie peeked inside.

Gareth stood opposite her, his big hands moving a scrap of sandpaper back and forth across an expanse of wood. He worked intently, all his focus on the project at hand.

The interior of the building was comprised of a single large room, partitioned here and there, but fully open to view. One quadrant stored lengths of lumber, another held shelves of small figures that appeared to be birds and animals. A large vat of some kind of liquid-soaked strips of wood. Other tables were laden with myriad hand tools.

The air smelled pleasantly of raw wood and tangy smoke from the open fireplace. An enormous skylight shed golden rays onto the floor below, catching dancing motes of dust along the way. Piled curls of wood shavings littered the floor at Gareth's feet.

Though she knew it was unwise, she moved forward into his line of sight. His head jerked up, and he stared at her, unsmiling.

She tucked her hands behind her back. "I take it this is your *work?*"

He put down the sandpaper and wiped his hands on his jeans. As he stepped from behind the workbench, she saw that the old, faded denim had worn in some very interesting places, emphasizing his masculinity in a throat-drying way.

"Did you eat?"

She nodded.

"And Annalise found you?"

A second nod.

"Do you remember anything?"

She swallowed hard. "No." Nothing concrete.

When he grimaced, she tried to squash an unreasonable feeling of guilt. He couldn't be any more frustrated than she was about her situation. "Sorry," she added, wondering why it was that women always seemed to feel the need to apologize and men seldom did.

He leaned against one of the rough-hewn posts that supported the vaulted ceiling, his hands in his pockets. The plain white T-shirt he wore was as sexy as any tux, and she had a gut feeling that he could wear either with ease.

As he surveyed her from head to toe, he frowned. "Why haven't you changed?"

"Is there a dress code?" Maybe she was a smart-ass in her previous life.

Finally…a small smile from the man with the stone face. "I thought you'd be eager to get out of those clothes."

Her stomach plunged at his suggestive words, but her brain wrestled with her libido. "I'll change later. Didn't seem to make sense to get all cleaned up when I was coming outside to explore. It's a beautiful day."

He nodded abruptly. "Glad you feel up to getting around. Does your head still hurt?"

"A little. I only took one pain pill. Didn't want to sleep the day away."

The conversation stalled. She worked her way closer. "What are you making?"

He paused, as if considering whether or not to answer. Then he shrugged. "A cradle."

"For someone in your family?"

"No."

Sheesh. It was like squeezing a stone to get water. "Then who?"

He rubbed a hand across the back of his neck, a gesture she was beginning to associate with his response to her. "A member of the British royal family."

She gaped. "Seriously?"

He cracked a smile, a small one, but definitely a tiny grin. "Seriously."

"Tell me. Spill the details."

He shook his head, his eyes dancing with humor. "If I told you, I'd have to kill you. That information is on a strictly need-to-know basis."

She pursed her lips, wondering why she could remember things she'd read in line at the grocery store while scanning the front page of a gossip rag, but not be able to visualize her own home. Rather than dwell on that unsettling fact, she put two and two together.

"Ohmigosh," she cried. "Are they pregnant? Is it—"

He put a hand over her mouth. "Uh, uh, uh… No questions. My lips are sealed."

They were so close together she could smell the soap he'd used in the shower…and the not unpleasant odor of healthy male sweat. For some weird reason, her tongue wanted to slip out and tease his slightly callused fingers. His eyes darkened and she could swear he was reading her mind at that very moment.

She gulped and backed up a step. A more lighthearted Gareth was definitely dangerous. "Does your improved mood mean that you believe me…about not remembering, I mean?"

His hand fell away. "I'll admit that deliberately falling to substantiate a claim of amnesia seems a bit far-fetched. I'm willing to give you the benefit of the doubt. For the moment, at least." His dark eyes seemed to see inside her soul.

She pretended to examine his workshop in order to give her ragged breathing time to return to a more normal cadence. "You must enjoy all this…the peace, the creativity." Her voice rasped at the end when she swallowed hard, caught suddenly by a memory of her own hands spreading paint across a canvas. Watercolors, maybe? The image left her.

He nodded, watching her with the intensity of a hawk stalking prey. "It keeps me off the streets," he deadpanned, seemingly relaxed.

But she had the notion that he was tense beneath his deliberately casual demeanor. She picked up a bottle of linseed oil and rubbed the label. "Why do you do it? Certainly not for the money."

"That's where you're wrong, Gracie."

She turned to face him, frowning. "What? Do you have some weird need to prove yourself and not lean on the family money?"

"You've been reading too many novels." He chuckled. "I'm quite happy to enjoy my share of the Wolff family coffers."

"And by the way," she said, "what *is* the family business?"

"Railroads originally, back in the 1800s. We've diversified since then. Most of the Wolff ancestors were good at making money from money."

"And now?"

"We took a hit, like everyone…when the economy tanked. But my father and my uncle are shrewd businessmen. We have interests in shipping, manufacturing, even agriculture to some extent."

"But you make furniture."

He nodded. "Indeed."

She put a hand on the piece of walnut he'd been sanding. Already, the finish was smooth to the touch. "Indulge me," she said, wondering if she was being far too nosy. "How much does a cradle for a royal cost?"

He shrugged, an enigmatic smile teasing the corner of his mouth. "Seventy-five thousand dollars…give or take. Depends on the exchange rate on any given day."

"Seventy-five…" Her mouth hung open. She didn't know what she, Gracie, did for a living, but it was a good bet she didn't make half that amount in a year. She didn't know why she was so sure, but she was. Maybe because hearing him say the number out loud was shocking.

He took pity on her. "I have a charity that I created a long time ago. My furniture pieces are one of a kind…and for whatever reason some people are willing to shell out big bucks for them. So I make the furniture, cash the checks and put all the money to good use."

"What's your charity?"

His face closed up. "You wouldn't have heard of it." Any good humor he'd exhibited had evaporated. "I need to get back to work."

"Tell me what else you make," she coaxed. "And for whom."

He let out an exaggerated, aggrieved sigh. "An armoire for a Middle Eastern sheikh. Windsor chairs for a Boston heiress. A desk for a former president…"

"That's amazing," she said simply. "You must be phenomenally talented. Is this what you studied in school?"

His expression darkened. "I earned a law degree at my father's urging. But I found out pretty quickly that I wasn't cut out for litigation. To show my dad what a badass I was, I enlisted in the army and did some time in Afghanistan."

"He must have been proud."

"He was terrified," Gareth said flatly. "And I regretted my rebellion almost from the beginning. Thank God nothing happened to me. I think it would have killed him."

Gracie saw the moment Gareth left her and went to some dark place. His eyes looked out across the room, unseeing. She struggled to find a new topic, one that didn't make her host look as if tragedy hovered far too close. A framed eight-by-ten photograph caught her eye. "Who's that?" she asked, moving closer.

Gareth's lips tightened. "Laura Wolff. My mother."

Again, a wisp of remembrance teased her. But it was gone before she could process what it meant. Gracie noted the resemblance in coloring between the woman and her son, but Gareth's strong profile must come from his father. His mother's features were delicate. She had an upturned nose and laughing eyes. "Does she live in the big house on top of the hill?"

"She'd dead."

He was trying to shock her into shutting up. She realized that. But she was hungry for information, anything to fill up the gray void that was her brain. "I don't suppose you want to tell me what happened."

"No," he said, his voice and expression harsh. "It's none of your damned business."

"I get that," she said quietly. "But you have to understand

that if I don't ask questions…if I don't try to piece together the world around me, I'm scared to death I'll never remember anything." Her chin wobbled, and she swallowed the embarrassing tears that ambushed her at odd moments. It was easy enough to distract herself for a few minutes, but the truth was, she was as lacking in self-knowledge as a newborn babe.

Gareth made a visible effort to pull himself out of whatever funk her volley of questions had put him in. And she saw genuine sympathy in his gaze.

He returned to his task, his big hands moving over the wood with a lover's caress. His eyes focused downward. "It's barely been twenty-four hours, Gracie. Give it time."

"How much time?" she asked, feeling frustrated at her impotence. "A day? A week? I should go home to Georgia. Familiar territory may be the only thing that jogs my memory."

He paused, looking up at her with reluctant compassion. "You need to stay for now. I can't in good conscience let you go home, because your father is gone. Until we get more information about you, or until a friend or relative comes forward to care for you, you're stuck with us."

"You could take me to a hotel in Savannah. I could explore the town like a tourist…see if anything pops."

"I'm not dumping you in an impersonal hotel all alone. And if you're honest, I doubt you really want me to."

She wrapped her arms around her waist, rocking back and forth on her heels. "My father didn't sound like a very nice man," she said slowly. "I'm embarrassed to say that, but it's true. And when I think about leaving here, it panics me…because I only have twenty-four hours of life in my data bank, and Wolff Mountain is all I know. Does that sound stupid?"

"Not stupid. But perhaps naive. You don't really know anything about this place…or at least not much. You've seen part of my house and some of Jacob's. But nothing here is likely to stimulate the return of your memory."

"Which is why I should leave," she said flatly, feeling a sharp ache in the pit of her stomach.

He abandoned his work and closed the gap between them. "I think you should relax."

"Easy for you to say."

His brief but striking smile returned. He brushed his thumb over her cheekbone, the fleeting caress as shocking as it was tantalizing. "Lucky for you, I'm always right."

Gracie's stomach plunged and her heart went haywire in her chest. She had no defenses against a Gareth who chose to be tender and teasing. Backing away slowly, she tried to smile. Did he notice the flush of color that heated her cheeks?

"I'll let you get back to work," she said hoarsely.

He nodded, his gaze hooded.

For several long heartbeats, they simply looked at each other.

And when it seemed as if something cataclysmic might shatter the tense silence, she fled.

Five

Gareth climbed the side of the mountain behind his workshop, pushing the pace, making his lungs labor. But he was unable to outrun the problem that waited below. And unfortunately, Gracie Darlington was potentially *more* than a problem. At last he stopped, bent forward with his hands on his knees and cursed.

Once before in his life, a beautiful, seemingly guile-free woman had used a strong physical attraction to persuade Gareth to trust her. Back then he had not been able to see past his own testosterone fueled hunger to the calculating bitch she really was. The resultant debacle cost Gareth dearly.

During a dinner party at the family home, his girlfriend had stolen a priceless piece of art, a small-enough-to-hide-in-a-purse Manet worth a quarter of a million dollars. The painting was eventually recovered, but the damage was done. On top of the tragedy in Gareth's childhood, this betrayal closed him off for good. He became cynical, antisocial and mistrustful of strangers. And he liked it that way.

His father had chastised him harshly in the aftermath of the unfortunate incident. Gareth's resultant humiliation led to his reckless run-away-from-home stint in the army. In all fairness, he'd only been twenty-four at the time. And his lack of judgment eight years ago had taught him valuable lessons about human nature. But even now, feeling an undeniable response to sexy Gracie, Gareth was on his guard.

He wiped his mouth, staring sightlessly at the ground, feeling the soft cushion of moss beneath his feet, listening to the quiet gurgle of the nearby creek.

His mind wrestled with frustration, both mental and physical. He'd awakened before dawn, his erection rigid and painful. Dreams, dark and hot, tormented his subconscious. And Gracie walked in those dreams. Smiled. Beckoned.

All around him, the early-spring abundance mocked Gareth's barren bed. The forest teemed with life. Gareth knew it well... had played in these same woods as a boy. It was a landscape as familiar to him as the small silver scar on the back of his right hand. For eighteen years he had lived and learned and grown, protected by geography and his father's phalanx of security guards from the dangerous outside world.

He wondered if Jacob and Kieran had resented the isolation as much as he had. The siblings were close, but in the way of men they seldom articulated feelings.

Even as adults they catered to their father's and uncle's paranoia in many ways, though they had each outgrown the fears the older men had bred in them as boys. And now, bit by bit, the cousins were all coming home.

Was it integrity or foolishness?

A bee buzzed gently around Gareth's ear. He batted gently at the insect then stretched. Losing himself in the forest was no way for a man to deal with the conundrum of a woman he wanted. But Gareth felt at home here, as much as in the elegant but oddly empty house he'd built and furnished in the last eighteen months.

He'd come home from the army, not a broken man, but a man who understood that it was possible to be lonely in a crowd. No one really understood what his life had been like growing up. His buddies on the front line didn't really care. Every day there was about survival. And that was Gareth's goal now...survival.

The furniture creation had begun on a whim, an extension of his boyhood love of carving. But in the grip of creative passion, he had gradually begun healing and had found a purpose for his life on the mountain.

Gracie could so easily destroy his newfound peace.

He firmed his jaw, took one last look at the budding green of tree and bush and turned his back on the bucolic scene. As he strode back down the mountain, his long legs made quick work of the journey despite the lack of a marked path.

He paused on the knoll above his house. Below him, framed in the deliberate swath he'd cut in the treetops, lay the valley floor. It seemed almost dreamlike, a fairy-tale place of warm hay, newly minted corn sprouts and the muted, busy hum of tractors. Normal people lived in the valley. Families with mortgages and financial worries and homes filled with noisy offspring.

Some days Gareth envied them. He was no longer a carefree, barefoot lad with stained, ripped shorts playing amidst blackberry thickets and flopping belly-first to watch salamanders in the creek. That boy had never hesitated to grab the world by the tail.

Thank God he had his workshop. At least when he was there, he could concentrate on the grain of fine wood, could smooth his hands over sleek curves, searching for any imperfections, forcing the oak or cherry or cedar to his own design.

As Gareth tromped with noisy footsteps onto the porch of his hideaway, the heavy basset hound dozing peacefully by the door shuffled suddenly into a new position, tucked his big head onto his paws and sighed deeply. His floppy ears were mottled with sawdust. It was enough to make Gareth smile despite his discontent. But only for a moment.

He was a man. Lonely. Frustrated. Torn between caution and desire. His entire body ached with the need to bury himself between a woman's soft thighs, to touch her breasts and ride her to oblivion. And not just any woman. Gracie. God, he could feel the moment of climax in his imagination.

As he picked up his handsaw, a hard-won measure of peace calmed him. The steps of his craft were familiar. Whenever he worked at his lathe with a lover's concentration, all else faded away. In his head there was always a vision of the finished piece. A beautiful chair, a sleek modern table, a sturdy chest. He'd tramped these hills in weeks past, locating materials, dragging them home. The art came from his Irish roots, the business sense a maternal genetic gift of Yankee drive and intuition.

But this afternoon, even the familiar routines of cut and turn, sand and polish, were not enough. After an hour and a half, he tossed his tools aside with a growl of displeasure. Nearly butchering a lovely length of chestnut told him it was time to stop. He poured a cup of coffee, and carried his mug outside.

The dog, Fenton, had scarcely moved. Gareth finished his drink, set the mug on the floor and clenched his hands on the split-log railing, heedless of splinters or rough shards of bark. He worked with such realities every day. His hands were a workingman's hands, callused, strong, not at all pretty.

A stinging discomfort pierced his introspection, and he realized his hand was bleeding. He'd gripped the railing so tightly that one thin sliver of wood had pierced his thumb. Absently he removed the piece and sucked at the tiny oozing wound.

He glanced up at the sky, feeling the warmth of the sun on his face. It had been a long, cold winter. And because of Gracie's advent into his life, he was, for the first time in a long time, questioning his self-imposed social exile. His father had forgiven him a long time ago. But Gareth had not been able to let go of the past. So many mistakes. So much pain for those he loved.

Was Gracie an arousing, fascinating gift, or a Trojan horse?

No divine intervention appeared from the fluffy clouds that resembled frolicking lambs. No jolt of understanding filled him with purpose.

He dropped his head forward, pressing it against a post, inhaling and exhaling, feeling on the precipice of disaster. He acknowledged what he'd been fighting to ignore all morning. Change was on the way. He could feel it in his bones, the sinews of his flesh.

Something was in the wind. He felt it brush his skin, smelled it in the air, tasted its unfamiliarity.

And her name was Gracie...

Gracie woke from a nap to find Jacob Wolff loitering in the kitchen, drinking a beer and reading email on his BlackBerry. He glanced up with a smile. "You look much better. How do you feel?"

She poured herself a glass of water. "Pretty good. The headache's almost gone."

"But your memory?"

She wrinkled her nose. "Still blank."

He stood and smoothed a hand over the front of his crisp white shirt. With his expensive haircut and knife-pleated black slacks, his appearance couldn't have been more different than Gareth's. But Jacob, handsome and sophisticated though he was, didn't stir Gracie's pulse in the least.

"Can I ask you something?" she said abruptly.

Jacob finished his drink and set the bottle on the counter. "Of course."

"This house is immaculate...and the fridge and freezer are stocked with food. But there's no one here except for Gareth."

Jacob chuckled. "We call it the silent army." At her upraised

eyebrow, he explained. "My father and uncle employ a significant number of people at the big house…everything from gar-
deners to housekeepers, chefs, mechanics. And my cousins and
I have access to those services as we choose."

"But Gareth isn't fond of people."

"So my father has set up an elaborate system whereby the
various service employees sneak down here and take care of
things either when Gareth is out of town or is working in his
shop."

"Well, that explains it," she said smiling. "I was beginning
to think he was Superman."

"He is, in many ways. Never underestimate him, Gracie.
He's been through a hell of a lot in his lifetime. And yes, he's a
bit of a curmudgeon on the outside. But he feels things deeply.
Perhaps too deeply for his own good."

"I asked him about his mother…your mother. He wouldn't
speak of her."

"That doesn't surprise me." He motioned toward the den.
"Do you mind if I give you a quick exam? For my own piece of
mind?"

"Of course not."

They sat side by side on the sofa as Jacob took her pulse,
checked her blood pressure and examined her head. "The knot
is smaller," he murmured. He took out a penlight and held her
chin steady.

Gracie blinked as the strong beam hit her pupil. "Will you
tell me?" she asked quietly. "About your mother?"

Jacob used his thumb to hold open her other eyelid. "Why is
it so important to you?"

"I want to understand Gareth. There was some reason I
showed up here in the beginning. Something that had to do
with him. My father knows, but he doesn't seem inclined to
communicate with me, especially now that he's left the country. I'm scared that my motives were questionable. And I don't

want Gareth to be angry when the truth comes out. I'll go home as soon as I can, but in the meantime, surely you see that the more I learn about him, the better chance I have of remembering why I came."

Jacob's expression was skeptical, and suddenly, the resemblance between the two brothers was more pronounced. "We don't talk about our family to outsiders," he said bluntly. "We've had our fill of sensational news stories and would-be novelists trying to benefit from our misfortune."

"I don't want to hurt Gareth…or anyone."

"But you don't know who you really are. You might be a reporter looking for a story. And as such, that means Gareth may be sharing his home with the enemy."

"Ouch," she said, wincing. "Isn't that a bit harsh?"

"You have no idea the things that have been written about the Wolff family over the years."

"I wouldn't do that. Please, Jacob. I'm floundering in this huge sea of nothingness. Toss me a life raft. I won't do anything with the information, I swear. I just want to know how your mother died."

His face grayed, his eyes dull. "I may as well tell you. It's nothing you couldn't find on the internet with a little digging." He paused and took a ragged breath. "She and my aunt were murdered. In the eighties, when we were all children. Gareth is the only one of us who was really old enough to remember them clearly. They were kidnapped, held for ransom and killed anyway…even when the money was paid. Is that what you wanted, Gracie? Well, now you know."

He stormed out of the room and out of the house, leaving her feeling sick. Thank God she hadn't pressed Gareth for details. Given the way the calm, friendly Jacob reacted in the telling of that horrible tale, Gareth would likely have exploded.

Her heart bled for him. What an unimaginable tragedy. One that affected two families. And clearly, the pain lingered even after twenty-plus years. No wonder the two old men gathered their young around them like broody mother hens. Their experience would have changed them irrevocably.

She jerked when Gareth's voice sounded behind her.

"Was that Jacob I saw leaving?"

"He came to check on me." She stood up, feeling as if guilt was inscribed on her face.

"And?"

Had he overheard part of the conversation? "And what?" she said, playing for time.

"Your head? Your leg?"

"Oh." She gave an inward sigh of relief. "He says I'm recovering very well."

"Would you like to swim?"

The odd segue wrinkled her forehead. "Um, yes…I suppose."

"I told Annalise to get you a suit. Can you change in ten minutes?"

"Of course."

She made it in eight. Gareth was standing in the kitchen wearing nothing but navy boxer-style swim trunks that clung to his body and left little to the imagination.

Her throat dried and her tongue felt clumsy in her mouth. She was suddenly stingingly aware that her swimsuit left her mostly naked, though for the moment she was veiled in a terry cover-up.

"This way," he said abruptly, leaving her to follow along in his wake.

The house was built into the side of the mountain, with several staircases leading to various levels. Gareth led them down and down until they passed through a set of glass doors and into a steamy, scented enclosure big enough to hold six or eight of her luxurious bedrooms.

The centerpiece of the room was an inviting pool, irregularly shaped to resemble a natural lake. All around the edge, tropical plants and flowers thrived in the misty air. Somewhere in the distance, soothing music played, with lots of flutes and Native American overtones.

The decking was cobblestone. Lounge chairs covered in batik-print fabric were scattered about.

At the far end of the pool, draped by thick palm fronds, flowed a waterfall, an actual waterfall.

Gareth tossed his towel on a seat. "What do you think?"

She scanned the whole area, quite sure her mouth was hanging open. "It's amazing. I've never seen anything like it."

"How would you know?"

She looked at him curiously, finally returning his smile when she realized that the taciturn Gareth Wolff was actually teasing her. "That's just mean," she said, her lips twisting in a wry grin.

"C'mon," he said abruptly. "Let's see if you know how to swim."

Fortunately for Gracie's peace of mind, Gareth dove in without ceremony and began doing laps. She walked around to the shallow end, preparing to shed her cover-up. When she thought Gareth wasn't watching, she took it off. The haute couture bikini in lime-green and saffron was as tiny as it was undoubtedly expensive.

She felt painfully exposed.

<u>Six</u>

Gareth almost swallowed his tongue when he got a first glance at Gracie in the next-to-nothing swimsuit Annalise had picked out. Gracie was slim, but sweetly curved in all the right places. Her pale, creamy skin befitted a natural redhead. Trying to disguise his avid interest, he watched her slip carefully into the pool.

She took a few steps before tentatively launching out in a creditable backstroke. Apparently he wouldn't have to play lifeguard. Too bad.

Her long legs kicked lazily. Her pert breasts rose above the water as she moved. Already, he was painfully hard, his erection taunting him with the knowledge that he'd not had a woman in his bed in recent memory.

Now Gracie was here…available…and he wanted her desperately, but could he trust the woman whose past was obscured?

After twenty minutes of punishing laps, he permitted himself to approach her. At arm's length, he took note of the way the shiny fabric clung to her like a second skin. The room was plenty warm, but Gracie's nipples thrust against the triangles of her bikini top.

He tried not to stare. "Would you like to try out the waterfall?" The hoarseness in his voice could be attributed to exertion.

She licked her lips, her eyes big. "Of course."

He took her hand, feeling her start of surprise. They moved against the water, walking deeper and deeper into the pool. When Gracie's feet left the bottom, she protested.

"It's too deep. I can't touch."

He put his hands on her narrow waist, imagining those fabulous legs winding around him. "Get on my back," he said.

They eyed each other from a distance of eighteen inches. He could see her chest rise and fall with each breath…could count the water droplets clinging to her eyelashes.

Slowly, clenching his hand tightly, she moved around until she could rest her hands on his shoulders.

"You can put your legs around me," he said.

"This is fine."

Her prim response made him grin.

"Hang on." He forged into deeper water until the waterfall was directly in front of them. The formation looked amazingly natural. The pool architect had constructed a pile of rocks that was home to colorful orchids and tiny, jewel-toned parakeets.

Gareth pulled Gracie around to stand beside him on the step hidden beneath the water. "You okay on your own now?"

She found her footing and nodded, her face turned up to the spray. "Never better."

Her delighted laughter as the cascading water drenched both of them tightened something in his gut. He wanted to take her here…in this wild setting. The hunger was fierce and relentless. He had to look away from her radiant face to catch his breath.

No matter how much he tried to remind himself that he'd been a fool for a woman once before, he couldn't shake the notion that Gracie was his. Even without her memory, there was a sweetness about her…a strength and a zest for life. She had shown remarkable courage in a difficult situation.

He moved them just out of the main torrent and touched her hand. "It's not my habit to ask, but you've had a rough two days."

Her smile faded to confusion. "Ask what?"

"May I kiss you?"

The shock on her face was unmistakable. But moments later, he saw the dawn of something else. Interest. Arousal. Caution.

He understood the caution. Hell, this was probably the stupidest idea he'd had in a while. But he couldn't help himself. "Gracie?"

A long, pregnant pause ensued. Just when he thought she was going to shut him down, she lifted her arms. "Okay."

He knew there was a good chance she was experimenting with him, hoping something might jog her memory. According to her father, she had no husband or boyfriend. But even still…

When their lips touched, her arms linked behind his neck, all rational thought evaporating in the cloud of steam that engulfed them. The pool at this end was heated by underwater jets, more like a hot tub in temperature. But Gareth was pretty sure he and Gracie would have generated steam even in an ice bath.

Her mouth was hesitant beneath his, her lips soft and curious. He tried to be gentle. He really did. But the taste of her intoxicated him. Their bodies melded, skin to skin. His tongue slid between her teeth, probing gently, dueling with hers.

She wasn't exactly embracing him. Her hands rested on his shoulders as if she wasn't sure if she would pull him closer or push him away. He kissed her firmly, without apology. He had asked. She had answered. He had nothing to feel guilty about. But he did.

Gracie Darlington didn't know anything about her past. And Gareth didn't know anything about her.

Heaving a deep breath, acknowledging the tremor in his own limbs, he broke the connection and stepped back as much as the step beneath his feet would allow.

Gracie stared at him glassy-eyed. "Wow."

His broken chuckle surprised even him. "Yeah."

"I think I'm in over my head," she said softly. "Not such a good swimmer, after all."

"Can you make it to the side of the pool?"

"You think you made me weak in the knees?" Her teasing smile relaxed a bit of the tension in his gut. "Braggart."

He shifted restlessly. "I'm going to do some more laps. Can you find your way back through the house?"

She nodded slowly, her gaze locked on his. "Thanks for the swim."

Gracie climbed out of the pool, aware that Gareth's gaze tracked her every motion. Though he moved through the water with the ease and speed of an Olympic swimmer, she knew he had his eyes on her.

She toweled off and then shrugged into the cover-up, glad to use it as armor. With one last wistful glance at the man in the pool, she wandered back to her bedroom, taking note of the decor and design of the house along the way. Every inch of Gareth's home was stunningly beautiful. Yet he lived here all alone, like a wounded beast hiding from the world.

After a quick shower, she dried her hair and surveyed her new clothing. Annalise had been kind enough to include basic makeup, so Gracie brushed on some eye shadow, darkened her lashes with mascara and covered her lips in pink gloss.

Feeling a bit too much like Cinderella, she picked out a cherry-red sundress with white appliquéd flowers at the hem and slipped it on. The woman in the mirror looked relaxed and happy...as long as no one looked too closely at the lost expression in her eyes.

Gracie gnawed her lip with indecision. What exactly was she supposed to do with herself for the next few hours? Perhaps it wouldn't hurt to browse through Gareth's extensive collection of books and DVDs. Who knew what small detail might tug at a memory?

But when she made her way back to the enormous den/living room, the low table in front of the entertainment center had been set with china and silver and an assortment of mouthwatering dishes.

Gareth stood by the fireplace, staring into the flames. He had changed as well. His dark slacks and cream Irish fisherman's sweater suited his wild masculinity.

She paused on the threshold. "Something smells wonderful."

As he crossed the room to stand beside her, she realized that her words had a dual meaning. Gareth smelled like the crisp, clean fragrance of his shower soap, a combination of lime and fresh evergreen. Though he was covered from neck to toe, she had a vivid memory of what that large, hard body looked like.

Perhaps he would attribute her flushed cheeks to the warmth from the fire.

He held out a hand. "Will you eat with me?"

She was flustered to realize that he meant for them to sit on the floor. That seemed altogether too intimate. Hesitating only a moment, she slipped out of her crimson sandals and situated herself on a comfy, velvet-covered pillow. Gareth joined her at the opposite corner of the table.

They ate in silence for several minutes. Beef tenderloin... asparagus with hollandaise sauce and fluffy mashed potatoes.

Gracie sighed, swallowing a bite of heaven on a fork. "My potatoes never turn out this well." She froze, fork in the air. "I remember," she said, her heart thumping. "My kitchen is yellow and white. I think I'm a decent cook."

Gareth had quit eating as well, his gaze intense. "What else?" he asked. "Take your time. Don't stress."

She closed her eyes, reaching with all her might for what was just on the other side of a frustrating curtain. Bit by bit a scene materialized in her head. "I was standing beside the stove, laughing. Another woman was there."

"Tell me about her."

Try as she might, the face wouldn't come into focus. She put down her fork, the food a hard knot in her stomach. "I don't understand," she whispered. "Why won't it come back?"

"The brain's a funny thing," Gareth said, his matter-of-fact tone soothing her nerves. "It will come when it comes."

"I've wondered about hypnosis," she said, doodling her fork in burgundy sauce. "I need to do *something*."

Gareth snorted. "I hardly think hypnosis qualifies as *something*...unless of course you're hoping to find out that you were a Persian princess in a past life."

"You're so open-minded," she mocked. "How do you know it wouldn't work? Maybe I should talk to Jacob about it."

"If Jacob thought hypnosis would solve your problem, I assure you he'd have already mentioned it. My brother is brilliant when it comes to the human body. I told you to quit worrying about it." He uncovered the last dish. "Eat some cherry pie. Pie helps everything."

"Says the man who probably never gains an ounce."

His gaze lashed her with heat. "You're perfect," he said bluntly. "Eat the damned pie."

She chewed and swallowed, barely tasting the scrumptious dessert. Gareth exhibited all the signs of a man in the throes of sexual frustration. And she was right there with him. The temperature in the room was rising ten degrees at a time...

He shoved back from their makeshift table and stretched out his legs, ankles crossed, hands behind his head. "I have an idea," he said. "I need to make a quick trip to D.C. in a couple of days. You could come with me."

"Why?" She frowned.

"I'm not going to leave you here unattended."

"You still don't trust me."

He shrugged. "I trust what I know of you. But that's not much, is it?"

"Why are you going to D.C.?"

"Some hotshot senator purchased an enormous gun cabinet from me. He wants to show off his new chest—and the creator—at a fancy-ass party in Georgetown."

"I'm shocked that you would agree."

"I didn't want to do it, so I told him that a personal appearance would mean another hundred grand for my charity. I never dreamed he would take me up on it."

She laughed out loud at the look of chagrin on his face. "Poor Gareth. It must seem like a fate worse than death."

"It would be a hell of a lot more enjoyable if you go with me."

"So I'm just a warm body to keep you from getting bored?"

The deliberate flirting was a skill that surprised her.

Gareth's eyes narrowed, reading the underlying message. "Be careful, Gracie. Don't start something you can't finish."

A huge yawn caught her off guard. "Sorry," she said, blushing.

He stood and pulled her to her feet. "Say good-night, Gracie."

She tilted her head, studying his face. "That's funny. I think my father used to say that to me."

He brushed a kiss across her cheek, fleeting, tantalizing. "Get some rest. We'll talk about the trip in the morning."

She put a hand to his cheek. "Are you afraid of me?" she whispered teasingly, deliberately moving closer so their bodies touched.

His head bent and he covered her mouth with his. The kiss shook her to the bone. It mixed raw carnality and seeking hunger with a tenderness that took the starch out of her knees. Everywhere she was soft, he was hard. But it was over almost before it began.

Disappointment flooded her chest as she let him scoot her down the hall. "I could help with the dishes."

"Go to bed. And stay there."

She had the distinct impression that he was trying to keep the two of them from doing something ill-advised. Her common sense lauded his fortitude, but deep inside, she wouldn't have minded if he had dragged her down to the lavish carpeting and had his way with her.

Her beautiful bedroom was beginning to feel like a prison. She changed into a silky negligee that felt naughty against her bare skin, and brushed her teeth. Jacob had said it was okay to take a pill before bedtime, so she filled a tumbler with water and washed one down. The medication worked its magic, and she fell into a deep, exhausted slumber.

Seven

Gareth awoke at the first scream. By the second, he was down the hall and into her room. She had left a light on in the bathroom, so he was immediately able to see, even in the dimly illumined bedroom, that Gracie was tangled in the covers, writhing as if she were fighting something or someone.

He sat down beside her, tugging back the blankets.

Before he could do more than that, she cried out, *"No!"*

The sheer terror in that one syllable made the hair stand up on his arms. She was sobbing, struggling with him as he tried to wake her. "You're okay, Gracie. Wake up. You're okay."

He repeated it over and over, his voice low but firm as he coaxed her out of her deep, tormented sleep. Finally, thank God, she took a shuddering breath and opened her eyes. Her pupils were dilated, and her entire body shook with tremors. When he was sure she was aware of her surroundings, he gathered her into his arms, warming her with his body heat.

"Shh," he said softly. "Everything's all right. It was a dream." He stroked her hair, twining a finger in a curl and rubbing the base of her skull. "Nothing can hurt you."

She wrapped her arms around his waist and buried her face in his chest. Only then did he realize what she was wearing. The feel of silk beneath his hand made his mouth go dry. *Damn Annalise*. His romantically minded cousin had tried to coax him out of his cave on many occasions—in the old days throwing her sorority sisters at him and more recently her coworkers.

He didn't need a woman to be happy. Sex…well, that was another story. But a man could take matters into his own hands if need be. Until Gareth found a woman he could trust, he wasn't interested in female companionship.

Liar. His libido jumped into the conversation, pointing out how soft Gracie was, how the smell of her hair made Gareth hard, even without her barely covered breasts mashed up against him. She had thrust herself into his life without compunction. He ought to be angry as hell. By all rights, he should send her packing.

But he wanted to keep her…just for a little while. She made his big house seem more like a home. Light and life shadowed her every step. And if she had any nefarious purpose in coming to Wolff Mountain, he'd yet to see any sign of it.

Finally she eased back, shoving the hair from her face with an unsteady hand. "Turn on the lamp," she pleaded, the words husky and quiet.

He did as she asked, relieved that the low-wattage bulb cast little more than a rosy circle of light. "Do you want to tell me about it?" he asked, still holding her with one arm.

Her lower lip trembled until she bit down on it and took a deep breath. "I was running in the dark. Something was after me. I knew if I could find my way home, I'd be safe. But every time I opened a door, nothing was there."

He pulled her closer again, his chin on her head, his fingers twined with hers. "I don't think we have to look too far to figure that one out. You're trying so damn hard, Gracie. You know it doesn't happen by sheer force of will. God knows if it did, you would already remember. I've never seen anyone so determined to make something happen. But Jacob said it may come in bits and pieces so gradually it will slip up on you. Or some little thing may trigger a release that gives it back to you all at once. You can't do this to yourself."

"I'm so scared that you'll hate me when I find out why I came." The words tumbled out   bald, unadorned—her expression similarly stark.

Gareth acknowledged the truth of her statement in his brain, but his body shied away from the unpalatable possibility that Gracie was as sleazy a person as her father. She couldn't be. Not when she felt so damned perfect in his embrace. "You'll be going home in a few days. Until then, you need to focus on something else." And in the meantime he wouldn't tell her that investigators were even now checking out the truth about Edward Darlington.

She gave a hiccuping sob and laughed unsteadily. "Easy for you to say. You're not the one with a major brain malfunction." She winced. "Were you sleeping?"

"It's 2:00 a.m.," he muttered. "Yes, I was sleeping." And having better dreams than hers.

She shivered. He ran his hands up and down her arms, feeling the gooseflesh. "Will you be okay now?"

She looked up at him…vulnerable, lost. "No. Will you stay? Please."

Gracie heard the words come out of her mouth and felt her cheeks flame with embarrassment. Could she be any more needy? She was clinging to Gareth like a port in a storm. The fact that she wasn't imagining the attraction between them didn't excuse her artless invitation.

Was she the kind of woman who slept with a man on a whim? Or had losing her memory simply stripped away her inhibitions?

Gareth went slack-jawed for a split second before his expression closed up, leaving no clue as to his emotions. He couldn't hide the erection that pulsed between them, but then again, he wasn't jumping at her offer.

And it *was* an offer. She knew it, and he knew it.

He stood up and ran his hands through his hair. "I can sit in that chair until you fall back asleep."

"But I could still have another nightmare after you leave," she pointed out.

"I haven't had sex with a woman in eleven months," he said flatly, clearly trying to shock her.

"Why?"

Her question seemed to perplex him. "Lots of reasons. I don't bring women here so I have to go somewhere and seek it out. Do the dance. Stay at her place. It's not worth it anymore."

"I see. But I didn't ask for sex."

His eyes flashed. "Don't be coy. We both know where this is headed. A man would have to be a real bastard to take advantage of a woman in your situation. And if I stay in this room with you—all night—you won't be sleeping."

If she had been standing, her knees would have buckled at his declaration of intent. He was bare from the waist up, his broad chest rippled with muscle. A pair of cotton pajama pants hung low on his hips, but she had a sneaking suspicion that he had donned those on her behalf.

"What if I take advantage of *you?*" she asked quietly. "You're an amazing man, Gareth Wolff. Very soon I'll be gone. Can you blame me for wanting to have you in my bed?"

The fabric at his groin pulsed visibly. His jaw was granite. "I won't make you any heartfelt promises. If you finally remember why you came, it won't make any difference. I can't give you softness and romance. I'm not that guy. This will be nothing more than two people scratching an itch…satisfying their curiosity."

His words hurt, though they were no more than she had expected. If she had some far-fetched idea that she could change this man, she was deluding herself. He'd been molded by tragedy, shaped by a childhood of fear and secrecy. He was as inflexible as the wood he crafted into beautiful objects.

He was fair and considerate. And he had been remarkably generous in letting her stay. But Gareth Wolff was not the kind of guy to be manipulated by a pretty face or a night of raw, make-me-forget sex.

She rose up on her knees, her body trembling in anticipation now, rather than fear. "I understand. I accept your terms." She held out a hand. "And I still want you."

The night, already still and silent, seemed to freeze in time. Gareth could have been a statue were it not for the quick up-and-down bob of his Adam's apple. His entire body was rigid. His hands clenched at his hips. For one long, aching minute, she thought she had lost.

And then he exhaled visibly, his gaze stormy. "I'll be right back."

He was true to his word, returning in mere seconds with a handful of plastic packets that he tossed on the bedside table. She could feel her heart beating in her ears as he shed his pants without modesty and put a knee on the mattress.

His body was magnificent, beautifully sculpted…all the way from his broad shoulders, to his trim waist, to that most masculine part of him that thrust upward in either invitation or intent, or both.

She was still on her knees, and he matched her pose. "Take it off," he said gruffly. "Knowing Annalise, that damn bit of sin and silk probably cost a fortune."

Gracie lifted her arms as he pulled the wisp of fabric over her head, leaving her clad in nothing but a matching scrap of lace at the hips. His chest heaved, one deep breath, before he put his hands on her waist. His gaze was hooded, his cheekbones slashed with a flush of red.

Face to face and chest to chest, their lips met. Tentative nips and tastes segued into harder, longer, drugging kisses. He was masterful, in control, clearly experienced in the ways of pleasing a woman. Gracie gasped, buffeted by waves of longing, dragged under by a hunger so strong she felt light-headed.

Beneath her questing hands, his skin was hot to the touch... as if his big body was a furnace ready to consume her. He tasted of mint and coffee, and pressed against him, she could feel the thunder of his heartbeat. He took her down to the mattress, spreading her thighs and settling between them.

She tensed. "I don't know how to please you...what you want."

He toyed with the band of lace that rode high on her thigh. "Time enough for that later," he said, his words guttural. "The important question at the moment is do I know how to please you?"

Without ceremony or warning, he scooted down in the bed and used his hands to spread her legs even wider. She shoved at his shoulders. "I don't think so..."

He glanced up at her, a glint of amusement in his dark eyes. "Oh, but I do..."

When he removed her panties and tasted her center, her hips came off the bed. The sensation was indescribable, and for a split second, she acknowledged the certainty that she had never allowed any man this liberty.

But Gareth wasn't waiting for approval. He set about destroying her completely with long, slow passes of his tongue. She was embarrassingly damp, even before he began his assault. Soon, her body shuddered wildly, lost to sensation. She grabbed handfuls of his soft, thick hair and clung helplessly while Gareth sent her rocketing to a climax so intense, she saw stars and fell softly back to earth.

Though she was scarcely aware of it, he moved up in the bed and gathered her in his arms. She wanted to weep at the beauty of what he made her feel. But she couldn't. Tears were for sadness, and with Gareth she was happy, perhaps happier than she had ever been in her life.

He stroked her hair, her back, the curve of her bottom. When she shivered, he covered them both with the comforter. His voice was a low, sexy rumble. "You're beautiful," he said softly. "And I love the way you come for me."

"Stop," she groaned, burying her face in his shoulder. "I'm not used to *talking* about it."

He kissed her brow. "So you want me to just *do* it. Okay, Gracie. I can oblige."

"That's not what I—"

Her inarticulate protest was lost as he made quick work of donning a condom and then entered her with a forceful thrust. Her breath caught in her throat. He was big and powerfully aroused. Her body struggled to accept him.

He stilled, clearly feeling the same incredible connection. "You okay, little Gracie?"

She nodded, mute.

Slowly, so slowly she wanted to beg him to hurry, he began to move in her. Her legs wrapped around his waist, deepening the penetration. She heard him curse.

He withdrew and thrust again, sliding in and out with a lazy rhythm that stoked the fires of a hunger she had thought quenched. But rapidly, her body responded again, eager for a repeat of the singeing pleasure only he could give.

Their skin slicked with sweat. Breathing labored. He reared up suddenly and looked down at her. "Promise me you won't regret this. Tell me Jacob won't have my hide." He was panting, but his eyes sparked with mischief.

She gazed at him sleepily, feeling a twinge in the vicinity of her heart. He was too damned gorgeous for his own good. "No promises," she dared to taunt. "Remember?"

His eyes narrowed. "Witch. If that's the way you want to play it…" He manacled her wrists in a gentle grip and held them over her head. "Beg me," he growled.

Her eyes widened. "For what?" Her tongue moistened her lips as her heart thudded wildly.

"You know damned well." He flexed his hips. "You may not remember the past, but I'll make sure you remember this, Gracie Darlington."

His head came down and his mouth found hers.

In between strangled gasps, she obeyed. "Please, Gareth. Make love to me." Even as she said the words, her heart wept. Gareth didn't love her…he didn't even know her. The only reason he was in her bed was to satisfy a need.

The delicious friction as his body stroked into hers brought her to the edge again. She felt him stretch her almost painfully as he gave a hoarse shout, and then she went with him, falling, falling into a blissful, dizzying tumble.

Gareth rolled to his back, lungs burning, eyes gritty. Good God. What had he done?

Gracie lay quietly against his side, one of her slender arms curled across his chest and one of her legs tucked between his. He tried for humor. "Not bad for a first go…"

Her lag in response time told him she was as off balance as he was. She moved restlessly. "Any man can impress an amnesiac." The tart bite in her joking words bemused him. Gracie Darlington was no pushover. Even hampered as she was by her hopefully temporary condition, she seemed determined to hold her own with him. He nuzzled her hair. "Come to Washington with me. The cherry blossoms are in bloom."

"I don't have anything to wear. Annalise outfitted me with casual clothes, but nothing that would work for a fancy dinner."

"She can shop anywhere. I'll call her in the morning and get her to send what you need directly to the hotel. It will be fun. You can forget about your problem and we'll paint the town red."

"My problem?" She shook her head. "It's a little more than a problem. I have no life, Gareth."

"Potayto…potahto…"

"You're such a compassionate man."

"It's one of my best qualities." He pulled her on top of him and arranged her like a doll, ready for action, but not quite there yet.

She blew a curl out of her eye. "Can I ask you something?"

He tensed, and then forced himself to relax. "I suppose." It was difficult to deny a woman anything when she was fulfilling every fantasy he'd had in recent memory.

"Why do you wear your hair so long?"

Not what he expected…not at all. "You don't like it?"

"On you, it's sexy and gorgeous and you know it." She leaned forward to winnow the fingers of one hand across his scalp, coincidentally squishing her small but lovely breasts against his chest as she moved. "But you and Jacob are so different. The family resemblance is striking. So I'm guessing there's a reason he looks like a rich doctor and you—not so much."

Gareth chuckled. She had a point. "You remember I told you I enlisted in the military for less than stellar reasons?"

"To rebel against your dad?"

"Yeah, but the army was good for me. Turned me from a boy into a man, you know the cliché. I was a damned good soldier. In almost every way. But conformity is not my strong suit. I swore to myself that when I got out, I'd never again have a buzz cut."

"And there's no middle ground?"

"I get it cut occasionally."

"For D.C.?"

He shook his head, running his palms over her soft, perfect ass. "I'll be playing a role for the senator. The untamed Wolff in a tuxedo. His party will be the talk of the season."

"That's pretty cynical."

"I'm a pretty cynical guy. People love a good story. And when they don't have one, they'll make one up."

She was silent for too long, her cheek resting over the steady bump of his heartbeat. "I'll have to go home after we return from D.C. My father will be back by then, surely. Will you go with me? Take me, I mean?"

"Yes. But you don't have to be afraid, Gracie. I'm guessing everything will come flooding back as soon as you're on home turf."

"And if it doesn't?"

"One day at a time." He reached out to grab protection. "You haven't answered me yet. Will you come with me? I'll take you to this great boutique hotel near the Capitol. A million thread count sheets. Pillows so soft you'll never want to get out of bed. Fresh flowers every day. A view of the Washington Monument…"

"Have you taken other women there?"

The note in her voice was hard to decipher. Nothing as simple as jealousy. If he hadn't known better, he'd say it was pained resignation. He shifted her off him long enough to sheath his eager erection. No amount of pillow talk had deflated it. "Does it matter?"

He lifted her again, fitting the head of his straining penis to the warm heart of her. She braced her hands on his chest, looking down at him. Her lips curved in a wry half smile. "Apparently not," she muttered.

"So you'll go with me?"

She nodded slowly, crying out as he joined them with one sharp upward thrust of his hips.

"Is that a yes?" He gritted his teeth and squeezed shut his eyes, trying desperately not to come like a green kid. Being inside Gracie was the closest he'd come in recent memory to peace. To sheer, God Almighty, too-good-to-be-true physical nirvana.

"Yes," she whispered. She sat up straight, lodging him to an incredible depth. Slowly, with all the confidence of a siren, she rode him to heaven and back.

His hands gripped her hips. "Slower," he pleaded. He didn't want this to end. Not ever. The desperation he felt might have alarmed him in a less fraught situation. As it was, he ignored the flashing lights in his brain, attributing them instead to mere frustration.

Gracie shuddered when he slid a finger over the spot where their bodies joined. He nudged the tiny swollen nerve center and she went rigid, clenching him with inner muscles in such a way that his eyes rolled back in his head, his climax hit him like a Mack truck, and they both fell, sated, into a messy tumble of arms and legs and ragged breathing.

Eight

"Are you insane?"

Gareth winced at the incredulity in his brother's voice. They were seated in Jacob's large office with its picture window that looked out at the forest. Rain droplets drizzled down the wide single pane. "What can it hurt?" he asked calmly. "She's making herself crazy trying to remember. A trip to D.C. will give her a break. A change of pace. Fresh scenery."

"If this is about you not trusting her, I'll let her stay here with me until you get back."

"It's not that," Gareth protested. "Or not entirely."

"You can't take someone with amnesia and let them loose in an uncontrolled environment. Anything could happen. She has no self-protection, Gareth. You might as well let a toddler play in traffic."

"Isn't that overstating things a bit? C'mon, Jacob. She can handle ordinary daily tasks. She's impaired, not stupid." He shot to his feet and paced.

"You're deliberately misunderstanding me." Jacob's face so like Gareth's own, creased with concern. "Gracie is terribly vulnerable right now, as anyone in her condition would be. She doesn't have a framework for making rational decisions. Emotionally she's a wreck, even if she hides it well."

Jacob's words pricked Gareth's conscience. He moved restlessly. "You're too late with your advice. We...talked last night. I invited her and she accepted."

"Good Lord. You've slept with her." Jacob rose to his feet, his hands-on-hip stance combative. "How could you? She's a woman in your care, under your protection. I've never known you to be so cavalier about an innocent."

Jacob knew him far too well for subterfuge. Gareth's instinctive urge to defend himself mingled with the sick certainty that Jacob was right on all fronts. "It just happened," he muttered.

Though in truth he'd been imagining sex with Gracie almost from the first instant he laid eyes on her. She made him feel emotions he'd thought long dead and buried. The warmth in her smile and the admiration he felt for her poignant fortitude thawed the ice castle to which he'd condemned himself. Even if her reasons for coming were unacceptable, Gareth still wanted her. At least for now.

Jacob still glared at him.

Gareth didn't care. "She had a bad dream. I comforted her."

"Shit, Gareth. That's the lamest excuse I've ever heard. You could have walked away. You *should* have walked away. You didn't have to screw her."

"It was her idea."

"And you went along with it like the saint you are."

"I tried to say no. She's very persuasive."

Jacob threw up his hands in disgust. "I give up. You've obviously lost your mind. But swear to God...if taking her on the road makes things worse don't expect me to mop up the pieces."

"You're a doctor. You took an oath to help people."

"But I never promised to cover for your sorry ass."

Gareth rubbed his neck. "She has to go home. After D.C. And she wants me to take her."

"Did you agree?"

"Yeah."

"You know she's scared."

"I get that. But there's still the matter of why she came in the first place. And what her father had to do with it."

Jacob shrugged. "Clearly she's not a threat. Even if she's a reporter, what kind of story could she write? You've never even taken her up to the house to meet Father. Is that intentional?"

"Of course it's intentional." Gareth joined his brother at the wide, plate-glass expanse that turned a dry medical office into an inviting arboretum. "He's not been feeling well. Her tenure here is extremely temporary. It seemed pointless to involve him."

"Where is she right now?"

"I left her sleeping. But I suppose it's getting late. I should go check on her."

"If she wants to go with you to Washington, it's her prerogative. But be damned careful, Gareth."

"I have it all under control. Don't worry."

Gracie awoke midmorning to memories of an incredible night. She would have chalked the heated visions up to wild dreams, were it not for the unmistakable dent in the pillow beside hers.

"Gareth?"

No answer. Feeling embarrassed and bashful, she slid out of bed and wrapped herself in the sheet, tiptoeing to the bathroom. She couldn't decide if she was relieved or disappointed that it was empty.

She shook her head as she climbed into the shower. It was practically lunchtime. No wonder Gareth hadn't lingered. He'd been considerate enough to let her catch up on her rest, but that didn't mean he'd waste a day watching her sleep. That image should have made her laugh, but instead, it inspired a wistful, haunting regret.

Last night she and Gareth had sex. And it was amazing. But in the light of day he was still a Wolff, and she was still an interloper with a murky agenda.

When she was dry and dressed in one of the cute outfits Annalise had provided—navy capri pants, a white sleeveless eyelet tunic, and red paisley slides—she pondered her options. Going with Gareth to Washington was fine, but after that, playtime was over. She had to get her life back in order. And clearly, doing so meant reconnecting with her father.

After a quick mini-meal of yogurt and cereal, she found her cell phone and turned it on. Three bars and a partial battery. That would work. With trepidation, she scrolled through her contacts and found the one marked "Daddy." Her heart beat madly as she hit Send.

"You have reached Edward Darlington, owner and operator of Darlington Gallery in Savannah, Georgia. I'm out of the country at the moment, and the gallery is closed. Hope to be back in my office next week. Please leave a message. Oh, yes... and if this is Gracie, don't give up, baby girl. Make it happen. Make me proud."

Beeeeeppppp...

Gracie stared at her phone with a scowl of frustration. Damn it. What in the heck was going on? Why had her father sent her to confront a Wolff? And Gareth Wolff in particular?

Make it happen. What did that mean? Had she come willingly? Or been coerced...? Closing her eyes, she replayed the message and concentrated on her father's voice. She caught snatches of conversation, whispered fragments of memory. Pleasing her father. She wanted to please him. But why? Because she was a dutiful daughter? Or was there a more selfish reason?

She could see shadowy images of a gallery...of paintings. But was she inventing a memory?

She flipped through the entries, hoping one name...any name, would look familiar. But none jumped out at her. Even reading a sampling of emails was futile. Most of them seemed to be business-related. Back-and-forth chitchats with clients wanting this or that.

The ones that were personal came from user names that meant nothing to Gracie.

Relax. Gareth's deep, comforting voice rang in her ears. She needed him. Now.

He wasn't in the kitchen or in the living room and his bedroom was empty, the bedspread made up neatly, pillows plumped, carpet perfectly vacuumed. *The silent army strikes again,* she thought with a grin.

She slipped on a light cardigan and made her way outside. The sun had faded, blocked by turbulent clouds. Shivering, she hurried to Gareth's workshop, and then stopped short. The doors were firmly shut. Was Gareth too chilled to leave them open, or did that signal his need for privacy?

She sneaked closer, and cautiously took a quick glance in the window. The large, mostly open room was completely empty of human inhabitants. A dog, curled up on a rag rug, raised his head, whined halfheartedly, and promptly went back to sleep. Clearly not a guard dog.

Clouds scudded more quickly now, and the smell of rain scented the air. It occurred to Gracie that she was in the middle of nowhere, with no one to turn to in an emergency, and with little true knowledge of the man whose home she had invaded.

Cowed by the gathering storm and her sensation of utter aloneness, she stumbled back to the house, slammed the heavy front door against the wind and stood with her back to it. Now what?

She prowled the halls of Gareth's house, studying paintings, sculptures, priceless wall hangings. For the first time, she noticed an eerie omission. Nowhere in the house could she find a single photograph, not even in Gareth's designer-perfect, strangely austere bedroom.

The homiest room in the entire dwelling, aside from the luxuriant solarium and pool, was the kitchen. Shiny pots with gleaming copper bottoms hung overhead along with ropes of garlic and dried tomatoes. Behind the stove and sink, handmade terracotta tiles with images of a dancing Kokopelli lent warmth and color.

But no refrigerator art…no framed photographs on the built-in desk, nothing.

And still no sign of Gareth.

Outside, the storm lashed the house with fury. She flinched once at a particularly synchronous bolt of lightning and thunder, but apparently she wasn't afraid of nature's pyrotechnics. In the quiet of empty rooms, she could hear the drumming of heavy rain on the roof.

With the right companion it would have been the perfect day to curl up in front of the massive fireplace and enjoy the flames while reading…or better still, making love.

She'd been trying to put last night out of her mind. Had she made a fool of herself? Begging Gareth to stay in her room… in her bed? Was that why he disappeared this morning? To give them both breathing space? Mortification heated her face, even though she was all alone with her painful thoughts.

At last, she landed in the library. It was a fabulous room, with three entire walls of built-in shelves running waist high to the ceiling and cabinets below. She scanned the titles, all neatly divided into categories. Gareth Wolff might give the appearance of wildness and lack of concern for convention, but in his workshop and in this book-filled room, she caught glimpses of his control.

For half an hour she flipped aimlessly through one volume

and another. Too restless to read in earnest, she finally knelt and opened a cabinet door. She found nothing out of the ordinary: stacks of magazines, writing and mailing supplies, a collection of baseball cards.

But moving on to the next section, she hit pay dirt. The photographs for which she'd unconsciously been searching. Albums of them. Expensive leather volumes of archival paper…covers imprinted in gold with dates from the 1980s.

Curiosity trumped caution. Scooping three of the big books into her arms, she stood, kicked off her shoes and carried the heavy volumes to the sofa. Curled up with an afghan, she began flipping pages. Like Pandora, she soon wished she had left well enough alone. Someone had painstakingly documented every print story about the Wolff family's tragedy.

The publications ranged from the *New York Times* to the most lurid of tabloids. Some accounts were strictly journalistic, others were prurient and speculative. One picture in particular caught her eye. It was black and white, fairly grainy, but heartbreakingly poignant.

Perhaps the photographer had been surreptitious in his labors, because she couldn't imagine Gareth's family allowing press at a funeral. In the image, two men of similar height and bearing stood flanking a matched set of flower draped coffins. Between them, tiny in stature, wearing a dark suit, was a young boy. Each man held one of his hands.

The caption read, "Financial titans Victor and Vincent Wolff grieve the loss of their wives. With them is seven-year-old son and nephew, Gareth Wolff."

Tears rolled down her cheeks and her heart broke. How awful, how impossibly tragic. She read on…

In a kidnapping scenario that has state police and federal law enforcement baffled, the spouses of multimillionaires Victor and Vincent Wolff were snatched at gunpoint during a shopping trip on a busy street in downtown Charlottesville, Virginia. No word from the perpetrators for three days, and then a demand for money. Despite the fact that the Wolff brothers handed over the ransom (reputed to be in the neighborhood of three million dollars), the women were later killed execution-style, with single gunshots to the head. Their bodies were found in an abandoned warehouse in suburban D.C. A reward is being offered for any information regarding this crime.

Gracie trembled, wishing she had never read a word. Who had assembled this morbid collection? Why would Gareth hold on to something so clearly painful? The tragedy had altered life for his entire family of eight. They had withdrawn from society and built walls, both literal and metaphorical.

A few of the clippings described how the brothers sold fabulous homes in central Virginia, bought a remote mountain and built a fortress to lock their offspring away from a dangerous world. Private tutors, a guard gate and little contact with the public. Ever.

No wonder Gareth hadn't wanted her here.

She laid aside the albums, leaving one open to the picture of little Gareth, and pulled her legs to her chest, resting her chin on her knees. The fire couldn't warm the cold that seeped deep into her bones. Did Gracie have a mother? Somehow she didn't think so. She glanced at the newspaper photo again, and for the flash of an instant, she saw another funeral. And a young girl hand in hand with her daddy. Was the young girl Gracie? Did she have that in common with Gareth?

In an instant, the memory was gone. If indeed it *was* a memory. Maybe she was trying so hard to regain her past that she had begun *inventing* recollections that were nothing more than wishful fiction.

The rain slashing the window doubled in intensity, drumming painfully at Gracie's shattered nerves. Where in heaven's name was Gareth?

Gareth jumped out of the Jeep and made a dash for the porch, shaking like a dog before opening the front door and ducking inside. He was soaked through to the skin, and he still hadn't decided how to handle Gracie and what happened last night.

Should he go with nonchalant avoidance? Or did they confront what they had done?

In his bathroom, he stripped out of his sodden clothes and changed into a soft flannel shirt and old jeans. This afternoon he needed to make some arrangements for the D.C. trip, but making sure Gracie was okay had to take priority. The sizzle of excitement he felt at the thought of seeing her was disconcerting.

He needed to back off a little and make sure she understood the score. And given Jacob's dire warnings, perhaps he ought to give her an out on traveling with him. After last night, the trip took on a whole new significance. Him and Gracie. In a hotel. Together.

Shit. He hardened in his jeans, making the relaxed fit not so relaxed after all. Leaving her in bed this morning had been sheer torture, but also a matter of self-preservation. Getting in too deep with a female relationship hadn't been a problem for a long, long time.

But Gracie, with her mysterious entrée into his life and her total lack of self-knowledge didn't fit the mold. He wanted to protect her. And at the same time, protect himself *from* her. Damned stupid and probably mutually exclusive outcomes.

Pausing only to towel dry his hair and run his hands through it, he left the steamy bathroom and went on a hunt, finding his quarry ensconced in front of a cozy fire in one of his favorite rooms in the house.

He stopped short in the doorway, lead in his gut. "What in the hell do you think you're doing?"

Her head snapped up, her expression wary. Mascara smeared one cheekbone, evidence that she had been crying. "I shouldn't have," she whispered.

Fury shook him. Conflicting emotions shredded his control. He had been ready to scoop her into his arms and carry her back to bed. Now he could barely look at her. "No, you damn well shouldn't have." Again and again she broke through barriers he'd erected, opening him up to emotions he hated. He didn't *want* to feel anything.

His icy-cold voice made Gracie blanch. Her eyes welled with tears, distress written on her delicate features. "I'm so sorry," she whispered.

"For what? Snooping?"

Her lower lip quivered. She scooted out from under the cashmere afghan and stood to face him. "No... Well, yes...for being nosy. But I meant I was sorry about your mother. So sorry. Gareth, you were only a baby."

"I won't discuss my mother with you." Gracie's simple compassion picked at the scab of a wound that was raw despite the passage of time. He couldn't allow her to expose the lack of healing. Not now. Not ever.

"But it was so long ago, and you're still hurting."

"And you're an authority on grief now? You and all your wonderful memories?"

She flinched, making him feel like a heel, but he was so angry he shook with it. No one else dared push at the walls that isolated him.

"Who made the albums?" she asked, her eyes raking his face with a sympathy he didn't want...didn't need.

"I did." He kicked the leg of the sofa with his toe. "None of the adults around me seemed to realize that I was the only one of the kids old enough to read. And newspapers were all over the house. I cut out the articles and saved them. I thought every word was true. And believe me, some of the worst stories made my stomach hurt."

"How do you mean?"

"I saw pictures of the bodies. My mother. My aunt. Eyes closed. Blood oozing from gaping holes in their heads."

"Dear God."

Gracie looked on the point of a breakdown, and he didn't care. Couldn't care. "A few of the tabloids hinted at drug deals and secret affairs…anything to sell papers. I was too young to know they were inventing things at random."

She took a step in his direction, but he held up his hand, his stomach twisting with nausea. "I didn't sleep for months. I'd wake up screaming, and my father never came. It was always a nanny. My dad was sedated in his bedroom, unable to deal with the grief, the guilt."

"The guilt?"

"He felt as if he'd failed in his duty as a husband. That he hadn't been proactive in protecting her."

Gracie held out her hands. "They were shopping, like a million women in America every day. People can't live in a bubble, Gareth."

"Oh, but you're wrong," he sneered. "With enough money you can hide indefinitely. He and my uncle did that to us. No Little League. No pizza parties at Chuck E. Cheese's. No trips to the zoo. Our entire world became this mountain. And it was years before we realized what we were missing…before we rebelled."

He hated rehashing this, hated that Gracie had seen the nasty underbelly of his life. But something in those big solemn eyes made him spill his guts uncensored as if hoping against hope that she could take away the agony of remembering.

He poured himself a shot of whiskey from a crystal decanter, enjoying the burn as it hit his throat. "Are you happy now?" he asked, seeing the sarcasm hit its mark on her expressive face. In her stocking feet she was so small, so slight, so defenseless.

Jacob was right. Anything could happen to her. And Gareth wouldn't be able to protect her. Evil lurked on every corner, even more so now than in 1985. He couldn't afford to fall in love with her. He wouldn't allow it.

She shrugged helplessly. "I'm not happy, Gareth. How could I be? I wish I could make those terrible memories all go away."

"That's just it," he muttered, downing a second reckless shot, though he seldom drank. "You've been making such a big damn deal about having amnesia, but there have been too many nights when I would have given anything to be able to forget."

"It must have been unbearable." Her compassion rolled over him in waves, and he hated the way it made him feel. Stripped raw. Completely naked.

He hurled the glass into the fireplace, hearing the gratifying sound as it shattered, enjoying the wide-mouthed shock on Gracie's face. "Get out of my sight," he said, jaw clenched. "I don't want to look at you."

Nine

Gracie sobbed, half crazed, as she blundered through the forest. She didn't even remember which way she came in the beginning, but she was leaving. There would be help at the bottom. A police station. Kind townspeople. Whatever…it didn't matter.

She couldn't stay here.

Briars scraped her legs. Sweat rolled down her temples. A fleeting sense of déjà vu tweaked her memory, but she was too distraught to care. The rain had stopped, and now that the sun was back out, the humidity turned the spring forest into an itchy, moist sauna.

The ground was soggy. She slipped time and again, falling on her butt, leaving mudslides as she tumbled down the mountain. In the midst of one headlong plunge, a thick root caught her foot and twisted her ankle painfully.

She cried out and fell to her hip, curling into a fetal ball. Even above the harsh sound of her breathing, she could hear crashing and cursing above her. It was impossible to outrun a wolf.

Gareth burst through a thicket of rhododendron and stopped

dead, his face ashen. "I'm sorry, Gracie. Hell, I'm sorry." He knelt beside her, eyes aghast. "You're barefoot. Holy God."

Her feet were a mess...cut, bleeding. And her ankle had already swollen to alarming proportions. She buried her face in her arms, embarrassed, hurt. "I wasn't thinking straight. And I know what you're going to say. *Stupid, irrational woman.*"

He lifted her carefully and started the trek back up the mountain. His arms were strong as tree trunks, his mighty legs covering the uneven ground with ease. "You're wrong," he muttered. "I was thinking what an ass I am."

This time, Jacob was not quite so welcoming when they showed up at his house. He glared at his brother. "Christ, you're hardheaded."

The two men faced off in a visual battle of wills. Gareth held Gracie tightly. She smelled his sweat, felt the faint tremor in his arms. "I don't need a lecture, Jacob. Take care of her...please."

Gracie knew that the final word had been dragged out of him. He was not in a conciliatory mood. She touched his arm. "I'm fine." The last thing she wanted was to cause discord between the two siblings.

Jacob cursed beneath his breath as he led them back to an examining room. Gareth deposited Gracie gently on the table. He touched her hair. "Should I stay?"

Before she could answer, Jacob held open the door. "No. We don't need you for this."

Again the two men bristled, but amazingly, Gareth bowed out and left the room.

Jacob turned to Gracie, his gaze a mix of professional assessment and personal concern. "Are you okay?"

Tears clogged her throat, but she was damned if she'd let them fall. "I did something stupid. It wasn't Gareth's fault."

"Yeah, right." The wry twist of his mouth said he didn't believe a word of her defense. "I know my brother, Gracie. He's hard as glass, not to mention stubborn. Let me look at you."

Even the gentle probe of his fingers was painful. Her ankle looked dreadful, but fortunately the X-rays showed no sign of a break. After cleansing the cuts and abrasions, Jacob wrapped her foot and lower leg tightly in an ACE bandage. He worked in silence, his expression grave. "You can walk short distances without hurting anything, but ice it today while you're resting. Ibuprofen will help." He covered her feet in soft cotton socks.

When he was done, he sat down on a rolling stool and crossed his arms over his chest.

In that moment his resemblance to his brother was uncanny. He sighed. "I think you should let me take you home, Gracie."

"Not yet," she whispered. "My father's out of the country, and I can't exactly call someone in my list of phone contacts and tell them the truth. I have no way of knowing which ones are personal and which ones are business related. They would think I'm insane. Besides…" She paused and fumbled for an explanation. "Gareth—"

"If you're hoping for something from him, you'll never find it. Gareth doesn't have much capacity for love or for trust. He was the only one of the six of us kids really old enough to re-member our mother and our aunt. He was the only one they deemed able to go to the funeral."

She bowed her head. "It makes me sick to think about it." She didn't mention the albums. Jacob might not know about them, and it wasn't her place to reveal that secret.

"Gareth endured what no child should ever have to face. Not only the loss of a parent, but the violence of it…the public forum. Kieran and I were only four and five. We were protected from the worst of it."

"But obviously you knew your mother wasn't coming back."

He shrugged. "Yeah. We got the speech about heaven and how much she loved us. I remember some bad dreams and feel-ing confused. But in the end, I was a kid…I got past it. Gareth wasn't so lucky."

"He's still hurting, Jacob. A lot."

"I know. And if you're not careful, his pain will damage you as well."

"He's kind when he wants to be. And gentle."

"Don't go to Washington with him," Jacob urged. "Don't fall in love with him."

"I don't plan to," she said, raising her head and meeting his gaze, hers bleak. "Fall in love, I mean. What would be the point?"

Jacob stood and put a hand on her shoulder. "Be strong, little Gracie. Concentrate on regaining your memory. You have a life waiting for you. I love my brother. He's a complicated, wonderful man. But he's no Prince Charming, despite the castle vibe around here."

He kissed her cheek just as Gareth knocked impatiently and entered the room.

Jacob held up his hands when his brother's eyes flashed with displeasure. "Doctor-patient privilege."

Gareth scowled until his eyes landed on Gracie's bandaged foot. His face softened, and he went to her, absentmindedly stroking her hair. "Did Jacob get you all fixed up?"

She nodded, her throat tight. "I could get used to having my own private physician on call." Her attempt at a joke fell flat, none of the three of them in a mood for levity.

Gareth scooped her up for the return trip to the Jeep. "I owe you one, Jacob."

Jacob followed them out. "Remember the ice. And elevate the ankle if you can. That will help with the swelling."

It was warm outside. And Gareth had taken the cover off the Jeep while he waited. He tucked Gracie into her seat. She smiled at her physician. "Thank you, Jacob. You're a wonderful doctor."

Gareth snorted as he got in and started the engine. "If he was that good, he'd have cured your amnesia."

"Gareth!" She punched his arm.

"Jacob knows I'm kidding."

The brothers stared at one another over Gracie's head. "He's my big brother," Jacob said. "I'm used to it."

Back at the house, Gareth carried her again, despite her protests. He bypassed his room and took her straight to hers, depositing her gently on the bed. "I'll get you some lunch."

She lay still, studying patterns in the wooden raftered ceiling. Her brain didn't want to think about anything more complicated than counting knotholes at the moment.

Gareth returned in short order with a tray set for two. The turkey and provolone sandwiches wouldn't have passed muster for a Martha Stewart photo shoot, but the single pink rose he'd tucked into a tiny crystal pitcher drew attention away from the efforts of a clumsy chef.

He set the tray on the bedside table and perched beside her, taking a linen napkin and laying it across her lap. She accepted the glass of lemonade he offered and downed a thirsty gulp. "I'm not hungry," she protested when he picked up a plate.

"You need to eat. Doctor's orders."

It was clear from his dogged expression that he would brook no protest. She tried to chew a few bites, but the food stuck in her throat. She dropped the half-eaten sandwich on her plate. "I really am sorry, Gareth. So sorry. I've intruded upon your life in so many ways, it appalls me. If you would rather I not go to Washington, Jacob will take me home."

He leaned forward and rescued a crumb from her chin. "Did he put you up to that?"

She bit her lip, shifting restlessly. "He's protective of you."

"And you, I think."

"Only in a professional capacity. You're his major concern."

"I'm a big boy. I can take care of myself. We'll stick with the original plan. A couple of days in the Capitol and then we'll see if your father has returned. I'm not taking you to Savannah until I know he'll be there to look after you." He sighed deeply and turned away from her, resting his elbows on his knees and dropping his head into his hands. "I owe you an explanation."

She touched his shoulder, felt the rigid muscles. "You owe me nothing."

He jumped to his feet and paced her elegant bedroom. "You're the only person who has ever seen those albums." She couldn't see his face, but his body language shouted his unease.

"How is that possible? They weren't exactly hidden."

He shoved his hands in the back pocket of his jeans, his brooding masculine beauty threatening to take her breath away. "For years, I kept the newspaper and magazine clippings concealed in boxes under my bed. When I was fourteen, I persuaded my tutor to help me order the special albums. He was a nice guy. One of my favorite teachers ever, actually. But he got married and moved away…"

She remained silent, reluctant to halt the flow of his painful introspection.

Gareth continued. "Bit by bit…in secret…I started arranging all the papers by date and securing them in the books. I'm sure it was unhealthy…this obsession I had with the kidnapping and murder. But I couldn't seem to let it go. One day my father caught me looking through my macabre collection and went practically apoplectic with rage. He ordered me to destroy the albums…called in one of the servants to take them away."

"Oh, Gareth…"

"I begged, pleaded… He didn't understand that those scraps of paper were all I had left of my mother. They were a connection, albeit a terrible one. A link that kept her alive in my memory."

"What happened then?"

"Our housekeeper saved the albums, secretly. Bless her dear old heart. Years later, when I was twenty-one, she produced them and said that I was old enough to decide their fate."

"So you kept them."

"I didn't *not* keep them. I had changed, matured. I thought about destroying them…for my own mental health. But I was caught between the past and the present. It felt disloyal to wipe away my mother's memory entirely."

"But that's not exactly what you would have been doing."

"I understood that intellectually. But for whatever reason, I couldn't do it…couldn't get rid of them. My solution and the proof of my sanity was that I never once opened them…not even that first day. I've kept them the way a recovering alcoholic tucks away a bottle of gin. As a test."

She felt sick. "And when you walked into the library today…"

"I saw that you had one of the albums spread on the sofa. I could see the picture from across the room. I overreacted. I'm sorry."

She clambered from the bed, wincing as her abused feet made contact with the floor. His body was stiff, but she embraced him anyway, arms around his waist, her cheek tucked to his chest. "If you apologize again, I'll smack you."

That coaxed a grin from him. "You're mighty fierce." He hugged her tightly, releasing some of her tension. "You don't have to be afraid of me. I'm not crazy, Gracie. Honest to God."

She smiled, releasing him. "No one ever said you were."

"I'll get rid of them if you think I should."

The import of that single sentence jangled in her brain. This was too intense, especially for someone who couldn't remember what she ate for breakfast last week. "I think they can go back into the cabinet for the moment. No harm, no foul. Do you want me to take care of it?"

"Already did," he said gruffly. "And no…I didn't look at them."

"It would have been okay if you had."

"Not to me. I'm done with that part of my life. My brothers and my cousins and I have moved on."

And it was time for her to do the same. She reached for her cell, and put it on speaker phone. "Listen to this."

"You have reached Edward Darlington, owner and operator of Darlington Gallery in Savannah, Georgia. I'm out of the country at the moment, and the gallery is closed. Hope to be back in my office next week. Please leave a message. Oh, yes and if this is Gracie, don't give up, baby girl. Make it happen. Make me proud."

Gareth's face darkened. "No offense, but I'm not a big fan of your dad. And I've never even met the guy."

"What do you think he wants? Do you by any chance paint in addition to making furniture?"

"No." His lashes flickered as if he had thought of something she hadn't. "And I don't have a clue what he wants. He owns a gallery. Maybe he's like the senator. Thinks that having me do a public appearance will help his bottom line."

"But that doesn't make sense. I don't even know you. And I approached you under less than ideal circumstances. Surely he knew the answer to any request like that would be a resounding *no.*"

"Maybe he thought your charm would win me over. You are kind of cute and cuddly."

"Kind of?" She pretended to scowl.

He surprised her with a hungry kiss. "Men are weak," he mumbled, kissing his way along her neck. "Maybe your dad is smarter than we think."

She wriggled free, suddenly less amused. "I have old messages from clients on my phone. Maybe he wanted to sell you something."

Exasperation marked his features. "I don't know. I wish the hell I did. But we'll find out. I promise you."

Ten

Gracie improved rapidly. Seventy-two hours later, her ankle was sore but in working order. Her head barely ached at all. Cuts and bruises had begun to fade, and Jacob was able to remove the handful of stitches from her leg.

Gareth disappeared for the most part. He holed up in his workshop, avoiding Gracie much of the day. When they *were* together, he seemed ill at ease, lending credence to her theory that he was not happy that he had shared so many intimate details of his life with her.

The evening meal was their only contact of any length, and even then he ate his food, drank his wine and conversed only at a bare minimum. After the first awkward day, Gracie gave up, retreating into silence herself and pretending that she had never seen Gareth Wolff naked.

She put the hours she was alone to good use, combing newspapers and magazines, as well as scouring the internet for information about the world in general and her place in it in particular. Her father's gallery had a website, but her name wasn't listed anywhere. She studied the photos, and though it all seemed vaguely familiar, even looking at the head shot of Edward Darlington produced nothing more than a nagging sense of anxiety.

Articles about Savannah caught her eye. She studied photographs of the old Southern city...read stories about its history. Little flashes, snippets of recollections, reassured her that the entire picture would soon slip into focus. Her life *wasn't* a blank slate. It was there, waiting. All she had to do was be patient.

Easier said than done when she lay in bed at night, her body yearning for Gareth's possession. She was poised on the blade of a two-edged sword. If she remembered everything, her time with Gareth would come to a messy end. But if the amnesia continued, she still had only a short window to savor his protectiveness and his sensual attentions. Very soon, she would go home and try to *find* her past, bit by bit.

Gareth sought her out on the fourth morning after the photo album contretemps. She was in the library searching for any book that might spark a memory. He braced his hands in the doorway as if not trusting himself to go in. "We're leaving at noon. Does that work for you?" His eyes were hooded. The dark smudges beneath them indicated restless sleep.

She wanted to help, but she didn't know how. Moving toward him with the caution afforded an unpredictable animal, she smiled hesitantly. "Will Jacob be taking us to the airport?"

A glint of humor danced across his face. "No."

"We're driving?" Several hours in the confined intimacy of a car seemed dangerous.

"No."

Hands on hips, she shot him a threatening stare. "Then how are we getting there?"

Gracie Darlington was about as threatening as a kitten. "You'll see." He loved teasing her. The pink in her cheeks and the flustered look in her eyes made him want to devour her one sensual inch at a time. He cleared his throat. "Your suitcase was delivered a little while ago. Annalise didn't want to send it to the hotel and risk anything getting lost. She assures me that you'll be covered for any fashion emergency…with the possible exception of a White House state dinner."

"What should I wear for travel?" The suspicion on her face hadn't abated.

He shrugged. "Comfortable. Smart casual. She sent a garment bag, too. You'll probably find what you need in there."

For a moment, the combative kitten appeared unusually upset. "I don't even know if I can afford to repay you," she fretted. "Your sister must have spent thousands of dollars."

He muttered a curse. "For God's sake. I have enough money to outfit you in something new every day from now until we both keel over dead. Forget about it." He reached for her hand, dragged her out into the hall, closed the library door and backed her up against it, crowding her deliberately with his considerable size advantage.

When she opened her mouth to continue the argument, he shut her up the quickest way he knew how. "Shh, Gracie." He loved the way her body went lax when his mouth captured hers. "I've missed you."

She nipped his bottom lip with sharp teeth. "I'm not the one who's been hiding out."

"I've been working," he said, setting the record straight. Wolff men didn't hide from anything. "I'm sorry if you felt neglected. I'll make it up to you this weekend."

She closed her eyes, a dreamy smile tilting lush, pink lips. "I may not know much, but I'm pretty sure someone must have warned me about men like you."

"I'm harmless." Her quick gurgle of laughter eased into a sigh of pleasure that hardened his shaft painfully and quickly. Staying away from her for several days had seemed the smart thing to do. Hearing her father's sleazy voice on the phone recording had reminded Gareth of all the reasons he shouldn't trust her.

So he went cold turkey. No Gracie. Period.

But he had ached, God, how he ached. Already his body knew hers, remembered the jolt of pleasure that threatened to pull him under when he entered her. Soft skin, soft breasts, soft everything. A softness so beautiful a man could bury himself in it willingly and never surface again.

He cupped her ass. "You need to know something, though."

Her pelvis was pressed to his with predictable results. "What?"

"I've booked two rooms at the hotel in D.C. You don't have to go there as my lover. We can be friends if that's what you want."

She pulled back and searched his face. "You're serious." It was a statement, not a question.

He tucked a silky curl behind her shell-like ear. "Jacob has been on my case. And I feel a certain need to protect you from myself."

"Is that even possible?"

"Hell if I know." He kissed her again. "I don't want you to think badly of me when this all ends."

The happiness on her face dimmed. "You haven't done anything wrong. Why would I think that?"

"I should never have made love to you."

She stiffened in his embrace. "That was my fault. And I've already apologized."

The strangled hurt in her voice made him swear again. "I don't want your regrets *or* your apology. All I want is you." He picked her up, pressing his erection against her in a move that made them both gasp.

She circled his waist with her legs. "I want you, too. And the trip to D.C. is *not* going to be platonic. You know it and I know it. But it would be nice if you could act a little happier about it."

"I don't feel happy," he admitted grudgingly. He lifted her up and down, rubbing his considerably aroused shaft against the spot he so badly wanted to feel, to see, to fill. "You've messed up my life, Gracie. Made me question things I've never questioned before."

She dropped her head back against the wood, baring her slender, delicate neck to his mouth. Skin that tasted like strawberries. "You'll be fine when I'm gone," she whispered.

The regret in her words hurt something deep inside his chest. He pushed the pain away. He knew how to do that…had been doing it for twenty-five years. "I'm not fine now." The words ripped from a throat raw with suppressed emotion. He dropped her to her feet and unzipped her jeans, dragging them and her panties down her legs.

"Gareth." She had her hands behind her, braced on the door. Nothing about her posture suggested that he stop what he was doing.

"Lift your arms."

She obeyed instantly, but protested. "Somebody could walk in…"

"Not today. I swear. Relax. We're alone." He was having trouble stringing words together coherently. When he had her naked, he stopped breathing and just looked at her. Narrow waist. Flaring feminine hips. Small but perfect breasts. A neat fluff of red-gold hair between her slender thighs.

She folded her arms across her chest, gnawing her lower lip. "It's embarrassing that only one of us is wearing clothes." Clearly she was trying for sophisticated humor, but her cheeks were fiery red.

He moved her arm and touched one breast, circled the pale pink nipple, watching in fascination as it tightened. "I'll catch up. But first, let me enjoy the view." He bent his head and tasted her there, sucking gently until Gracie cried out.

Her hands tangled in his hair, pulling him closer. "Shouldn't we go to your bedroom…or mine…?"

He unfastened his pants and freed himself, hardly able to touch the tight, sensitive skin. "No time," he groaned, desperately glad he had stuffed a condom in his pocket. He couldn't fool himself. This was what he'd had in mind since he awoke hard and hungry that morning.

He rolled on the protection, wincing when Gracie brushed her hand over him intimately.

She touched his cheek with gentle affection, almost unmanning him. "I want you so much," she said softly. "You make me shake with it. I look at you and I melt inside."

He lifted her a second time, aligning their bodies, probing at her slick entrance with the head of his shaft. "I need you, Gracie." The confession was wrung from him…and he regretted it almost immediately. But in the bliss of burying himself deep inside her, he ignored the thought.

He forged the physical connection, meeting no resistance, relishing the snug, tight fit. All the way to the head of her womb, heartbeat to heartbeat. He resented the condom that separated them. Wanted to fill her with his seed, mark her at the most primitive level.

Her forehead rested on his, her breathing ragged. "I won't ever forget this," she whispered. "I won't ever forget you."

Again, the understanding of deferred pain hovered just out of reach. He shook his head, refusing to think beyond this moment. "Don't talk, Gracie. Let me make you come."

He thrust hard, banging her bottom against the unforgiving door in a reckless rhythm. She chanted his name. "Gareth. Gareth. Gareth." Her arms tightened around his neck in a stranglehold. "Don't stop," she panted. "Please don't stop."

As if he could. Blinded now, eyes closed, he felt the end barreling toward him. His hips flexed. He felt Gracie's inner muscles clench in orgasm as he shouted his release. All the oxygen departed his lungs. His brain exploded.

Afterward, staggering, he shuffled them down the hall toward his room, her body clinging to his like a limpet, his legs trembling as he tried to find a handhold on reality.

Gracie had amnesia. Even after an interlude that left her reeling with weepy joy. But she was pretty sure no one had ever banged her against a door, pardon the pun.

For a moment, when Gareth entered her, a flash of some sweet memory tangled with the present urgency. She was no virgin. There had been at least someone in her life before. She was sure of it. But memory or no memory, she was positive no one had ever made her feel the way Gareth did. No one had ever made her *want* with such intensity.

She was torn between wanting to giggle and battling a barrage of inexplicable, hot-behind-the-eyes tears. They didn't fall. She blinked them back with dogged ferocity. She had Gareth. For this moment in time, he was hers.

When he dumped her on the bed and dropped facedown beside her, she rolled to look at the clock. "We're going to be late."

He half lifted his head, blinked in the direction she pointed and groaned. "They'll wait…"

"They who?"

His muffled answer segued into a gentle snore. Allowing herself sixty seconds to snuggle against him, she heaved a deep sigh, slid out of bed and scuttled into the hall.

The unmistakable evidence of their spontaneous combustion met her gaze. Panties here, bra there… No one could mistake what had happened. She retrieved her clothing and ran for her room, locking the door and leaning against it with a frantically beating heart.

No one was around to witness her chagrin. She was all alone. But she shivered nonetheless. Gareth continued to surprise her.

She made quick work of a shower and dug into the new bounty Annalise had provided. A navy pantsuit in silk shantung struck her as appropriate travel wear. The matching silk camisole was cream with navy piping.

This time, Annalise had also provided a carry-on stocked with expensive cosmetics. Gracie dressed, applied makeup with a light touch, and packed up her things. The only items of any value she'd had with her when she first arrived on Wolff Mountain were her wallet and cell phone. She tucked those in a bag and went to meet Gareth.

She wasn't about to invade his personal domain, so she perched on a chair in the den and waited for him to show up. It wasn't long. But when he appeared, she couldn't hold back a blush.

Gareth eyed her with a grumpy stare. "You left."

"You said we were leaving at noon. I had to get ready."

He surveyed her from head to toe. "Annalise has great taste, but I like you better naked."

She gaped at him, but shut her mouth sharply and refused to rise to the bait.

Gareth grinned. "No comment?"

She shook her head. "My big suitcase is in the bedroom. Everything else is right here."

In a matter of moments Gareth had loaded their bags into the Jeep and they were on their way. He looked strong and handsome in a crisp white dress shirt and dark slacks. The open collar and rolled up sleeves suited him.

They took a different route this time, bypassing the cutoff to Jacob's place and instead, climbing higher up the mountain. This was the closest she had come to the magnificent home where Gareth had spent his formative years. The enormous house was amazing.

She knew why Gareth had not taken her there. He didn't trust her to be around his family. And knowing that hurt. Still, she would love to see inside the massive structure. It demanded respect because of its sheer size, but it was beautiful as well.

She could come right out and ask him to give her a tour when they got back. But given her father's cryptic words, she didn't want Gareth to think she had any mischief in mind. Surely her father didn't expect her to steal the family silver or to try her hand at safe-breaking.

It was a measure of her good mood that she could joke about it, even with herself.

The Jeep angled sharply, and she grabbed on to the door. "You can't tell me there's an airstrip up here."

Gareth shot her an amused glance. "Of course not. Don't be ridiculous."

They shot through an opening in the trees. Gracie's eyes widened even as instinctive apprehension made her muscles tense. No airstrip, but instead, a helipad. The chopper itself was black and yellow. The body was sleek and shiny, with lots of glass, and on the side, the words Wolff and Sons, Inc. painted in sharp relief.

"Um, Gareth?"

He didn't give her time to freak out. "C'mon."

A uniformed attendant greeted Gareth respectfully and made short work of stowing their bags. The pilot, who had been standing nearby smoking a cigarette, gave a salute and climbed into the vehicle, starting up the rotors with a *whoosh* of sound.

Gareth grabbed Gracie's hand and helped her board, tucking her into a seat and fastening her seat belt. "Wear these," he said, placing large noise-deadening headphones over her ears. Instantly she could hear the radio-transmitted conversation between the pilot, his copilot/attendant and Gareth.

It was crystal clear who was boss. Though Gareth's manner

with his employees was joking and relaxed, they treated him deferentially.

Without warning, the chopper lifted straight up into the air, hovered just long enough for Gracie to get to an incredible vantage point from which to see the house and then they were off, headed northeast and covering ground rapidly.

Gracie was either fascinated or terrified or both. She felt like a bird, streaking high above the earth. Below her, Virginia's fertile farm fields lay like patchwork quilts on the land. Cars were no more than ants scurrying along twisted silver highways. Lakes and rivers marked the landscape. Once she got past her initial frozen fear, she loved it.

The copilot passed back two boxed lunches. Gareth dug into his, polishing off the chicken salad sandwich quickly and swigging a root beer. Gracie's meal was similar, but it included her favorite lemon/lime soda and one large chocolate chip cookie. Clearly someone had studied her preferences.

She ate a few bites and waited to see if her stomach could handle eating and flying at the same time.

Gareth touched her hand. "You okay?" He mimed the words instead of speaking into the headset.

She nodded. Their seats were close, their hips practically touching. He took a small blanket and tucked it around her shoulders. She appreciated the gesture, because the air was definitely cold.

In record time, it seemed, she began to recognize what she knew as Washington landmarks. The pilot made a wide sweep over the Potomac, and soon they were descending slowly and at last settling gently as a cloud onto the rooftop of a multistory building.

Another trio of helpful young men gathered the luggage and spirited it away. As Gareth bid farewell to the crew, Gracie frowned at the chopper. When he joined her, she waved at the lettering. "Why does it say *and sons?* What about your cousin? She's a girl."

He chuckled, putting his arm around her waist and ushering her toward a nearby door. "Annalise is terrified of helicopters. Hates that we use one at all. She doesn't want to have any part of it…thinks it would be bad luck to have her name or sex included."

Suddenly, Gracie recalled Annalise bemoaning the need for a private jet. Wow. This family could give Bill Gates a run for his money.

Inside the hotel, the air was lightly scented, the thickly carpeted hallways silent but beautifully decorated with sconces and sparkling chandeliers. The cordial manager, a sophisticated blonde with eyes for no one but Gareth, met them in the lobby.

She held out a hand, immaculate nails painted scarlet. "We're delighted to see you again, Mr. Wolff. Your suite is ready for you."

Eleven

Gracie disliked the woman on sight. The tall, leggy female was a little *too* friendly, and if Gracie had been someone important in Gareth's life, the woman's total lack of acknowledgment would have been insulting.

Gareth didn't seem to notice. He shook the woman's hand briefly, his arm still wrapped protectively around Gracie's waist. "Hello, Chandra. The place looks welcoming, as always."

She practically gushed. "How nice of you to say so. We're always delighted to get your reservation." She afforded Gracie a single dismissive glance. "As you requested, we've given you the Jefferson suite. I think you'll find the amenities extremely comfortable. And your *companion*—" a little dig there "—will be equally pampered."

Gareth smiled lazily. "Gracie and I will be very happy, I'm sure."

The other woman blanched and visibly lost several degrees of confidence. Did the lovely Chandra have designs on Gareth Wolff?

The manager grimaced slightly. "Shall I escort you upstairs? Help you get settled in?"

Gareth nuzzled Gracie's cheek, making no bones about his intentions. "I can handle it from here." He took the two key cards. "Thanks, Chandra."

Gracie allowed herself to be propelled across the marble foyer to the small, elegant elevator. As they rode up to the penthouse floor, she studied the crimson paisley wallpaper in the enclosed space. One wall was mirrored, and in its reflection, she saw Gareth's eyes on her. Recognized the sensual intent on his face.

"Quit staring," she muttered.

"I like the view." His lazy smile sent bubbles of anticipation sparkling through her veins.

When the brief ride ended in a smooth stop, he stood back and waited for her to exit. For some reason, she was as nervous as a virgin bride. Their door—the only one in the hallway— was directly opposite the elevator. Gareth used the key card and opened it.

Soft classical music drifted into the foyer from the spacious living room directly in front of them. Lavish flower arrangements, massive bouquets of everything from roses to freesias to tiny Dutch iris, graced the entrance hall cabinet, the coffee table and a duo of marble and cherry pedestals.

Gareth put out the Do Not Disturb sign and locked the dead bolt. He tossed his wallet, phone and keys on the escritoire. "Alone at last." His mocking half smile was perhaps self-directed, but it made Gracie's toes curl in her Italian calfskin pumps.

She licked her lips. "I'm impressed. Though I can't say for sure at this point, I have a feeling that I'm a Holiday Inn Express kind of girl. You know…mass-produced artwork, breakfast in the lobby, that kind of thing. You may have spoiled me forever."

He took her hand. "Come look."

French doors opened out onto a small, private balcony hedged in with black wrought-iron grille work. To their right, the mall, decked out in spring green, stretched from the Capitol building to the Washington Monument, with all the iconic museums in between. The afternoon sun hung low in the sky, shedding warm light over tourists with cameras and joggers enjoying the gentle breeze.

Gracie braced her hands on the railing, peeking down to the street below. "I wish I could remember if I've ever been here," she said, overcome with a pensive melancholy. "It all seems so wonderfully familiar, but I suppose that might simply be the sum total of movies and television programs I've seen."

Gareth massaged her shoulders, his big body trapping hers against the metal that still held the warmth of the day's heat. "Why does it matter either way?" he asked, his tone matter-of-fact. "Embrace the experience. Soak in the sights and sounds. Enjoy being here with me…"

His breath was warm on her nape as he kissed the sensitive spot behind her ear. Gripping the bar at her waist, she tipped her head to one side, offering access, offering an invitation.

Gareth wasn't slow to accept. But his actions were circumspect at first…given their public venue. His hands grasped her hips as he nibbled a course from her ear to her collarbone. With tantalizing slowness, he reached around to unbutton her jacket and slip it from her shoulders, tossing it carelessly on a nearby patio chair.

The spaghetti-strap chemise she wore was thin, as was the delicate ivory bra beneath. There was no hiding her excitement as he brushed the tip of first one breast and then the other. He didn't linger. To the casual observer, they were no more than a man and a woman enjoying the fresh air.

She felt the heat of him, the intensity. The scent of expensive aftershave—something new she hadn't noticed before—teased her nostrils. It was a potent aphrodisiac. Mingled with the essence of the man himself, it hit her at a most basic level.

Speaking of abandoned pleasures and pheromones and wicked temptation…

"When do we have to be at the senator's home?" she croaked, trying desperately for common sense, for self-preservation. They'd had sex only a few hours before, and yet between them shimmered a need so intense she felt it as a physical pain.

"Eight o'clock," he murmured, caressing her bottom. "Hours from now. We have all the time we want."

Her body went boneless, slumping backward, moving unconsciously into his embrace. "I don't have much time left," she whispered. "Don't make me wait."

He growled. He actually growled. The masculine sound sent gooseflesh all over her body. His chest heaved. "Inside, Gracie Darlington. Let me have my way with you."

Stunning her into an awed silence, he scooped her into his arms and carried her back to the luxurious room with the antique settee and the thick Persian rug. Hesitating only momentarily, he strode through the door to the right and found his own quarters, his set of bags stowed in the enormous, open armoire.

He flipped back the chocolate duvet, slipped off her shoes and deposited her carefully on a nest of pillows. "We've done hard and fast," he said, already stripping out of his clothes. "Now I'm going to make you ache, make you yearn." He paused, magnificently naked. "Imagine that we're all alone in the world. Nothing exists outside this suite. No phones. No meddlesome relatives. Only you and me."

And no memories that, when recovered, would almost surely come between them.

The sight of Gareth's nude body literally took her breath away. Muscle and bone and sinew combined to create a man who emanated confidence and beauty in equal measure. He was fully erect, and her mouth dried, imagining the moment when all that power would penetrate her, fill her, claim her.

She sat up on her elbows. "I'll pretend I have amnesia," she teased. "The only memories I want are the ones of you and me in this room."

"I like how you think." He chuckled, coming down on the bed beside her and unzipping her elegant slacks. "Close your eyes," he murmured. "Relax. Let me give you pleasure."

Her eyelids fluttered shut, even as the butterflies in her stomach increased tenfold. She wasn't by nature a passive person, and ceding control didn't come naturally. Some things a person never forgot.

Gareth's hands were warm and slightly rough as he bared her legs, removing her lace panties in the process. She was still partially dressed from the waist up, but he seemed intent on exploration.

His breath tickled her thigh. Moments later she felt his lips and tongue at the heart of her, teasing her with an intimate caress that arched her back in shocked reaction. "Be still," he commanded.

The words were stern, but his hands on her body were infinitely gentle. She gripped fistfuls of the sheet and cried out when he brought her close to the brink, only to change his course and kiss his way down to her ankle.

She trembled all over, her breathing choppy.

Again he issued an order. "Raise your arms."

It never occurred to her to disobey. She felt him move up and over her, his weight straddling her thighs, but not crushing her. He took the camisole and slithered it up her arms and over her head, pausing to kiss her hard on the lips. Before she could respond, he was dealing with her bra, spiriting it away so easily she might have been perturbed if her brain had been working clearly.

She felt his hands on her waist, her rib cage, her breasts. Breathing became difficult, almost impossible. Every cell in her body was wondering…anticipating. Where would he go next?

A light brush of his thumbs on her nipples furled them tightly.

The similar caress he bestowed on her collarbone made her move restlessly. With her eyes closed, every response intensified. She felt deliciously helpless, though he had not restrained her in any way.

"Open your mouth," he whispered, tracing the curve of her ear with a fingertip. His lips moved over hers...teasing, seductive. He slipped his tongue inside to taste, to tangle with hers. She tried to hold him, but he pulled back. "No touching, no talking." The silky insistence in his words made her shiver.

The life she couldn't remember was hazy, unimportant. With Gareth on his mountaintop and Gracie in Savannah, all the light would disappear from her days. She didn't need her memories to know that. Despite her body's demands, the sexual mood faded. Tears stung her eyes, and she wanted to curl into the covers and sob out her frustration, her confusion...her premonition of dread.

Gareth was no fool. He sensed her emotional disengagement almost instantly. "What's wrong?" he asked. The words were husky with alarm. "Tell me, Gracie. Whatever I did, I'm sorry." Her lashes lifted, and he saw such pain in her beautiful eyes it made his gut hurt. He smoothed a hand over her pale cheek. "I shouldn't have assumed...and after I told you we could come here as friends. God, I'm a fool. Forgive me, Gracie."

She shook her head, a single tear spilling over and marking a wet path to her chin. "It's not that. I want you. I do..."

"But...?" He was a man who fixed things, who solved problems, and he hadn't a clue what to do. He missed her smile desperately.

Her lower lip trembled badly, and he saw her bite down hard to stop the quiver. "I don't think I'm the kind of woman who can do light and easy. I want to. I've tried. But I think I'm falling in love with you."

The words hit him like a sledgehammer. The swift jolt of

joy was immediately obscured by suspicion. He was vulnerable when it came to Gracie Darlington. And a vulnerable man was a weak man.

He rolled to his side and leaned on his elbow facing her, head propped on his hand. "That's impossible. Your situation is making you—"

She stopped him with a hand on his lips. Even that was enough to harden his flagging erection. "Don't discount what I feel," she said, her eyes bleak. "This is my problem, not yours. I have no business getting close to you…to any man, until I regain my memory."

The *any man* reference lit a fury in him that was as fierce as it was unexpected. "Your father told you there's no husband or boyfriend. You don't believe him?"

She pulled a corner of the comforter over her shoulder. "Yes, of course I believe him. But I have this gigantic void that scares me to death. I want to know, but I'm afraid of what I'll find out." Her gaze beseeched him to understand, but damned if he did.

"How is enjoying sex with me a threat?"

"You have everything, Gareth. Family, wealth, an ego the size of Texas. And all that adds up to your incredible confidence. Not a bad thing, but pretty intimidating for a woman who has nothing but a few phone messages from a man who will never deserve a father-of-the-year prize."

"Intimidated?" That word jumped out at him. "Bullshit. You've held your own with me every step of the way. And I want to believe that you came to my mountain without any intent to do wrong. You're a darling, Gracie. By nature and by name. Everything about you is sweet and innocent and untainted by greed."

"You *want* to believe it, but you're not willing to make that last step. Because maybe I'm a darned good actress. And you can't bear the idea that I might play you for a fool and cause you to betray your family."

"No one is that good an actor."

She needed to believe he'd had a change of heart, he could tell. But the moment was lost. Gracie was smart enough to sense that his tiny slivers of doubt that still remained could prick the bubble of their happiness. And he needed to give her some space. With his body protesting every step of the way, he rolled out of bed and pulled on his pants. In the bathroom he found a thick terry robe and took it to her. "Here. Go settle in. Take a bath if you want to…or a nap. Order room service."

She sat up, exchanging the comforter for the robe. With the collar turned up and her hair tousled, she looked far too young to be the object of his baser instincts. Her slim hands tugged the sash into a solid knot. "What will *you* do?" The words were husky.

He shrugged. "I have some phone calls to make. Email to check. If you feel up to it, we'll leave about seven-fifteen. I've ordered a car. The senator's home is in Maclean, Virginia."

She scooted out of bed and bent to gather her things. As she knelt, the robe tightened across her bottom. Gareth swallowed and had to turn away. He was appalled to realize how close he was to an attempt to talk her back into bed.

He pretended to study a pamphlet about hotel room security while Gracie found each piece of the clothing Gareth had removed from her body. When she was done, she hovered in the doorway. "I'm sorry, Gareth."

"Go," he said, his throat tight. "We'll talk later."

As soon as he heard the door to her bedroom close, he jotted a quick note, placed it prominently on the table in the foyer and escaped. The walls were closing in on him, and this time he couldn't disappear into his workshop to find peace.

He strode out the front door of the hotel, ignoring Chandra's attempt to waylay him. Pressure built in his chest like a geyser. Somewhere deep inside him a fault line vibrated. *I think I'm falling in love with you.* Good God. What did a man say to that? She wasn't thinking clearly…that's all. Amnesia was a scary thing. Gracie was deluding herself.

He wasn't the kind of man she needed for the long haul. He was selfish and cynical. No woman in her right mind would want a guy who still battled demons from the past. Gracie was soft…trusting. And she should have a partner to cherish her and make her the center of his world.

Gareth wanted her body. And he enjoyed her quick wit and her sharp tongue. But *love?* No. Not now. Maybe not ever. Especially not when he had yet to determine why she came to Wolff Mountain and what she wanted from him.

Once upon a time, he'd been a naive, horny young man. He'd fancied himself falling in love. Even after all that had happened to him as a child, he'd been willing to lay his heart on the line. To open himself up to the possibility of a future.

The resultant debacle had ripped a jagged hole in his ability to trust. Intimacy. Love. Those two words were babble in a foreign tongue. He liked women. Liked Gracie even more. But if what he offered wasn't enough for her, it was too damn bad.

He'd take her home as promised. Let her find her roots, her life. And then he'd return to his mountain and remind himself that he liked solitude and an empty bed at night.

He didn't need Gracie Darlington to be happy. Not at all.

Twelve

Gracie ran water into the lovely Jacuzzi tub and added a handful of scented bath salts. The resulting aroma fogged up the gilt-edged mirrors that hung over matching marble sinks. She was glad to have her image obscured. Every time she looked at her reflection, the woman in the glass shook a disapproving head.

Coward. Tease. There weren't enough pejorative adjectives to cover the way she felt about herself at this moment. She had told Gareth she was falling in love with him, and then had put on the brakes. Her behavior looked manipulative at best. She wanted to embrace the opportunity life had tossed in her lap. She wanted to embrace the big, hardheaded, fascinating Gareth Wolff.

But she was scared. She had a hunch that a broken heart was even harder to mend than a broken brain.

As she took off her robe and slipped into the deliciously warm water, she felt her face burn. Not from the temperature, but from the remembrance of Gareth's slightly panicked expression when she mentioned the "L" word. Had she subconsciously been testing the waters? Hoping at some pathetic level that he would fall at her feet and proclaim his reciprocal pledge of adoration?

She snorted, blowing a clump of bubbles across the tub. Surely the real Gracie Darlington wasn't so needy. Grabbing a razor, she extended one leg and started turning the skin into a smooth expanse ready for a lover's questing touch.

It was possible that she had spooked him badly enough to make *him* be the one to back away. She'd heard the door to their suite close only moments after she fled his bedroom. No doubt, he was putting physical distance between them.

Commitment-phobic guys were famous for nipping relationships in the bud, rather than getting trapped into situations that made them uncomfortable. Judging from Gareth's expression when she dropped her little bomb, he'd been *very* uncomfortable.

It hurt. No two ways about it. The physical intimacies they had shared in the last week seemed like so much more than sex. But even with a few synapses misfiring, she knew enough to realize that men were contrary animals. They saw the world through a different lens. And she'd be wise to remember that.

So, the question was: did she have enough guts to see this thing through to the end, when the truth about Gracie Darlington was revealed? And could she bear to see hatred in Gareth's eyes if that truth was unpalatable or even worse, hurtful?

She had promised to spend the evening with him. Even in a crowd, the connection that sizzled between them would be difficult to ignore. It wasn't fair to Gareth to send out mixed messages. Either she wanted him, or she didn't. It was that simple.

Tonight, when they returned to the hotel, she had to advance or retreat. Once and for all.

When the water cooled, she jumped into the shower to wash her hair, then stepped out and dried off with a velvety towel. Annalise had provided more than one choice for the evening. All three gowns, with familiar names on the sewn-in labels, were sultry, vivid, and skin-baring. They ranged the gamut from red satin to emerald chiffon to a basic black jersey with a halter neck. Black seemed the safest choice. It looked like nothing on the hanger, but surprisingly, morphed drastically when Gracie slid it over her head.

She stared into the mirror, turning this way and that. It would be impossible to wear a bra. In fact, other than a thong panty, anything between her skin and the dress would show. The V-neckline plunged modestly in front, but the reverse side of the dress was nonexistent, nothing but a cowl fold at her lower back.

A smattering of sequins and bugle beads drew attention to her breasts. The expensive fabric clung to her waist and hips, flaring out only slightly as it made its way to the floor.

She thought about changing, but vanity won out. The woman in the mirror was beautiful…confident…sexy. Gracie wanted badly to be that woman.

Her hair was almost dry. She finger combed the loose curls into a deliberately tousled array, stepped into black stilettos, and pirouetted. Not bad for a woman who couldn't remember if she'd ever worn a designer label.

Moments later she grimaced when her stomach growled on cue. She'd been nervous in the helicopter and hadn't finished her sandwich. Dinner would be late. Though she didn't want to cross paths with Gareth, at least not just yet, she dialed room service and ordered soup and crackers. The mini meal arrived with stunning swiftness, making her wonder if Gareth's presence in the hotel was the equivalent of a red alert.

It wasn't the smartest idea she'd ever had…getting dressed and then trying to eat soup. But she managed not to ruin anything. Afterward, she paced her beautiful room restlessly, torn between wanting to confront Gareth and get it over with and hiding out until the last possible second.

He took the decision out of her hands. The in-house phone on the bureau rang. It was him.

"Hello?"

"It's time, Gracie."

The ominous words sent her stomach into a free fall until she realized he was talking about the senator's party. She smoothed a hand over her stomach. "I'll be right there."

When she opened the door into the living room, her heart stuttered and skipped a couple of beats. Gareth's back was toward her, his wide shoulders straining the fabric of a crisp, obviously tailor-made tux. He'd gotten his hair trimmed while he was out. It still brushed his collar, full and wavy and dark, but she doubted he could put it into his customary stubby ponytail at the moment.

He turned around, and she saw his eyes widen. But she was too dumbstruck to give it much thought. He was magnificent. The white shirt drew attention to his sun-browned skin. Knife-pleated slacks molded to his powerful thighs, and the requisite bow tie and cummerbund almost made him appear civilized.

But she only had to look at his hawklike features and piercing eyes to see the predatory male animal he really was.

Her thighs tightened in instinctive, feminine reaction. Gripping her tiny evening bag, she forced herself to walk forward instead of beating a hasty retreat. "You look wonderful," she said quietly. "I'm sure the senator will be impressed."

Gareth found himself unable to speak for a full ten seconds. What had happened to his pretty, girl-next-door, memory-challenged Gracie? The woman in front of him was a goddess. Confident, sensual, serene in her infinite beauty.

He cleared his throat. "The senator is known as a womanizer. Perhaps taking you tonight is a bad idea. He probably gobbles up sweet young things like you for breakfast."

"I read my driver's license. Thirty doesn't sound all that

young." She approached him, one long, toned, slender leg appearing briefly through the mile-high slit in her narrow skirt. "But it's a good thing I have you to protect me." As she slid an arm through his, he almost groaned. His erection was heavy… painful. Every muscle in his body clenched in helpless desire. Appearing at some fancy society dinner and being paraded around like a damned lapdog was so far down the list of things he wanted to do tonight, it was criminal. Reminding himself of the charitable payoff was the only way he could follow through with what promised to be torture…in more ways than one.

He clasped her fingers with his. "The car is waiting." His conversation had been reduced to banalities. But damned if he could do better. All the blood in his body had rushed south. It was a miracle he could walk upright.

In the elevator her reflection in the mirror taunted him. Narrow white shoulders, shapely breasts, a flat belly and just the hint of a dip in the fabric that covered her most vulnerable femininity. Was she naked beneath that man-killer dress?

He noticed the omission of a wrap. "Won't you be cold?" he asked hoarsely. Still no more than a four-word sentence.

"You can keep me warm." Her smile was dauntingly close to making him come with no more than a look.

"You're not playing fair, Gracie Darlington."

She sobered. "You're right. I'm not. My only excuse is extreme confusion. But things are clearer to me now than they were this afternoon."

He resisted the urge to slide a finger inside his collar and loosen his tie. "How so?"

She leaned into him and slid her silly little purse into his pocket. Her slim arms encircled her neck. "I was scared."

"And now?"

Her hips brushed his. He wondered if she felt his urgency.

Apparently so. Her eyes widened. She looked up at him. No artifice. No coquettish invitation. Nothing but unveiled, completely vulnerable feminine need. "Forget what I said about love," she whispered. "To hell with who I am, who I was. All I want is to enjoy this thing between us for as long as we can. No looking forward. No looking back. No regrets."

He cursed long and low. "You're killing me, woman. Do you really expect me to walk around with a boner all night?"

Her lips caressed his chin. "Suffering builds character."

"Then you might as well nominate me for sainthood," he said gruffly. "Because if I make it through the evening without shoving you into a coat closet and taking you hard and fast, it will be a miracle."

She didn't have a chance to respond. The elevator slid to a halt in the lobby with a muffled *ding,* and the door slid open. For once, Chandra was not in sight. Gareth was glad.

The limo waited out front. Gareth gave the chauffeur the address, helped Gracie into the car and followed right behind her. He made no pretense at polite, socially acceptable behavior. With one quick flick of a button, he raised the privacy screen. Seconds later, he hauled Gracie into his lap and kissed her urgently. Tinted windows kept the world at bay.

It was almost like holding her naked. Every hill and valley of her body was his to explore, the thin fabric more of an enhancement than an impediment. The skirt of her dress succumbed to gravity, baring her legs. He slid a hand up her thigh and found only a tiny excuse for panties. His handkerchiefs were bigger.

The satin between her legs was damp. He rubbed gently, dangerously close to losing control. "You want me." He needed to hear the admission, needed to know that he wasn't the only one going crazy with lust...with hunger so intense it obscured all other realities.

"Yes." Her voice was little more than a reedy breath of air.

He stroked a pert nipple, now sure that nothing stood between him and her bare skin but the dress. "God, you are beautiful." He tangled a hand in her loose curls, wrapping one around his finger and seeing how it clung to his skin. Tugging gently, he half lifted her and helped her straddle his lap. The dress had to be shoved higher. He couldn't risk tearing it. Not now. With the skirt rucked up to her waist, he could see that the panties were hot pink, his new favorite color.

The naughty position made her vulnerable to his touch. His thighs stretched hers deliberately, opening her to him completely. He could have removed the panties…thought about it. But certain boundaries had to remain if he was to fulfill his role tonight.

Deliberately he stroked his thumb over her clitoris. She moaned and writhed as if trying to get away. No way in hell. He had her right where he wanted her. Again, he repeated the caress.

"Gareth…"

"Hmm?" He probed with two fingers at the opening of her channel, hampered by the cloth, wishing this erotic play was going to lead directly to the intimate contact he craved.

She didn't say anything else. Her eyes were closed. She was wrapped up in the pleasure he was giving her. That knowledge filled him with fierce satisfaction. The evocative bouquet of her perfume mingled with the scent of feminine arousal.

"Look at me." As her eyelashes fluttered open, he locked his gaze on hers, demanding obedience. "Put your hands on my shoulders."

She did as he asked…immediately. Without a word.

"See how long you can hold out," he urged. "Show me your strength, your power."

He moved his thumb back and forth, changing things up with quick strokes of his fingers. Gracie whimpered and begged, coming nearer every second to completion. But as soon as he knew she was close, he cupped her with his palm, petting her and lulling her body into submission.

She fought him. She called him names. And finally, when he

was close to the breaking point himself, he nudged firmly and sent her shooting into a climax that was beautiful and humbling to watch.

He'd long since resigned himself to an evening of agony. Now the night would be layered with sexual suffering as well.

Holding her close, he stroked her bare back, traced the delicate spine, buried his face in her hair. The city streets swept by unnoticed. Gareth had the means to keep the car going indefinitely—all the way to L.A. if he chose—but the journey had an end. And Gareth had made a commitment he was forced to honor.

Reluctantly he sat her up straight. Wincing at the sight of her sprawled legs, he turned her, straightened her dress and pulled her to his chest. "You okay?"

She nuzzled her cheek against his starched shirt, right over the spot where his heartbeat thundered. "Yeah."

They rode in silence, just like that, for miles. The Welcome to Virginia sign made him curse inwardly. He didn't want to let her go. Not now. Maybe not ever.

By the time the limo rolled to a smooth stop, Gracie had returned to her seat, fixed her makeup and hair and huddled in her own corner, staring out the window.

The senator's mansion was impressive by any standards; white columns, softly weathered brick, a curved driveway filled with cars and guests. Gareth felt his gut tighten. He'd been in social settings as upscale or more than this one since he'd been a child. But the thought of being trotted out like a dancing monkey filled him with loathing.

And the worst part was it was his own damn fault. He hoped that three hours would cover drinks and dinner and the obligatory mingling. All else aside, he wanted to take Gracie back to the hotel as quickly as possible.

He reached across the seat and touched her hand. "I don't know what your background is…" He chuckled ruefully. "And neither do you. But in my experience, the super elite are pretty much like anyone else. You'll meet the vain, the cocksure and the genuinely charming. I'll do my best to stay by your side, but the senator can be pretty bullheaded when he wants something. So if we get separated and you're at all uncomfortable, grab a glass of wine, hide in a corner and I swear I'll rescue you."

"And if I embarrass myself with a devastating faux pas?"

He grinned, already focused on thoughts of having her tonight. "Don't worry. After a few rounds of drinks, I guarantee you no one will notice."

Thirteen

Gracie decided that the best way to handle the evening was to approach it as a movie. Her role was a tiny bit part that might end up on the cutting-room floor. Gareth was the star. And her job, at least for tonight, was to trail in his wake and be there if he needed her.

As she placed her hand in his to be helped out of the car, their fingers clung. When she was standing on the flagstone driveway, he lifted her hand to his mouth and kissed the back of it, lingering long enough to make her knees weak. Though she tried hard not to show it, she was still reeling from Gareth's drive-time entertainment. She had let him reduce her to a mass of quivering need, begged him with no thought for pride and then collapsed in his arms, sated…wrung out…head over heels in love.

A love he didn't want. A love she would keep to herself from now on.

But sadly, there was no time for a post mortem, inward or otherwise. Their car was already pulling away. Gareth ushered her up a flight of steps flanked by topiaries sculpted in the shape of eagles. Tiny white lights entwined in the branches sparkled in the amazingly balmy night.

The senator and his two-decades-younger wife received guests in the elegant foyer. "Mr. Wolff. I'm delighted to finally meet you." The suave politician was tanning-bed bronze, twenty pounds overweight and had a smile that didn't quite reach his calculating eyes. "This is my wife, Darla. And your lovely guest is…?"

Gracie shuddered. This man gave her the creeps.

Gareth squeezed her hand unobtrusively. "Gracie Darlington. A very good friend of mine."

"We're so happy to have you visit our home." The simpering Darla sized up Gareth with an experienced eye, her avid expression as she looked him over disturbingly akin to Chandra's. Definitely a *fresh meat* nuance in her gaze.

Fortunately guests were bottlenecking on the steps, so Gareth and Gracie were allowed to shuttle back through the hallway to the formal salon where hors d'oeuvres were being served. She found herself tucked close to his side to keep from getting crushed in the melee. Where was a fire marshal when you needed one?

They snagged a table tucked to the side of a strangely out-of-place palm tree, and Gareth shook his head in bemusement. "Want some champagne?" he asked.

Gracie nodded. "I have a feeling we'll need more than one glass apiece."

He kissed her cheek. "You are so right. But we'll start with one."

In a surprisingly short time given the crush around the food table, he returned with a duo of expensive crystal flutes and a single plate of food piled high. Scallops wrapped in prosciutto, wedges of baked brie, skewers of fat boiled shrimp and grilled eggplant.

They stood elbow to elbow at the tall linen-covered table and demolished the bounty, Gareth consuming two-thirds of it. He smiled sheepishly as he filched the last shrimp. "Forgot to order room service. I'm starving."

Her lips quirked. "We could have snacked in the car," she said demurely, feeling her chest flush with remembrance.

His eyes darkened. Patting his mouth with a thick napkin, he cocked his head and stared at her. "Some of us did. You're awfully cheeky for a woman who was screaming my name thirty minutes ago."

"Gareth!" She glanced around to see if anyone was close enough to hear. "Behave yourself," she said, pinching his muscular forearm through the fabric of his jacket.

"That's no fun."

She watched as his eyes scanned the room. The monstrous cabinet he had created for the senator held a position of honor on the far wall. It still amazed her to think of the talent hidden in Gareth's large, masculine hands. But then again, she probably shouldn't be surprised at all. He played her body like a maestro.

Uniformed staff unobtrusively moved the crowd in the direction of the dining room. The long, narrow space held a magnificent dinner table surrounded by antique chairs, the seats covered in crimson-and-cream-striped damask. Handwritten place cards mingled with heavy silver and exquisite china.

Gracie found herself seated between a charming ambassador and a famous baseball player. The fact that she knew the pitcher's name told her she was a sports fan. Just one more piece in the puzzle. She was nervous, though she understood the functions of the place setting pieces and the flow of a formal dinner. Perhaps her father's gallery hosted the occasional soiree, though on a far less exalted level.

Gareth's assigned spot was across the table from her, just far enough away to make conversation difficult. He, on the other hand, was surrounded by a pair of Botoxed socialites who hung on his every word. Though he conversed easily through at least five interminable courses, Gracie already knew him well enough to see the tension in his big frame…and his distaste for the way his dinner companions continued to touch him with seemingly innocent motions.

It was a distinct relief when the senator rose to his feet and quieted his guests with the clink of a fork against his wineglass.

He smiled expansively, clearly in his element as the cynosure of all eyes. "It gives me great pleasure tonight to introduce you to the incomparable Gareth Wolff." He paused for the muted smattering of applause. "Gareth…if I may call him that?"

The raised eyebrows and jovial urbanity directed at his reluctant star demanded a positive response.

Gareth nodded stiffly.

The senator continued. "Gareth, in addition to being part of the well-known Wolff financial empire, is a master craftsman in wood. He creates only special order pieces, and has a waiting list of several years. After much cajoling on my part—" polite laughter on cue "—Gareth agreed to build the gun cabinet you have all seen tonight, one that is a close replica of a piece once owned by the incomparable Teddy Roosevelt. I couldn't be more pleased with the result, and it is my distinct honor to introduce to you tonight…Mr. Gareth Wolff."

Gareth rose to his feet, and for the first time, Gracie understood that Gareth Wolff was part of this world, despite his proclivity for seclusion. He was born to it, bred to be a mover and shaker. His stance was relaxed but compelling, his personality dominant in the hushed silence. His dark coloring made him seem like an exotic predator in a room full of colorful, insubstantial social animals.

With one hand in the pocket of his tux, he swept his arm out in a motion that encompassed the senator's largesse. "It's an honor to be here tonight in the senator's lovely home. And many thanks to our hostess, Darla."

The woman actually tittered nervously.

Gareth smiled at her. "Not only has the senator met my outrageous purchase price, all of which, as you know, goes to charity, but he has also donated an equally large check for my delivery fee." That last, self-deprecating, tongue-in-cheek remark amused the crowd.

Gracie watched them, noted the way all eyes were on Gareth, the women with sexual appreciation, the men with respectful admiration. Even the senator didn't appear to mind that Gareth's sheer charisma had hijacked center stage.

Gareth continued. "Most of the major fundraising in this country is financed by the generosity of men and women like yourselves. You make a difference in so many ways, and I respect your willingness to share with those in need, those less fortunate. Tonight, I'm especially grateful to the senator and his wife. I'll look forward to meeting more of you as the evening progresses."

Gareth sat down to uproarious applause. Gracie was impressed and humbled. If there had been any doubt in her mind before, now there was none. She had no permanent place in the life of a man like Gareth Wolff. Though her own past was still an unknown, she sensed that her calendar was not studded with such evenings, and that hobnobbing with the social elite was not something she did on a regular basis.

When dinner drew to a close, the crowd moved en masse to an actual ballroom. It was impossible to gauge the square footage of the senator's home, but Gracie had seen enough of it to know that the man in question clearly had a private fortune to supplement his earnings as a public servant.

Gareth joined her, an arm around her waist. He stood out in the crowded room. "You having fun?"

His droll question made her smile. "It's been an educational evening. I'll give you that." She leaned her head against his shoulder briefly. "You were very charming. I won't be surprised if several of these women slip checks into your pocket."

"Not the men?" His eyes danced.

"Perhaps. But you have every female in this house panting after you. And if they have to give money to get close to you, I'm sure that's what they'll do."

He turned her to face him, his hands on her shoulders, warming her bare skin. "Jealous, Gracie Darlington?"

The question was teasing. He clearly expected a riposte from her in return. But the truth was—yes—she was jealous. Not because of any specific woman's attentions to Gareth, but because she knew that the females gathered here tonight were the sort of pool from which a man in Gareth's position would select a wife…if he ever did. She shifted slightly, forcing his hands to fall away. "Just making an observation," she said lightly. "I'm not in a position to be jealous. And besides, that's why we're here, isn't it?"

Gareth frowned. Opened his mouth to say something. But in that instant, Darla appeared by his side, her face alight with enthusiasm. "I'd like to share the first dance with our guest of honor… Hostess's prerogative, you know." She barely glanced at Gracie. "What do you say, Mr. Wolff? And may I call you Gareth? By the way, a half dozen of my girlfriends are planning to make donations tonight. I'm sure you won't mind a few turns around the dance floor in return. Right?"

As her high-pitched prattle continued, she drew Gareth out into the throng of dancers. Gracie watched them go, heartsick… alone. But when an older man with a bad hairpiece moved zealously in her direction, she hastily slid out a side door and found the ladies' room.

After using the restroom and checking her makeup, she sat on an ornate ottoman for a long time, giving Gareth a chance to make his obligatory rounds. Finally she sucked up her courage and returned, like a weary Cinderella, to the ball.

* * *

Gareth saw her as soon as she entered the room. The knot in his stomach eased. He'd known the instant she vanished, had fretted like an old woman until she reappeared.

If he had his way, he would make a beeline for her right now. But the fact that he now had a sheaf of checks in his pocket, which at first glance totaled well over two hundred thousand dollars for his charity, kept him on the job. Reluctant. Frustrated. But resigned. Probably less than five percent of the crowd gave a damn about what was important to Gareth. But if they were willing to toss cash around like confetti, he wasn't going to stop them.

As he watched, Gracie found a seat on the sidelines and waved at him, her face serene, her expression amused at his expense. He grinned at her wryly over the shoulder of his current dance partner. Gracie knew how much he hated this. What she probably didn't understand was how much her presence made it all bearable.

During every interminable song, in the midst of every cloying conversation, he subverted his impatience with the knowledge that tonight he'd have Gracie in his bed, wrapped naked in his arms.

Another woman cut in, her determined gaze brooking no opposition as she elbowed her predecessor out of the way. Gareth sighed inwardly, ground his teeth and manufactured a smile that was beginning to fray at the edges. "Tell me your name," he said, consigning the woman to hell and back. "It's a pleasure to meet you."

It was after eleven when Gracie visited the bar for one last glass of wine. During the course of the evening she had exchanged banalities with a host of people whose names she would never remember. She was ready to find a chair and hide out until Gareth cut loose and decided it was time for them to leave.

A half dozen times he had moved in her direction, clearly expecting to dance with her, only to be waylaid at the last moment by one of the senator's guests.

Not all of Gareth's admirers were female. Almost as many men approached him, not to dance of course, but to pull him aside, offer a cigar out on the terrace, or merely to engage him in conversation.

Gracie was disappointed, but not hurt. She wanted to dance with Gareth, but this evening was not about romance. That would come later. Just the thought of being alone with him in their fancy hotel room made her breath catch. These glitzy people might have dibs on him for the evening, but when it was time to go, she had him for the whole night.

As she sipped her wine and contemplated how much her feet hurt in her beautiful shoes, a pleasant-faced older woman approached her.

"Hello, my dear. I'm Genevieve Grayson. My husband works as a lobbyist for the beef industry." She paused, smiled diffidently and continued. "You seem a bit lost, and I know how that feels. I've passed many an hour at these kinds of functions, waiting patiently as my spouse does his job. I just wanted to say hello."

Gracie was touched. "Hello, Genevieve. How kind of you." Perhaps that last glass of wine had been a mistake. The room seemed to be spinning slightly. "You must be a very patient woman. I can't imagine doing this on a regular basis. Not that the senator's dinner party isn't lovely, but I confess I'm more of a *curl-up-with-a-book* kind of gal."

Genevieve asked the bartender for a gin and tonic and sipped it slowly. "He's thinking about retiring soon…my husband, that is. We have our eye on a beautiful horse farm out in rural Virginia. I have visions of the two of us sitting in rocking chairs watching the sun set."

"Sounds lovely."

Genevieve's absent gaze was wistful. "Perhaps only a fantasy, unfortunately. He thrives on the high-octane energy in Washington. I'm not sure how he'll take to being put out to pasture."

"I hope everything works out for you."

They stood in silence for several moments. Gracie appreciated the woman's kindness to a stranger, but even this minimal conversation was tiring after a long day, a long week. Her stomach rolled. Perhaps she should eat something.

Genevieve seemed to call herself back to the present. "So, Gracie. Are you and Gareth Wolff an item?"

"Just friends." Gracie grimaced inwardly. How many women this evening had wondered the same thing? Obviously Genevieve's motive in asking was no more than simple curiosity, but Gracie felt self-conscious nevertheless.

"He's a very impressive man."

"Yes, he is. I admire him very much."

"Tell me, Gracie. What do you do when you're not socializing with one of the East Coast's most eligible bachelors? Are you an artist like Gareth?" Genevieve's gentle interrogation was nothing out of the ordinary. Simple dinner party conversation. Queries a six-year-old could answer.

Gracie froze. Deer-in-the-headlights froze. She and Gareth should have come up with a plan for this eventuality. But they had been too busy indulging their hunger for each other. "Well, I…"

Her face must have shown distress, because Genevieve backed off immediately. "I'm sorry, my dear. My husband always accuses me of being nosy. If you'd rather not say, I certainly understand. All of us inside the beltway certainly understand secrecy."

"Oh, no," Gracie said, legs trembling. "It's not that at all. I have nothing to hide. It's just that…"

Her throat closed up. Nausea rose and crested in her belly. Embarrassment rolled over her head like a suffocating shroud.

How had she not prepared for this eventuality? She could have lied. Pretended to be a lawyer, a teacher…anything.

Genevieve took her arm. "It's okay," she said in a soothing voice. "I didn't mean to upset you. Let me take your glass so it doesn't spill."

Gracie's hands were ice-cold. Her vision tunneled. She must have looked like hell, because Genevieve's placid expression went from cordial to panicked.

Gracie tried to breathe through the constriction in her chest. "Gareth," she whispered. "I need Gareth."

Her world went black.

Fourteen

He saw her go down. For a split second his brain couldn't process what was happening. "Sorry," he muttered, thrusting the woman in his arms away and sprinting across the dance floor.

The older woman who had been conversing with Gracie had managed to catch her somewhat, supporting Gracie's dead weight long enough to keep her from hitting her head as she collapsed to the floor.

Gareth scooped up the unconscious Gracie in his arms, cursing his stupidity. "Help me find a bedroom," he demanded, his tone harsh.

The woman never missed a beat. They walked quickly down a hallway into a quiet wing, ending up in a beautifully appointed guest room that was thankfully empty.

Gareth laid Gracie carefully on the bed. Put his hand on her chest momentarily. She was breathing. One small part of his brain had wondered if Jacob missed something…if the previous head injury had resulted in death. *Dear God…*

He closed his eyes for a split second, his composure in shreds.

As he turned around, the woman held out her hand. "I'm Genevieve," she said.

Shaking her hand briefly, he turned back to where Gracie lay so still and lovely in her black dress, the color emphasizing her pallor. "What happened?"

"I don't really know." Genevieve shrugged, her face unhappy. "We were having a nice conversation when she suddenly became overwrought."

"In what way?"

"I asked her about herself...you know...what she does for a living, and she became very agitated before passing out."

Gareth cursed furiously.

Genevieve blanched. "I'm sorry. Is this my fault somehow?"

He fisted his hands, wondering if he should call 911. "No," he muttered. Gracie wouldn't want her personal business to end up the source of gossip. "She's been through a very difficult time lately. I thought an evening out would be good for her. Apparently I was wrong."

Gracie stirred on the bed, her colorless lips moving silently as she began to wake up.

"What can I do to help?" Genevieve asked.

He rummaged in his pocket for a card. "Please call the car service. This is my driver. Ask him to come to the back door ASAP." He paused, knowing he owed this woman a debt and an apology. "Thank you for being kind to her. I'm sorry if I was rude."

Genevieve touched his arm gently. "I saw your face, young man. This woman is your life." With no more than that, she exited the room.

Gareth sat down on the bed and pulled Gracie into his arms, holding her tightly. "I've got you," he said, his eyes stinging. "I've got you."

Her lashes lifted, revealing a cloudy, confused gaze. "Gareth?"

"You're fine. Everything's fine. We're going home."

"But I wanted to dance with you."

He hadn't thought he could feel any worse. "Maybe another time," he said, the words torn from his throat. "Let's get you home."

Genevieve was as good as her word. As soon as Gareth spirited Gracie to the back of the house, carrying her with utmost care, the car appeared at the back door. Genevieve waved them off and promised to give Gareth's goodbyes to the senator.

Gareth would have taken Gracie away under any conditions, but the hour was late, and Gareth had certainly fulfilled his obligation.

In the limo he reached into the mini fridge for a bottle of water and unscrewed the cap. "Drink this," he said softly, holding her across his lap and wondering if he'd ever be able to let go. "You scared the hell out of me."

Her blue eyes met his. "I'm so sorry if I embarrassed you in front of the senator," she said miserably. "I never should have come."

"Correction," he said tersely. "I never should have brought you."

Her tiny gasp and the wounded look on her face reduced him to cursing again. "Hell, Gracie. You know that's not what I meant. I'm worried about you, damn it. Clearly neither of us has taken the consequences of this amnesia thing seriously enough. What happened in there? Why did you faint?"

She insisted on leaving his lap, her shoulders bowed in defeat. "It was nothing," she murmured, her face turned toward the window as they streaked along through the night, cocooned in intimacy. "A stupid nothing."

He caressed her arm. "Tell me. Please."

"She asked me what I did…when I wasn't dating the East Coast's most eligible bachelor. All I had to do was make up something, but for some reason, her simple question caught me off guard. I'd probably had too much wine…and I didn't eat enough of my dinner. What can I say? I was an idiot."

"Stop that," he said firmly. "You're not to blame. I brought you here. Took you out of a safe environment. Exactly what Jacob warned me not to do."

"But I *wanted* to come," she insisted. "I wanted this one special time with you before I have to leave."

"Not so special anymore, is it?" He brooded quietly in his corner, wishing he could turn back the clock.

At the hotel, she battled him, insisting on going inside under her own steam. The only reason he didn't overrule her was that the argument took what little strength she had left and winnowed it away.

In their living room, he hesitated, unsure of the appropriate course of action. He wouldn't make love to her, not tonight. She needed to rest. But would she rather be alone?

She swayed on her feet, her skin paper-white, her eyes haunted. Not a trace of his spunky, combative houseguest remained.

"Maybe you'd be more comfortable in your own bed," he muttered. "No need to set an alarm. All I had planned for tomorrow was some touristy stuff. Or we can go home if you'd rather."

Her gaze was uncomprehending, her eyes bleak.

"Come here." He picked her up. She didn't protest as her head lolled against his shoulder.

In her room, he stood her on her feet only long enough to slide the dress from her body and tuck her between the sheets wearing nothing but those sinful panties. Seeing her almost-nude beauty shook him.

Earlier in the limo, a wanton and fabulous Gracie had dazzled him with her strength, her fiery femininity. Now she was a broken doll. And it was his fault.

* * *

Gracie woke in the dark, struggling to break free from the tentacles of a bad dream. She bit her lip, refusing to cry out and wake Gareth. She'd done enough damage as it was. He didn't need her to lean on him, to suffocate him with her neediness.

And if she was going to enjoy his lovemaking in whatever short time they had left, she surely didn't want a man who felt sorry for her.

After donning a thigh-length silk robe, she crept stealthily into the living room and opened the armoire that hid a small fridge. Taking out a bottle of sparkling water, she unscrewed the lid and sipped it slowly, wondering if her life would ever get back to normal.

She was trapped in a strange limbo. Too broken and confused to recognize the past, too distraught to contemplate the future.

She crossed the room, eased open the glass doors and stepped out onto the small balcony. It was cold now, the flagstones icy beneath her feet. She welcomed the discomfort, needing to shake off the lingering effects of the nightmare.

Traffic noise, even at this hour, hummed in the distance. This beautiful historic city had seen its fair share of heartache and pain. With equal measures of hope and triumph in between. Gracie intended to emulate that pattern. Life had dealt her a dual blow…erasing her memory and filling the resultant void with an intense yearning for a man who would not, could not be hers.

She had to trust that whatever followed, wherever the path led her, she would survive, both literally and emotionally. She was strong; she felt that in the marrow of her bones. And she was never going to admit defeat when it came to retrieving her memories, even if some of them were gone for good.

And as for Gareth…

Well, Shakespeare had it right. It was better to have loved and lost than never to have loved at all.

She shivered violently, her numb fingers clenched around the glass bottle. The thought of returning to her solitary bed held little allure. But she dared not risk adding pneumonia to her list of physical ailments.

As quietly as she had exited, she padded back inside, locking the French doors and pulling the diaphanous fabric panels into place. When she turned around, her heartbeat spiked in alarm. A man loomed in the shadows of the room. Gareth.

She set the water bottle on a table and wrapped her arms around her middle. "You scared me," she said softly.

"Then we're even. What are you doing out of bed?"

"I'm sorry I woke you." It wasn't an answer to his question, but she didn't mention the dream. If a woman planned to stand on her own two feet, she had to start somewhere.

Gareth closed the distance between them. For the first time, she realized he was wearing nothing but a pair of navy silk boxers. His broad chest looked even more impressive au naturel than it had in a designer tuxedo. With rumpled hair and the dark shadow of a beard marking his roughly sculpted jawline, he looked nothing like the senator's honored guest. He stopped mere inches from her, their bodies almost touching.

"Come to bed with me," he said, the words a low rumble that stroked her nerves and weakened her knees.

"I can't, Gareth." She wanted to. She craved the oblivion that she would find in his arms, the soul-searing relief of climax, the physical bliss his claiming would bring. But she hadn't slept well the past few nights without Gareth in her bed. And she ached with a fatigue that was as much mental as physical.

"Not for that. You need to let me hold you." He stopped, backed up verbally. "I need to hold you," he said, dropping his forehead to hers as he slid his arms around her waist. "Good God," he exclaimed. "You're freezing."

She wanted to cry when he picked her up, his strength effortless as he carried her back to his bed. He tucked her beneath the covers and slid in beside her. The sheets still held the heat from his body. She curled into a ball, her head pillowed on her hand. Gareth spooned her from behind, his natural warmth so comforting she wanted to purr.

"Thank you," she whispered.

"For what?"

His unmistakable erection pulsed between them, but he neither acknowledged his physical state nor made any attempt to coax her into a more intimate embrace.

She yawned, sleep slurring her words. "For rescuing me tonight."

He chuckled, holding her close, his hard, hair-covered arm tucked firmly beneath her breasts. "A woman as strong as you are is more than capable of rescuing herself." He played with a curl behind her ear, his fingers sending shivers of sensation down her neck. "Go to sleep, Gracie." He kissed the back of her neck. "Go to sleep."

She obeyed him instantly, her body going lax, her breathing slowing to a calm, steady cadence. Holding her like this was both pleasure and pain. His body recognized the opportunity for what it was. His better instincts reminded him that she was fragile, in need of healing.

As the clock marked off the hours, he pondered his options. The life he'd built for himself had no permanent place for a woman. And even if he managed to rewrite his own hard-and-fast rules, Gracie might not need him anymore once she returned to her home turf.

He could love her if he allowed himself that leeway. But he hadn't. Not yet. Caution still held the reins. He knew what it was like to love and to lose, and he was in no hurry to experience that pain again.

He cupped one of her small, firm breasts. She fit into his arms perfectly. But into his life? That was another story.

Who *was* Gracie Darlington? And did it really matter if she had amnesia? The world was full of couples who married only to realize that they didn't know the other person at all. Was it ever possible to really know someone?

He loved the qualities Gracie had shown him. Her sweet spirit. Her compassion. Her refusal to whine or complain in the face of adversity. Surely nothing sinister lurked in the wings.

Marriage? He lifted a mental eyebrow, stunned that the word had popped into his head, even obliquely.

Resting his cheek against her shoulder, he tried to let sleep claim him. Hard as a pike, hungry as a lion, he forced himself to relax, to be lulled by the rhythm of her breathing.

The world outside their room ceased to exist as he closed his eyes and breathed in the scent of her hair.

Fifteen

Gracie had disappeared when he woke up. But the pillow beside him still bore the imprint of her head. He yawned and stretched. She couldn't have been gone long.

After showering rapidly, he went in search of her…and found her standing on the balcony again, this time dressed in crisp white slacks and an off-the-shoulder turquoise peasant blouse. She looked fresh and beautiful, and he wanted her so badly, he shook with it.

He scowled, unused to being at the mercy of his body. Enduring periods of celibacy had always been his choice. But with Gracie, his self-control ceased to exist. If he had his way, they would never leave the suite. Spending the day in bed held a raw, seductive appeal.

She smiled at him when he stepped outside. "Good morning." Her eyes were clear, the shadows gone.

He gave her a hard kiss, one that left her flustered and rosy cheeked. "Good morning, yourself. Are you ready to hit the town? I thought we'd take in some of the museums."

"Sounds fun."

"Do you have any feel for whether you've ever explored the Smithsonian?"

"Not a clue. So I'm ready to be entertained."

He would have liked to interpret her words on a carnal level, but he'd promised himself to give her an uncomplicated, enjoyable day. Tomorrow they would head back to the mountain... and soon, on to Savannah. He shoved the thought aside. "Grab what you need. I have a driver picking us up in fifteen minutes."

Gracie managed to shut out all memories of the previous night's debacle. For a few short hours, she intended to have nothing on her mind but a handsome man, a fun day and a chance to spread her wings.

Gareth had hired a driver for their outing, insisting that Gracie was not up to walking the distances required to go from museum to museum. It was patently untrue. She felt full of energy and ready to tackle the world. But if Gareth insisted on pampering her, who was she to quibble?

After breakfast at a street-side café, they made their way via a maze of one-way streets to their first stop. The Museum of American History. Gracie recognized items in many of the exhibits: Dorothy's ruby-red slippers, Julia Child's kitchen, the Star-Spangled Banner, Michelle Obama's inaugural gown. But she had no clue if she had stood in these exact same spots before or if she knew the cultural icons in other contexts.

Later, they picnicked on the mall, seated side by side on a park bench, the sun beaming down with benevolent warmth. The driver had picked up a preordered basket filled with all sorts of goodies. As they ate, Gracie smiled, enjoying the feeling of normalcy. All around them, life ebbed and flowed. "I like it here," she said, sipping a Coke and stretching her legs to admire the espadrilles Annalise had picked out.

Gareth extended an arm behind her along the back of the seat

"I'm glad," he said simply. "I thought we'd take in one more stop and then get you back to the hotel to rest."

"I'm not an invalid."

His expression was stubborn. "We're not having a repeat of last night. Jacob can't be here, and I take my medical responsibilities very seriously."

"If it makes you feel better. But I'm okay, I swear." Drumming up her courage, she spoke quietly, looking straight ahead, not at him. "May I ask you something?"

She was close enough to feel the tension that gripped his body. "If you must."

The half-joking tone was probably more truthful than he wanted her to realize. "Will you tell me about your charity?"

The silent pause that lingered between them could have spanned the length of the grassy mall. "What do you want to know?"

"Did you start it on your own? What does it do? Why didn't you talk about it directly last night?"

"Are you sure you're not a reporter?"

Again, the quasi-humor didn't quite ring true. "I'm curious about you," she said. "I'll admit it." Perhaps she shouldn't have pushed, but she really did want to know.

He exhaled, rolling his shoulders and grimacing. "It's called W.O.L.F."

"An acronym?"

He nodded. "Working Out Loss and Fear. It's a foundation that provides counseling opportunities for children who have lost a parent in violent or tragic circumstances—war, cancer, automobile accidents…"

"Kidnapping? Murder?"

She saw him flinch. The terrible words seemed out of place in such a beautiful day.

"That, too," he said, the words tight. "I started it when I turned eighteen. On that birthday, I inherited a bequest from my maternal grandmother. It had been held in trust for me, and there was also an amount from my mother, as well. With the help of the family lawyers, I fleshed out what I wanted and they made the legalities work."

"And you run it?"

He shook his head. "Not anymore. I have an excellent board who oversees the process of reviewing applicants and dispersing funds."

"Couldn't you have collected even more money last night if you had given a sales pitch for the charity?"

"Probably. But I swore when I started W.O.L.F. that I would never exploit my mother's death, even for good. I don't want her to be remembered for the way she died. In life she was happy and upbeat and incredibly giving. That's the image I try to carry in my head."

But clearly, such intent was not always successful. Gareth held within him a remnant of the young boy who had stared in horror at grisly crime scene photos he should never have witnessed.

She allowed the conversation to lapse. Gareth's willingness to answer her questions truthfully marked a milestone.

They tossed their trash and walked across the grass to the National Gallery of Art. Gareth took her arm as they climbed the broad, wide steps. "You clearly know something about the art world," he said, "since your father owns a gallery. So I thought this might shake something loose."

She stopped dead, halting his progress as well. "Can't we just have fun?" she pleaded. "Please don't look for miracles at this point. I can't take the pressure of you always wondering if I'm getting better. It makes me crazy."

He raked a hand through his hair, remorse flickering in his eyes. "Sorry. Of course we can. Once we go through that door I'll follow your lead. I want this to be a day you'll always remember."

"Is that a joke?"

He actually reddened, his foot-in-mouth comment hanging in the air between them. "No," he muttered. "And I'm not saying another word."

The museum fascinated Gracie. She wandered from gallery to gallery, Gareth trailing in her wake. He kept his vow, remaining silent as she absorbed the centuries of artistic genius housed within the massive walls.

When they came to the impressionists, Gracie halted, struck by a yearning that caught her off guard. She knew these works... knew them well. One in particular caught her eye...*Girl With a Watering Can*. She moved closer, studying the brush strokes, the smears of color that added up to a masterpiece.

Suddenly a dam inside her brain breached, letting in a rush of certainty. "I've been here," she whispered. "I know it."

Gareth didn't comment. But he stood at her shoulder, bolstering her confidence with his quiet presence. She wanted to run her hand over the canvas, but the uniformed guard stationed in the doorway of the room was a deterrent.

Fascinated...scared...hopeful, she examined the painting. "I think I have a copy of this in my bedroom...over my dresser."

"What else?" he prompted.

She bit her lip, concentrating so hard, her head ached. "The dresser is oak. And the drawer pulls are antique glass."

His arms went around her from behind. "Take your time. Don't force it."

She closed her eyes, the better to concentrate on a fuzzy image that threatened to dissolve like smoke in the wind. "I have a picture of my mother on my dresser. I don't think she's alive. There's no sense of immediacy in my memory of her."

Gareth's big frame surrounded hers, protective...supportive. "It will come, Gracie. Even if you have to go back to Savannah to complete the picture, it will come."

Long moments passed in silence as she reached for what

could not be touched. "That's all," she said, frustrated, but no longer despairing. The clarity of this most recent memory convinced her that it was only a matter of time until she had everything back that she had lost.

Disheartened, but philosophical, she turned in his arms to face him, her hands at his waist. "I want you to know," she said slowly, "that I'm sorry. Sorry to have invaded your privacy. Sorry to have arrived on your mountain with some agenda of my father's in hand. It pains me to know that he convinced me to do it. Even if I don't know what 'it' is."

He kissed her softly, unconcerned with the groups of people milling around them. "I wouldn't have missed the chance to know you, Gracie Darlington. So I say to hell with your apologies. We'll deal with the truth, whatever it is."

"What if I'm more like my father than we know? What if I'm manipulative and nosy and self-serving?"

"You're not. Don't be ridiculous." He tugged her hand and led her out into the enormous rotunda. "Let's go back to the hotel. You don't realize what a toll these bits and pieces of memory take on you. This is supposed to be a fun day. Not stressful. Let it go for now."

She allowed herself to be persuaded, though the instinct to prowl through the museum again was strong.

In the limo, Gareth leaned back, his gaze focused outside the window. Gracie wanted to know what he was thinking, but she was afraid to ask. The unknown hung between them, an impenetrable curtain that might or might not mask an unpalatable truth.

His profile had become as familiar to her as the image of her own features in the mirror. She sensed a restlessness in him and wondered if he was missing his mountain.

In their suite, he confronted her, stone-faced, hands stuffed in his pockets. "I have some calls to make," he said abruptly.

"I thought you might want to shower and freshen up. Later, I'd like to take you out for the evening if you feel up to it."

She waved a hand impatiently. "Of course I do. What's wrong, Gareth? You've been brooding ever since we left the museum. Did you think I'd remember more than I did? I tried. Honestly I did."

"It's not that."

"Then what?"

He shrugged, dark eyes turbulent with emotion. "I don't have a good feeling about taking you home to Savannah. I'm hardly in a position to throw stones when it comes to sensitivity, but your father appears to be an ass. I'm not at all sure he'll give you the support you need until you have your memory in place."

"We don't really have a choice," she said, the tight knot of dread and regret in her stomach something she couldn't control. "I have to go home. Familiar territory will bring it all back. I have to believe that, and I have to pick up the pieces of my life. You know it's the only way."

She wanted him to fight for her. To say he couldn't bear for her to leave.

But Gareth was not the kind of man to spill his emotions in a messy declaration. "I don't have to like it," he muttered. Without warning, he slid a hand beneath the hair at her nape and dragged her toward him. His lips settled over hers in a rough, seeking kiss.

"Gareth…" She felt the violence in him, the mixture of frustration and sexual hunger. Though he held her gently as he ravaged her mouth, his body thrummed with tension.

Finally he broke free and pushed her away. "Seven o'clock. Be ready."

She stepped into her lavish shower stall, wishing she had the guts to invite Gareth to share it. Instead she washed quickly and got out, her skin tingling, her blood pumping, her breath choppy and shallow.

Though the bedroom was warm, she had gooseflesh as she dressed for her lover. Coffee-colored lingerie accented with pink rosettes. Thigh-high nylons in a lighter shade of mocha. And the dress. The one she'd not had the guts to wear the night before.

Red satin. The kind of dress worn by a courtesan. A temptress. A dangerous woman.

The mandarin collar was modest. But any propriety ended there. The sleeveless sheath fit her as if it had been sewn onto her where she stood. Wearing a bra was impossible. The sumptuous fabric clung to her body like a second skin. The unapologetic scarlet should have clashed horribly with her hair, but instead, it warmed her coloring and made her skin glow.

With a shaky hand, she applied eyeliner and shadow, making her eyes mysterious and dark. A dab of perfume, wrist to wrist, earlobe to earlobe. Soon, she was ready. A ragged laugh escaped her as she realized there would be no limousine high jinks in this ensemble. She'd be lucky if she was able to sit down at all.

In another time, she would have carried a black lacquer cigarette holder...or a painted fan. Perhaps if Gracie emulated those women of the past, the outrageous females who dared not to conform to society's expectations, she might be able to enjoy the evening without heartbreak.

Before leaving her room, she dialed her father's number one more time and got the same message. Anger burned in her gut, along with hurt and suspicion. He was avoiding her. No question about it. But the day of reckoning was fast approaching, and if necessary, she would force him to apologize for whatever stupidity he had tried to perpetrate on the Wolff family in general and Gareth Wolff in particular.

She didn't wait to be summoned. A full twenty minutes early she stepped into the living room and scanned the space. Gareth wasn't there. A bottle of Perrier gave her something to hold on

to and at the same time soothed her nerves along with a dry
throat.

When Gareth appeared, she was prepared. "I'm ready," she
said, conscious of her double meaning and wondering if he heard
her not-so-subtle invitation.

This time she was able to look at him in his tux without
swooning. He was every bit as handsome and charismatic as he
had been the evening before, but she was not going to let him
see how desperately she wanted him. At least not yet.

"You look lovely, Gracie." Something about the poleaxed
expression on his face filled her with simultaneous satisfaction
and amusement. With the right dress, a woman held the power
to topple kingdoms.

Chandra was present in the lobby, tracking their departure
with a jaundiced eye. Gracie called out a cheery, deliberate
greeting and tucked her hand through Gareth's arm, proof that
she was not above a little petty grandstanding.

The limo driver held open the car door, his face a respectful,
expressionless mask.

Gareth looked down at Gracie, humor vying with sensual
intent in his beautiful, dark brown, almost-black eyes. "Can you
actually bend in that thing?"

She went up on tiptoe and kissed his chin. "Guess we'll see."

With as much grace as possible, she eased inside, settling
onto the smooth leather seat and tucking her legs to one side.
Gareth followed her in, his gaze not missing the way the skirt
molded to her thighs and left little to the imagination.

They politely ignored each other for several miles. Finally
she caved. "Where are we going?"

He stretched out his long legs, ankles crossed, and tucked his
hands behind his head. "Dinner and dancing."

Her heart skipped a beat. "Seriously?"

"We didn't get our shot at the ball last night. Seemed a shame.

So I called around to find a hotel that has live music and a dance floor."

Her eyes misted. "That's very sweet."

"Or very manipulative."

Her eyebrows lifted. "Meaning?"

"Dancing is little more than a civilized man's public foreplay."

"I might buy that if I were going out tonight with a civilized man."

"Touché." His lips twitched, and she was ridiculously glad she'd managed to coax him out of his earlier somber mood.

As they pulled up in front of an old, established hotel with a burgundy awning, Gareth slid out of the car and extended a hand to draw her to her feet. He paused for a moment to brush a soft kiss across her cheek. The innocent caress lit a fire deep inside her.

Without speaking, he led her inside where the ambiance was old Washington. Lavish decor with the slightly faded appeal of a genteel lady past her prime.

Every employee bowed and scraped in Gareth's wake. Soon he and Gracie were seated at a table near the crackling fire. Over salads and what she suspected was horribly expensive wine, he studied her face, his own unsmiling.

Finally she protested. "What? Do I have crumbs on my chin?"

He leaned his head on his hand, sober, speculative. "I can't figure out how a woman so innocent-looking can turn a man inside out without even trying."

"Do I really do that to you?" she asked boldly. He was speaking of carnality when she craved something far different. But even still, she was gratified to know he could admit weakness in her presence.

"That and more. Let's dance."

Sixteen

Gareth hovered on the cusp of a blinding revelation. His brain tried to make sense of what he felt for the slender, strong-willed woman in his arms, but it was all he could do to keep from dragging her into the nearest dark corner and pressing his aching erection into her until oblivion claimed them both.

In her heels, she stood tall enough to rest her head against his shoulder. They swayed together, the music a faint counterpoint to the thudding of his heartbeat. His hands roved her back, tormented by the layer of slick fabric that separated him from her bare skin. Every man in the room stared at him with envy and at Gracie with barely concealed lust.

He couldn't blame them.

She was a burning in his veins, a sweet torment he would gladly endure. It came to him in that moment that he could never let her go. No matter the reason she had to come to him in the beginning, she was his now…body and soul.

Caution rang a warning bell in his subconscious. But with Gracie pressed against him, chest to chest, thigh to thigh, all he could think about was taking her. Claiming her. Proving to her that new memories were all she needed.

One song ended, then another. Reluctantly he escorted her back to the table. The filet mignon and lobster tails he had ordered for both of them were no more than cardboard in his mouth. He watched her eat…saw the way her small white teeth bit delicately into a crust of bread, the gut-wrenching way her tongue ran across her bottom lip to catch a drip of clarified butter.

They barely spoke. Words seemed unnecessary. Gracie glowed as if lit from within. Close. He came so close to saying the words that would make him vulnerable to her…promises that couldn't be withdrawn. But something held him back.

He had time. All the way to Savannah, in fact. Instead of taking the chopper, he would drive her. Just the two of them… for hours. Making her laugh. Binding her to him in every way he knew how. So that whatever secrets she was hiding couldn't tear them apart.

The truth washed over him, making his eyes burn. He loved her. The walls he had built to protect his heart had fallen brick by brick. Gracie was warmth and light and happiness. He would tell her. Soon. When he'd had a chance to get used to the idea.

Surely the words were superfluous tonight. Surely she could see what she did to him.

Dinner dragged on with the agonizing gait of a snail. After key lime tarts and rich coffee, he dragged her out onto the dance floor one last time, his control fraying. With little compunction, he slid his hands over her ass, cupping those curves and dragging her as close as was humanly possible.

Gracie came willingly it seemed, as unconcerned as he was with anything or anyone around them.

They moved together in drugged silence, perfectly in sync until the band had the temerity to take a break.

At last the waiter produced a check, signaling the end to

Gareth's time upon the rack of impossible desire. Barely concealing the shaking in his hands, he scrawled his name on the signature line, included a large tip, and scooted his chair from the table with unconcealed impatience.

He tugged her hand, drawing her to her feet. "Time to go, Gracie."

In the car, he was unable to touch her. His fuse was so short as to be nonexistent. He drummed his fingers on his knees, his skin too tight, his collar strangling him.

Getting from the car to their suite took an eternity.

When at last the door closed behind them, sealing her with him in undisturbed intimacy, he stripped off his jacket, ripped away his tie and cummerbund and kicked off his shoes.

Gracie watched him, big-eyed, her hands clenched around a silly little evening bag.

He tugged it from her grasp and tossed it aside. "Tell me you want me," he whispered, twining his hands in her curls and massaging her scalp.

"I do," she said.

Her simply phrased response sounded a bit too weddinglike for his peace of mind. He ignored the odd shiver her words produced and kissed her roughly. He tried to wedge a leg between her thighs, but the siren's dress was too damned tight.

Reaching around her for the zipper, he lowered it without waiting for permission. The rasp of the teeth in a downward slide sounded abnormally loud in the stark silence. The fabric gaped, but Gracie clutched it with her hands, apprehension shadowing the cornflower-blue of her eyes.

He unfolded her fingers one by one. "Don't be afraid of me, Gracie. Not now. Not ever."

With one smooth slide of his hand, she was all but naked, standing in a pool of crimson fabric, her pert nipples a paler shade of ruby. Fiery hair, high breasts, long shapely thighs.

He held her hand as she stepped free of the gown and came

to him eagerly, her arms sliding around his neck. Her shocked cry as his heavy shaft prodded her belly echoed inside his head.

Slowly, carefully, he backed her toward his room. *Her* room tonight, as well. And along the way, he kissed her. Long, slow, intimate kisses that tested his control.

Gracie's lips mated with his, her enthusiasm increasing his own ardor exponentially. Heated whispers. Soft sheets and scented pillowcases. A curved breast gripped by hard fingers. Pale, slender thighs parting instinctively.

His passion consumed him, threatened to tear away the veneer of polite society and rage unchecked in this room filled with shocked gasps, quiet sighs and muttered curses.

Everywhere she was soft, he was there. The inside of an elbow. A delicate earlobe. The moist petals at her center. He wanted it all…ached to claim every inch of her for his own.

Shuddering…shaking…he hooked her legs over his forearms. He saw on her face the moment she realized how the new position increased her vulnerability…opened her to him without reservation.

The condom was a frustrating but necessary stop on the road to heaven. Hovering over her, the head of his shaft nudging impatiently for entrance, he sucked in a gulp of oxygen and tried to formulate the words. Words she deserved to hear. But his throat closed up and his ability to speak was incinerated in the rush of ravenous hunger that drove him to the brink of insanity.

Gracie's eyes were closed. Her breasts rose and fell with the rhythm of her breathing. Against the pure white of the sheet, her hair glowed like fire. And that sweetly curved mouth, those perfect lips, parted in a whimper of pleasure as he fingered her deliberately.

She was swollen, wet and more than ready for his possession. And still he waited. Was he testing her or himself? Or was he simply relishing a night that was waning with reckless speed?

He positioned his shaft...rubbed her intimately. "Watch us, Gracie."

Her lashes lifted in slow motion, the glaze of need in her eyes telling him that the time for play was over. In deadly earnest, he lunged forward, drawing a shout from him and a faint cry from her. The sensation was indescribable. Her body received him with the tight squeeze of a too-small glove.

Heat rocketed down his spine, pooled in his loins. He withdrew and drove in again, losing himself in sheer bliss. How long had it been since he felt this raw, unshakable need? Maybe never.

Again and again he rocked into her, going so deep he felt the mouth of her womb. He would give his entire fortune, gladly, to be able to love her like this all night, never pausing, never falling off the edge.

But only a robot could withstand the intense pleasure. Only a eunuch could be immune to the way her tight passage milked him, her inner muscles caressing his shaft, giving him an excruciating pleasure he hadn't known existed until now. In a faraway corner of his mind he acknowledged that such perfect union was far more than physical. That the mating of two souls was as integral a part of this cataclysm as damp flesh and aching lungs.

He felt the end stalking him...fought it off with slow strokes that tormented them both. Gracie's legs were on his shoulders now, giving him compete access, total trust.

When he snapped, his vision blurred, his heart stopped. And then he could do no more than hang on as he shot to the stars and then fell helplessly into her arms.

Dimly, uncomprehending, he sensed her completion as it sparked from his. He held her tightly as darkness claimed him.

Gracie slipped from the bed in the wee hours to use the bathroom and sponge the evidence of their lovemaking from her body. She felt used and abused in the best possible way, her muscles lax with remembered pleasure, but at the same time sore and spent.

In her absence, Gareth had rolled onto his back, but he never stirred when she climbed back under the covers. His big body radiated heat. She snuggled into his embrace, one leg resting across his hard thigh.

Suddenly wide-awake, she moved her hand bravely across his abdomen and found his groin. His shaft, already partially erect, flexed and grew. He murmured in his sleep. As she held him in a loose grasp, he hardened to steel wrapped in velvety skin. The drop of moisture that wet the head of his erection signaled his eagerness.

"Gareth?"

Her whispered invitation bore no fruit other than the pulsing, rigid length of him.

Filled with a dangerous mixture of bravado and desperation, she scooted around and over him, taking him in her hand once again and guiding him into her body. She needed him so badly. The hourglass was almost empty. And who knew what moment would be their last?

Rising and falling on her knees, she pleasured herself on his erection. Eventually Gareth rose from the depths of sleep and moved with surety, surging upward and filling her beyond the realms of possibility.

Despite their earlier excess, the climax was near painful… drawn out…shiveringly intense.

She was half-asleep already when she felt him draw the covers over both of them, warming chilled skin and cocooning them in down-filled layers.

When she finally surfaced from a deep, restful sleep, she sensed someone watching her. Cracking one eye open, she witnessed Gareth's grin. He was lying on his side, leaning on an elbow, head in his hand. "I had the most *amazing* dream," he drawled.

She licked her lips, wondering what to say that would perhaps not implicate her. "I don't know what you mean."

"Liar." How a single word could convey amusement, affection and lust in equal measures baffled her. He grinned. "I'm not complaining, mind you. A guy can never have too many good dreams."

She smiled lazily, recognizing the dual gifts of happiness and contentment as they took up residence in her heart. No words could convey her mood.

His smile faded into something less lighthearted while his hand, hidden beneath the covers, parted her legs. "Feel like dreaming again?" he asked huskily, his breath warm at her throat as he moved over her.

Her stomach growled audibly. "I need breakfast," she complained, giggling when he groaned in protest. Already she felt him pushing deep.

"Later, darling Gracie."

His unexpected transposition of her names caught her off guard. A man like Gareth Wolff didn't make free with careless endearments. So she savored the unexpected sweetness and tucked it away in her heart.

Surely by now his determined possession should not have been as shocking, his take-no-prisoners approach to lovemaking less overwhelming.

But nothing about this barely blossoming relationship was predictable. Moments later when she arched in stunned pleasure and found her release, it was as shiningly perfect as the first time he'd taken her and as sweetly sensuous as the last.

They were late for checkout. Fortunately for Gracie, such mundane concerns were not on Gareth's radar. When they made their way to the rooftop, the helicopter and pilot awaited them despite their tardiness.

Gracie was more able to enjoy the return trip to Wolff Mountain than on the first leg of their journey. Any nerves borne of a new experience had settled in the interim. As the pilot and Gareth chatted via their radio headsets, Gracie was content to take in the spectacular view. Like a bird on a mission, the chopper flew a steady, swift path south and west. In no time, they were settling onto the helipad and disembarking.

The Jeep, keys inside, awaited them. Gareth stowed their bags and after seeing that Gracie was tucked in, jumped behind the wheel and slung gravel as he turned and headed back through the forest at a fast clip.

As they broke through a gap in the woods, the magnificent Wolff fortress came into view. Gareth, face carved in mysterious lines, slowed the vehicle to a stop. With the engine still running, he half turned to face her. His hand covered hers, fingers linking with hers.

She was shocked to see his teeth worry his lower lip. All around them nature burst forth in a panoply of spring exuberance. Gracie's heart followed suit. Gareth felt *something* for her. She knew it. Without false modesty or brain-addled, amnesia-created, pie-in-the-sky dreams, she sensed his caring at a most basic level.

He played with a lock of her hair, his eyes trained on the house above them, the home where he had grown up so harshly, so quickly. "I want you to meet my father tonight," he said. "I think the two of you will like each other."

Her heart bounced and swelled, dancing with amazement and joy. "I'd love to," she said softly, trying not to let him see how much this significant gesture of trust gave her hope for the future—their future. Was it possible that she and Gareth were more than lovers passing in the night? She hoped so...dear God, she hoped so.

He held her hand the rest of the way to his house. With the sun beating down on her head and the breeze tossing her hair in her eyes, she was momentarily blinded. Gareth was her lode-stone, her anchor.

Jacob's car was parked in front of the house when they pulled up. Gareth hopped out. "I see we have a welcoming committee. Hopefully he's brought lunch. I'm starving."

But when they entered the cool, dimly lit foyer and then made their way to the living room, Gracie knew that Jacob was not here to provide a picnic. His face was somber, his eyes hooded.

He never even glanced at Gracie. Instead he went to his brother and wrapped his arms around him, holding tight. Gareth returned the embrace and then broke away to stare at his sibling in puzzlement. "What's wrong?"

Jacob swallowed, his Adam's apple bobbing visibly as he strove for control.

Fear like she had never known crashed over Gracie, threatening to swallow her whole.

Gareth paled, his gaze locked on his brother's face. "Tell me, damn it."

"I thought about not showing you," Jacob said, his voice harsh with suppressed emotion. "You're not going to like it." He half turned and gestured to what Gracie had not been able to see until this moment. Strewn across the surface of the coffee table was a series of tabloids, Gareth's unmistakable face plastered on the cover of each one.

But even more shocking were the small, square insets on all of the papers. Blurry, grainy head shots of Gracie. Her stomach clenched.

Gareth's mouth opened and snapped shut. He reached for the worst of the gossip rags, one where Jacob had folded back the page to reveal the article inside. With no one to stop her, Gracie stood at his elbow and read with shocked dismay.

Edward Darlington, owner of Darlington Gallery in Savannah, Georgia, spoke to our reporter at a charity golf tournament in Cannes this past weekend. It seems that Mr. Darlington is on the verge of scoring a coup for his modest gallery. Darlington's daughter, Gracie, has recently become intimately involved with the reclusive eldest son of the renowned Wolff family, whose considerable fortune has suffered very little at the hands of the American economy. Mr. Darlington hints that he will soon be allowed to exhibit the small but remarkable collection of oil paintings completed by Gareth's Wolff's mother, Laura, prior to her violent and untimely death in the mid-1980s...

The story went on for another sentence or two, but Gracie turned away, unable to read another word. Sick to her stomach, she cringed when Gareth turned on her and stared through eyes that chilled her with black ice. "How did he find out about the paintings?" His voice shook. At his sides, his hands clenched, as though he wanted to strike her. "And was this your intent from the beginning? To fake amnesia...worm your way into my bed... God, you're self-serving...both of you."

Jacob touched his arm. "Give yourself a minute. I know this stings."

"Stings?" Gareth's expression was incredulous. "It doesn't sting. It makes me want to put my hands around Edward Darlington's neck and squeeze until he's a dead man."

He stared at Gracie, his expression fierce as a thunderstorm waiting to strike. "And you. You *know* I don't exploit my mother. I told you that. You've been playing me from the beginning, haven't you? And God knows I fell for it."

Seventeen

Gracie backed up to the wall, her arms wrapped around her waist. "I didn't know," she whispered hoarsely. "I'm so sorry."

Jacob still barely looked at her. All his attention was focused on his big brother, the man who was in so much pain it was terrible to watch. Jacob spoke soothingly. "Clearly the man's an ass. He's using this as a publicity stunt to draw business to his gallery. No one will take him seriously. We've never exhibited Mother's work, and we won't start now. He's trying to pressure you into agreeing to a gallery showing, but little does he know you're a stubborn bastard."

Gareth stalked Gracie, grabbing her shoulders in a bruising grip and shaking her. "Get out of here," he yelled. "Now."

She clung to him, her heart shattering at his feet. "I didn't know. I swear I didn't know."

The rage melted from his face to be replaced by something far more frightening. He thrust her away. "But that's just it, Gracie Darlington."

It hurt unbearably to hear him say her name with such loathing.

He bit out the words. "You *did* know at one time. And how *convenient* that you forgot."

Tears streamed down her face. "It's not really such a bad thing, is it? He went about it the wrong way, trying to bully you, but the showing could be a beautiful tribute to your mother. I never meant to hurt you. I wouldn't. I couldn't."

"I thought I knew how low a woman could sink. But you're a bitch of the first water. It was lies from the very beginning, every bit of it."

She fell to her knees, willing to beg, to humble herself on behalf of her idiot father. "I love you," she cried. "Why would I hurt you?"

But it was too late. The wolf had gnawed off his own foot to spring free of the trap. Whatever tender feelings he might have had for her were cauterized in an instant.

He stared downward, disgust and fury shriveling her where she knelt. "Don't make me call the authorities," he said coldly, every inch the firstborn of the manor.

Sensing the utter futility of any appeal, she stumbled to her feet and fled. The keys were still in the Jeep. She could barely see through the burning wash of tears. Cranking the engine, she threw the vehicle into Reverse, turned and shot down the road, hysteria dictating every motion.

The driveway was kinked with twists and turns that negotiated the mountainside. At the third switchback, she lost control and slammed into a tree.

"Gracie. Wake up. You're okay. Open your eyes."

Sluggishly, wrapped in a cloud of dread, she complied. Jacob sat beside her in the passenger seat, his gaze watchful. He took her wrist in an impersonal grip and checked her pulse. "That was a stupid thing to do. The Jeep is a mess, and you're lucky you didn't get hurt."

"Where's Gareth?" Just saying his name out loud was like scraping her throat with razor blades.

Jacob shrugged. "He headed up the mountain. I've known him to disappear for days at a time. He won't come back until you're long gone. I've been charged with escorting you off the property and taking you to the airport. I'll pay for a first-class ticket and arrange for one of our employees to meet you at the other end and stay with you until your father returns."

"But I…"

He got out and motioned for her to follow. "We need to collect your things. Get in my car."

At Gareth's house, she held her breath, hoping he had relented, but knowing in her heart that he would never forgive her.

Jacob stood in the doorway of her bedroom while she packed. It didn't take long. Gracie took nothing of Annalise's bounty except for a couple of casual outfits. She didn't know what to expect during the journey home, and it seemed prudent to have a change of clothing. When she had added her few personal items, the things she had brought with her when she first arrived, she zipped shut the small carry-on and stood quietly. "I'm ready."

Jacob nodded tersely.

The forty-five-minute drive to the airport was accomplished in dead silence. Nothing looked familiar to Gracie. And she no longer cared.

At the departure gate, Jacob pulled to the curb, engine idling. With his face set in grim lines, the resemblance to his brother was striking. He scowled at Gracie, not a shred of the compassionate doctor in evidence. "Don't contact him," he said bluntly. "No phone calls. No texts. No emails. If you ever try to approach our property again, you'll be charged with trespassing. Do you understand?"

A dagger of unbearable pain lodged beneath her heart, making it difficult to breathe. "I understand." Her voice was dull. Every scrap of life had been beaten out of her. No memory. No future. No Gareth.

As soon as she stepped out of the car with her bag, Jacob drove away without a backward glance.

She wandered the airport terminal in a fog of agony, feeling as if she had lost a limb. To have something to hide behind, she purchased a copy of *People* magazine. All the faces on the cover were familiar. It was too damn bad that the rich and famous were more accessible in her memory bank than her family and friends.

When the flight boarded, she huddled in her first-class window seat and tried to block out the world. After one abortive attempt at conversation, her travel companion, a balding middle-aged man, left her alone.

Gracie rested her head against the glass, eyes closed. If she could have ended her life at that moment, she might have considered it. The yawning chasm of emptiness inside her chest threatened to swallow her whole.

Perhaps she dozed. Or perhaps the pain simply became too much to bear and she lapsed into a stupor of grief.

But when the plane touched down and the flight attendant insisted Gracie leave the plane, she managed to get to her feet and shuffle in the wake of the other passengers.

As she exited the concourse, a tall man with a deep artificial tan and a cautious smile waved at her. "Over here, Gracie."

And just like that, it all came flooding back. Every bit of her lost memory. In an instant. He was her father.

Twenty-four hours ago such a development would have elated her. Now all she felt was a dull acceptance. If Gareth had been standing beside her, he would undoubtedly have been skeptical in the extreme.

Fortunately she didn't have to explain herself to anyone. Her father thought she was pretending to have amnesia while on

Wolff Mountain, so as far as he was concerned, nothing had changed.

He took her arm as they made their way outside. "I'm glad you're home, baby girl. Those Wolff men are scary. I've had to hire a lawyer…can you believe it? They made all kinds of threats…just because I joked with some sleazy reporter."

"I thought you were gone."

He pulled out into traffic and glanced at her. "Came in on a flight half an hour ago. When I saw a woman holding a sign with your name on it, we had a little chat and I sent her on her way. You want to stop for lunch? My treat?"

Gracie turned away from him, too desolate to be indignant. Her father was shallow, ego-driven and about as thick-skinned as a rhino. If he picked up on her distress, he showed no sign.

Even with no response from her, he stopped at the restaurant anyway. While her father polished off a substantial meal, Gracie pushed around several bites of syrup-soaked pancake on her plate and waited for the interminable stop on her journey home to be over.

Suddenly she was struck by a revelation. "You never had any intention of letting me manage the gallery, did you?" Only now did she remember that he had promised the job as an incentive to get her to invade Wolff Mountain and coax Gareth Wolff into giving them his mother's paintings for the gallery. "You knew I would fail," she accused. "This was all nothing more than a futile goose chase. Why, Daddy? Why would you do that to me?"

He set down his coffee cup and sighed, his put-upon expression designed to make *her* feel guilty instead of the other way around. "Misty's the new manager, sweetheart. And if you think about it, it makes perfect sense. She needs the job…you don't."

Misty was her father's less than brilliant girlfriend. "And *why* don't I need the job?" Gracie asked. She'd worked at the gallery in one capacity or another for years. Knew the business inside and out. Becoming manager was something she had wanted for a long time. So she had acceded to her father's audacious request that she track down Gareth Wolff and ask about Laura's paintings. Gracie had actually been the one to stumble across the mention of them in an old art journal she'd picked up at a flea market.

Edward took her hand in his, surprising her with the open affection. Her father rarely made the effort to play his parental role. "You're a gifted artist, Gracie. You should be creating art...not selling it. Every penny of the money your mother left you is still sitting in the bank. Take some of it. Go away. Find your muse. And when you come home, I'll be begging *you* to let me exhibit your work."

She took the flattery with a grain of salt. Edward knew he had screwed up, and he knew she would not be easily appeased. What he didn't know was that she was too heartsick to work up a head of steam over his transgressions. Fighting with him was simply more than she could endure right now.

An hour later, she was alone in her bedroom. The air was stale and musty, so she threw open the windows and curled up on one of the cushioned gable seats searching for solace.

Everything surrounding her was comfortable and familiar. And she had never felt so alone in all her life.

Two weeks of grieving were all she could tolerate. Nothing was going to change unless she took the reins and quit letting the days wash past her...unnoticed, unappreciated.

She wasn't the first woman to lose a man she loved. And she wouldn't be the last. Life moved on.

But what hurt the most—the regret that was hardest to shake—was that Gareth thought she had been willing to use his mother's art for personal gain. And it was true. Not knowing Gareth or his personal history, she hadn't thought the idea so terrible at its inception. In fact, Gracie had gone to the Blue Ridge sure she could persuade Gareth Wolff to share his mother's talent with the world. Thinking of him alone and hurting in his mountain hideaway made her ill. Knowing that she had added to his pain was almost more than she could bear.

When she could stand it no more, she took her father's advice. Loading up her yellow VW bug, the one that had been returned to her from a small town in Virginia with no note, no acknowledgment at all, she fled the city.

With her she had a month's stash of food and several boxes of art supplies. She had rented a small, isolated cabin in the north Georgia mountains, and for the next thirty days, she planned to do nothing but paint, sleep and paint again.

Halfway up the state, she came close to a crisis. A huge part of her wanted to drive northward, not stopping until she reached a certain mountain in Virginia. She actually pulled over in a rest stop and folded out a map to see how long it would take her.

But at the last minute, she acknowledged the futility of such a plan. Not only would she face the very real possibility of being arrested, but even worse, the likelihood that Gareth might throw her out himself. The God's honest truth was, she couldn't bear to see hate in those beautiful, dark eyes that had shown her such tenderness and care.

She had cried enough tears to fill a small lake. There were none left. Only a dull acceptance of what could not be changed.

The sun was almost gone when she spotted a turnoff on the narrow two-lane road. Now she traversed a rough, hard-packed dirt lane. Forty-five minutes later, when it seemed as if she might drive off the end of the world, she found her lodging, a small, unimpressive house in the heart of the forest.

Peeling paint, a leaning porch and ill-kempt landscaping made her wonder if she had been scammed. Fortunately the inside was more prepossessing. Though had she not been so bone tired, she might have spared a moment's amusement for the mental juxta-position of Gareth's incredible home with this dump.

The first night in the cabin was unsettling. She was a city girl, used to the sounds of sirens and traffic and quarreling neighbors. Here the solitude was oppressive, the deep, impenetrable night threatening.

On Wolff Mountain, the conditions were similar. But there she'd had Gareth to share her bed, to keep her safe and warm. Now she was on her own.

She slept little, choosing instead to curl up on the screened-in porch in a cushioned wicker chair and listen to the chirp of crickets and the rustle of nocturnal animals. Occasionally she dozed, but it was not until the faint light of morning dawned that she was finally able to crawl back into her bed and fall into a deep, exhausted slumber.

The pattern continued over the next week. Sleeping much of the day…eating a single meal in the evening, and working as the night hours waned. Sometimes she dragged a small lamp out onto the porch. At other moments she labored by candlelight.

Her water colors remained untouched. Instead she used pen and ink, filling page after page of heavy paper with black slashes, most of which translated into the same subject.

As her hands flew over the pages, her mind was unfortunately free to wander. Her world was topsy-turvy, changed beyond recognition. She couldn't continue with the life she had known for so many years. The potential for a future with Gareth was obliterated. Where did she go from here?

On the eighth day of her walkabout, it rained. Not a gentle sprinkle, but a raging, stormy deluge. In the wake of her usual nighttime insomnia, she slid into bed, pulled the covers over her head and fell asleep to the drumming of the storm on the tin roof overhead.

Dreams swirled in her subconscious, memories of Gareth making love to her. Vivid images of the two of them talking, laughing, wanting, taking. Hunger and heat.

She moaned, restless and aching. The dream was sweet a

first, but then terrifying and wretched. Gareth turned his back on her, walking away until he was no more than a speck on the horizon.

Thunder rumbled again, but with an oddly insistent beat. It took her long minutes to shake off the vestiges of sleep and recognize that someone was beating on her door.

Heartsick…exhausted…she contemplated not answering the summons. But perhaps there was a neighbor with an emergency…someone who needed her help.

Cautiously she peeped around the edge of the front window draperies and felt her limbs go numb as her heart ceased to beat. It was Gareth. Wasn't it? She hardly recognized him.

Swinging open the door with an unsteady hand, she stared at him. "Why are you here?" she demanded.

Eighteen

Gareth considered himself an intelligent man, but the lessons he had learned since Gracie left the mountain were hard-won. Giving up his grief and bitterness was no easy task. But in Gracie's absence, he had seen a man in the mirror who was a ruthless bastard. A man who suffered.

He'd walked miles in the mountains, trying in vain to outrun his demons. And at night he'd tossed and turned in restless dreams, aching for Gracie as if he had lost a limb.

His current quest was half closure, half penance. First to Savannah for a heated conversation with Edward Darlington, then on north and west to track through an obscure area with few directional signs and many roads that didn't show up on his GPS.

He was exhausted, frustrated and frankly, miserable. He drank in the sight of Gracie like a tonic. He felt dizzy, disoriented. None of his recollections of her came close to the real thing. Though she was thinner perhaps, and pale, too pale, she was so beautiful it hurt to look at her. He leaned against the door frame, his knees embarrassingly weak. "May I come in?"

She debated saying no. He saw the refusal form in her eyes, and yet at the last minute, he was granted a reprieve. But instead of answering him, she merely stepped back and allowed him to brush past her. He inhaled her familiar scent and his gut clenched. Another part of him tightened, as well, but he knew such a craving would not likely be appeased. Not when he had acted like a complete and total jackass.

"Nice cabin," he said, running his hand over a questionable support beam. With an inward wince, he admitted to himself that sarcasm probably wasn't the best approach.

"Why are you here?" She reiterated the question bluntly.

In her face he could see no sign of welcome. He had hoped… God, he had hoped that she would still feel at least an iota of the love she had professed. But he'd done a damned good job of riding roughshod over her tender heart, and he couldn't blame her if she hated him.

He paced the small living room, noting the bunch of wildflowers in a milk-glass vase, the remnants of a snack on a rickety end table. "I had your father investigated," he said bluntly.

Some strong reaction flashed in her eyes before she recovered and presented him with an impassive gaze. "And?"

"He's not a criminal. I suppose you would say his worst sin is an overabundance of ego."

"You're hardly one to throw stones in the arena."

"A fair point," he acknowledged. "Do you have anything to drink? I'm parched."

He followed her into the kitchen, waiting as she poured a cup of lukewarm coffee and handed it to him…black…the way he liked it. He downed half the cup and grimaced. The sludge tasted as if it had been brewed hours ago.

He set the unfinished drink on the scarred Formica counter and scowled. "Why didn't you just ask to see my mother's paintings?"

Her glare was incredulous. "I had amnesia."

"So that part was true?" In the aftermath of her leaving, he'd had a hell of a time deciding which aspects of Gracie Darlington were gold and which were dross.

"Yes," she muttered. "It was all true. Believe me, if I had remembered why I was there, I would have told you. You would have kicked me out and the two of us would have remained strangers."

"But instead, you became my lover."

She went white, her eyes agonized. And then just as quickly, the expression vanished. With a shrug, she nodded. "Apparently so."

"Did you ever get your memory back?" He had vacillated between wondering if she had regained her past and doubting that she had ever lost it in the first place.

Gracie perched on a stool, dark smudges beneath her eyes. After a wide-mouthed yawn, she rubbed her hands on the knees of her flannel sleep pants. They were cotton-candy-pink with little bunnies hopping across the fabric. "As soon as I saw my father, I remembered everything. Not that it mattered at that point."

"I'm glad." He stopped short, the words he had come to say bottled up in his chest. "I had a serious girlfriend once."

His abrupt change in topic left her visibly confused. "Okay..."

"She used me to get to my father and steal a priceless painting during a family dinner."

Though he didn't deserve it, her eyes softened. "I'm sorry."

"I was afraid of making the same mistake with you." The admission hurt his chest.

"What mistake?"

"Confusing lust with love. Opening my family to harm."

Her pretty face, usually so open and easy to read, baffled him with its lack of expression. She shrugged. "I'm sorry my father was such an idiot. And I regret the fact that I let him coax me into doing something as stupid as infiltrating your privacy. I've apologized before. I don't know what else I can do."

"Why *did* you come to Wolff Mountain, especially knowing how unlikely it was that I would agree to your proposal?"

"My father promised me that if I could get you to place your mother's work in the gallery, he would appoint me manager."

"And he wouldn't have done that anyway?"

"No. Not even if I had succeeded in my mission with you. When I got back, he had already installed his bimbo girlfriend as manager. Apparently she needs the job more than I do."

"I'm sorry."

"For once, he was probably right. I have an MFA degree. But I convinced myself that the percentage of artists who make a full-time career from painting was so small, there was no point in trying. As manager of the gallery, I would still be using my degree, but without the personal risk. Essentially I wanted my father to give me the job so I could settle down and move on with my life."

"You're awfully young to settle down. Are you any good?"

His blunt question dragged a laugh from her. "You be the judge." She left him only long enough to retrieve a sketch pad from another room. "I've done all these since I've been here."

Gareth flipped the pages slowly, at once impressed and humbled. She was damned good. The only real surprise was that in every one of the admittedly outstanding sketches, the subject was him. Gareth.

He studied each of them, noting how she had captured his expressions so succinctly. Arrogance. Humor. Anger. Hostility. It didn't escape his notice that very few of the pages revealed any softer nuance in him. Perhaps if she had drawn his face during lovemaking, she could have seen what was in his eyes. As it was…no wonder she had greeted him today with such a marked lack of emotion. The man in the images was certainly not lovable as far as Gareth could see.

A blank page came next, and when he flicked at it, preparing to close the pad, he realized that here was another sketch still unseen. He turned the page. And his heart stopped. *Dear God.*

His mother's eyes gazed back at him with amusement and compassion.

Gareth looked up, shock flooding his belly. "How did you…"

Gracie moved past him and perched on the arm of the sofa, her feet tucked beneath her. "The photo in your workshop. I recreated it from memory…at least the portion that was your mother. The more I sketched, the more I realized how much you look like her. She must have loved you very much. Her first child. A precious boy."

With a fingertip, he traced the features of a woman who had once meant the world to him. But in an instant, unbidden, another picture, a newspaper photo, momentarily threatened to replace his current nostalgic mood. With all his mental acuity, he forced it back.

He refused to let those old images hurt or define him. Not anymore. The likeness Gracie had created of his beloved mother warmed his heart and further cracked the shell he had built around himself. "It's perfect," he said, his throat tight and painful. "The spittin' image…" He paused. "Is it for sale?"

Gracie nodded.

"How much?"

"Seventy-five thousand dollars. A check made out to my charity."

He managed a grin, the first time he had really felt like smiling since he'd chased Gracie out of his life. "And what charity would that be?"

"I'll think of one."

He sobered, laying aside the collection of Gracie's art. "I'll never be able to make it up to you for the way I reacted that day. I'm ashamed, Gracie. And so damned sorry."

She picked up a snack plate and carried it to the kitchen, ensuring that it was impossible for him to see her face, though the two rooms were connected. "I think we've both spent far too much time on apologies."

He followed, taking her arm and forcing her to confront him. Without shoes, she was small, defenseless. Her big blue eyes looked up at him with wary calm.

She seemed cool as ice. He was the one whose hands trembled. He swallowed his pride along with the lump in his throat. "I understand loyalty to a parent, Gracie. Believe me. I've made decisions over the years, choices to please my father that anyone looking in would have questioned…and often did. I no longer fault you for coming to Wolff Mountain. You had to try."

"And the newspaper interview?"

"It felt like betrayal," he said simply, reliving for a moment that terrible afternoon. "I'd planned to tell you that night that I loved you. But instead, it seemed as if I had made the same mistake all over again…that I had been ruled by my libido at the expense of my family."

"Were there any follow-up stories?"

"No. It was a nonarticle in the first place. Just one stupid guy shooting off his mouth and saying asinine things."

"He is my father and will always be my father. No matter how badly he screwed up or will screw up in the future, I can never abandon him."

"Does that same level of forgiveness and acceptance extend to me, as well?"

He held his breath, the balance of his life in the palms of her small, feminine hands.

The fact that she couldn't meet his gaze gave him his answer. "I'll go," he said curtly, almost beyond social niceties. The agony of his chest being torn in two as he left his heart in those same small hands almost crippled him. He made it to the door before she stopped him.

"I don't want you to leave," she said, breathless as she

wrapped her arms around him from behind and hung on. "Of course I forgive you."

He stopped, whirled and grabbed her up in his arms. "I love you, Gracie," he said hoarsely. "God knows you have no cause to believe it, but it's true."

Her arms were around his waist, her cheek to his chest. Frustrated with her silence and his inability to read her face, he scooped her up and carried her to the sofa. With her in his lap, he began to think the world might once again make sense.

He tipped up her chin, the better to see her crystal clear eyes. But the blue was muted today, veiled in a way that made him afraid.

She grimaced faintly, pressing a kiss to his chin and curling into his embrace. "I love you, too."

"Come back with me," he urged. "The house is empty now. You stole the life away from it."

"No." Her answer was simple. Quiet. "You're welcome to stay here for a few days. In my bed." She seemed to realize that her invitation needed clarification.

"And after that?" Anger clenched his muscles.

"You have a life and I have mine. Parallel lines, Gareth. No intersection."

"That's where you're wrong." He could outstubborn her any day. "I'm not letting you go."

"You never had me...not really. We were playing a game, that's all. The scullery maid and the prince. Can you imagine my father and yours if they ever met? It's a ludicrous thought. We live in totally different worlds."

"But you're willing to have sex with me for old times' sake? Is that it?"

"You needn't make it sound so tawdry. There's no reason we can't maintain a physical relationship until you find the right woman to marry."

"And then you'll let me go...just like that?" He thrust her

away and stood to pace, ridiculously hurt. Did she think so little of him?

Her bullheaded attitude convinced him he had to take another tack. "Let's go to bed then. Right now."

"I...uh..."

He took her hand and dragged her to her feet. "Where's your room? Through here?" It wasn't too hard to locate his target in such a tiny cabin.

The covers on her bed were tumbled. Either she was a little on the messy side or she had still been asleep when he arrived.

Without waiting for an engraved invitation, he stripped her out of her practical sleepwear, divested himself of his own clothing and bent her over the bed, hands at her hips. He almost forgot the condom, remembering only at the last second to bend down and pull one from his jeans pocket.

When he was sheathed in latex, he surged into her from behind, feeling the long, slow slide home on a million different levels. Her body accepted him easily now, warm and moist and slick with welcome.

He touched the back of her head, ruffling her curls. "Is this what you had in mind, Gracie? Friends with benefits?"

She was mute, her sharp gasps as he rammed into her repeatedly the only response. From this angle, the view was unbearably erotic.

"Look at us in the mirror," he urged. His tanned hands on the white skin of her ass made a memorable picture. "This will never be enough," he muttered, almost beyond speech. "You're wrong. Dead wrong."

He reached beneath her to cup her breasts and play with them, slowing his drive to completion only by exerting every inch of his iron will. Her nipples budded at his touch. He used his other hand to pinch lightly at her labia. She cried out and came, squeezing his shaft so tightly at the peak of her climax that he shuddered and saw stars.

"Gracie. God, Gracie." Gripping her ass once again, he moved desperately in her, stroke after steady stroke. The tempo increased, his body tensed. Without warning, his world exploded as release snatched him up and tumbled him onto a rich, blissful, panting shore.

He had collapsed on top of her at the end. Boneless with pleasure, he shifted her all the way onto the bed and climbed in with her. Gracie was already asleep, which struck him as odd since it was morning, but he'd not had much rest in the last week, so he succumbed to postcoital fatigue and joined her.

Nineteen

Gracie awoke at noon, completely disoriented, but feeling as if something momentous had happened. The broad hair-roughened chest to which she was currently plastered gave her the first clue.

Gareth had found her. She reprimanded her silly, nonsensical heart for its cartwheel of jubilation and told herself to enjoy his apology visit without regret for the future.

Her movements wakened him. He rubbed his eyes and sat up, the sheet barely protecting his modesty. "I'm starving," he said, running a hand over her hip and caressing her butt.

She managed a smile. "I can feed you. Give me a minute to get dressed."

He rolled over her, trapping her with his thighs and resting his weight on his arms. "Do you understand what just happened?" His expression was sober as he looked down at her.

She chewed her lip, wondering why he was not putting a truly magnificent erection to good use. "Make-up sex?"

He bit her neck, sending shivers in wild seismic patterns all over her body. "Beyond that."

"No."

"I showed you how wrong you are."

"Not following." How could a woman concentrate when a man had his *you-know-what* pressed tantalizingly close to her most needy spot.

"I love you. You love me. We're not going to skulk around having some Romeo and Juliet affair. We're going to get married."

Like a beached fish, Gracie struggled to breathe. "Excuse me?"

"You heard me." He used his swollen penis to nudge her gently.

"Not gonna happen. Now that I have all my memories back, I get the full picture. I'm firmly middle-class and you're stinkin' rich. Your father would have apoplexy if you brought me up to the castle. Admit it. That's why you never introduced us to start with."

"Wrong again. I wanted him to meet you, but I was afraid you were up to no good. Now that I know the truth, I can tell you that he'll welcome you with open arms."

"I still have an unpredictable, not always clear-thinking father."

"Let me tell you a secret, Gracie Darlington." He entered her half an inch or so and withdrew. "As we speak, UPS is delivering a dozen of my mother's painting to the Darlington Gallery in Savannah…in preparation for an exhibition entitled *For Those We Love*. Dear old Edward is free to show them however long he likes…as long as the foundation gets the requested fee."

She searched his face, stunned to see he was telling the truth. "But you were so angry with him. He was insensitive about your mother's death, her life, your memories."

Gareth sank deep, his mouth finding hers in a deep carnal kiss as he claimed her. "He created you, my love. And for that I'll forgive him almost anything."

Gracie couldn't stem the tears that wet her cheeks. "Thank you," she whispered.

He moved with a power that left no question as to his passion, his adoration. "You're mine," he muttered, the muscles in his arms straining as he supported his upper body. His hips flexed. "Mine."

Gracie gave herself up to the moment, overwhelmed not only by his incredibly generous gesture to her father, but by the openness she sensed in him, the lack of bitterness, the almost palpable contentment.

The end sparked at one instant this time, both of them groaning with pleasure as they came together, perfectly in sync, exquisitely attuned to one other.

Lazily, feeling like the luckiest woman in the world, she ran a hand over his shorn head. The hair was no more than a half an inch long all over. "Why did you cut it?" she asked. "When I looked out the window, I wasn't sure at first that it was you." Though he was still incredibly handsome, his new appearance was more hero and protector than wild man and dangerous predator.

Gareth dragged them both to a seated position against the headboard, Gracie's back to his chest. In the mirror opposite the bed, she could see his expression clearly.

He ran a hand over his head, his smile rueful. "In ancient days, men sometimes cut off their hair as a sign of penitence and devotion. I hurt you badly, Gracie. The very person to whom I owed the greatest debt…for bringing me back to life. For loving me. This was the only way I knew how to make you see what was in my heart."

"Oh, Gareth…"

Their gazes met in the mirror, hers tremulous, his amazingly tender as he rubbed the wetness from her cheeks with a gentle touch.

He grinned suddenly. "Well, the haircut wasn't the *only* thing I thought of. Wait here. Don't move."

He left the room; she heard the front door open and close, which made her laugh out loud, because he was buck naked.

Moments later he was back, this time scooting up beside her so they faced each other.

She leaned toward him and used both hands to caress his head. "I'm getting used to it already. It makes you look like even more of a badass than you did before."

He hugged her tightly, his arms bands of steel that made it hard to breathe. "I'll never hurt you again, Gracie Darlington."

Reluctantly he released her, handing over a small parcel clumsily wrapped in tissue, but without tape or bow. She took it with a quizzical smile and peeled back the paper.

"Oh, Gareth." That was her new refrain. But what else was there to say when he had given her the most exquisite box. The wood was cherry, the dimensions two inches by three inches and barely an inch deep. The lid was inlaid with an intricate pattern of turquoise and silver and onyx. "You made this?"

He nodded. "Open it."

She slid the lid to one side, revealing a small compartment and an even smaller wad of tissue. Inside the tissue was a diamond ring, the square cut center stone flanked by two perfect emeralds. She was speechless.

"It was my mother's," he said hurriedly. "And if it makes you feel bad to wear it, we'll find something else. But I've already talked to Kieran and Jacob. They gave me their blessing to pass this on to you…since I was the one who remembered her best."

She gulped as he slid the lovely ring on to her finger.

Gareth's expression was more open and vulnerable than she had ever seen it, his heart laid out for her to see. "Marry me, Gracie. Bring light and life and children to our mountain."

She rested her head against his shoulder, already contemplating the memories they would create together. "Yes, my dear wolf," she said. "Always and forever, yes."

* * * * *

A TOUCH
OF PERSUASION

BY
JANICE MAYNARD

Published in Great Britain 2012
by Mills & Boon, an imprint of Harlequin (UK) Limited,
Eton House, 18-24 Paradise Road, Richmond, Surrey TW9 1SR

© Janice Maynard 2012

ISBN: 978 0 263 89210 9
ebook ISBN: 978 1 408 97779 8

51-0812

Harlequin (UK) policy is to use papers that are natural, renewable and recyclable products and made from wood grown in sustainable forests. The logging and manufacturing processes conform to the legal environmental regulations of the country of origin.

Printed and bound in Spain
by Blackprint CPI, Barcelona

Janice Maynard came to writing early in life. When her short story *The Princess and the Robbers* won a red ribbon in her third-grade school arts fair, Janice was hooked. She holds a BA from Emory and Henry College and an MA from East Tennessee State University. In 2002 Janice left a fifteen-year career as an elementary teacher to pursue writing full-time. Her first love is creating sexy, character-driven, contemporary romance. She has written for Kensington and NAL, and now is so very happy to also be part of the Harlequin family —a lifelong dream, by the way!

Janice and her husband live in beautiful east Tennessee in the shadow of the Great Smoky Mountains. She loves to travel and enjoys using those experiences as settings for books.

Hearing from readers is one of the best perks of the job! Visit her website at www.janicemaynard.com or e-mail her at JESM13@aol.com. And of course, don't forget Facebook (www.facebook.com/JaniceMaynardReader Page). Find her on Twitter at www.twitter.com/Janice Maynard and visit all the men of Wolff Mountain at www.wolffmountain.com.

For Deener,
Your energy, enthusiasm and *joie de vivre* challenge the rest of us to embrace life more fully!
I am glad you are my friend!

One

Kieran stood on the front porch of the small, daffodil-yellow house and fisted his hands at his hips. In the distance, the sounds of a lawn mower mingled with childish shouts and laughter. The Santa Monica neighborhood where he had finally tracked down Olivia's address was firmly, pleasantly middle class.

He told himself not to jump to conclusions.

The article he'd clipped from one of his father's newspapers crackled in his pocket like the warning rattle of a venomous snake. He didn't need to take it out for a second read. The words were emblazoned in his brain.

Oscar winners Javier and Lolita Delgado threw a lavish party for their only grandchild's fifth birthday. The power couple, two of the few remaining MGM "Hollywood royals," commanded an A-list crowd that included a who's who of movie magic. Little "Cammie," the star of the show, enjoyed pony rides, inflatables and a lavish afternoon buffet

*that stopped just short of caviar. The child's mother, Olivia
Delgado, stayed out of the limelight as is her custom, but
was seen occasionally in the company of rising film star
Jeremy Vargas.*

Like a dog worrying a bone, his brain circled back to the
stunning possibility. The timing was right. But that didn't
mean he and Olivia had produced a child.

Anger, searing and unexpected, filled his chest, choking
him with confusion and inexplicable remorse. He'd done his
best to eradicate memories of Olivia. Their time together
had been brief but spectacular. He'd loved her with a young
man's reckless passion.

It couldn't be true, could it?

Though it wasn't his style to postpone confrontation,
he extracted the damning blurb one more time and studied
the grainy black-and-white photo. The child's face was in
shadow, but he knew her family all too well.

Did Kieran have a daughter?

His hands trembled. He'd been home from the Far East
less than seventy-two hours. Jet lag threatened to drag him
under. Things hadn't ended well with Olivia, but surely she
wouldn't have kept such a thing from him.

The shocking discovery in his father's office set all of
Kieran's plans awry. Instead of enjoying a long overdue reunion with his extended family on their remote mountaintop
in the Virginia Blue Ridge, he had said hello and goodbye
with dizzying speed and hopped on another plane, this time
to California.

Though he'd be loath to admit it, he was jittery and panicked. With a muttered curse, he reached out and jabbed the
bell.

When the door swung open, he squared his shoulders
and smiled grimly. "Hello, Olivia."

The woman facing him could have been a movie star

herself. She was quietly beautiful; a sweeter, gentler version of her mother's exotic, Latin looks. Warm, sun-kissed skin. A fall of mahogany hair. And huge brown eyes that at the moment were staring at him aghast.

He probably should be ashamed that he felt a jolt of satisfaction when she went white. The urge to hurt her was unsettling. "May I come in?"

She wet her lips with her tongue, a pulse throbbing visibly at the side of her neck. "Why are you here?" Her voice cracked, though she was clearly trying hard to appear unconcerned.

"I thought we could catch up...for old times' sake. Six years is a long span."

She didn't give an inch. Her hand clenched the edge of the door, and her body language shouted a resounding *no*. "I'm working," she said stiffly. "Now's not a good time."

He might have been amused by her futile attempt at resistance if he hadn't been so tightly wound. Her generous breasts filled out the front of a white scooped-neck top. It was almost impossible not to stare. Any healthy man between the ages of sixteen and seventy would be drawn to the lush sexuality of a body that, if anything, was more pulse-stopping than ever.

He pushed his way in, inexorably but gently. "Perhaps not for you. I happen to think it's a damn good time."

She stepped back instinctively as he moved past her into a neat, pleasantly furnished living room. Though it was warm and charming, not an item was out of place. No toys, no puzzles, no evidence of a child.

On the far wall, built-in bookcases housed a plethora of volumes ranging from popular fiction to history and art appreciation. Olivia had been a phenomenally intelligent student, an overachiever who possessed the unusual combination of creativity and solid business sense.

A single framed picture caught his eye. As he crossed the room for a closer look, he recognized the background. Olivia had written her graduate thesis about the life and work of famed children's author and illustrator Beatrix Potter. On one memorable weekend, Olivia had dragged Kieran with her to England's Lake District. After touring the house and grounds where the beloved character Peter Rabbit was born, Kieran had booked a room at a charming, romantic B and B.

Remembering the incredible, erotic days and nights he and Olivia had shared on a fluffy, down-filled mattress tightened his gut and made his sex stir. Had he ever felt that way since?

He'd tried so damned hard to forget her, to fulfill his duty as a Wolff son. A million times he had questioned the decisions he made back then. Leaving her without a word. Ending an affair that was too new…too fragile.

But he had ached for her. God, he had ached. For Olivia…elegant, funny, beautiful Olivia…with a body that could make a man weep for joy or pray that time stood still.

He shoved aside the arousing memory. There was a strong chance that this woman had perpetrated an unforgivable deception. He refused to let his good sense be impaired by nostalgia. And let's face it…this meeting should be taking place on neutral ground. Because without witnesses, there was a good chance he was going to wring Olivia's neck.

Again, he studied the photo. Olivia stood, smiling for the camera, holding the hand of a young child. Kieran's world shifted on its axis. He lost the ability to breathe. My God. The kid was a Wolff. No one could doubt it. The wide-spaced eyes, the wary expression, the uptilted chin.

He whirled to face his betrayer. "Where is she?" he asked hoarsely. "Where's my daughter?"

Two

Olivia called upon every parentally bestowed dramatic gene she possessed to appear mildly confused. "Your daughter?"

The man facing her scowled. "Don't screw with me, Olivia. I'm not in the mood." She saw his throat work. "I want to see her. Now."

Without waiting for an invitation, he bounded up the nearby stairs, Olivia scurrying in his wake with her heart pounding. She'd known on some level that this day would come. But in her mind, she'd always thought that *she* would be the one orchestrating the reunion.

Kieran Wolff had been her first and only lover. Back then she'd been a shy, lonely, bookish girl with her head in the clouds. He had shown her a world of intimate pleasures. And then he had disappeared.

Any guilt she was feeling about the current situation evaporated in a rush of remembered confusion and pain.

On the landing he paused, then strode through the open door of what was unmistakably a little girl's bedroom. A Disney princess canopy bed…huge movie posters from a variety of animated children's films…a pair of ballet slippers dangling from a hook on the door.

For a moment, Olivia was reluctantly moved by the anguish on his face, but she firmed her resolve. "I repeat the question. What are you doing here, *Kevin?*"

A dull flush of color rose from the neck of his open-collared shirt. Short-cropped hair a shade darker than hers feathered to a halt at his nape. He was dressed like a contemporary Indiana Jones, looking as if he might be ready to take off on his next adventure. Which was exactly why, among other reasons, she had never contacted him.

He faced her, his gaze an impossible-to-decipher mélange of emotions. "So you know who I am." It was more of a statement than a question.

She shrugged. "I do now. A few years ago I hired a private investigator to find out the truth about Kevin Wade. Imagine my surprise when I learned that no such man existed. At least not the one I knew."

"There were reasons, Olivia."

"I'm sure there were. But those reasons mean less than nothing to me at this point. I need you to leave my house before I call the police."

Her futile threat rolled off him unnoticed. He was intensely masculine, in control, his tall lanky frame lean and muscular without an ounce of fat. Amber eyes narrowed. "Maybe *I'll* call the police and discuss charges of kidnapping."

"Don't do this," she whispered, her throat tight and her eyes burning. "Not after all this time. Please." The entreaty was forced between numb lips. She owed him nothing. But he could destroy her life.

"Where is the child?" His unequivocal tone brooked no opposition.

"She's traveling with her grandparents in Europe." Not for anything would Olivia reveal the fact that Cammie's flight wasn't departing LAX for several hours.

"Tell me she's mine. Admit it." He grasped her shoulders and shook her, his hands warm, but firm. "No lies, Olivia."

She was close enough to smell him, to remember with painful clarity the warm scent of his skin after lovemaking. Her stomach quivered. At one time she had believed she would wake up beside this man for the rest of her life. Now, in retrospect, she winced for the naive, foolish innocent she had been.

In high heels she could have met him eye to eye, but barefoot, wearing nothing but shorts and a casual top, she was at a distinct disadvantage. She pushed hard against his broad chest. "Let me go, you Neanderthal. You have no right to come here and push me around."

He released her abruptly. "I want the truth, damn it. Tell me."

"You wouldn't know the truth if it bit you in the ass. Go home, *Kevin Wade*."

Her deliberate taunt increased the fury bracketing his mouth with lines of stress. "We need to talk," he said as he glanced at his watch. "I have a conference call I can't miss in thirty minutes, so you have a choice. Tonight at my hotel. Or tomorrow in a room with two lawyers. Your call. But the way I'm feeling, a public forum might be the best option."

The sinking sensation in her belly told her that he would not give up easily. "I don't have anything to say to you," she said, her bravado forced at best.

He stared her down, his piercing golden eyes seeming to probe right through her to get at the truth. "Then I'll do all the talking."

Olivia watched, stunned, while he departed as quickly as he had come. She trailed after him, ready to slam the front door at the earliest opportunity, forcefully closing the door to the past. He paused on the porch. "I'll send a driver for you at six," he said bluntly. "Don't be late."

When he drove away, her legs gave out beneath her. She sank into a chair, her whole body shaking. Dear God. What was she going to do? She was a terrible liar, but she dared not tell him the truth. Kieran Wolff—she still had trouble thinking of him by that name—was not the laughing young man she remembered from their graduate days at Oxford.

His skin was deeply tanned, and sun lines at the corners of his eyes gave testament to the hours he now spent outdoors. He was as lethal and predatory as the sleek cats that inhabited the jungles he frequented. The man who helped dig wells in remote villages and who built and rebuilt bridges and buildings in war-torn countries was hard as glass.

She shuddered, remembering the implacable demand in his gaze. Would she be able to withstand his interrogation?

But there were more immediate details to address. Picking up the phone, she dialed the mother of Cammie's favorite playmate. The two families' backyards adjoined, and Cammie was spending part of the afternoon with her friend. Olivia had been terrified that Cammie would come home while Kieran was in the house.

Twenty minutes later, Olivia watched her daughter labor over a thank-you picture for her grandparents. Despite Olivia's reservations about the recent birthday party, the worst that had happened to her precocious offspring was the almost inevitable spilled punch on a five-hundred-dollar party dress…and a sunburned nose.

The dress had been a gift from Lolita. Olivia warned her mother that the exquisite frock was highly inappropriate for a child's birthday party. But as always, Lolo, as she liked to be called by her granddaughter, ignored Olivia's wishes and bought the dress, anyway.

Cammie frowned at a smudge in the corner of the drawing. "I need some more paper," she said, close to pouting. "This one's all messed up."

"It's fine, sweetheart. You've done a great job." At five, Cammie was already a perfectionist. Olivia worried about her intensity.

"I have to start over."

Sensing a full-blown tantrum in the offing, Olivia sighed and produced another sheet of clean white paper. Sometimes it was easier to avoid confrontation, especially over something so minor. Did all single mothers worry that they were ruining their children forever?

If Cammie had a father in her life, would she be less highly strung? More able to take things in stride?

Olivia's stomach pitched. She wouldn't think of Kieran right now. Not until Cammie was safely away.

She would miss her baby while Cammie was gone. The hours of reading storybooks. The fun baking experiments. The leisurely walks around the neighborhood in the evenings. The silly bathtub bubble fights. They were a family of two. A completely normal family.

Was she trying to convince herself or someone else?

She desperately wanted for Cammie the emotional security Olivia had never known as a child. The simple pleasure of hugs and homework. Of kisses and kites.

Olivia had been raised for the most part by a series of well-meaning nannies and tutors. She had learned early on that expensive Parisian dolls were supposed to make up for long absences during which her parents ignored her. The stereotypical poor little rich kid. With a closet full of expensive and often inappropriate toys, and a bruised heart.

Olivia remembered her own childish tantrums when her parents didn't bring presents she wanted. Thinking back on her egocentric younger self made her wince. Thank heavens she had outgrown that phase.

Maturity and a sense of perspective enabled her to be glad that her parents were far more invested in Cammie's life than they had ever been in their own daughter's. Perhaps grandparenthood had changed them.

Olivia's determination to live a solidly middle class life baffled Lolita and Javier, and they did their best to thwart her at every turn, genuinely convinced that money was meant to be spent.

The weekend party was an example of the lifestyle Olivia had tried so hard to escape. It wasn't good for a child to understand that she could have anything she wanted. Even if Olivia died penniless—and that wasn't likely—Cammie stood to inherit millions of dollars from her grandparents.

Money spoiled people. Olivia knew that firsthand. Growing up in Hollywood was a lesson in overindulgence and narcissism.

Cammie finally smiled, satisfied with her second attempt. "I wish Lolo had a refrigerator. My friend Aya, at preschool, says her nana hangs stuff on the front of the refrigerator."

Olivia smiled at her daughter's bent head. *Lolo* owned several refrigerators, all in different kitchens spread from L.A. to New York to Paris. But it was doubtful she ever opened one, much less decorated any of them with Cammie's artwork. Lolita Delgado had "people" to deal with that. In fact, she had an entourage to handle every detail of her tempestuous life.

"Lolo will love your drawing, Cammie, and so will Jojo." Olivia's father, Javier, wasn't crazy about his nickname, but he doted on his granddaughter, probably—in addition to the ties of blood—because she gave him what he craved the most. Unrestrained adoration.

Cammie bounced to her feet. "I'm gonna get my backpack. They'll be here in a minute."

"Slow down, baby…." But it was too late. Cammie ran at her usual pace up the stairs, determined to be ready and waiting by the door when the limo arrived. Olivia's parents were taking Cammie to Euro Disney for a few days in conjunction with a film award they were both receiving in Florence.

Olivia had argued that the trip was too much on the heels of the over-the-top birthday party, but in the end she had been unable to hold out against Cammie's beseeching eyes and tight hugs. The two adults and one child, when teamed against Olivia, made a formidable opponent.

Cammie reappeared, backpack in hand. Olivia had her suitcase ready. "Promise me you'll be good for your grandparents."

Cammie rolled her eyes in a manner far too advanced for her years. "You always say that."

"And I always mean it."

The doorbell rang. Cammie's screech nearly peeled the paint from the walls. "Bye, Mommy."

Olivia followed her out to the car. In the flurry of activity over getting one excited five-year-old settled in the vehicle, Lolita and Javier managed to appear both pleased and sophisticated as they absorbed their granddaughter's enthusiasm.

Olivia gave her mother a hug, careful not to rumple her vintage Chanel suit. "Please don't spoil her." For one fleeting second, Olivia wanted to share the truth about Kieran with her parents. To beg for guidance. She had never divulged a single detail about her daughter's parentage to anyone.

But the moment passed when Javier bussed his daughter's cheek with a wide grin. "It's what we do best, Olivia."

The house was silent in the aftermath of the exodus. Without the distraction of Cammie, the evening with Kieran loomed menacingly. Olivia wandered from room to room, too restless to work. Cammie would be going to kindergarten very soon. Olivia had mixed emotions about the prospect. She knew that her highly intelligent daughter would thrive in an academic environment and that the socialization skills she acquired with children her own age would be very important.

But it had been just the two of them for so long.

And now Kieran seemed poised to upset the apple cart.

When Olivia felt her eyes sting, she made a concerted effort to shake off the maudlin mood. Life was good. Her days were filled with family, a job she adored and a cadre of close, trusted friends. Kieran wasn't part of the package. And she was glad. She had made the right choice in protecting Cammie from his selfishness.

And she would continue to do so.

The remainder of the day was a total loss. She had a series of watercolors due for her book publisher in less than two weeks, but putting the finishing touches on the last picture in the set was more than she could handle today. She loved her work as a children's illustrator, and it gave her flexibility to spend lots of time with Cammie.

But the concentration required for her best efforts was beyond her right now. Instead, she prowled her small house, unable to stem the tide of memories.

They had met as expatriate grad students at a traditional English country house party hosted by mutual friends. With only six weeks of the term left, each knew the relationship had a preordained end. But in Olivia's case, with stars in her eyes and a heart that was head-over-heels in lust with the handsome, charismatic Kevin Wade, she'd spun fairy tales of continuing their affair back in the U.S.

It hadn't quite turned out that way. During the final days of exam week, "Kevin" had simply disappeared with nothing more than a brief note to say goodbye. Thinking about that terrible time made Olivia's stomach churn with nausea. Her fledgling love had morphed into hate, and she'd done her best to turn her back on any memory of the boy who broke her heart. And fathered her child.

After a quick shower, she stared at her reflection in the mirror. Even if Olivia wanted to follow in her mother's footsteps, she would never have stood a chance in Hollywood. She was twenty pounds too heavy, and though today's pool of actresses was more diverse, many directors still preferred willowy blondes. Olivia was neither.

By the time the limo pulled up in front of her house, Olivia was a wreck. But since birth, she'd been taught "the show must go on" mantra, and to the world, Olivia Delgado was unflappable. For six years, she had spun lies to protect her daughter, to make a life so unexceptional that the tabloids had long since left her alone.

An unwed mother in Hollywood was boring news. As long as no one discovered the father was a Wolff.

Tonight Olivia would be no less discreet.

She had dressed to play a part. Confident and chic were the qualities she planned to convey with her taupe linen tank dress and coral sandals. Though she had not inherited an iota of her parents' love for acting, she had inevitably learned from them along the way what it meant to present a serene face to the world, no matter if your life was in ruins.

Kieran Wolff's hotel was tucked away in a quiet back street of Santa Monica. Exclusive, discreet and no doubt wildly expensive, it catered to those whose utmost wish was privacy. The manager, himself, actually escorted Olivia to the fifth floor suite.

After that, she was left to stand alone at the door. Instead of knocking, she took a few seconds to contemplate fleeing the country. Cammie was everything to her, and the prospect of losing her child was impossible to imagine.

But such thoughts were defeatist. Though she might not be able to go toe-to-toe with the Wolff empire when it came to bank accounts, Olivia did have considerable financial means at her disposal. In a legal battle, she could hold her own. And judges often sided with a mother, particularly in this situation.

She had no notion of what awaited her on the other side of the door, but she wouldn't go down without a fight. Kieran Wolff didn't deserve to be a father. And if it came to that, she would tell him so.

Deliberately taking a moment to shore up her nerve, she rapped sharply at the door and took a deep breath.

Kieran had worn a trail in the carpet by the time his reluctant guest arrived. When he yanked open the door and saw her standing in the vestibule, his gut pitched and tightened. God, she was gorgeous. Every male hormone he possessed stood up and saluted. A man would have to be almost dead not to respond to her inherent sexuality.

Like the pin-up girls of the 1940s, with legs that went on forever, breasts that were real and plenty of feminine curves right where they should be, Olivia Delgado was a vivid, honey-skinned fantasy.

But today wasn't about appeasing the hunger in his gut, even if he *had* been celibate during a recent, hellacious foray into the wilds of Thailand. Bugs, abysmal weather and local politics had complicated his life enormously. He'd been more than ready to return to central Virginia and reconnect with his family. Not that he ever stayed very long, but still…that closely guarded mountain in the Blue Ridge was the only place he called home.

With an effort, he recalled his wayward thoughts. "Come in, Olivia. I've ordered dinner. It should be delivered any moment now."

She slipped past him in a cloud of Chanel No. 5, making him wonder if she had worn the evocative scent on purpose. In the old days, she had often come to his bed wearing nothing but a long strand of pearls and that same perfume.

He waited for her to be seated on the love seat and then took an armchair for himself a few feet away. In the intervening hours, he'd rehearsed how this would go. Having her here, on somewhat public turf, seemed like a good idea. He was determined to keep his cool, no matter the provocation.

They faced off in silence for at least a minute. When he realized she wasn't going to crack, he sighed. "Surely you can't deny it, Olivia. You were a virgin when we met. I can do the math. Your daughter is mine."

Her eyes flashed. "My daughter is none of your business. You may have introduced me to sex, but there have been plenty of men since."

"Liar. Name one."

Her jaw dropped. "Um…"

He chuckled, feeling the first hint of amusement he'd had since he saw the article about the party. Olivia might look like a woman of immense sophistication and experience, but he'd bet his last dime that she was still the sweet, down-to-earth girl he'd known back at university, completely unaware of her stunning beauty.

"Show me her birth certificate."

Her chin lifted. "Don't be ridiculous. I don't carry it around in my purse."

"But you probably have it at the house, right? In order to register her for kindergarten?"

She nibbled her bottom lip. "Well, I…"

Thank God she was a lousy liar. "Whose name is on the birth certificate, Olivia? You might as well tell me. You know I can find out."

Suddenly she looked neither sweet nor innocent. "Kevin Wade. Is that what you wanted to hear?"

The sharp pain in his chest took his breath away. "Kevin Wade…"

"Exactly. So you can see that no judge would think you have any rights in this instance at all." Her eyes were cold, and even that realization was painful. The Olivia he had known smiled constantly, her joie de vivre captivating and so very seductive.

Now her demeanor was icy.

"You put my name on her birth certificate," he croaked. It kept coming back to that. Kevin Wade was a father. Kieran had a daughter.

"Correction," she said with a flat intonation that disguised any emotion. "In the hospital, when I gave birth to my daughter, I listed a fictional name for her father. It had nothing to do with you."

He clamped down on his frustration, acknowledging that he was getting nowhere with this approach. Unable to sit any longer, he sprang to his feet and paced, pausing at the windows to look out at the ocean in the far distance. One summer he had lived for six weeks on a houseboat in Bali. It was the freest he had ever felt, the most relaxed.

Too bad life wasn't always so easy.

Olivia continued to sit in stubborn silence, so he kept his back to her. "When you hired an investigator, what did you find out about me?"

After several seconds of silence, she spoke. "That your

real name is Kieran Wolff. You lost your mother and aunt to a violent abduction and shooting when you were small. Your father and uncle raised you and your siblings and cousins in seclusion, because they were afraid of another kidnapping attempt."

He faced her, brooding. "Will you listen to my side of the story?" he asked quietly.

Olivia's hands were clenched together in her lap, her posture so rigid she seemed in danger of shattering into a million pieces. Though she hid it well, he could sense her agitation. At one time he had been attuned to her every thought and desire.

He swallowed, painfully aware that a king-size bed lay just on the other side of the door. The intensity of the desire he felt for her was shocking. As was the need for her to understand and forgive him. He was culpable for his sins in the past, no doubt about it. But that didn't excuse Olivia for hiding the existence of his child, his blood.

"Will you listen?" he asked again.

She nodded slowly, eyes downcast.

With a prayer for patience, he crossed the expanse of expensive carpet to sit beside her, hip to hip. She froze, inching back into her corner.

"Look at me, Olivia." He took her chin in his hand with a gentle grasp, lifting it until her gaze met his. "I'm not the enemy," he swore. "All I need is for you to be honest with me. And I'll try my damnedest to do the same."

Her chocolate-brown eyes were shiny with tears, but she blinked them back, giving him a second terse nod. He tucked a stray strand of hair behind her ear and forced himself to release her. Touching her was a luxury he couldn't afford at the moment.

"Okay, then." He was more a man of action than of words. But if he was fighting for his daughter, he would use any means necessary, even if that meant revealing truths he'd rather not expose.

He leaned forward, elbows on his knees, and dropped his head in his hands. "You were important to me, Olivia."

A slight *humph* was her only response. Was that skepticism or denial or maybe both?

"It's true," he insisted. "I'd been with a lot of girls before I met you, but you were different."

Dead silence.

"You made me laugh even when I wanted you so badly, I ached. I never meant to hurt you. But I had made a vow to my father."

"Of course you had."

She could give lessons in sarcasm.

"Sneer if you like, but the vow was real. My brothers and cousins and I swore to my father and my uncle that if they would let us go off to college without bodyguards, we would use assumed names and never tell *anyone* who we really were."

"So it was okay to sleep with me, but you couldn't share with me something as simple as the truth about your real name. Charming."

This time it was Olivia who jumped to her feet and paced. He sat back and stared at her, tracking the gentle sway of her hips as she crisscrossed the room. "I was going to tell you," he insisted. "But I had to get my father's permission. And before I could do that, he had a heart attack. That's when I left England so suddenly."

She wrapped her arms around her waist. "Leaving behind a lovely eight-word note. *Dear Olivia, I have to go home. Sorry.*"

He winced. "I was in a hurry."

"Do you have any clue at all how humiliated I was when I went to the Dean's office to beg for information about you and was told that Kevin Wade was no longer enrolled? And they were not allowed to give out any information as to your whereabouts because of privacy rules? God, I was embarrassed. And then I was mad at myself for being such a credulous fool."

"You weren't a fool," he said automatically, mentally replaying her words and for the first time realizing what he had put her through. "I'm sorry."

She kicked the leg of the coffee table, revealing a hint of her mother's flamboyant temper. "Sorry doesn't explain why suddenly neither your cell phone nor your email address worked when I tried to reach you."

"They were school accounts. My exams were over. I knew I wasn't coming back, so I let them go inactive, because I thought it was the easiest way to make a clean break."

"If you're trying to make a case for yourself, you're failing miserably."

"I never wanted to hurt you," he insisted.

"They call them clichés for a reason." The careful veil she'd kept over her emotions had shredded, and now he was privy to the pure, clean burn of her anger.

"Things were crazy at home," he said wearily. "I stayed at the hospital round-the-clock for a week. Then when Dad was released, he was extremely depressed. My brother Jacob and I had to entertain him, read to him, listen to music with him. I barely had a thought to myself."

She nodded slowly. "I get it, Kieran." He watched her frown as she rolled the last word on her tongue. "I was a temporary girlfriend. Too bad I was so naive. I didn't realize for a few weeks that I had been dumped. I kept making excuses for you, believing—despite the evidence to the contrary— that we shared something special."

"We did, damn it."

"But not special enough for you to pick up the phone and make a call. And you had to know I was back home in California. Yet you didn't even bother. I should thank you, really. That experience taught me a lot. I grew up fast. You were a horny young man. I was easy pickings. So if that's all, I'm out of here. I absolve you of any guilt."

Fortunately for Kieran, the arrival of dinner halted Olivia's headlong progress to the door. She was forced to cool her heels while the waiter rolled a small table in front of the picture window and smiled as Kieran tipped him generously. When the man departed, the amazing smells wafting from the collection of covered dishes won Olivia over, despite Kieran's botched attempts to deal with their past.

Neither of them spoke a word for fifteen minutes as they devoured grilled swordfish with mango salsa and spinach salad.

Kieran realized he'd gotten off track. They were supposed to be talking about why Olivia had hidden the existence of his daughter. Instead, Kieran had ended up in a defensive position. Time for a new game plan.

He ate a couple of bites of melon sorbet, wiped his mouth with a snowy linen napkin and leaned back in his chair. "I may have been a jerk," he said bluntly, "but that doesn't explain why you never told me I had a daughter. Your turn in the hot seat, Olivia."

Three

Olivia choked on a sliced almond and had to wash it down with a long gulp of water. The Wolff family was far more powerful than even Olivia's world-famous parents. If the truth came out, she knew the Wolff patriarchs might help Kieran take Cammie. And she couldn't allow that. "You don't have a daughter," she said calmly, her voice hoarse from coughing. Hearing Kieran's explanation of why he had left England so suddenly had done nothing to alleviate her fears. "I do."

Kieran scowled. Any attempts he might have made to appease her were derailed by his obvious dislike of having his wishes thwarted. "I'll lock you in here with me if I have to," he said, daring her to challenge his ability to do so.

"And how would that solve anything?"

Suddenly her cell phone rang. With a wince for the unfortunate timing, she stood up. "Excuse me. I need to take this."

Kieran made no move to give her privacy, so she turned her back on him and moved to the far side of the room. Tapping the screen of her phone to answer, she smiled. "Hey, sweetheart. Are you in New York?"

The brief conversation ended with Olivia's mother on the other end promising to make Cammie sleep on the flight over to Paris. Olivia's daughter had flown internationally several times, but she wasn't so blasé about jet travel that she would simply nod off. Olivia had packed several of the child's bedtime books in her carry-on, hoping that a semi-familiar routine would do the trick.

When Olivia hung up and turned around, Kieran was scowling. "I thought you said she was in Europe."

She shrugged. "That's their ultimate destination."

"So this morning when I came to your house, where was she?"

"At the neighbor's."

"Damn you, Olivia."

It was her turn to frown in exasperation. "What would you have done if I had told you, Kieran? Made a dramatic run through the yard calling her name? My daughter is now traveling with her grandparents. That's all you need to know."

"When will they be back?"

"A week…ten days… My mother isn't crazy about abiding by schedules."

His scowl blackened. "Tell me she's my daughter."

Her stomach flipped once, hard, but she held on to her composure by a thread. "Go to hell."

Abruptly he shoved back his chair and went to the mini bar to pour himself a Scotch, downing the contents with one quick toss of his head. His throat was tanned like the rest of him, and the tantalizing glimpse of his chest at the opening of his shirt struck Olivia as unbearably erotic.

Sensing her own foray into the quicksand of nostalgia, she attacked. "If you want to have children someday, you should probably work on those alcoholic tendencies."

"I'm not an alcoholic, though God knows you could drive a man to drink." He ran a hand through his hair, rumpling it into disarray. She saw for the first time that he was exhausted, probably running on nothing but adrenaline.

"You don't even own a house," she blurted out.

Confusion etched his face. "Excuse me?"

"A house," she reiterated. "Most people who want a family start with a house and a white picket fence. All you do is travel the globe. What are you afraid of? Getting stuck in one place for too long?"

Her random shot hit its mark.

"Maybe," he muttered, his expression bleak. "My brothers have been begging me to come home for a long time now. But I'm not sure I know how."

"Then I think you should leave," she said calmly. "Get back on a plane and go save the world. No one needs you here."

"You didn't used to be so callous." His expression was sober. Regretful. And his cat eyes watched her every move as if he were stalking prey.

"I'm simply being realistic. Even if I *had* given birth to a child that was yours, what makes you think you have what it takes to be a father? Parenting is about being *present*. That's not really your forte, now is it?"

She heard the cruel words tumbling from her lips and couldn't stop them. If she could drive him away in anger, he would go and leave Olivia to raise her daughter in peace.

"I'm here now," he said quietly, his control making her ashamed of her outburst. "Cammie is my daughter, I want to get to know her."

Olivia's heart stopped. Hearing him say her daughter's

name did something odd to her heart. "How exactly do you mean that?"

"Let me stay here with you for a little while."

"Absolutely not." She shivered, imagining his big body in her guest bed…a few feet down the hall from hers.

"Then I want the two of you to come to Wolff Mountain with me for the summer and meet my family. This afternoon I talked to the CEO of my foundation, Bridge to the Future. He's lining up people to take my place until early September."

"Thank you for the invitation," she said politely. "But we can't. Perhaps some other time." *When hell freezes over.* If she let Cammie go anywhere near the Wolff family compound, Olivia stood a chance of never seeing her daughter again. Kieran's relatives made up a tight familial unit, and if they got wind that another wolf had been born into the pack, Olivia feared that her status as Cammie's mother would carry little weight.

He shoved his hands in his pockets. "At the risk of sounding like one of your father's action hero characters, I'm warning you. We can do this the easy way or the hard way. I can get a court order for a DNA sample."

Olivia shivered inwardly as she felt her options narrowing. She could buy some time by stonewalling, but ultimately, the Wolff would prevail. "My daughter and I have lives, Kieran. It's unrealistic of you to expect us to visit strangers for no other reason than your sudden odd conviction that you are a daddy."

"Your work is portable. Cammie doesn't start school until the fall. I'll make a deal with you. I won't claim her as mine…. I won't even tell my family what I know to be true. But in exchange, you agree to let me see her as much as possible in the next few weeks."

"She's not yours." The words were beginning to sound weak, even to her ears.

He came toward her. The silent intensity of his stare was hypnotic. When they were almost touching, chest to chest, he put his hands on her shoulders, the warmth of his touch searing her skin even through a layer of fabric. "Don't be afraid of me, Olivia."

His mouth moved over hers, light as a whisper, teasing, coaxing. The fact that her knees lost their starch should have made her angry, but there was no room for negative emotion in that moment. For no other reason than pleasure, her lips moved under his. Seeking. Responding.

He made an inarticulate murmur that encompassed surprise and masculine satisfaction. Then the kiss deepened.

His leg moved between her thighs as he drew her closer. "You haven't changed," he said roughly. "I've dreamed about you over the years. On nights when I couldn't sleep. And remembered you just like this. God, you're sweet."

She felt the press of his heavy erection against her belly, and everything inside her went liquid with drugged delight. How long had it been? How long? No longer a responsible mother, she was once again a giddy young woman, desperate for her lover's touch.

Unbidden, the memories came flooding back....

"You're a virgin?"

Kevin's shock worried her. Surely he wouldn't abandon her now. Not when they were naked and tangled in her bed. "Does it matter? I want this, Kevin. I really do. I want you."

He sat up beside her, magnificently nude, his expression troubled. "I haven't ever done it with a virgin. You're twenty-two, Olivia. For God's sake. I had no idea."

With a confidence that surprised her, she laid a hand on his hard, hairy thigh, her fingertips almost brushing his thick penis. "I told you I had led a sheltered life. Why do you think I wanted to cross an ocean to finish my school-ing? I'm tired of living in a cocoon. Make love to me, Kevin. Please."

His hunger, coupled with her entreaty, defeated him. Groaning like a man tormented on a rack, he moved be-tween her legs once more, his erect shaft nudging eagerly at her entrance. Braced on his forearms, he leaned down to kiss her...hard. "I know I'll hurt you. I'm sorry."

"No apology needed," she whispered, sensing the mo-mentous turning point in her life. "I need this. I need you."

He pushed forward an inch, and she braced instinctively against the sharp sting of pain.

"Easy," he whispered, his beautiful eyes alight with ten-derness. "Relax, Olivia."

She tried to do as he asked, but he was fully aroused, and she was so tight. His whole big body trembled violently, and she wanted to cry at the beauty of it. Another inch. Another gasped cry to be swallowed up in his wild kiss.

She felt torn asunder, violated, but in the best possible way. Never again would her body be hers. Kevin claimed it, claimed her.

When he was fully seated, tears rolled silently down her cheeks, wetting her hair, sliding into her ears.

He rested his forehead on hers. "Was it that bad?" he asked, clearly striving for humor, but unable to hide his distress over what had transpired.

"Try moving," she said breathlessly. "I think I can handle it."

"Holy hell." His discomfiture almost elicited a giggle, but when he followed her naive suggestion, humor fled. Slowly, inexorably, her untried body learned his rhythm. Deep inside her a tiny flame flickered to life.

She moaned, arching her back and driving him deeper on a down thrust. It was easier now, and far more exciting.

Her long legs wrapped around his waist. Skin damp with exertion, they devoured each other, desperately trying to get closer still.

Kevin went rigid and cursed, closing his eyes and groaning as he climaxed inside her. She was taking the pill, and he had been tested recently, so no condom came between them.

As he slumped on top of her, she wrinkled her nose in disappointment. She had been so close to something spectacular. But the feeling faded. Taking its place was a warmth and satisfaction that she had been able to give him pleasure.

He rolled to his side. "Did you come?"

She nibbled her lip. Would it hurt to lie? It wasn't a habit she wanted to start. "Not exactly. But I know it takes practice. Don't worry about it...really."

He chuckled, yawning and stretching. "For a novice, you're pretty damned wonderful. Hold still, baby, and let's finish this."

Without ceremony, he put his hand between her legs and touched her. She flinched, still not quite comfortable with this level of intimacy, and also feeling tender and sore. His fingers were gentle, finding a certain spot and rubbing lightly. Her hips came off the bed.

"Um, Kevin?"

"What, honey?"

"You don't have to do this. To tell you the truth, I'm feeling sort of embarrassed."

"Why?" The strum of his fingers picked up tempo.

"Well, you're...um...finished, and it's a little weird now." *Her voice caught in her throat. "That's enough. I feel good. Really."*

He entered her with two fingers and bit the side of her neck. "How about now?"

Her shriek could have peeled paint off the walls, but she

*was too far gone to care. The attention she gave herself now
and again when the lights were out barely held a candle to
this maelstrom. Kevin gave no quarter, stroking her firmly
until her orgasm crested, exploded and winnowed away,
leaving her spent in his arms.*

She cried again.

He made fun of her with gentle humor.

*Then they turned out the lights and spent their first night
together, wrapped in each other's arms.*

Kieran cupped her breast with his hand, and just like
that, Olivia was fully in the present. What shocked her back
to reality was the incredible realization that she was a hairs-
breadth away from letting him have her again. No protest.
No discussion. Simply mindless pleasure.

And while that may have been okay six years ago, now
she had a daughter to think about. Sexual reminiscing with
Kieran Wolff was not only self-destructive and stupid, but
also detrimental to her role as a parent.

"Enough," she said hoarsely, tearing herself from his
embrace and warding him off with a hand when he would
have dragged her back for another kiss. "I mean it," she said.
"We're not doing this. You can't seduce me into agreeing to
your terms."

"Give us both more credit than that, Olivia. What happened just now proves that we've always had chemistry…
and still do."

"If you're expecting to pick up where we left off, you're
destined for disappointment."

"Is that so? From what I could tell, what just happened
was a two-way street."

"It's late," she said abruptly. "I have to go."

He crossed his arms over his chest and leaned a hip
against the back of the sofa, his eyes narrowed. From the
look of him, no one would guess that sixty seconds ago he'd

been kissing her senseless. "You can't run from me, Olivia. Closing your eyes and thinking about Kansas is a child's game. I want some answers."

Her phone chimed to signal a text, and she pulled it from her pocket, glancing at it automatically. Her mother's words chilled her blood.

Kieran touched her shoulder as she sank to a seat. "What is it? What's wrong?"

"The flight was delayed. My mother has a stalker fan, and he showed up at the airport."

He squatted beside her, his mere presence lending comfort. "What happened?"

"When he tried to burst through a checkpoint, calling her name, TSA arrested him."

He frowned. "I don't like the thought of Cammie being exposed to something like that."

"First of all, my parents take security very seriously, and second of all, this is none of your business. I'm her mother. It's up to me to keep her safe."

From his vantage point crouched at her side, their gazes collided. "You don't have to do this alone anymore," he said quietly, the words like a vow. "Any child with my blood running in her veins has the protection of the entire Wolff clan at her back."

She swallowed hard, near tears, missing her daughter and feeling out of her depth. "A child is not a belonging. She's her own person. Even if she *is* only five."

"You think I don't know that? I was a year younger than she is now when my mother was killed." He sprang to his feet, pacing once more. "My brother Gareth was the only one of us really old enough to understand and remember the details, but I lived it, and those terrible days are buried somewhere in my psyche…the confusion, the loneliness, the knowledge that my world was never going to be the same.

No child should lose a parent, Olivia, even if she thinks she has only one."

Guilt reached inside her chest and squeezed hard. Kieran Wolff had hurt her badly. Did she have the right to make her daughter vulnerable to his undeniable charm? Conversely, was she wrong to deny her child a father, even an absentee one? The same questions had haunted her for half a decade.

Her head ached. "We'll visit for a long weekend," she said, her voice tight. "As soon as Cammie gets back from Europe. But that's all it will be. All it will ever be. And if you break your word to me, I'll take her away and never speak to you again."

His lips quirked in a half smile. "Mama Bear protecting her cub. I like seeing you in this maternal role, Olivia. It suits you."

She gathered her purse and the light sweater she'd brought with her. "No one and nothing in this world means more to me than Cammie. And you'd do well to remember that. Good night, Kieran. Pleasant dreams."

He followed her to the door, having the temerity to press another hard kiss to her lips before allowing her to leave. "I'll dream," he said, brushing her cheek with the back of a hand. "But I have a feeling that pleasant won't be the right word for it."

Four

Kieran had never liked waiting. The ten days that elapsed between his confrontation with Olivia and her arrival at Wolff Mountain were interminable. Every moment of every day he imagined a dozen excuses she could make to keep from showing up.

As an adolescent he'd imagined the walls of the monstrous house closing in on him, as if he were trapped in a castle dungeon. Even now, his homecoming was tainted with confusion. Mostly he felt the agitation of being stuck in one place. He liked the freedom of the open road.

But if he were honest with himself, he had to admit that Wolff Mountain drew him home time and again despite his conflicted feelings about its past…his past.

Having his brothers close went a long way toward passing the time. They shared meals at the "big house," and Kieran was introduced to Gracie, Gareth's new wife.

Kieran's older brother was happier than Kieran had seen him in years, and it was clear that he adored his bride.

In the mornings, Kieran hiked the mountain trails with Gareth, and after lunch every day, he helped Jacob add on a new room to the doc's already state-of-the-art clinic. Kieran welcomed the physical exertion. Only by pushing himself to the point of exhaustion was he able to sleep at night. And even then he dreamed... God, he dreamed.

Olivia...in his bed, beneath him, her fabulous mane of hair spread across the pillows like a river of molten chocolate shot with gold. Her honey smooth skin bare-ass naked, waiting for him to touch every inch of it with his lips, his tongue, his ragged breath...

He'd dreamed of her before... At least in the beginning. When he first lost her. But the pain of doing so had ultimately led him to pretend she didn't exist. It was the only way he had survived.

But now, knowing that he and Olivia would soon be sharing a roof, the chains he'd used to bind up his memories shattered. He'd taken more cold showers in the past week than he had as a hormone-driven teen. And in the darkest hours of the night, he wondered with no small amount of guilt if he was using his own daughter as leverage to spend more time with the woman he'd never been able to forget.

Olivia wasn't coming here to be his lover. She'd made that crystal clear. Her single concession was to allow Cammie a visit. And that was only because Kieran threatened court proceedings.

He still felt bad about that, but Olivia's stubbornness infuriated him. Why couldn't she just admit that in the short time they were together, they created a life? He knew the truth in his gut, but he needed Olivia to be honest...to tell him face-to-face. Until he heard her say the words out loud, he wouldn't be satisfied.

With Cammie as his child, everything changed. It meant that when he was laboring in some godforsaken corner of the world, he could dream about returning home to someone who was his, a child who would love him and hug his neck.

Kieran's family loved him, but coming home to Wolff Mountain was painful. So painful, in fact, that he made it back to the States only a couple of times a year. No matter how hard he tried, the memories of his mother, though vague and indistinct, permeated the air here. And those same memories reminded him of how helpless he had felt when she died.

Seeing his father and uncle and brothers and cousins crying had left an indelible mark on an impressionable four-year-old. Until then, he'd believed that men never cried, especially not his big, gruff daddy. Kieran had been confused, and fearful, and so desperate to make everything better.

The day of the funeral he pretended to take a nap while the adults were gone. While the nanny was on the phone with her boyfriend, Kieran slipped into his mother's bedroom and ransacked the large walk-in closet that housed her clothes. He tugged at the hems of blouses and dresses and evening gowns, ripping them from the hangers and piling them up haphazardly until he had a small mountain.

The fabrics smelled like her. With tears streaming down his face, he climbed atop his makeshift bed, curled into a ball of misery and fell asleep, his thumb tucked in his mouth.

Kieran inhaled sharply, realizing that he had allowed himself the bittersweet, two-edged sword of memory. That's why he came home so seldom. In another hemisphere he could pretend that his life was normal. That it had always been normal.

Returning to Wolff Mountain always pulled the Band-Aid off a wound that had never healed cleanly. He remembered being discovered on that terrible funeral day and escorted out of his parents' bedroom. No one chastised him. No one took him to task for what he had done. But three days later when he worked up the courage to once again sneak into his mother's closet, every trace of her was gone... as if she had never existed. Even the hangers had been removed.

That day he'd cried again, huddled in a ball in the corner of the bare closet. And this time, there was no comfort to be found. His world had shredded around him, leaving nothing but uncertainty and bleakness. He hated the stomach-hollowing feelings and the sensation of doom.

No child should ever have to feel abandoned, and sadly, Kieran and his brothers had been emotional orphans when their father fell apart in the wake of Laura Wolff's death. It took Victor Wolff literally years to recover, and by then, the damage was done. The boys loved their father, but they had become closed off to softer emotions.

Kieran cursed and kicked at a pile of loose gravel in the driveway. *Was* Cammie his daughter? A tiny shred of doubt remained. He found it almost impossible to believe that Olivia had gone from his bed to another man's so quickly. But he had hurt her badly...and she might have done it out of spite.

The girl in the photograph at Olivia's house looked like a Wolff, though that might be wishful thinking on Kieran's part. And as for the Kevin Wade on the birth certificate, well... Olivia might have done that to preserve her privacy. Using the name of a man who didn't exist to protect her rights as a mother.

But God help him, if Olivia had lied...if she had kept him

from his own flesh and blood, there was going to be hell to pay.

His cell phone beeped with a text from the front gate guard at the foot of the mountain. Olivia's car had arrived.

She had flatly refused Wolff transportation, either the private jet or a ride from the airport. Her independence made a statement that said Kieran was unnecessary. It would be his pleasure to show her how wrong she was.

When a modest rental vehicle pulled into sight, he felt his heart race, not only at the prospect of seeing Olivia, but at the realization that he might be, for the first time, coming face-to-face with his progeny.

The car slid to a halt and Olivia stepped out. Before she could come around and help with the passenger door, it was flung open from the inside, and a small, slender girl hopped into view. She had brown hair pulled back into pigtails and wore a wary expression as she surveyed her surroundings. Though Kieran didn't move, she spotted him immediately. Try as he might, Kieran could see no hint that she resembled his family. She looked like a kid. That's all. A little kid.

She slipped her hand into Olivia's. "It's like Cinderella's castle. Do we get to sleep here?"

"For a few nights."

Kieran wondered if Olivia was intimidated by the size and scope of the house. She had grown up as the only child of famous, wealthy parents, but this structure—part fortress, part fairy tale—was beyond imagination for most people. All it was missing was gargoyles on the parapets. With turrets and battlements and thick, gray stone walls, it should have looked unwelcoming, but somehow, it suited this wild mountaintop.

"Who's that, Mommy?"

Kieran stepped forward, but before he could speak,

Olivia gave Kieran a warning look. "His name is Kieran. He's a friend of mine. But you can call him Mr. Wolff."

"She'd better call me Kieran to avoid confusion, because she's going to be meeting a lot of Mr. Wolffs."

Olivia's lips tightened, but she didn't argue.

Kieran knelt beside Cammie. "We're glad to have you and your mommy here for a visit. Would you like to see the horses?" He took a punch to the chest when he realized the child's eyes were the same color as his own, dark amber with flecks of gold and brown.

He glanced up at Olivia, his heart in his throat. *Tell me,* his gaze signaled furiously.

Olivia didn't give an inch. "I think it would be best if Cammie and I rested for a while. It was a long, tiring flight and we're beat."

"But, Mommy," Cammie wailed. "I love horses."

Kieran straightened. "Surely a quick trip to the stables wouldn't hurt. And after that you'll nap with no argument, right, Cammie?"

The child was smart enough to know when a deal was worth taking. "Okay," she said, the resignation in her voice oddly adult. She slipped her hand into Kieran's. "C'mon, before she changes her mind."

Olivia followed behind the pair of them, realizing with chagrin that she would have been better served letting Kieran stay with them in California. On his turf, already Olivia felt at a disadvantage. And she hadn't missed Kieran's poleaxed look when he saw her daughter's eye color. It was unusual to say the least. And a dead giveaway when it came to parentage.

Behind the massive house stood an immaculate barn with adjoining stables. Inside the latter, the smell of hay mingled not unpleasantly with the odor of warm horseflesh.

Kieran led Cammie past the stalls of mighty stallions to

an enclosure where a pretty brown-and-white pony stood contentedly munching hay. He handed Cammie a few apple chunks from a nearby bin. "Hold out your hand with the fingers flat, like this."

She obeyed instantly, her small face alight with glee as the pony approached cautiously and scooped up the food with a delicate swipe of its lips. "Mommy, look," she cried. "It likes me."

Kieran put a hand on her shoulder. "Her name is Sunshine, and you can ride her as long as you're here."

"Now?" Cammie asked, practically bouncing on her feet. "Please, Mommy."

Over her head, the two adults' gazes met, Olivia's filled with frustration, Kieran's bland. "Later," Olivia said firmly. "We have plenty of time."

She had been afraid that she would have to meet a phalanx of Kieran's relatives while she was still rumpled and road weary, but he led them to a quiet, peaceful wing of the house where the windows were thrown open to embrace the warm, early summer breezes.

"This will be your room, Olivia." Kieran paused to indicate a lovely suite decorated in shades of celadon and pale buttercup. "And through here…" He passed through a connecting door to another room clearly meant for a child. "This is yours, Cammie."

Olivia saw her daughter's eyes grow wide. The furnishings had been made to resemble a tree house, with the sleep space atop a small pedestal accessed by rope netting, which coincidentally made any possibility of falling out of bed harmless.

Cammie kicked off her shoes and scampered up the rope apron like the monkey she was. "Look at me," she cried. "This is awesome. Thank you, Kieran."

Soon she was oblivious to the adults as she explored the

tree trunk bookcase, the two massive toy chests shaped like daisies and the enormous fish tank.

Olivia drew Kieran aside. "Are you insane?" she asked, her low whisper incredulous. "This must have cost a fortune. And for three nights? You can't buy my compliance, Kieran. Nor hers."

"The money isn't an issue," he said quietly, a small smile on his face as he watched Cammie scoot from one wonder to the next. "I wanted my daughter to feel at home here."

"She's not your daughter." The denial was automatic, but lacked conviction.

Kieran barely noticed. "She's smart, isn't she?"

"Oh, yes. Talking in full sentences before she was two. Reading at three and a half. Learning how to use my laptop almost a year ago. I can barely keep up with her."

"A child needs two parents, Olivia." He wasn't looking at her, but the words sounded like a threat.

"You grew up with only one," she shot back. "And you've done all right."

He half turned and she could see the riot of emotions in his eyes. "I wouldn't wish my childhood on anyone," he said. The blunt words were harsh and ragged with grief.

Shame choked her and she laid a hand on his arm. "I'm so sorry, Kieran. I really am."

He took her wrist in his hand, bringing it up to his mouth and brushing a kiss across her knuckles. "Tonight. When she's asleep. We'll talk in my suite. One of the housekeepers can babysit and make sure she's okay." His grip tightened. "This isn't optional, Olivia."

Once again she was thrown by the way he mingled tenderness with masculine authority. Kieran wasn't a man who could be "handled." He expected to be obeyed, and it incensed her. But at the same time, she knew she dared not cross him and risk having him blurt out the truth to

Cammie. That she had a father. A flesh and blood man who wanted to know her and be part of her life. What kind of mother would Olivia be if she stood in the way of that?

What else did Kieran want? Was this weekend visit going to appease him? Would he sue for joint custody? Or perhaps at the urging of his paranoid father, would he insist on full custody and try to lock Cammie up here in the castle until she was old enough to escape?

That's essentially what Kieran and his brothers had experienced. They had been hidden away from the world until they were allowed to go away to school with aliases.

Olivia couldn't live like that. And she certainly didn't want her daughter to endure such isolation. So she had no choice but to convince Kieran that being a father was too much for him to handle.

He left them finally, and Olivia and Cammie fell into an exhausted sleep, both of them in Olivia's bed. For a five-year-old, even with a private playground at her disposal, sometimes the most comfortable place to be was curled up in Mommy's arms.

Shadows filled the room when they awoke. Someone had slid a note under the door indicating that dinner would be at seven. As Olivia and Cammie washed up and changed clothes, a smiling young maid brought by a tray of grapes, cheese and crackers.

Olivia blessed whoever had the foresight to be so thoughtful. When Cammie got hungry, she got cranky, and her resultant attitude could be unpredictable.

Fortunately Cammie was on her best behavior that evening. And it helped that the whole Wolff clan was not in residence. Only Kieran's father, Victor, Kieran's brothers, Gareth and Jacob, and the newest member of the family, Gareth's wife, Gracie, were seated around the large mahogany dining table when Olivia and Cammie walked into the room.

Olivia put a hand on her daughter's thin shoulder. "Sorry if we're late. We took a wrong turn in the third floor hallway."

Victor Wolff, one of the clan's two patriarchs, lumbered to his feet, chuckling at Olivia's lame joke. "Quite understandable. No problem. We're just getting ready for the soup course." His gaze landed on Cammie and stayed there, full of avid interest. "Welcome to the mountain, ladies. Kieran rarely brings such lovely guests."

"Thank you, sir." Olivia took a seat, and settled Cammie beside her, surprised to find that she was nervous as hell. It certainly wasn't the formal dinner that had her baffled. She'd conquered dining etiquette as a child. No, it was the barely veiled speculation in the eyes of everyone at the table when they looked at Olivia and Cammie.

Only Kieran seemed oblivious to the undercurrents in the room. After digging into his pan-fried trout, caught in one of the streams on the property, he waved a fork at his father. "So tell me, Dad…what big projects do you and Uncle Vincent have lined up for the summer?"

He sat to the left of Olivia, and in an aside, he said, "My dad always likes to keep things humming here on the mountain. One year he repainted the entire house. Took the workmen six weeks and untold gallons of paint. Another time he added a bowling alley in the basement."

She smiled, hyperaware of Kieran's warm thigh so close to her own. "I imagine with a place this size there is always something that needs your attention."

Victor nodded. "Indeed. But this time I'm branching out. I've decided to plant a portion of the back of the mountain in Christmas trees."

Cammie's face lit up, her attention momentarily diverted

from her macaroni and cheese. "I *love* Christmas. My mama covers the whole house with decorations."

Victor smiled at her. "How old are you, young lady?"

"Five," she said casually, returning her attention to her meal.

Victor honed in on Olivia then. "My son hasn't told us much about you, Olivia. Have you known each other very long?"

The food she had eaten congealed into a knot in her stomach. She had been dreading just such a line of questioning. It took all she had to answer in a matter-of-fact voice. "We met when Kieran and I were doing graduate work at Oxford. You were taken ill soon after that, and he and I lost touch."

"I see." Olivia was very much afraid that he *did* see.

Her phone buzzed in the pocket of her skirt. Javier and Lolita tended to worry when she and Cammie were out of their reach, and they called often to check in. Since there was a lull before dessert, she smiled at the group in general and said, "Excuse me, please."

When she returned a few moments later, Kieran jumped up to move out her chair. He leaned over as he seated her, whispering in her ear, "What's wrong? You're pale as a ghost."

She wanted to hold on to him for comfort, and that scared her. So she swallowed her dismay and produced a smile. "Everything's fine. That was my mother checking up on us."

Kieran frowned, obviously unconvinced. "Olivia's parents are Javier and Lolita Delgado."

A rippled murmur swept the table. Gareth Wolff lifted an eyebrow. "I remember seeing her in *Fly by Night* when I was sixteen. She's amazing."

Jacob joined in the verbal applause. "And I'll never forget

when your dad played his first big role in *Vigilante Justice*. I thought he was the coolest dude ever."

Hearing Kieran's reserved brothers speak so enthusiastically about her parents made Olivia realize anew how much the older couple was beloved around the world. As their daughter, she saw them in a different light, but she understood the admiration and passion they generated in audiences.

Unfortunately not all of it was positive.

Biting her lip, she decided to share her unease. "My mother has a stalker fan who has been causing some problems. She just told me that he has hacked into her private email account and started sending her weird messages."

All four Wolff males wore matching expressions of ferocity. "Like what?" Kieran demanded, sliding an arm across the back of her chair.

Olivia slanted a worried glance at her daughter, but Cammie was engrossed in playing with a kitten that had wandered into the dining room. Olivia lowered her voice, anyway. "He's threatening violence. To my mother and to the people she holds dear. I could tell my mother is really spooked."

"It's a good thing you're here," Victor boomed, his florid face indignant. "How long are you staying?"

"Just until Monday."

Kieran brushed her arm with his fingertips. "I could only get her to agree to a three-night visit, but I'm hoping to change her mind." In front of God and everyone at the table, he leaned in and kissed her gently on the lips.

Olivia stiffened and turned red with mortification. Kieran's family only grinned.

Victor signaled an end to the dinner by rising unsteadily to his feet. "Well, keep us posted. I'd be happy to help in any way I can."

Gracie moved around the table and gave her brother-in-law a hug. "Nice of you to bring some estrogen to this male enclave." She smiled at Olivia. "I hear you're a children's book illustrator. I'd love to pick your brain about that if you have time. I'm a painter."

"I'd be happy to," Olivia said. "But at the moment, I need to get Cammie ready for bed. When we cross time zones, it's tough to keep her routine intact."

Kieran took her arm as they left the dining room. "Remember," he said. "My suite. Don't make me hunt you down."

She shivered, looking into his eyes for any sign of weakness. But there was none. His gaze was steady, confident, implacable. Her time of reckoning was nigh.

Cammie was irritable and uncooperative, perhaps picking up on Olivia's unsettled mood. It was close to ten o'clock when the child finally went to sleep in her tree house bed.

One of the older housekeepers took a seat in front of the television in Olivia's sitting room and promised to be vigilant in keeping an eye and ear out for Cammie. Olivia knew that her daughter rarely woke up after falling asleep, so she had no real reason to procrastinate any longer.

She slipped into the bathroom and changed out of the dress she had worn to dinner. Instead, she opted for soft, well-worn jeans and a light cashmere pullover sweater in pale mauve. Her mass of hair seemed unruly, so she swept it up in a thick ponytail.

The woman in the mirror had big eyes and a troubled expression. She'd been waiting for six years to face what was coming. But knowing the day had finally arrived made it no easier.

Somehow she had to prevent Kieran from seeing how much she still responded to him sexually. Giving him that

advantage would weaken her, and she couldn't afford that...
not when Cammie's life and well-being were at stake.

Kieran's suite of rooms was across the hall from hers.
Was the arrangement designed to let him see more of his
daughter or to remind Olivia that she could no longer hide
from him?

She wiped damp palms on her jeans and knocked.

Five

Kieran had wondered if she would come. It wouldn't have surprised him if she had used jet lag or some other excuse to postpone this meeting, yet here she was. In casual clothes and with her hair pulled back, she seemed scarcely old enough to be the mother of a five-year-old child. "Come in," he said, feeling his muscles clench as she slipped past him. "Would you like some wine?"

"Yes," she said, her voice husky and low. "White, please."

He handed her a glass of the zinfandel he remember she liked and motioned for her to be seated. His suite, like the one he had chosen for her, included a bedroom, a lavish bath and this sitting room.

Olivia perched primly on a comfy chair, her knees together, ankles and feet aligned. Her curvy ass filled out the jeans she wore in a mouth-drying way. And that sweater. Jesus. Had she dressed this way deliberately to throw him off track?

Kieran remained standing, finishing his drink and setting the glass aside. "Cammie is mine," he said slowly, still stunned by the notion. "Without a doubt. But you told me six years ago that you were taking the pill."

She grimaced. "I was. But one morning I forgot to take it, and I found it lying by the sink when I got ready for bed that night. I swallowed it down right away, but obviously the damage was already done."

"Hmm." He was itchy, nervous, unsettled as hell. Tiptoeing through a minefield, that's what this was. He cleared his throat. "We're done with dancing around this, Olivia. I need to hear you say it. Tell me that Cammie is my daughter."

When she remained stubbornly silent, he sighed. "Do you want to know the real reason I didn't contact you after I left England?"

Shock flashed across her face, and she nodded cautiously, looking at him as if waiting for bad news from a doctor.

He ran both hands through his hair, searching for the right words. "After we had been together for a couple of weeks, you began telling me stories from your childhood… about what it was like to be the daughter of world famous celebrities. How there were always bodyguards and races to avoid paparazzi. You said you hated the isolation and never being able to play at a friend's house. You told me you weren't allowed to go to school, but instead, had private tutors. Do you remember saying all that?"

She nodded, frowning. "Of course."

"Well, what I couldn't tell you was that your story mirrored my own in many ways. We both suffered growing up, and I understood completely your feelings of being trapped, of wanting to fly the coop. You said on more than one occasion that all you wanted out of life was to be normal. To raise any children you might have like regular people."

Grimacing, she took a sip of wine. "You really listened."

"I did. And that's why I never called. It's not ego talking when I say that I knew you were falling in love with me. I felt the same way. You weren't like any girl I had ever dated, and I wanted you so badly I couldn't think straight half the time."

"You never said anything."

"I thought you'd be able to tell how I felt when we were making love. And I didn't want to bare my soul when you knew me as Kevin Wade. If I told you I loved you, I wanted you to know I was Kieran."

"And when your father had his heart attack?"

"It shook me. The night before I had called him and asked permission to tell you the truth. He was terribly upset, and the next morning I got the call that he'd been taken to the hospital. It felt like I had caused the heart attack, and maybe I did."

"So you decided before you ever left England that we were over?"

"If I'm being honest…yes. I knew I could never give you what you needed, and I didn't want to hurt you. My family is not normal. So it seemed kinder in the long run to end things before we both got in too deep. No matter how far I try to run from it, I'll always be a Wolff, and the money will always make me and those I love a target. You have this dream of being a PTA mom and having a white picket fence. There's not a place for me in that scenario."

He thought his explanation would make her feel better. Instead, she looked furious.

"What gives you the right to make decisions for me, to map out my life?" she said angrily. "I had nothing but lies to go on, Kevin Wade. You're an arrogant ass." Her eyes flashed fire at him and her chest heaved.

How the hell did he become the bad guy, when he was

only trying to protect her from hurt? "Tell me that Cammie is mine," he demanded through clenched teeth.

Her lustrous eyes were wounded, her lips pale where she had pressed them together so hard. "Your sperm may have generated her life, but Cammie is *my* daughter."

His heart caught in his throat and he sank onto the sofa, not for the world willing to admit that his knees had gone weak. "So you're admitting we made a baby?"

Olivia's face softened, and she came to sit beside him. Not touching but close. "Of course we did. Have you *looked* at her?"

Fury built in his belly. "How could you keep her from me for five long years? Damn it, Olivia. Do you have any idea what I've missed?" He vaulted to his feet, unable to bear her presence so close. He didn't know whether to kiss her in gratitude for giving him a child or to strangle her for her deception.

He was shaking all over, and the weakness and turmoil he experienced infuriated him. Grief for the time he would never recoup mingled with wonder that a part of him lay asleep in a nearby room.

"When can we tell her?"

Olivia went white. "It's not the kind of thing you blurt out. Maybe you should get to know her first."

"In three days?" He was incredulous that she didn't understand his urgency. "Guess again. I'm keeping her here this summer."

"You can't."

"Oh, yes," he said in dead earnest. "I can and I will. Both of you will move in here for the duration."

"You can't order me," she whispered, anguish marking her face.

He shrugged. "I'm not being unreasonable. Your work

can be done anywhere. She's not in school yet. If you don't agree, I'll take you to court. I know plenty of judges who frown on parents who kidnap their own kids."

"I didn't kidnap her. That's a terrible thing to say."

"You kept her existence a secret from her father. Semantics, Olivia. I'm calling the shots now."

"You're bluffing."

He felt a tingle of sympathy for her distress, but only that. She'd do well to understand that he fought for what was his. "It wouldn't be such a terrible thing, would it? To spend time here on the mountain?"

Clearly unconvinced, she frowned stubbornly as she stood up and crossed the room to stand nose to nose with him. "I can't turn my life upside down overnight. You're a bully."

He grinned, feeling suddenly lighthearted and free. A daddy. He was a daddy.

Olivia cocked her head. "What's so funny?"

"You. Me. Life in general."

"I don't see any humor in this situation at all," she huffed.

He scooped her up, lifting her until his belt buckle pressed into her stomach. Her arms went around his neck. "Thank you, Olivia, for giving me Cammie." He kissed her nose.

"She's not a *thing* to give. But you're welcome."

He slid his lips across hers, tasting the flavors of the coffee and lemon pie she had consumed earlier. "One summer," he coaxed.

"One weekend," she countered.

He palmed her ass, pulling her into his thrusting erection. The clothes separating them were a frustration. So he set her on her feet and began undressing her.

Olivia went beet-red and batted at his hands. "What do

you think you're doing?" she sputtered. "Sex won't make me change my mind."

"The decision's already made." He groaned aloud as he peeled away her sweater and revealed a mauve demi-bra barely concealing its bounty. "Sweet heaven. Please don't stop me, Olivia. I need you more than my next breath." His body was one huge ache that concentrated in his hard erection.

Her eyelids fluttered shut as her shoulders rose and fell in a deep sigh. He removed the remainder of her clothing posthaste. The well-washed jeans, the socks and shoes, the scanty bra and, finally, the lacy thong.

Was it possible that he had forgotten how gorgeous she was? Full breasts with light brown centers topped a narrow waist and hourglass hips. He must have been insane six years ago. How had he left her?

He weighed both her breasts in his hands. "Look at me, Olivia."

She opened her eyes and what he saw there humbled him. Sadness, resignation, need. "This won't solve anything, Kieran."

He nodded, refusing to let the future taint the moment. "Then don't think. Just let me make you feel."

A bleak smile lifted the corners of her lips. "Do you think you're that irresistible? You have a bad habit of wanting to run the show."

"I'll work on my failings," he promised, ready to agree to anything as long as she stayed in this room with him for the next half hour.

"What makes you think I'll be lured into your bed given our history?"

"It's *because* of our history that I believe it. We could never keep our hands off each other, and you know it."

"I won't have Cammie be hurt or confused by any relationship we might initiate."

"Of course not. This is no one's business but ours."

"Someone might come in," she said, nibbling her bottom lip.

"I locked the door, I swear."

"And the housekeeper?"

"I told her you'd be back no later than eleven-thirty."

Her face flamed again. "Oh, my God, Kieran. Don't you think she knows we're across the hall having sex?"

"We're *not* having sex," he pointed out ruefully.

"You know what I mean."

His hands moved to her waist, petting her, soothing her. "She thinks we went for a walk in the moonlight. And she's a romantic soul. Quit worrying."

For one interminable heartbeat he thought Olivia would refuse him. But finally she nodded as if coming to some unknown decision. Her hands went to his belt buckle. "If we have a curfew, I suppose we'd better not waste any time."

"I agree," he said fervently, batting her hands away and ripping off his clothing in two quick swipes as he toed off his shoes.

Her eyes rounded in a gratifying way as she took stock of his considerably aroused state. "I seem to have forgotten a few things about you," she said, cupping him in her hands.

He sucked in a breath between clenched teeth. "I'm on a hair trigger, Olivia. It's been a while. Maybe you shouldn't touch me."

"There you go again, bossing me around." She dropped to her knees on the plush carpet and licked him daintily.

The shock of it ricocheted through his body like streaks of fire. He cursed, gripping her head, and with one snap of his wrist breaking the band that held her ponytail in place.

That fabulous hair tumbled across her cheeks, around his straining penis. The eroticism of the image sent him over the edge, and he came with a ragged shout.

They collapsed to the floor and Olivia lay beside him, a small, pensive smile on her face.

He rubbed his eyes with the heels of his hands. "Was that meant to prove something?"

"Maybe. I'm not a kid anymore, Kieran. I'm a woman, and I've been running my life for six years without your help."

"But you have to admit that when we do things together, the results are pretty spectacular."

"Is that a sexual reference?"

"Could be, but in this case I was talking about Cammie."

She curled into him, hooking one long, slender leg over his thigh. "I can't argue with that."

He stroked her hair. "We don't have to be adversaries."

"As long as you understand that you can't ride roughshod over my feelings and opinions. And we don't have to be a couple."

"Fair enough."

She touched him intimately. "If you're trying to manipulate me with sex, it won't work."

His erection flexed and thickened. "Understood."

"Then I think we're on the same page."

He stood and pulled her to her feet. "Bed this time," he grunted, reduced to one syllable words. He lifted her into his arms and deposited her in the center of his large mattress. The old Olivia would have pulled a sheet over herself immediately, but this more mature version lifted one knee, propped her head on her hand and smiled.

It was the smile of a woman learning her own power. Kieran was not immune. He sprawled beside her and entertained himself by relearning every curve and dip of her feminine body.

Olivia melted for him, her soft gasps and tiny cries filling him with determination to pleasure her as she had never been pleasured before. He brought her to the brink with his hands and then moved between her legs. At the last moment he remembered the need for a condom. He wasn't taking any chances this time.

Not that he considered Cammie a mistake, but because he needed to learn how to be a father. One child was enough for the moment.

He sheathed himself in the latex and positioned the head of his penis against Olivia's warm, moist flesh. She was pink and perfect, her sex swollen where he had teased her.

Her eyes were shut. "Look at me," he insisted. When she obeyed, he drove into her, eliciting groans from both of them. Her body squeezed him, begged him not to leave. Panting, he withdrew and surged deep again. "We're good this way," he muttered. "So damn good."

The truth of the statement tormented him.

He was not a family man. After a lifetime of living caged up, he needed the freedom he found in anonymous villages on the other side of the world. Olivia was important to him, and Cammie was part of him, flesh and blood.

But what did it matter when he was condemned to be alone? Loving meant loss, and he'd had his share of that.

Olivia's sultry smile was drowsy. "Does it have to end?"

Even the question was enough to send heat streaking down his spine, sparking into his balls and rushing through the part of him that longed for release. His jaw clenched, the muscles in his neck corded and he shouted half in relief, half in awe when his body shuddered in the throes of a climax that left him weak.

Dimly he was aware that Olivia joined him at the end.

Panting, half addled from the scalding deluge of release, he rolled to his back, dragging her on top of him, their bodies still joined.

"Stay the night." The words were muffled as he buried his face in her cleavage.

"I can't," she said, disentangling their limbs and rolling to sit on the side of the bed.

"I could come to your room."

Her body stilled, her back to him. "No."

As he watched, only momentarily sated, she dressed rapidly and finger-combed her hair. He frowned, already missing the feel of her in his arms. "Dismiss the housekeeper and come back. We could set an alarm so you'll be in your room by morning."

"I have responsibilities," she said, not meeting his gaze.

"And that precludes meeting your needs as a woman?"

She stopped at the door and faced him across the room. In her eyes he saw regret and resolution. "I can't afford to get involved with you again. Sharing a daughter will be hard enough. Let's view tonight as one for Auld Lang Syne and put it behind us."

"I'm not a fan of that plan. It wouldn't hurt for Cammie to see us getting along."

"We can be civil without starting something we can't finish. I'm here for a very short time. And unlike you, I don't happen to see recreational sex as an appropriate lifestyle."

Now he was pissed. "Who said anything about recreational sex?"

He strode to where she stood backed up against the door and got in her face. "I'm attracted to you, Olivia Delgado. I like you. And as of today, I know we share a child. Any intimacies we indulge in are far from casual."

She licked her lips, her eyes huge. "You're bullying me again," she whispered.

Damn it. He was hard. And hungry. And mad as hell that she seemed to see him as some kind of a lowlife. He backed up two feet and crossed his arms over his chest. "You have more power than you think. But I won't be pushed away."

She reached behind her for the knob and opened the door. Since he was buck naked, and knowing that one of the housekeepers sat just across the hall, he didn't have a prayer of stopping her.

But his chest was tight when he closed the door and banged his forehead against the unforgiving wood. She was making him crazy. Two steps forward…one step back. Perhaps it was time for a change of plan. He would get to know his daughter, and in the meantime, maybe Olivia would acknowledge the fire that burned between them and return to his bed on her own.

Six

A strange house. Odd night sounds. And dreams that were riddled with images of Kieran Wolff. No wonder Olivia slept poorly. She had no more defenses against him now than she had as a naive university student. All he had to do was crook his little finger and she fell into his arms without protest.

It was infuriating and humbling and, if she were honest, exciting. Her days since Cammie was born had been pleasant. And the white-picket-fence life she had so deliberately created was good. Really good. But what woman—still two years shy of thirty—should be willing to settle for that?

Kieran's recent intrusion into her life was a jolt of adrenaline. Now she was scared and aroused and worried and challenged, but she wasn't bored.

Finally, at 4:00 a.m., she fell into a deep sleep, only to be awakened at the crack of dawn when Cammie crawled into bed with her. Crossing three time zones was not an easy adjustment for a child.

Olivia yawned. "Good morning, sweetheart."

"What are we going to do today?" Cammie snuggled close, her small, warm body a comfort Olivia never tired of.

"I think Kieran wants to hang out with us. Is that okay?"

In the semidark, her daughter's face was hard to read. "Yep. I like him."

That was it. Four short words. But hearing her daughter's vote of confidence relieved at least some of Olivia's concern.

Olivia dozed off again. When she woke, Cammie was gone, and light streamed into the room. Good Lord. She was a sweet kid, but mischievous at times. Olivia stumbled from her bed and rushed through the connecting passageway to Cammie's whimsical bedroom. She stopped short when she realized that Cammie was sprawled on the floor on her stomach alongside Kieran, who was aligned in a similar position.

Both of them were playing with an expensive model train set. A small black engine *choo-chooed* its way around a figure-eight track. Seeing the two of them side by side wrenched something inside her chest and brought hot tears to her eyes. She blinked them back, refusing to dwell on what might have been.

Kieran looked up, his gaze raking her from head to toe, taking in the flimsy silk nightie that ended above her knees, her thinly covered breasts, her tousled hair. "Rough night, Olivia?"

His bland intonation was meant to bait.

"Slept like a baby," she said, glaring at him when she thought her daughter wouldn't see. Kieran looked delicious…clear-eyed and dressed casually in jeans and an old faded yellow oxford shirt with the sleeves rolled up. His big masculine feet were bare, and Olivia discovered that there was no part of him that didn't make her heart beat faster.

He motioned to a nearby tray. "Cook sent up fresh scones and homemade blackberry jam. And there's a carafe of coffee."

Cammie had barely acknowledged her mother's presence, too caught up in the new entertainment. Olivia shifted her feet, reluctant to parade in front of her host to get a much-needed cup of caffeine. The awkward silence grew.

Kieran took pity on her. "Go take a shower if you want to. I'll pour you some coffee and set it on the nightstand. Okay?"

"Thanks," she muttered, escaping to the privacy of her room. In twenty minutes she had showered and changed into trim khakis and a turquoise peasant shirt that left one shoulder bare. She hadn't needed to wash her hair this morning, so she brushed it vigorously and left one swathe to lie over the exposed skin.

The coffee awaited as promised. She drank it rapidly and went in search of a second cup. What she saw stunned her. Cammie, often shy around strangers, sat in Kieran's lap in a sunshine-yellow rocker as he read to her from an Eric Carle book.

The two of them looked up with identical expressions of inquiry. Cammie's typical smile danced across her face. "You look pretty, Mommy. Kieran's going to take us to the attic."

Olivia glanced down ruefully at her fairly expensive outfit. "Do I need to change?"

Kieran laid the book aside and shook his head. "The Wolff attic is more of a carefully maintained museum than a dusty hiding place. You'll be fine."

While Cammie took another turn with the train, Kieran spoke, sotto voce to Olivia. "She's right. You look lovely."

He brushed a kiss across her cheek. "I wanted you when I woke up this morning."

The gravelly statement sent goose bumps up and down her arms. She glanced at Cammie, but the child was oblivious to the adult's tension. "You shouldn't say things like that. Not here. Not now."

He shrugged, unrepentant, and suddenly she saw the source of Cammie's mischievous grin. Circling Olivia's waist with one arm, he pulled her close and whispered in her ear, his hot breath tickling sensitive skin. "If you had stayed in my bed last night, neither of us would have gotten any rest. Remember the evening after the Coldplay concert? We didn't sleep that night at all."

His naughty reminiscence was deliberate. In a hotel room high above the streets of London, they had fallen onto the luxurious bed, drunk on each other and the evening of evocative music. Again and again he had taken her, until she was sore and finally had to beg off.

The resultant apology and intimate sponge bath had almost broken his control and hers.

"Stop it," she hissed. "That was a lifetime ago. We're different people."

"Perhaps. But I don't think so." He bit gently at her earlobe, half turned so Cammie couldn't see his naughty caress. "You make me ache, Olivia. Tell me you feel the same."

She broke free of his embrace. "Cammie, are you ready for the attic?"

Kieran grimaced inwardly, realizing that he had already strayed from his plan. As long as he pushed, Olivia would run. Only time would tell if another tack would woo her in the right direction.

As they climbed the attic stairs, Cammie slipped her little hand into his with a natural trust that cut him off at the knees. Frankly it scared him spitless. What did he know about raising a kid? He'd been too young when his mother died to have many memories of her. And when his father imploded into a near breakdown, the only familial support Kieran had known was from his uncle, his two brothers and his cousins, all of whom were grieving as much or more than he was.

He halted Cammie at the top of the stairs. "Hold on, poppet. Let me get the switch." It had been years since he had been up here, but the cavernous space hadn't changed much. Polished hardwood floors, elegant enough for any ballroom, were illuminated with old-fashioned wall sconces as well as pure crystalline sunbeams from a central etched glass skylight. Almost thirty years of junk lay heaped in piles across the broad expanse.

Olivia's face lit up. "This is amazing…like a storybook. Oh, Kieran. You were so lucky to grow up here."

Though her comment hit a raw nerve, he realized that she meant it. Seeing the phenomenal house through a newcomer's eyes made him admit, if only to himself, that not all his memories were unpleasant. How many hours had he and Gareth and Jacob and their cousins whiled away up here on rainy days? The adults had left them alone as long as they didn't create a ruckus, and there was many a time when the attic had become Narnia, or a Civil War battlefield, or even a Star Wars landscape.

He cleared his throat. "It's a wonderful place to play," he said quietly, caught up in the web of memory. Across the room he spotted what he'd been looking for—a large red carton. He dragged it into an empty spot and grinned at Cammie. "This was my favorite toy."

"I remember having some of these." Olivia squatted down beside them and soon, the Lincoln Logs were transformed into barns and bridges and roads.

Kieran ruffled Cammie's hair. "You're good at building things," he said softly, still struggling to believe that she was his.

"Mommy says I get that from my daddy."

His gut froze. "Your daddy?"

"Uh-huh. He lives on the other side of the world, so we don't get to see him."

Kieran couldn't look at Olivia. He stumbled to his feet. "Be right back," he said hoarsely. He made a beeline for the stairs, loped down them and closed himself in the nearest room, which happened to be the library. His throat was so tight it was painful, and his head pounded. Closing his eyes and fisting his hands at his temples, he fought back the tsunami of emotion that had hit him unawares.

A child's simple statement. *We don't get to see him....* How many times had Olivia talked to Cammie about her absentee father? And how many times had a small child wondered why her daddy didn't care enough to show up?

His stomach churned with nausea. If he had known, things would have been different. Damn Olivia.

As he stood, rigid, holding himself together by sheer will, an unpalatable truth bubbled to the surface. He *did* live on the other side of the world. He'd logged more hours in the air than he'd spent in the States in the past five years. What would he have done if Olivia had found him and told him the truth?

His lies to her in England had been the genesis of an impossible Gordian knot. One bad decision led to another until now Kieran had a daughter he didn't know, Olivia was afraid to trust him and Kieran himself didn't have a clue what to do about the future.

When he thought he could breathe again, he returned to the attic. Cammie had lost interest in the Lincoln Logs, and she and Olivia were now playing with a pile of dress-up clothes. Cammie pirouetted, wearing a magenta tutu that had once belonged to Kieran's cousin Annalise. "Look at me," she insisted, wobbling as she tried to stand up in toe shoes.

Kieran stopped short of the two females, not trusting himself at the moment to behave rationally. "Very nice," he croaked.

Olivia looked at him with a gaze that telegraphed inquiry and concern. "You okay?" she mouthed, studying him in a way that made him want to hide. He didn't need or want her sympathy. She was the one who had stripped him of a father's rights.

He nodded tersely. "I'll leave you two up here to play for a while. I have some business calls to make."

Olivia watched the tall, lean man leave, her heart hurting for him. In hindsight, she wondered if she and Kieran might have had a chance if he hadn't lied about who he was, and if she had been able to get past her anger and righteous indignation long enough to notify him that she was having his baby.

It was all water under the bridge now. The past couldn't be rewritten.

She and Cammie were on their own for most of the afternoon, despite Kieran's insistence that he wanted to get to know his daughter. After lunch and a nap, Olivia took her daughter outside to explore the mountaintop. They found Gareth's woodworking shop, and Cammie made friends with the basset hound, Fenton.

On this beautiful early summer day, Wolff Mountain was twenty degrees cooler than down in the valley, and Olivia fell in love with the peace and tranquility found in towering trees, singing birds and gentle breezes.

She and Cammie ran into Victor Wolff on the way back to the house. He was slightly stoop-shouldered, and his almost bald head glistened with sweat. From what Olivia had gleaned from the private investigator and from a variety of internet sources, Victor had been a decade and a half older than his short-lived bride…which meant he must now be banging on the door of seventy.

The old man stared at Cammie with an expression that made Olivia's heart pound with anxiety. He shot a glance at Olivia. "The child has beautiful eyes. Very unusual."

Olivia held her ground, battling an atavistic need to tuck her baby under her wing. "Yes, she may grow up to be a beauty like my mother."

Cammie had no interest in adult conversation. She started picking flowers and dancing among the swaying fronds of a large weeping willow that cast a broad patch of shade. Victor's eyes followed her wistfully. "I may die before I get to see any grandchildren. Gareth is the only one of my sons who is married, and he and Gracie have decided to wait a bit to start their family."

"Are you ill?" Olivia asked bluntly.

He shook his head, still tracking the child's movements. "A bad heart. If I watch what I eat and remember to exercise, my son, the doc, says I probably have a few thousand more miles under the hood."

"But you don't believe him?"

"None of us knows how many days we have on this earth."

"I'm sorry about your wife, Mr. Wolff. I can't imagine how hard that must have been losing her so young."

He shrugged. "We argued that day. Before she left to go shopping. She wanted to let the boys take piano lessons and I thought it was a sissy endeavor. I told her so in no uncertain terms."

"And then she died."

"Yes." He aged before her eyes. "I've made a lot of mistakes in my life, Olivia."

"We all do, sir."

"Perhaps. But I almost ruined my sons, keeping them locked up like prisoners. My brother, Vincent, was the same. Six children between us, vulnerable little babies. I was terrified, you know. My brother and I both were."

"That's understandable." She began to feel a reluctant sympathy for the frail patriarch.

Suddenly his eyes shot fire at her, and the metamorphosis was so unexpected that Olivia actually took a step backward. "Kieran's a good boy. It's not his fault that the memories here keep him away."

"We all have our own demons to face," Olivia said. "But children shouldn't have to suffer for our mistakes."

"Are you talking about me or about you?"

His candor caught her off guard. "I suppose it could be either," she said slowly. "But know this, Mr. Wolff. I will do anything to protect my daughter."

He actually chuckled, a rusty sound that seemed to surprise him as much as it did her. "I like you, Olivia. Too bad I didn't have a daughter to take after my dear Laura."

Olivia couldn't think of a response to that, so she held her peace, walking beside Kieran's father as the three of them made their way back to the house.

Seven

Kieran saw the three of them approach the house. He was watching from an upstairs window. Part of him resented the fact that his father was sharing time with Olivia and Cammie, something Kieran had intended as the primary focus of the weekend. But anger boiled in his veins, and he was afraid that if he snapped and confronted Olivia in Cammie's presence, the child would be frightened.

Still, it was time for a showdown, and since nothing appeared to mitigate the harshness of the rage that gripped him, Olivia had better beware.

Dinner was an awkward affair with only the four of them. Jacob had been called way unexpectedly, and Gareth and Gracie were still in the honeymoon phase of their marriage, enjoying time together at home alone.

Cammie behaved beautifully at the overly formal table, conversing easily with Kieran and smiling shyly when Victor Wolff addressed her. Olivia was pale and quiet, perhaps sensing that a storm was brewing. The courses passed slowly. At last, Victor pushed back from the table. "I'll leave you young people to it. If you'll excuse an old man, I'm going upstairs to put on my slippers and sit by the fire."

Cammie wrinkled her nose as he left. "A fire? That's silly. It's summertime."

Kieran smiled, loving how bright she was, how aware of her surroundings. "You're right about that, little one. But my father has his eccentricities, and we all adjust."

"X cin…" She gave up trying to replicate the difficult word.

Olivia leaned over to remove crumbs from her daughter's chin with a napkin. "It means that Mr. Wolff has lived a long time and he sometimes does strange things."

"Like when Jojo puts hot sauce on his ice cream."

Olivia grinned. "Something like that."

Kieran saw himself suddenly as if from a distance, sitting at a table with his lover and their child. Anyone peering in the window would see a family, a unit of three. A mundane but extraordinarily wonderful relationship built on love, not lies.

But appearances were deceiving.

So abruptly that Olivia frowned, he stood up and tossed his napkin on the table. "Why don't I tuck Cammie in tonight? Is that okay with you, Olivia?"

He saw the refusal ready to tumble automatically from her lips, but she stopped and inhaled sharply, her hands clenching the edge of the table. "I suppose that would be fine. What do you think, Cammie?"

"Sure. Let's go, Kieran. Do you have any boats to play with in your bathtub?"

After they were gone, the silence resonated. Olivia realized that she was inconveniencing the waitstaff as long as she sat at the table, so she got up, as well. There were so many rooms in the huge house, it was easy to get lost. Not wanting to be too far away from Cammie, she found a staircase that led to the second floor and walked toward her suite. When she could hear laughter and splashing from the bathroom, she paused in the sitting room to call her mother.

Lolita's well-modulated voice answered on the first ring. "Hello, darling. How's the visit with your school friend?"

Olivia might possibly have fudged a bit on the details of her trip. "Going well. But I'm worried about you and Dad. Anything else from your psycho fan?"

"Don't be so cruel, Olivia. Men can't help falling in love with me. It's the characters on the screen, of course, but I play them so well, they seem genuine and warm, especially to someone who has already experienced a disconnect with reality. We should have compassion for the poor soul who is obsessed with me."

Olivia's mother had no problem with self-esteem. But her nonchalance seemed shortsighted. Olivia might have been even more worried were it not for the fact that Javier Delgado took his responsibilities as a husband very seriously. He was narcissistic to a fault, but he did love his tempestuous wife, and he had the bodyguards and manpower to prove it.

"Still, Mom, please be vigilant. Don't let down your guard."

"It's a tempest in a teapot, Olivia. Just a sad man wanting attention. Quit worrying."

"Has he sent more emails?"

"A few. The police are monitoring my computer."

"What did the notes say?"

"More of the same. Threats to me and the people I love. But you and Cammie are in a safe place for now, and your father and I are well taken care of. Everything's fine."

The conversation ended with Olivia feeling no less concerned than she had been earlier. As much as she hated to admit it, her parents would always be targets because of their celebrity and their wealth. Which was exactly why Olivia had struggled so hard to make a home for herself and her daughter away from the limelight that surrounded Lolita and Javier. Even letting Cammie travel with her grandparents was a leap of faith, but Olivia wanted the three of them to be close, so she bit her tongue and prayed when necessary.

The noise of Cammie's bedtime rituals moved from the bathroom to the bedroom. Olivia walked through the door in time to see Kieran tuck his daughter into the raised bed, giving her a kiss in the process. "My turn," she said.

Feeling awkward beneath Kieran's steady gaze, she hugged Cammie and tucked the covers close. "Sweet dreams."

Cammie's eyes were already drooping. "Nite, Mommy. Nite, Kieran." The two adults stepped into the hall. Kieran's expression was brooding, none of the lightheartedness he'd exhibited in Cammie's presence remaining. "Put some other shoes on," he said. "We're going for a walk."

Kieran saw on her face that she recognized the blunt command for what it was.

She frowned. "When you have a child, you can't waltz away whenever you want. She's too small to be left alone."

"I'm not stupid, Olivia." Her patronizing words irritated him. "Jacob returned a little while ago. Cook is fixing him some leftovers. He's bringing a stack of medical journals with him and has promised to sit up here until we get back."

"I don't know why we have to leave the house."

"Because it's a beautiful night and because I don't think you want to risk having our conversation overheard."

That shut her up. He was in a mood to brook no opposition, and the sooner he stated his piece, the better.

About the time Jacob appeared upstairs, Olivia returned wearing athletic shoes as instructed. She had changed into jeans and a long-sleeve shirt in deference to the chill of the late hour. Even in summer, nights on the mountain were cool.

They chatted briefly with Jacob, and then Kieran cocked his head toward the door. "Let's go."

Outside, Olivia stopped short. "You haven't told me where we're going."

"To the top of the mountain."

"I thought we *were* on top."

"The house sits on a saddle of fairly level land, but at either end of the property, the peak splits into two outcroppings. One has been turned into a helipad. We're headed to the other."

She followed him in silence as he strode off into the darkness, deliberately keeping up an ambitious pace. If she ended up exhausted and out of breath, perhaps she wouldn't be able to argue with him.

When the trail angled sharply upward, she called out his name. "Kieran, stop. I need to rest."

He paused there in the woods and looked at her across the space of several feet. Her face was a pale blur in the darkness. The sound of her breathing indicated exertion.

"Can we go now?" He was determined not to show her any consideration tonight. Nothing would dissuade him from his course of judgment.

She nodded.

He spun on his heel and pressed on. They were three miles from the house when the final ascent began. "Take my hand," he said gruffly, not willing to place her in any actual danger.

The touch of her slender fingers in his elicited emotions that were at odds with his general mood of condemnation.

He pushed back the softer feelings and concentrated on his need for retribution.

Clambering over rocks and thick roots, they made their way slowly upward. At last, breaking out of the trees, they were treated to a vista of the heavens that included an unmistakable Milky Way and stars that numbered in the millions.

Despite his black mood, the scene humbled him as it always did. Every trip home he made this pilgrimage at least once. To the right, a single large boulder with a flat top worn down by millennia of wind and rain offered a seat. He drew her to sit with him. Only feet away, just in front them, the mountain plunged into a steep, seemingly endless ravine.

Olivia perched beside him, their hips touching. "Are you planning to throw me off?" she asked, daring to tease him.

"Don't tempt me."

"It's a good thing I'm not afraid of heights."

"We'll come back in the daylight sometime. You can see for miles from up here."

They sat in silence for long minutes. Perhaps this had been a mistake. The wild, secluded beauty of this remote mountain was chipping away at his discontent. Occasionally the breeze teased his nostrils with Olivia's scent. All around them nocturnal creatures went about their business. Barred owls hooted nearby, their mournful sound punctuating the night.

Olivia sat quietly, her arms wrapped around her.

He rested his elbows on his knees, staring out into the inky darkness. "You committed an unpardonable sin against me, Olivia. Robbing me of my daughter—" His voice broke, and he had to take a deep, shuddering breath before he could continue. "Nothing can excuse that...no provocation, no set of circumstances."

"I'm sorry you missed seeing her grow from a baby into a funny, smart girl."

"But that's not really an apology, is it? You'd do the same thing again."

"The father of my child was a liar who abandoned me without warning or explanation. And later, when I did discover the truth, I found out what kind of man you are. An eternal Peter Pan, always searching for Neverland. Never quite able to settle down to reality."

"You think you have me all figured out."

"It's not that hard. All I have to do is look at the stamps on your passport."

"Traveling the world is not a crime."

"No, but it's an inherently selfish lifestyle. I'll admit that your work is important, but those bridges you build have also created unseen walls. You've never had to answer to anyone but yourself. And you like it that way."

The grain of truth in her bald assessment stung. "I might have made different choices had I known about Cammie."

"Doubtful. You were hardly equipped to care for a baby. And by your own admission, you've returned to Wolff Mountain barely a handful of times in six years. You may feel like the wronged party in this situation, Kieran, but from where I'm standing, both of our lives played out as they had to—separate…unrelated."

He couldn't let go of the sick regret twisting his insides with the knowledge that he had never been allowed to hold his infant child. "You call me selfish, Olivia, but you like playing God, controlling all the shots. That hardly makes you an admirable character in this scenario."

"I did what was necessary to survive."

"Lucky for you, your parents had money."

"Yes."

"Because, otherwise, you'd have been forced to come

crawling to me, and that would have eaten away at your pride."

"I would never have come to you for money."

He pounded his fists on his knees. "Damn you. Do you know how arrogant you sound?"

"Me? Arrogant?" Her voice rose. "That's rich. You wrote the book, Kieran. All you do is throw your weight around. I won't apologize for protecting my daughter from an absentee father."

"Military families deal with long absences all the time and their children survive."

"That's true. But those kids suffer. Sometimes they cry themselves to sleep at night wishing with all their hearts that their mommy or daddy was there to tuck them in. It's a tough life."

"But you never gave us a chance to see if we could make it work."

"You had sex with me for six weeks and never told me your real identity. What in God's name makes you think I would have put myself out there to be slapped down again? You hurt me, Kieran…badly. And when I found out a baby was on the way, it was all I could do to hold things together. If you had at least contacted me, who knows what might have happened. But you didn't. So forget the postmortems. What's done is done."

"I want to tell her I'm her father."

"No."

"I have legal rights."

"And you have plane tickets to Timbuktu at the end of the summer. Telling her would be cruel. Can't you see that?"

"She needs me. A girl should have a daddy to spoil her and teach her how to ride a bike."

"And you'll do that via Skype? Is that what you had in mind?"

"God, you're cold."

"What I am is a realist. We're not talking about how much Cammie needs *you*. This is really about you needing *her*, isn't it? And if you'll stop and think about it, the mature thing to do would be to walk away before she gets hurt."

"I want her to stay for the whole summer."

"She would fall in love with you and then be crushed when it was over. Absolutely not."

"We're getting nowhere with this," he groused. "It's a circular argument. I have a proposition. My cousin Annalise is returning tomorrow. She's great with children, and Cammie will love her. I have to make an overnight trip the following morning to New York to meet with a charitable board about the September project. I want you to come with me and we'll see if we can work this thing out."

"There's nothing to work out."

"Let me put it this way…either you agree to go to New York and hash things out on neutral ground, or I tell Cammie the truth when she wakes up in the morning."

"You can't."

"Try and stop me." He was beyond pleasantries, fighting for his life, his future.

Olivia leaped to her feet and he grabbed for her wrist. "Be careful, damn it. You're too close to the edge of the cliff."

She struggled instinctively, and then froze when his words sank in. "Take me back to the house." Unmistakable tears thickened her voice.

He stood up and backed them both from the precipice. "Don't make this so hard, Olivia," he murmured, sliding his hands down her arms. "We're her parents. Together. I don't want to fight with you."

"But you want to torture me."

"Not that, either." Her nearness affected him predictably.

"I want to make love to you, but I don't have a death wish, so I suggest we get off this ledge."

He steered her down the winding, narrow path until they were once again cloaked in the pungent forest of fir and pine. When he halted and slid his hands beneath her hair to tilt her face toward his for a kiss, she didn't protest. But her lips were unmoving.

His thumbs stroked her cheeks, wiping away dampness. "You have to trust me, Olivia." He could feel the tremors in her body as he pulled her closer. "I won't hurt Cammie. I won't hurt you." He said it almost like a vow, but as the words left his lips, he realized the truth of them.

Traditional or not, Olivia and Cammie were his family... as much or more than Gareth, Jacob and Victor. He would protect them with every fiber of his being, to the death if necessary. If he could make Olivia understand how deep his feelings ran, how desperately he wanted to take care of both the women in his life, perhaps she would be more inclined to believe his sincerity and his resolve.

With aching slowness he claimed her mouth, tasting her, nipping at her tongue. At last, her arms circled his neck and her sweet lips dueled with his. There was less tenderness tonight, more unrestrained passion. Frustration and conflict segued into ragged hunger and rough caresses.

He jerked her shirt over her head and fumbled with the bra, dragging it down her arms and tossing it away haphazardly. Red-hot desire hazed his vision, and he trembled as if he had a fever.

Her lush breasts took on gooseflesh in the night air, and her nipples pebbled into small, hard stones. He took them in his mouth, one after the other, and suckled her, dragging on her tender flesh with his mouth and plumping her breasts with worshipful hands.

Olivia moaned, a sound that went straight to his groin

and sent scalding heat to scorch him alive. He ripped at her jeans, shoving them down her hips only enough to touch her between her legs. She was damp and ready for him.

Freeing his own eager sex, he fumbled in his pants pocket for a condom, rolled it on and then lifted her and braced her against the nearest tree. It was animalistic and raw and absolutely necessary.

With a grunt of determination, he thrust up and into her warm, hot passage. The sensation of being caressed by wet silk made him groan aloud. "I can't get enough of you," he said, the words muffled against her neck. "God, you make me burn."

After that, conversation evaporated in the white-hot conflagration of his drive to completion. Olivia's fingernails bit into his shoulders as she clung to him in desperation. He gripped her ass and lifted her high, angling his hips to fill her more deeply.

She cried out and trembled, heart pounding against his as she climaxed wildly, her inner muscles milking him. Her release triggered his. Keeping his hands under her ass to protect her from painful contact with the tree, he thrust recklessly, not caring if his hands suffered in the process. Nothing could have separated him from her in that moment.

She kissed him softly, and the simple caress was his undoing. Shaking, breathing hoarsely, he came with a rapid fire punch of his hips, feeling his strength drain away as he reached the end.

Legs embarrassingly weak, he went down, rolling onto his back in a sea of pine needles, settling Olivia on top of him as they both recovered. "Stay the summer," he begged.

She put her hand on his lips. "Stop. Let it go for now. I'll travel to New York with you. That's two more nights, total. After that, Cammie and I have to go home. I have a project to finish, and she has play dates scheduled with friends. We have a life, Kieran. But I'll consider returning later in the summer for a visit. Don't push me on this."

It was hard to be angry when she laid on top of him, every voluptuous inch of her his for the taking. Lazily he rubbed her firm, generous ass. She was the most intensely *female* woman he had ever known. As though her entire body was created for the purpose of male fantasy.

His erection was already perking up, but he had only brought one condom. Bad mistake. Instead of feeding his own hungry obsession, he reached between them and touched the tiny bud of nerves that made her quiver and pant. Deliberately he brought her to the brink again. She tried to fight him, but her body defeated her.

"Come for me, baby," he urged, relishing the feel of her dew on his fingers. He might ache, unappeased, for hours, but it was worth it to hear her call his name as she spiraled into bliss and then slumped onto his chest.

Eight

Olivia wanted to remain in the dark. Deep in the woods, she could pretend that she wasn't scared of repeating mistakes that should have been far behind her.

She wasn't lying to Kieran when she said she didn't want Cammie falling in love with him only to experience a child's broken heart when he left. But that was only half the truth.

Olivia couldn't, shouldn't, wouldn't fall in love with him again, either, and that's what was bound to happen if she remained on Wolff Mountain for the summer. Though she'd die rather than admit it, Kieran *was* irresistible. Look how she'd tumbled into his arms with barely a protest. Only physical distance could protect her. In New York, she planned to make her position clear.

Neutral ground, Kieran had said. The proposition sounded sensible on the surface. But Olivia had been to

New York several times, and she knew that with the right man, the city would be magical.

She could always make celibacy a condition of the trip, but that would be self-deceptive in the extreme. She *wanted* Kieran…looked forward to spending an uninterrupted night in his arms. And by reminding herself that when it was done, it was done, she could protect her heart.

Maybe in August she and Cammie would make one final quick trip for Kieran to see his daughter. Then he'd fly out across the globe, and she and Cammie could get back to their normal lives.

Why did that thought have to hurt so much?

Olivia had grown up in chaos, being dragged around to movie sets all over the world, hiding in her bedroom when her flamboyant parents indulged in one of their theatrical shouting matches. All she had ever wanted was a peaceful, normal existence to raise her child. And if she looked seriously, surely there was some nice guy out there who would want to marry her and add to the family.

Try as she might, such a picture never came into focus.

Kieran held her hand as they made their way back to the house. Their feet made scarcely a sound as they walked.

Her fingers clung to his, wishing she had the right to be with him like this forever. He was a loving man, and an honorable one, despite his youthful misjudgments. He loved his family, and he was clearly on his way to loving Cammie, as well.

But ultimately he saw Wolff Mountain as a trap, one that had robbed him of his childhood. And though he might visit from time to time, he was never going to settle in one place.

They entered through the back of the house, treading quietly in deference to sleeping servants. When they entered the room where Jacob kept watch, he stood up and stretched. "I was about to give up on you."

Kieran grimaced. "Sorry. The time got away from me. It's a beautiful night."

Jacob's gaze settled on Olivia. He was a quiet, intense man, and his piercing eyes, like the X-ray machines he used, seemed to see right through her. "You need to watch out for my brother," he joked. "We used to call him the 'were-Wolff,' because he loved roaming the woods at night."

She blushed, feeling as if Jacob could see exactly what she and Kieran had been up to. "I enjoyed the walk," she said. Her red cheeks were probably a dead giveaway, but she kept her expression noncommittal.

In the wake of Jacob's departure, an awkward silence bloomed. Kieran's jaw was rigid, and hunger still tightened the planes of his face. "Will you come to my room?" he asked.

She shook her head, backing away. "I need to get some sleep. Cammie will be up early. Good night."

Her retreat was embarrassing to say the least, but she needed distance. His masculinity dragged her in, demanding a response, and for tonight, she needed to regroup and figure out how to protect her vulnerable heart.

Late the following morning Kieran's cousin Annalise arrived. She blew in on a burst of wind and rain, her laughter contagious and her genuine welcome hard to resist.

"So glad to meet you both," she said, squatting in Prada pumps to hug Cammie.

She was tall, dark-headed and gorgeous. And when she looked at Cammie, she was clearly shocked.

Olivia squirmed under her assessing gaze, but refused to be lured into saying something she would regret. "How was the family vacation?"

Annalise hugged her cousins, as well. Kieran and Jacob had showed up to eat lunch with her before going back to their construction project at Jacob's clinic. Gareth had gone home to see Gracie. "Daddy and the boys are still fishing in Wyoming, but I reached my fill of tying lures and fighting mosquitoes. Plus, I had to get home to see Kieran. It's like a sighting of the Loch Ness monster. You don't want to miss it."

"Very funny." Kieran suffered her teasing with an easy grin, slinging an arm around her shoulders as they walked to the dining room. "Admit it, brat. You just had to come home and meet my guests."

She wrinkled her classically beautiful nose. "You got me." She gave Olivia a rueful glance. "It's a well-known failing of mine," she said, patting Cammie's head as she seated herself at the table. "Whenever we were little, the guys tortured me by pretending to have secrets I wasn't privy to. I'd badger them unmercifully, until half the time they admitted that they had made it all up."

"It must have been hard being the only girl."

"You have no idea." She paused, expression concerned. "Where's Uncle Victor?"

"He had a rough night," Jacob said. "But he hopes to be with us for dinner."

Over a lunch of cold salads and fresh fruit, Olivia watched Annalise interact with her family. There were three more males not present, the brothers Annalise spoke of, as well as Vincent Wolff, who was Victor's twin. Clearly Annalise was close to Kieran and Jacob. She teased and kidded them with open affection.

The six young cousins had been raised in isolation in this huge house after the violent deaths of their mothers. It was no wonder they had formed a bond. Tragedy had marked this family and shaped its face.

When the meal was concluded, the men were itching to get back to work. Annalise turned to Olivia, her face alight with enthusiasm. "Why don't we go swim in Gareth and Gracie's pool?"

"A pool?" Olivia looked askance at the window where lightning flashed and water rolled down the panes.

"Indoors, silly." Annalise laughed.

Kieran frowned. "Does Cammie know how to swim?"

"We're from southern California. Of course she does." Olivia noted Kieran's response, as did Annalise. He had reacted with a parent's automatic concern. Olivia wondered how long it would be before someone in Kieran's family came right out and demanded to know if Cammie was a Wolff.

The pool was amazing. Built to resemble a natural tropical lake, it featured a waterfall, twittering parakeets and water that was heated just enough to be luxuriously comfortable.

Cammie loved it. She swam like a fish, and soon she was all over the pool. Gracie joined them soon after they arrived. The small redhead had a quiet smile and a look of contentment about her that Olivia envied.

At one point, Annalise threw back her head and laughed in delight. "I *love* having women here," she exclaimed, beaming in her gold bikini that seemed more suited to sunbathing at a resort on the French Riviera rather than actually getting wet.

Gracie nodded. "Me, too. After our honeymoon, Annalise was gone, and I have to confess that I was lonely sometimes for girl talk."

"How long have you two been married?" Olivia asked.

"Less than two months. I'm still getting used to this amazing house."

Gareth's Western-themed home was spectacular, though not as large as Wolff Castle, of course. And Olivia had glimpsed Jacob's more modern house through the trees. She frowned. "Why has Kieran never built his own place?"

Annalise shrugged. "Doesn't need one. He's here less than a dozen nights during the year. Two days at Christmas if we're lucky. Other than that, he's always on the go. The constraints of our situation were hard on all of us kids growing up, but Kieran chafed at them more than anyone. At the first opportunity, he struck out for freedom and has never really looked back. You can't cage a man who wants to roam."

Was that pity Olivia saw in Annalise's eyes? Olivia hoped not. It was bad enough for Olivia to acknowledge to herself that a future with Kieran was impossible. She didn't want or need anyone's commiseration, no matter how well meant.

When Gracie hopped out of the pool to dry off and get back to her painting, Olivia spoke quietly to Annalise, all the while keeping tabs on Cammie's high energy stunts. "Kieran has asked me to go to New York with him overnight. He thought you wouldn't mind keeping Cammie. Did he volunteer you too freely?"

"Of course not." Annalise straightened one of the flimsy triangles of her bathing suit top. Though she was the complete antithesis of Olivia's mother in looks, she possessed the same star quality. A woman no one, particularly no man, could resist. She smiled. "Cammie is a delight, and I'd be happy to look after her."

Standing next to her, waist deep in silky water, Olivia felt frumpy and large, though Kieran certainly seemed to have no complaints about her less than reed-thin figure. His appreciation for her…assets was flattering.

She signed inwardly. "Just one night, and we won't be late the following day, because Cammie and I will have to catch the red-eye back to the West Coast. That reminds me, I need to shift our tickets one day later."

"Why don't you take the family jet? Did Kieran not offer?"

"He has. Several times. But I prefer to make my own travel arrangements."

"Because you don't want to feel beholden to him?"

"It's not that. I've tried to raise Cammie away from the over-the-top lifestyle my parents enjoy."

"How's that workin' out for you?"

Olivia shook her head ruefully. "Sometimes I think it's a losing battle."

"So you didn't like growing up with all the bells and whistles?"

"I liked the toys and activities as much as the next kid. But I had friends whose parents were what I thought of as *normal.* Nine-to-five jobs, cookouts on the weekend. T-ball games. That wasn't part of my life, and I wanted it for Cammie."

"Sometimes we don't appreciate what's in our own backyard. There's something to be said for not having to worry constantly about money. And there's also the satisfaction that comes from helping people less fortunate. Our family has never wanted for anything, but I like to think we aren't spoiled. Our fathers instilled in us a sense of responsibility, *noblesse oblige,* if you will."

"If I can do as much for Cammie, I'll be happy."

Annalise twisted the ends of her long hair and squeezed out water. "She's a great kid, already. For a single mom, you've done a great job. It can't have been easy."

Here it comes. Olivia braced herself, waiting for Annalise to demand an explanation of Cammie's parentage. But the other woman merely smiled.

"Thank you," Olivia said awkwardly. She followed Annalise out of the pool and began drying off.

"If you ever need a friendly ear, I'm here." For once, the bubbly personality shifted to reveal a deep vein of seriousness. Her eyes, like Jacob's, seemed to see all.

"I appreciate that." For a moment, Olivia was tempted. She wanted to share with another female the fears and heartaches that came with being Kieran's lover, with bearing his child. But Annalise was Kieran's cousin, part of his family. Olivia had not even allowed Kieran to claim his daughter yet, so it would be unethical at the very least to share their secret.

She wrapped a towel around her waist and stretched out on a lounge chair to watch Cammie play. Annalise did the same. From speakers tucked away somewhere in the foliage, pleasant music played. Olivia yawned, ruefully aware that her unsettled sleep had everything to do with Kieran. When she wasn't actually with him, she was dreaming about him. What did that say about her subconscious desires?

Annalise's long legs were tanned and toned, making Olivia realize it had been some time since she herself had hit the gym. It was tough with a child. An older woman in Olivia's neighborhood came most mornings for several hours to watch Cammie so Olivia could work. Cammie still napped in the afternoons, and after that it was time to fix dinner, play games and enjoy bath time.

The routine worked well for them, and Olivia wasn't willing to leave her child with an evening babysitter to go work out. Perhaps after Cammie started kindergarten it would be easier.

Cammie did a handstand in the shallow end, making sure both women were watching. They clapped and cheered her success.

Olivia grinned, pleased that her daughter was enjoying

this visit. "Cammie found one of your old ballet costumes in the attic. I hope it was okay for her to play with it."

"Of course." Annalise yawned, leaning back her head and closing her eyes. "Tomorrow I'll show her my secret trove of Barbie dolls. I had to keep them hidden or the boys would pop off their heads."

"That's terrible." But Olivia chuckled in spite of herself.

Annalise lifted one eyelid, her expression morose. "Don't get me started."

Nine

Olivia and Kieran left for New York at first light. Though Olivia had worried about abandoning Cammie, it was clear the child was having the time of her life. Victor Wolff doted on her. Jacob promised her a tour of his clinic and a lollipop, and Gareth and Gracie had sent up a note inviting Cammie to swim again.

And then there was Annalise. She and Cammie had bonded like long lost sisters. If anything, Cammie was the more sensible of the two. Annalise had planned out a twenty-four-hour agenda of fun that would be impossible to fulfill, but she delighted in making Cammie laugh at her antics.

Kieran and Olivia said their goodbyes and departed via helicopter to a small airstrip near Charlottesville. There, the Wolff family jet sat waiting, its brilliant white fuselage gleaming in the sunlight. Though Olivia was well accustomed to luxury and pampering, the level of wealth enjoyed by Kieran and his clan far surpassed anything she had experienced.

Fortunately she had packed liberally in preparation for her trip to Wolff Mountain. Knowing nothing of Kieran's family or what to expect socially, she had gladly paid for extra bags so her wardrobe and Cammie's would cover all eventualities. Which meant that she had plenty of choices for this impromptu New York trip.

Inside the plane, a handsome male attendant offered Olivia her pick of beverages along with a midmorning snack, in case her breakfast had been inadequate. She declined the fruit parfait with murmured thanks. Her earlier meal had been more than generous. Victor Wolff's current chef had once served in the White House, and with three full-time cooks to assist him, the menu offerings were varied and delicious.

Kieran grabbed a bag of cashews and went forward to chat with the pilot. As Olivia fastened her seat belt in preparation for takeoff, she had time to appreciate her plush seat. It was more of an armchair, really. She stretched her legs and felt a little frisson of excitement wend its way through her veins.

Rarely did she take time all to herself for something as frivolous as a vacation. Tending to a rambunctious child, even when she and Cammie traveled with Lolita and Javier, generally meant little downtime.

Closing her eyes with a smile of contentment, she let her mind drift. It was a shock when she felt a warm hand settle on her shoulder. When she looked up, Kieran grinned at her, his expression more lighthearted than she had seen him at any time since their university days.

He sat down in the seat adjacent to hers and clicked his belt. "Are you a good flier, or one of the white-knuckled types?"

"I love it," she said simply. "How about you?"

"It gets me from A to B quickly, and for someone in my line of work, that's the main thing. But I also love the freedom and the sense of adventure. I've never lost that. Don't guess I ever will."

Olivia's heart sank. This Kieran, chomping at the bit to take off, was the man who circumnavigated the globe. She could see in his body language the expectation, the energy.

The day dimmed suddenly and her anticipation of the trip palled. It was painful to see the evidence of what she had only surmised. Her lover, the father of her child, was a road warrior, an adventurer. He would never be content to live inside Olivia's mythical white picket fence.

Soon, the noise of takeoff overrode the possibility of conversation. Olivia closed her eyes again and pretended to sleep. Her emotions were too close to the surface. She could fall in love with him again so easily. Not with the nostalgic reminiscence of a young woman's rosy fantasy, but in a solid, real way. How could she not? He was caring and honorable. With Cammie, he showed a gentle side that ripped at Olivia's heart.

Kieran loved his daughter, even knowing as little of her as he did. He was committed to being her dad. Only Olivia's fears and reservations stood in the way. That and her determination to protect herself from the pain of losing him again. The devastation six years ago still rippled inside her, waiting to be resurrected. Terrifying in its power.

As Kieran spoke to the attendant, Olivia studied his profile. Classic nose, sculpted chin. Straight teeth that flashed white in a tanned face when he smiled. His body was fit and healthy; his long limbs and broad shoulders were a pleasing package of masculine perfection.

Her mouth dried and her thighs tightened as she remembered last night's lovemaking. When they were together, he made her feel like the most important, most desirable woman in the world. His frank hunger and sensual demands called to the essence of her femininity.

Though she was well capable of taking care of herself, she enjoyed his protectiveness, his innate gentlemanly core of behavior. In a crisis, Kieran Wolff would be a rock.

At one time, being his wife had been her dream. Now she knew that even if he put his name on a piece of paper, the dream would end in pain and frustration. Olivia knew herself. She needed a lover who would be there on the ordinary days and not just in the midst of an emergency.

Kieran could handle the crises. No doubt about that. But Olivia was pretty sure that he would just as soon not have to deal with the mundane aspects of family life.

Taking out the trash, paying bills, mowing the grass. Ordinary husbands and fathers did those things.

Too bad Kieran Wolff was not ordinary. And too bad that *ordinary* was what Olivia had always wanted.

To Olivia's surprise, she actually slept. Kieran woke her in time to peek out the nearest window and see the Statue of Liberty as they flew past. Soon, the landing gear deployed, the pilot set them down with a tiny bump and it was time to go.

A limousine awaited them on the tarmac.

In no time at all, Kieran and Olivia were speeding toward the city amidst a maze of taxicabs. He took her hand, surprising her. As he lifted it to his lips for a kiss, he smiled lazily. "We're going to drop you downtown. Do you mind entertaining yourself for a couple of hours while I get this meeting out of the way?"

"Of course not, but I…"

"What?"

She bit her lip. "I owe you an apology. I thought this *business trip* was only an excuse to get me alone."

They were sitting so close, she could inhale the after-shave he had used that morning. In a severely tailored charcoal-gray suit with a pale blue shirt and matching tie, he looked nothing like the man she had come to know. If he had reminded her of Indiana Jones before, now he looked more like a character from Wall Street. She wasn't sure she liked the transformation.

He tugged her closer, one strong arm encircling her waist as he claimed her mouth with an aggressive kiss. When she was breathless, her heart pounding, he released her and sat back. "Sucking up to the fat cats is a necessary evil for the work I do."

"What do you mean?"

"I'm meeting this morning with the heirs of a wealthy socialite. The dead mother wanted to fund a variety of charitable works around the world. But her charming children thought the ten million she left each of them was an insult, so they went to court. Fortunately the judge couldn't be bought and he upheld the will. Unfortunately for me, the kids sit on the foundation board, so I have to deal with their greedy, petulant demands to get what I need for my next project."

"The one in September?"

He nodded. "We're going to design and build an orphanage in the Sudan. A variety of church agencies will do the staffing and oversee operations."

"Isn't it dangerous there?"

He shrugged. "Have you looked around the Big Apple? You can get killed crossing the street."

Before Olivia could respond, the car pulled up in front of a row of small, and obviously expensive, designer shops. She wrinkled her nose. "I'd really rather go to Macy's, the original on 34th Street. You know…from the movie. Is that too far out of our way?"

"No. But I thought given your Hollywood roots you'd enjoy the upscale shopping."

She shrugged. "I'm really more of a Macy's kind of gal."

"Whatever you say." The ride to midtown didn't take long. When Kieran hopped out to open Olivia's door and escort her to the sidewalk, he tucked a stray hair behind her ear, his gaze filled with something she wanted to believe was more than affection. "Here's my card with all my numbers. Have fun," he said softly, brushing a kiss across her lips.

Her arms wanted to cling, to beg him to stay. She forced herself to back up. "Go to your meeting. I'll be fine."

He winced when a cacophony of horns protested the illegally parked limo. "I'll call you when we're done."

Kieran tolerated the meeting with less than his customary patience. The "awful offspring," as he had nicknamed them in his mind, were no more difficult than usual, but today he was in no frame of mind to placate them. All he could think about was getting Olivia back to a hotel room and spending twenty-four hours in bed.

It was a great fantasy, but, of course, the gentlemanly thing to do would be to show her a good time out on the town first. Even that would be fun with Olivia.

And then there was the issue of Cammie. Once he made his case for claiming his rights as a father, would the mood be ruined? He wasn't sure where Olivia stood at the moment. Sometimes it seemed as if she was ready for him to tell Cammie the truth. But on other occasions, she bowed up, determined that Kieran was not father material.

To further strain his mood, the meeting ran long. At twelve-thirty, he finally stood and excused himself. The major business had been completed. All that was left was the minutiae that didn't require his presence.

He called downstairs, and the limo was waiting when he strode out into the sunshine. Unfortunately the lunch hour rush had traffic backed up in all directions. When they finally reached Macy's, after sending Olivia a text that they were on the way, Kieran's head was pounding from hunger and tension.

Olivia jumped in quickly, all smiles. A lot of women would be bitching about his late arrival. Instead, she seemed happy to see him. Kieran reacted to her greeting automatically, but inside, he dealt with a stunning realization. He had become addicted to her smile. In fact, he couldn't imagine going a day without seeing that look on her face.

The knowledge shook him. Since the death of his mother and his father's involuntary emotional abandonment, Kieran had never really allowed himself to *need* anyone. He prided himself on being self-sufficient, a lone Wolff.

He took Olivia's hand in his, clearing his throat to speak. "I know several great restaurants where we can have lunch. Do you have a preference?"

She patted the large shopping bag at her feet. "When your meeting ran late, I picked up several things at the gourmet shop around the corner. I thought we could have a picnic in Central Park. What do you think?"

Suddenly the irritations of the past several hours rolled away. "Sounds perfect." He gave the driver a few directions, and soon they were hopping out in front of the Metropolitan Museum of Art. As they crossed Fifth Avenue and entered the park, he took Olivia's heavy bag. "Good Lord. What all did you buy?"

She laughed, shoving her hair out of her face as the wind whipped it carelessly. Her beautiful creamy skin glowed in the sunlight, revealing not a flaw or an imperfection. He suspected that Olivia, growing up as she had in the shadow of her outrageous mother, had no clue that she was equally stunning. It would be his job and his pleasure to convince her.

With no blanket to stretch on the grass, they instead sat on a bench overlooking the lake, in a patch of shade that lent dappled shadows to their alfresco feast. Olivia wore a white sundress scattered with yellow-and-orange sunflowers. When she took off her small sweater, Kieran's food stuck in his throat.

Her body was like a centerfold's, curvaceous, even voluptuous. With her sienna hair and chocolate eyes, she reminded him of a young Sophia Loren. The dress was not particularly immodest, but the crisscrossed vee of the neckline was hard-pressed to contain her full breasts. He imagined licking his way from her collarbone down each rich slope, and his body hardened painfully, visualizing what it would be like to peel back the cloth and reveal pert nipples.

Nestled against the cleavage was a yellow diamond pendant that he remembered from their university days. Her parents had given it to her for her twenty-first birthday. Olivia had been loath to wear the expensive bauble on a daily basis, but he had lobbied for enjoying the gift and not worrying about losing it.

He tore his gaze from her charms and guzzled his Perrier, wishing fervently that they had dined in a more private locale. All around them life ebbed and flowed…the dog walkers, the teenage lovers, the nannies pushing expensive strollers. Seeing the babies made him frown.

How *would* he have reacted if Olivia had let him know she was pregnant? Back then, he'd been full of piss and vinegar, chomping at the bit to make a name for himself in the world, especially a world that had nothing to do with the Wolff empire. Parenthood wasn't even on his radar.

As soon as Victor recovered from the heart attack that had brought Kieran home from Oxford, Kieran had hit the road, determined to explore the globe despite his father's concerns about safety. Where Kieran went, no one knew or cared who he was. He waded through rice paddies, canoed down rivers of sludge in mosquito-infested jungles, hiked soaring peaks where the air was so thin a man gasped to breathe.

And every mile took him farther and farther away from the mountain that had been his prison, albeit a luxurious one. He'd kept in touch via the occasional email and phone call, learning that Gareth and Jacob were acting out their own rebellions. As far as the civilized world knew, Kieran Wolff had ceased to exist.

Gradually his nomadic existence with no purpose began to pall. His first project had come about almost by accident. He'd been in Bangladesh during a monsoon, and the resultant water damage had left a huge cleanup effort. Kieran had pitched in to rebuild bridges that connected remote villages to the help they so desperately needed.

After that, he'd found his architectural skills in demand from place to place. He used to joke that he was a cross between Johnny Appleseed and Frank Lloyd Wright. His work gave him a sense of peace and fulfillment, something he'd never been able to find at home.

But what if he had known about Cammie?

The question buzzed in his brain like an annoying gadfly.

Olivia brushed bread crumbs off her skirt and stretched out her legs, crossing them at the ankles. Her toenails were painted a deep coral that matched her dress. Kieran wanted desperately to kiss each delicately arched, perfect foot.

God knows he'd never been a fetishist, but somehow, Olivia was turning everything he thought he knew about himself on its ear. She made him ache and sweat and laugh all in the space of a single conversation. How had he ever made the decision to leave her six years ago?

The answer was easy. For once in his life, he'd done the mature thing. When Olivia talked back then, he had listened. Hearing about how much she hated the unsettled childhood she had experienced and how badly she wanted to settle down and be *normal* made him realize he had to give her up before either of them got in too deep.

The Wolffs were not a normal family.

But his altruistic decision had, in the end, caused Olivia even more pain. She believed he didn't want her. Surely she couldn't doubt that now. He needed the summer to prove to her that he had wanted her back then and he wanted her still.

Cammie's existence changed everything. Kieran and Olivia *were* involved. Only time would tell how deeply.

He sighed inwardly, wondering if such a thing as salvation existed. He was more than happy to pay atonement, but Olivia had to accept his offering. "What now?" he asked abruptly. "A Broadway matinee? A harbor tour? More shopping?"

Olivia half turned to face him, her face shadowed with worry. "We can't ignore the elephant in the room. You brought me here to hash out our situation. We might as well deal with that, and maybe then I'll be able to enjoy the rest of the day."

He shrugged, stretching his arms along the back of the bench and staring out across the water. "You know my position. I want you to stay for the entire summer, and I want to tell Cammie that I'm her dad."

Olivia nibbled her bottom lip, hands twisting in her lap. "I have work to finish, Kieran. I need to get back to my studio."

"Tell me about that," he said, wanting to know everything concerning her life, what made her tick. He'd been impressed with her talent for whimsical watercolors when they first met, and he'd recognized an ambition and drive for perfection that mirrored his own.

"I illustrate children's stories for two publishers here in New York. It's a flexible job, which means I can be there for Cammie when she needs me. One of my last books was nominated for an award."

"You've done well, then."

She nodded. "I never wanted to live off my parents. I like my independence and the security of knowing I'm providing for my daughter."

"So why can't you work on the mountain?"

"It's not as easy as that, Kieran. I have paints and papers and supplies. And besides…"

"Yes?" He had a feeling he wasn't going to like this one.

"I haven't changed my mind about what your leaving would do to Cammie. She sees you as a buddy now, but it would be so much worse if you were her father. I haven't told you this, because I didn't want to cause you pain, but she has always begged me for a daddy, ever since she was old enough to know that she was supposed to have two parents and not just me. If we told her the truth, she would jump to the conclusion that you were going to come back to California and live with us."

The image of his baby daughter begging for a daddy haunted him. Regret sat like a boulder on his chest. "So that's your final word?"

She stared at him, solemn, wary. "Are you going to take me to court?"

He stood up and turned away from her, afraid of what she might see on his face. "Oh, hell. Of course not." Impotence and rage tore at him, but what made it worse was that he had no target for his anger.

Olivia joined him, wrapping an arm around his waist and laying her head on his shoulder. "Don't be mad…please. I'm trying to do what's best. Maybe not for you or for me, but for Cammie."

He tugged her close with his left arm, still staring at boaters on the lake that sparkled like diamonds in the sun. "I'm not mad," he said gruffly.

"Let me go home tomorrow," she said. "I'll finish my project. Cammie and I have some fun summer activities planned. Then in August we'll come back for another visit before you have to leave for the Sudan."

He thought of all the long, lonely weeks that stretched between now and then. "Will you promise to think about letting me tell her who I really am?"

Her body stiffened in his embrace and finally relaxed. "I'll think about it," she said softly.

"That's all I ask." He wanted more…so much more. But for now he would bide his time.

Ten

Olivia felt terrible. Kieran was being firm, but reasonable, and she was the one refusing to compromise. But how could she? Nothing Kieran suggested had any basis in reality.

At least they had solved the question of whether or not she and Cammie would go home. Olivia badly needed physical distance to recoup her equilibrium. If she stayed with Kieran much longer, she would end up agreeing to anything solely to see his smile and to feel his body wrapped around hers.

He had shed his suit jacket in the limo earlier, and had rolled up his shirtsleeves. To the casual observer he was a big city businessman taking a lunch break in the midst of a busy day. But Olivia knew better. Like a chameleon, he had assumed the camouflage that enabled him to get what he wanted.

Kieran Wolff might appear civilized at the moment, but in reality, he was a man's man—steel-cored, physically honed, mentally sharp. Olivia had no doubt that he could accomplish anything he put his mind to...which didn't bode well for her ability to hold out against his wishes in the long run. He might very well be planning to wear down her resistance by any means necessary...including intimacy.

She had little defense against him, though she'd tried to keep her distance. Men could have sex for the sake of sex. Why couldn't women? If Olivia kept her head, she could enjoy the time with Kieran but not let her good sense be swayed by his magnetism.

Two choices, both risky. Leave and take Cammie away, provoking Kieran's anger and possible vengeance. Or stay, and keep her heart intact by regarding any sexual relationship as temporary and recreational.

She gulped inwardly. There was no doubt that she and Kieran were going to end up in bed together before the day was out. Not because he was going to lure her there, but because she wanted him desperately. One more day. Surely she could keep her messy emotions at bay for one more day. And then a brief visit in August. After that, Kieran would be safely on the other side of the world, and there would be no chance of Olivia doing something embarrassing like going down on her knees and begging him to stay and love her *and* her daughter.

He released her and gathered up their lunch debris, tossing it in a nearby receptacle. "Have you ever taken a carriage ride in the park?" he asked.

"No. But I'd rather do that at night, I think."

"Okay. Then what shall we do now? Anything you want. I'm at your disposal."

"How about we check into our hotel and not waste any more time?"

Her boldness shocked him. Heck, she shocked herself. It was almost amusing to see the slack-jawed surprise on

Kieran's face. Almost, but not quite. Limbs trembling and stomach doing flips, she awaited his answer.

Kieran stood there in the sunlight, gorgeous as a big jungle cat, and equally dangerous. "Are you serious?"

She approached him slowly, her feet having a hard time making the steps. "Completely. I want to be with you for as much time as we have. I want to sleep in your bed and wake up beside you. I want it all."

All constituted a heck of a lot in her book, surely more than he was willing or able to give. But he would think she was referring to sex, and that was okay. No reason for him to know that she was so much in love with him that the thought of returning to California was an actual pain in her chest.

He took her wrist and reeled her in, snaking an arm behind her waist and pulling her against his chest. "You're going to get me arrested," he muttered, his mouth moving over hers with sensual intent. "I'm not sure I can resist taking you here...now." He dragged her off the path near a clump of trees. Privacy was still not an option, but at least they weren't smack in the middle of the walkway.

His erection thrust between them, full, hard, seeking.

Her knees went weak, and if he hadn't been supporting her, she might have melted to the ground in a puddle of need. No one was paying any attention to them. But this game was dangerous. "Isn't the hotel close?" she panted.

"Not close enough." He bit her bottom lip and pulled it into his mouth, sucking until she shuddered. She wanted to climb inside his clothes, rip them from his body.

"Call the car," she begged.

He smelled of starched cotton and warm male skin. His hands cupped her ass. "I could tell the driver to circle the city...over and over and over. Have you ever made love in a limo, Olivia?"

Dizzy, needing oxygen, she leaned into him. "No. Have you?"

"Never had the pleasure. But damned if I couldn't be persuaded right about now."

She whimpered when he pulled away and barked an order into his cell phone. The planes of his face were taut, his eyes glittering with arousal. "C'mon. He's picking us up in five minutes."

Hand in hand, they walked rapidly. His breathing was audible and as choppy as her own.

Unfortunately the car ride from the edge of the park to the Carlyle was long enough for only one heated kiss. Suddenly a uniformed gentleman was opening Olivia's door and they were engulfed in the bustle of check-in. Twenty minutes later, in a luxurious suite that was blessedly quiet and totally private, Kieran faced her, arms folded across his chest. "Take off your dress."

The blunt command, combined with the intensity of his regard made her thighs quiver and her sex dampen. Never contemplating refusal, she shed the tiny shrug sweater and reached behind her for the zipper. When she stepped out of the dress and tossed it on a chair, she saw his eyes widen and his Adam's apple bob up and down.

The dress didn't require a bra, so she stood facing him in nothing but a lacy red thong and high heels. Her generous breasts were firm and high. The urge to cover them with her hands was there, but she resisted, wanting to please him.

His whispered curse was barely audible. She saw his fists clench at his hips. "Walk toward me."

The distance between her and the door where he stood was considerable, more so because she was naked and he was eyeing her like a condemned man who hadn't seen a woman in months.

When she was halfway across the room, he held out a hand. "Stop. Turn around. Take down your hair."

She had tucked it up in a loose chignon during lunch when the heat of the day made the weight of her long hair uncomfortable. Now she reached for the pins and removed them, dropping them into a cut glass dish on the coffee table. Deliberately she ran a hand through the masses of heavy, silky strands and shook her head.

When she was done, she looked at him over her shoulder through lowered lashes. "Does this meet with your approval, Mr. Wolff?"

His jaw firmed. "Are you sassing me, Olivia?"

"Would I do that?" Her eyes widened dramatically.

"Face me. Touch your breasts."

They were playing a game of chicken, and Kieran had just upped the stakes. Olivia felt her throat and cheeks flush, but she reversed her position and hesitantly placed her hands on her chest. Her voice was gone, locked down by the giant lump in her throat.

"I said *touch* them. Put your fingers on your nipples."

Good Lord. She licked her lips, dizzy and desperate for his touch. Feeling awkward but aroused, she did as he demanded, feeling her sensitive flesh bud and tighten as she stroked herself. The sensation was incredible, pleasuring herself as Kieran watched with a hooded gaze.

"Beautiful." He breathed the word like a prayer, the three syllables almost inaudible.

When her skin became too sensitive to continue, her hands dropped to her sides.

Kieran didn't move. How did he do it? She was so hungry for him, her whole body trembled.

But he wasn't finished. His gaze blazing with his heat, he narrowed his eyes. "Go to the bedroom. Don't look back. Lie down on the bed on your stomach."

She flinched in momentary fear. But it was a gut reaction. Kieran would never hurt her or make her uncomfortable. This was all about pleasure. His and hers.

Turning away from him was difficult. She knew he watched her, hawklike, as she walked slowly toward the doorway that led into the rest of the suite. Once, she stumbled, but she finally made it into the bedroom. For a moment, she stood in indecision. Was she supposed to turn back the covers?

The bedding was expensive and ornate. Making a rapid decision, she folded back the top layers and lay, facedown, on the smooth crisp sheet. Her heartbeat sounded loud and irregular in her ears. Her arms were by her sides. Ten seconds passed. She raised her arms over her head.

What did he want? What were his plans?

Moments later she heard the sound of his footsteps on the carpet. Nearby a rustle and then the rasp of a zipper. A soft clink when the belt buckle slid free. The sounds of a man undressing.

An activity that was at once commonplace and yet deeply erotic, particularly when the woman in his bed was not allowed to witness the disrobing. She imagined his long, muscular limbs, narrow hips, jutting arousal.

The bed shuddered when he put a knee beside her hip and joined her on the mattress. Without warning, he took her two wrists and bound them together with what felt like his necktie. She struggled instinctively. He paid her no mind.

The silk fabric tightened, and then she felt him lean down as he whispered in her ear. "You're at my mercy now. Everything I ask of you, you'll do, and in exchange, I'll make you burn."

"Kieran…" The word ended on a cry as he ran his tongue around the shell of her ear and winnowed his fingers through her hair. With a slow, steady touch, he massaged her scalp. His fingertips skated to her nape, the back of her ear. Her whole body craved his attention, but he was set on a course that was drugging, slow and steady.

Gradually, almost imperceptibly, he moved south, digging his thumbs into the tense muscles of her neck and shoulders. Her spine caught his focus. He ran his tongue the length of it and then rubbed gently on either side.

At her ass, he made a sound, a cross between a groan and a curse. Quivering, helpless, she felt him plump the cheeks, trace the cleft, reach beneath her and brush the part of her that ached the most.

When she spread her legs, begging wordlessly, he chuckled and abandoned the ground he had barely conquered. "Patience, Olivia."

She felt his hands beneath her hips, lifting her, turning her. Now she could see him, and the sight took her breath and shredded it. His broad chest was tanned and rippled with muscle. An arrow of fine, dark hair traced the midline, all the way down to where his shaft reared proudly against his abdomen.

His erection was thick and long, and a drop of moisture glistened on the tip. "Please," she begged without pride. "Please don't make us wait."

"Waiting is half the fun. I want you crazed when I finally take you, so lost to reason that nothing exists but you and me and this bed."

It was as if he were a hypnotist. Her body responded to his words atavistically, ceding control without a qualm. But by the look on his face, *his* control was more fragile than he was willing to admit. His jaw was tight. The dark flush of color staining his cheeks made him look wild and uncivilized…a man close to the edge.

He bent over her, no part of his body touching hers except

his lips. "I love your mouth," he said, tracing the soft flesh with his tongue and sliding through to taste her.

She tried to link her bound wrists over his head to trap him close, but he moved away, using one big hand to pin hers to the mattress. "Naughty, naughty," he teased.

Suddenly very serious, he kept his gaze locked on hers as he slid his free hand down her stomach and between her thighs. Two large fingers entered her, testing her readiness. Her hips came off the bed, her heartbeat racing as sweat beaded her forehead.

He never looked away and neither could she. All the secrets of a man's desires were there in his eyes if she could only translate them. Was this all he wanted from her? Dare she hope he needed more?

Stroking lazily, he turned interrogator. "Tell me about the men in your life, Olivia. Who has benefitted from what I taught you back in England?"

His finger brushed her clitoris and she gasped. "None of your damned business, Wolff man. I haven't quizzed you about your women in every port."

Back and forth. Back and forth. That brazen fingertip brought her closer and closer to the edge. "There haven't been that many," he said slowly, looking at his hand's mischief and not her face. "I work long hours when I'm overseas. Not much time for play."

"But a man like you can't go without sex for long. Back in university you wanted it twice a day, three times if we were lucky."

"That's because I was obsessed with you."

The blunt confession gave wings to her heart. But she reined in her excitement. The pertinent word in that sentence was in the past tense. *Was.* Kieran had been a horny young adult male. And Olivia had fallen into his bed like the proverbial ripe peach.

As a fully mature man, he was no less sexually primed, but he'd had any number of women since he left England so suddenly. And even now, being with Olivia was probably more about expedience and availability than any deep-seated obsession.

Kieran's early experiences in life had clearly stunted his ability to express deep emotion. He was a passionate man, but she doubted whether he was capable of true romantic love. That would mean putting a female first in his life, and she had seen no sign of such willingness in his behavior.

He clearly *wanted* her, but for Olivia, that would never be enough.

His hand moved, and she gave up analyzing the situation. Today was about physical pleasure. Her heart was safely locked away.

Kieran released her wrists. Sliding far down in the bed, he used his hands to widen the vee of her legs. When she felt his hot breath on her thighs, she tensed in panic. They had never explored this kind of intimacy when she was younger. "No, wait…" she blurted out. "I don't like this."

"How do you know?" he asked, a lazy smile tilting the corners of his mouth.

"Seriously, Kieran." She pushed at his shoulder. "I mean it. Stop."

He reared up, all humor erased from his face. "I'll stop. If you insist. But it would give me great pleasure to do this with you."

She nibbled her lower lip, caught between unease and cautious interest. "What if I can't come, because I'm too self-conscious?" Blurting out what she was thinking wasn't something she planned, but he might as well know the truth.

"Relax, Olivia. It's not an exam you have to study for. I want to make you happy. That's all. You don't have to do a thing."

Her hand fell to the sheet. "Well, I…"

Anticipating her consent, he resumed his earlier position. She felt the softness of his hair on her leg, jerked briefly as his hot breath feathered over her belly. "You're beautiful," he murmured.

She closed her eyes, arching her back at the first gentle pass of his tongue. When she moaned, helpless in the grip of shivering sensation that spread in warm ripples throughout her lower body, he repeated the motion. The sensation was indescribable. Like a warm, electric shock that built and built until she called out his name in a frenzy of need. "Kieran. Oh, God. Kieran."

His muffled response was neither decipherable nor important. She was lost, caught up in a whirlwind that slammed into her, dragged her over the edge of a perfect climax and dropped her helpless into his embrace.

When she recovered, he had moved up beside her and was leaning on an elbow watching her with a totally masculine satisfaction. "Still don't like it?" he asked drolly. One eyebrow lifted in a questioning stance.

She tried to corral her ragged breathing. "Don't brag."

He placed his hand, palm opened flat, on her belly. "Watching you come like that ranks as the highlight of my year."

"The year's only halfway done," she quipped, trying not to let him see how completely undone she was. "Too early to tell." She put her hand on top of his and laced their fingers together.

"Don't be so modest. I'm sure they heard you in Brooklyn."

"Kieran!" Mortification washed over her and she rolled to her side, bending her knee and resting her leg across his hairy thighs. They were hard and corded with muscle. His deep tan extended everywhere except for a narrow band of white at his hips and the tops of his thighs.

She imagined him, laboring out beneath a blazing tropical sun, shirtless, wearing only cargo shorts and boots. Did he ever get lonely always living among strangers? The question hovered on her lips, but she knew it was self-serving. Obviously his lifestyle suited him. Otherwise, he would have come home long ago.

He lifted her without warning and settled her astride his hips. His hunger unappeased, he flexed and grew at least another centimeter beneath her fascinated gaze. She put both hands on him, measuring the length and breadth.

Hard steel pulsed beneath his velvet skin. Even if she had been with a dozen lovers in the interim, she couldn't imagine that any of them would have been as beautiful in body and spirit as Kieran Wolff. Perhaps such a virile man might balk at the feminine adjective, but Olivia chose not to retract it, even in her own private discourse.

Kieran's body was perfect. Even the smattering of scars that were part and parcel of the hard physical labor he performed only served to make his physique more interesting.

She saw him reach for a condom, and her heartbeat accelerated.

Extending his hand, he challenged her. "Will you do the honors?"

Eleven

Kieran waited, amused and impatient, as Olivia fumbled with the condom. The earnest intent on her face filled him with tenderness and another feeling not so easy to diagnose. He brushed aside the unfamiliar emotion and concentrated on the physical.

While she labored, he played with her breasts displayed so temptingly in front of his face. He tweaked a nipple, noticing with interest that his gentle pinch washed her face with color. A similar firm caress on the other breast deepened the crimson.

Olivia finished her task, her face damp with perspiration. "There. All set."

He tested the fit and nodded. "Good thing I brought a dozen."

"A dozen?"

The strangled squeak in her voice made him chuckle despite the fact that the skin on his penis was tight enough to cause every vein to bulge. He'd been in this state, in varying degrees, for over an hour now. In fact, he might set some kind of damned record for extended foreplay.

Not that he hadn't enjoyed himself immensely. God, she was sweet. And hot as a firecracker. Though she probably didn't see it in herself, she was one of the most innately sensual women he had ever met.

With his hand, he positioned himself. "You ready, honey?"

Her eyelids were at half-mast, her lips swollen from his kisses. The skin at her throat bore the marks of his passion, and her nipples puckered as if begging for his kisses. He leaned up and obliged, just as he thrust as hard as he could manage into her welcoming heat.

Their foreheads actually bumped together.

"Hell," he said ruefully, the pain giving him a moment's respite from total insanity. "Rub my head." His hands were clenched on her curvy ass, and he had no plans to let go.

She kissed his forehead. "Poor baby."

Her innocent motion seated him more deeply. "Hold still," he said through clenched teeth. "Damn it, I'm about to come."

"Isn't that the object of this exercise?"

He groaned, caught between incredulous laughter and the imminent explosion in his loins. Had any woman ever made him experience both in such measure? His heart caught, and he buried his face in her neck, panting, trying to stay the course. "You're killing me."

Reaching behind her, she found his sac and delicately played with him. It was like being hit by a lightning bolt. He lost control of himself, of her, of the entire flippin' situation.

Pumping his hips wildly, he thrust upward again and again, deaf, blind, mute...except for the caveman grunts that were all he could manage. Olivia clung to his shoulders as he fell to his back. Her breasts glided across his face, sweet-smelling, soft and warm.

God, he never wanted to stop. He wanted to mark her as his, to stake a claim. She found his lips and kissed him. That was all it took. He shot so hard that his balls pulled up, a vise tightened around his forehead and he saw nothing but blackness and yellow sparks for long, agonizing seconds.

At last, he lay spent, Olivia draped over him like a weary nymph.

"Good God in heaven."

She nodded, her breasts smashed against his heaving chest, her cheek resting atop his thundering heart. "I hope you're in good shape. I'd hate to have to call the concierge for the number of the closest cardiac center."

He stroked her ass, deciding he might never move. "You're something else, Olivia Delgado."

One eyelid lifted and then fluttered shut. "Mmm…"

"Don't go to sleep on me."

"Is that literally or metaphorically?"

Given her current posture, it was a fair question. "Either, I suppose." He yawned and stretched. "Any idea what time it is?"

"Do we care?"

"I may not have been entirely truthful." When she stiffened in his arms, he could have kicked himself for his unfortunate phraseology. "I promised we could do this for twenty-four hours, but I think I'm going to need sustenance."

"Room service?"

He patted her butt. "I was thinking of something a bit more upscale. After all, we *are* in the greatest city in the world. We should go somewhere incredibly expensive and over-the-top."

"And you know such a spot?" She slid off him, sat up and clutched the sheet to her chest.

Her sudden modesty was baffling. But then again, he never claimed to understand women. "I've heard Jacob talk about a place he likes."

"Jacob, the strong silent doctor? Somehow I thought he was above us mere mortals who need to eat."

"Jacob has his weaknesses. New York style cheesecake, for one. He's usually here in the city for medical conferences every year or so. In fact, he did a consult at Lenox Hill Hospital last Christmas."

"He's scary smart, isn't he?"

Kieran grinned. "Oh, yeah. Perfect score on the SATs. Four years of college in two and a half." He paused, and cocked his head. "Do we have to talk about my brother any longer, or can I interest you in a shower?"

"I'll race you."

He was treated to a delicious view of Olivia's backside as she dropped her only covering and darted into the bathroom. When he followed her, she was already hidden from view, water running. "Room for two?" he asked, stepping in without an invitation.

When Olivia sputtered with maidenly affront, he grinned. "I'll take that as a yes."

Olivia discovered that even a man who slept in grass huts and swallowed the occasional disgusting, edible bug could drum up romance if he put his mind to it, starting with a tuxedo that appeared as if by magic, delivered by a uniformed bellman.

When Kieran strode out of the bedroom clad in crisp black and white, fumbling with a bow tie, her breathing hitched. He was gorgeous. No other word to describe him.

"Help me with this damned thing," he said. "They're a necessary evil, but I'm out of practice."

She stood behind him and wrapped her arms around his neck, deftly folding the fabric into the desired configuration. "Out of practice?" She nipped his earlobe with her teeth. "I don't think so."

He turned and scooped her off her feet, twirling her in a circle before setting her back down. "I love reviews from satisfied customers."

"Customer? Good grief. Am I going to get a bill for services rendered?"

"I haven't decided yet. This afternoon was only my warm-up. I'll have to let you know."

He slid his hands beneath her hair and steadied her head while he dove deep for a hungry, forceful kiss.

On tiptoe, Olivia clung to his forearms and tried not to get the vapors. Kieran Wolff was like hundred-proof whiskey: guaranteed to go straight to a woman's head.

The night was clear and relatively cool so they decided to walk. The restaurant Kieran had chosen was only a couple of blocks away on a side street around the corner from East 76th.

He didn't hold her hand. But he did wrap an arm around her shoulders and tuck her close to his side. She felt warm and cherished, and for the span of an evening's stroll, she allowed herself to knit cobwebby dreams about happily ever afters.

When they arrived, Olivia paused on the sidewalk. "Do you mind if I call Cammie? She'll be in bed by the time we finish dinner."

"Of course not."

Olivia took her cell phone from her purse and punched in the contact info she'd saved for the Wolff house. An em-

ployee answered, and seconds later, Cammie's excited voice
came on the line.

"Hi, Mommy. Me and Annalise are dressing up for
dinner."

"Oh?" She grinned at her daughter's enthusiasm.

"We're going to be…" A muffled conversation ensued
to the side and then Cammie said loudly, "…flappers."

"That sounds fun. Will you ask Annalise to take a picture for me?"

"Yes, ma'am. May I speak to Kieran now?"

Olivia hesitated, taken aback. Usually Cammie chattered
away forever on such a phone call. "Sure," she said, handing her cell toward Kieran. "She wants to talk to you."

He blinked, and then smiled, barely masking his pleased
surprise. But he hit the button for speakerphone, a thoughtful gesture that made Olivia ashamed of her odd jealousy.
"Hey there, ladybug. What's happenin'?"

"I got to play with your wooden submarine today,"
Cammie said. "It's way cool, and Annalise tried to torpedo
me a bunch of times, but I got out of the way."

Kieran laughed out loud. "Tomorrow morning, ask her to
show you the secret tunnel. It's a little spooky, but a brave
girl like you will like it."

Suddenly the line went silent, but in the background they
could hear Cammie's excited squeal.

Annalise picked up the call. "How are you lovebirds getting along in New York?"

Kieran's lips quirked. He gave Olivia a rueful smile.
"Behave, brat," he told his cousin firmly. "We're fine.
Should be home by lunch tomorrow. I'll bring you a dozen
bagels if you're nice to me."

"Oooh…bagels. Big spender."

Olivia giggled. "I can do better than that, Annalise.

Thanks again for keeping Cammie. Give her a kiss and hug for me."

They all said their goodbyes, and Kieran took Olivia's arm. "Ready to eat?"

She nodded, relieved to know that Cammie was happy and content. "I'm starving."

Patrice's was delightful, with snowy linen tablecloths, fresh bouquets of Dutch iris and freesias, and a modest string ensemble tucked away in a far corner. Even the lighting was perfect.

Olivia sank onto a velvet-covered banquette and leaned back with a sigh of appreciation. "Order for me," she said. "I'm in the mood to be surprised."

Kieran wondered how surprised Olivia would be if he were honest about his intentions. After dinner, he planned to hustle her back to the room and hold her captive there until they were forced to check out the following morning. He'd let her sleep…occasionally. But the sand in his hourglass was running out rapidly, so he didn't plan to waste a minute.

As they'd entered the restaurant earlier, practically every head had turned, the women's faces reflecting envy, and the men's expressions frankly lustful. Olivia was oblivious. How could she not recognize the impact she made? He'd never met a woman more genuinely modest and unselfconscious, especially not one with Olivia's stunning beauty.

The dress she wore tonight was deceptively simple…a slender column of deep burgundy with a halter neck and a back that plunged to the base of her spine. Her hair was pinned on top of her head in one of those messy knots women managed to create. The only accessory she had chosen to wear was a pair of dangling earrings comprised of tiny ruby and jet beads.

He knew her body intimately, and he was pretty certain she was wearing nothing beneath the sinuous fabric that clung to her body like a second skin.

A waiter interrupted Kieran's musings. By the time their order was placed, the sommelier appeared to offer a wine selection. Kieran perused the extensive list. "We'll have champagne," he said. "To celebrate." He indicated a choice near the top of the price list.

Olivia propped her chin on one hand and gazed at him curiously. "What are we celebrating?"

"How amazing you look in that dress."

His sincere compliment flustered her. She straightened and fidgeted, looking at their fellow diners. "Thank you."

"I mean it," he said. "You outshine your mother any day."

"Oh, please," she huffed. "I could stand to lose a few pounds, my mouth is too wide and my chest is too big."

He burst out laughing.

"What?" she cried.

"You really have no clue, do you?"

"I'm not sure what you mean." She played with her silverware, refusing to meet his gaze.

"First of all, my naive chick, as far as a man is concerned, there's no such thing as a chest that's too big. God in his infinite wisdom created breasts in all shapes and sizes, and yours are a work of art."

Her head snapped up at that, a small frown between her brows. But she didn't speak.

"Second of all," he continued, "just because your mother is petite and thin doesn't make her more beautiful than you. The camera may love the way she looks, but you are fabulous just the way you are. You're incredibly feminine and knock-'em-dead gorgeous. Every man in this room wishes he were sitting in my chair."

Her cheeks went pink. "You're a tall-tale raconteur, but thank you. That's very sweet."

He threw up his hands. "I give up. But know this, Olivia Delgado. I wouldn't change a thing about you." As the words left his mouth, he understood just how true they were. She was his ideal woman. And if he were in the market for a wife, he'd have to look no farther.

But he wasn't…in the market, that is. He was a man destined to travel alone. Despite that reality, he hoped to forge a bond with Cammie this summer that could withstand the long separations. He might not be the best dad in the world, but he would ensure that his daughter knew her father loved her.

Over a meal of stuffed quail and apple-chestnut dressing, they conversed lazily. Though he drank guardedly, the wine went to his head, and all he could think about was getting Olivia naked again. She, on the other hand, seemed content to enjoy the formal, drawn-out dinner.

Finally the final bite of dessert was consumed, the last cup of coffee sipped. Kieran summoned the waiter, asked for their check and waited, fingers drumming on the tablecloth, for Olivia to return from a trip to the ladies' room.

As he watched her make her way between the carefully orchestrated maze of tables, someone reached out a hand to stop her. Olivia's face lit up, and the next thing Kieran knew, his lover was being kissed enthusiastically on the mouth by a tall, handsome man in a dark suit.

Feeling his temper rise, Kieran got to his feet. Olivia didn't even look his way. Now she was hugging the mystery guy and patting his cheek. The waiter had the temerity to block Kieran's field of view for a few seconds as he provided the bill. Kieran scribbled his name with leashed impatience on the credit card slip and started toward the couple on the far side of the room.

"Olivia?"

She stayed where she was, only now the fellow had his arm around her waist. By the look of things, Olivia's admirer was dining alone. And in the meantime, trolling for other men's girlfriends?

Kieran tamped down his annoyance. "Am I missing the party?" he asked, not managing entirely to squelch his pique.

She reached for his hand. "Come meet someone, Kieran. This is my dear friend, Jeremy Vargas. We've known each other forever. We used to be in school together on the MGM lot. He's here in New York rehearsing for a stint in a Broadway play…during a brief lull between shooting a string of great movies. Jeremy, this is Kieran Wolff, my…" She stumbled, licked her lips and trailed off.

"Olivia and I are seeing each other." Kieran shook the man's hand, taking in the firm grip and easy smile that said Jeremy Vargas was confident and in no way threatened by Kieran's glower. "Nice to meet you," Kieran said, lying through his teeth.

Vargas might be a stage name, because Jeremy didn't appear to have a drop of Latino blood. He was the quintessential Hollywood golden boy, blond hair, blue eyes and a killer smile.

Olivia recovered and beamed her approval back and forth between the two of them.

Jeremy continued to embrace Olivia. "It's a pleasure, Kieran. You've snagged a great girl."

"A great *woman*." Was he the only one who noticed the note of over-familiarity in Jeremy's voice? And did Jeremy know about Cammie?

Olivia finally freed herself from the other man's proprietary hold and stood beside Kieran. "I wish we'd known you were here. We could have shared a meal."

Like hell. Kieran suddenly remembered where he had heard Vargas's name. He was mentioned in the article about Cammie's birthday party…as Olivia's date.

Intellectually Kieran knew that Olivia hadn't been a nun for the past five years. She was a passionate, gloriously beautiful woman. But seeing with his own eyes that other men weren't blind to her beauty put a sour taste in Kieran's mouth.

One day soon, when Olivia was ready to expand her white picket fence, perhaps with a second baby on the way, she wouldn't have any trouble finding men to line up for the role of husband and father.

Kieran brooded on the way back to the hotel. Damn Jeremy and his inopportune arrival. "Have you and Vargas dated?" he asked abruptly, tormented by the fact that she had an entire life apart from him.

"He's like a brother." The blunt response shut him up. After that, Olivia was mostly silent. Kieran wasn't sure if she was sleepy from too much champagne or if she was re-membering all the reasons she wanted to keep him at arm's length.

In their hotel room, he paced, stripping off his jacket and tie, and swallowing a glass of ice water, hoping it would cool him down. Olivia removed her earrings. When that innocent tableau turned his sex to stone, he knew he was in trouble.

He cleared his throat. "Are you ready for bed?"

Twelve

Olivia dropped the earrings on the table. "For bed or for sex?" She met his gaze squarely, no pretense, no games. Her big brown eyes were rich and dark, masking her secrets.

"I want to make love to you." The words ripped his throat raw. He'd never said them to any woman.

Her face softened as if she read his inner turmoil. "I don't expect you to change for me, Kieran. You are who you are. I am who I am. We're two people who met at the wrong time and the wrong place. But we created a child and we have to put her first."

When he stood rigid, torn between honesty and seduction, she came to him and held out her hand. "Let's have tonight. Tomorrow will take care of itself."

He allowed himself to be persuaded. There was no choice, really. If he didn't have Olivia one more time, he would die, incinerated by the fire of his own reckless passion.

This time, he vowed to give her tenderness. He'd been

rough with her earlier, rough and earthy and carnal. What she deserved was a man who would worship at her feet.

He dropped to his knees, heart in his throat. Encircling her hips with his arms, he laid his head against her belly. She had carried his child, her lovely body rounded and large with the fruit of their desire. God, how he wished he had been with her, had been able to see her flesh expand and grow in lush, fertile beauty.

Her swollen breasts had nursed their baby. If life had played out differently, Kieran would have been there to watch. To be a part of something wonderful and new.

Regret was a futile emotion, one he'd learned a long time ago to push down into a dark, unacknowledged corner of his gut. The only important thing was the here and now. He lived for the moment...*in* the moment.

Olivia trembled in his embrace.

She stroked his hair. The light caress covered his skin in gooseflesh. What he felt for her hurt, reminding him of a dimly remembered anguish from his childhood. Women were soft and warm and wonderful. But loving them meant vulnerability. A man could not afford to let down his guard.

Without speaking, he snuggled her navel with his tongue, wetting the fabric of her dress. Carefully he bunched the cloth in his hands and lifted the long, slim skirt until he could see what had tantalized him all evening. A wispy pair of black lace panties, a thong, which explained why he'd thought she might be naked.

Despite his vow of gentleness, he gripped the thin bands at either side of her ass and ripped the fragile undergarment. It fell away, exposing her intimate feminine flesh.

Her smooth, honey-skinned thighs were scented with the distinctive perfume he'd come to recognize as her favorite.

Olivia tugged at his hair. "You're embarrassing me," she whispered. "Quit staring."

He stood abruptly and scooped her into his arms. "Whatever the lady wants." As he strode with her into the bedroom, Olivia nestled her head against his shoulder. The trust implicit in her posture dinged his conscience. He had failed her once before. This time he had to do what was right. He wanted the world to know he was Cammie's father, but if Olivia truly believed that was a mistake, Kieran might be forced to humble his pride and step back.

Retreat had never been his style. But for Olivia, he would try.

Beside the bed he stood her on her feet and, without ceremony, removed her dress. She stepped out of her shoes and put her cheek to his chest, hands on his shoulders. "Thank you for bringing me to New York," she whispered. "I think we needed this…for closure. I didn't want bad feelings between us."

He ignored her comments that intimated a swift and unwelcome end to their physical relationship. "Let me love you," he said hoarsely, the "L" word rolling more easily from his lips this time. "Lie down, Olivia."

Stripping off his clothes, he joined her on the bed. When she held up her arms, he couldn't decide if the smile on her face was a lover's welcome or the erotic coaxing of a siren, luring a man to doom.

Foreplay wasn't even an option. That had gone up in smoke during a four-course dinner with Olivia sitting across from him wearing a dress designed to turn a man's brain to mush. He found a condom, rolled it on and moved between her legs.

Their eyes met. As he entered her slowly, her lashes widened. Her breath caught. Her throat and upper chest flushed with color. He put his forehead to hers, filled with a maelstrom of inexplicable urges.

Half a millennium ago, he would have slain dragons for

her, might even have used his travels to bring home chests of gold and jewels. But Olivia didn't want the knight on the white charger. She was looking for a more stable fellow, perhaps the village miller or the town carpenter.

If Kieran truly wanted to make her happy, he would head out on his next crusade and leave her to build a life between the castle walls. Without him.

The room was silent save for their mingled breathing. He moved in her so slowly that her body seemed to clasp him and squeeze on every stroke. It was heaven and hell. Giving a man what he hadn't known he needed and in the next breath reminding him that the gift had an expiration date.

He braced most of his weight on his arms, but his hips pressed against hers, pinning her to the mattress. Her hair, fanned across the pillows, made an erotic picture that seared into his brain, never to be forgotten.

As he picked up the tempo, her legs came around his waist. Lifting up into his strokes, she arched her back and took what she wanted. Sensual and sweet, she looked like the girl he had first met on a rainy Saturday in the English countryside. She'd been alone, away from the hustle and bustle of an overcrowded house party, standing in the lane beneath a giant black umbrella, fumbling with a map and muttering mild imprecations beneath her breath.

Why hadn't he recognized what had landed in the palm of his hand for one brief spring? The vibrant, fragile butterfly that had been his relationship with Olivia....

How had he been so foolish as to crush those wings by his abrupt departure?

She touched his forehead, rubbing at the unconscious frown that had gathered between his brows. "You'll always be my first love," she said, gasping as he thrust deep. "No matter what happens next."

First love. Was that his only role? That and sperm provider?

Gentleness fled, chased away by frustration and self-directed anger. Damn the past. What about the future?

His body betrayed him then, slamming into hers with a violence that shook the bed. Olivia cried out as she climaxed, her eyes closed, her hands fisted in the sheets.

He felt his own orgasm breathing hot flames down his neck and tried to battle it back. But it was too late. Molten lava turned him inside out, gave birth to a shout of exultation laced with surrender, and trailed away, leaving a dark, inexplicable confusion.

Easing onto his back, he tried to corral his breathing. Olivia lay unmoving beside him, her chest rising and falling rapidly.

"We should get married," he said, the words coming from out of nowhere and surprising him as much as they apparently did Olivia.

Her body jerked, and she stiffened. "What? Why?"

Because I love you madly and can't imagine living my life without you. Any version of that response would have been acceptable to Olivia. But Kieran hadn't read the same script.

He ran a hand over his face and sighed. "It would be good for Cammie, I think. Assuming you're eventually going to tell her that I'm her father. If you and I were married, all the times I'm gone, she would have the security of knowing that we're a family."

"That won't make her miss you less."

"Maybe not. But she would know that I'm coming home to her eventually."

Eventually. Olivia hated that word. And she hated the fact that her stupid heart threw her under the bus again and again. Kieran wasn't in love with her. He felt *something* for her…affection, maybe…and a sense of duty. But that was never going to be enough. Not when Olivia wanted to give him every bit of her passion and devotion.

Kieran didn't need her. They weren't a couple.

"I don't like the idea," she said flatly. "I deserve to have a man in my life who loves me and can't live without me. What you're describing would be dishonest. Children are more intuitive than you realize. She would know the truth. I promised to think about you and Cammie. Give me time. Let me go home. In August I'll give you your answer."

He didn't respond, and to her chagrin, she realized that he had fallen asleep. Disheartened, she turned her back to him, and did the same.

When she woke up, Kieran wasn't in the bed beside her. A whiff of aftershave lingered in the air, so she surmised that he had risen early to shower. Perhaps after their awkward conversation the night before, he'd had no inclination to initiate any early-morning fooling around.

She leaned up on an elbow to look at the clock. Still plenty of time before their scheduled flight. The jet would be on standby, ready to go at their convenience. But Kieran had promised Annalise that he and Olivia would be back by lunchtime, so Olivia needed to get dressed.

When she appeared in the sitting room thirty minutes later, Kieran stood in front of the window, hands behind his back, looking down at the quiet street below.

He turned to face her, his expression grave. "Where's your cell phone?" he asked.

She grimaced. "I forgot to charge it last night. The battery's probably dead."

"Sit down, Olivia." He came to join her on the sofa, taking her hands in his and studying her face, his eyes filled with compassion. "Your parents have been trying to reach you. They finally called the house to relay a message, and Father contacted me."

Her heart thudded with fear. "What's wrong?"

"I need you to be brave," he said. "We'll get through this."

"Oh, my God…was there an accident?" Her blood turned to ice in her veins.

"Not that. They're fine."

"Then what?"

She actually saw on his face the struggle to choose a correct phrase. And Kieran's loss of words scared her more than anything had in a long, long time. "Just tell me," she croaked. "I can take it."

His thumbs rubbed absently over the backs of her hands, the repetitive motion not at all soothing given that his expression was torn and troubled. "Your mother's psycho stalker fire-bombed your house last night. It burned to the ground. Everything is gone."

She saw his lips moving, but the roaring in her ears drowned it out. Her eyes closed as hysteria welled in her chest. "No. You're wrong," she said, batting his hands away when he tried to hold her. "That's not possible. Cammie's baby album is there…and my paintings. All her toys…" Agony clogged her throat, exacerbated by the way Kieran looked at her. It couldn't be true.

"Take me there," she said. "Take me now. I want to see it." She was shaking all over, and the last words came out on a cry of pain.

Kieran took her shoulders and dragged her close, ignoring her wildly flailing fists, stroking her hair. "Hush, baby," he said. "I'm right here. It's going to be okay."

She cried in broken, gasping, wretched sobs that hurt her chest. A great, yawning chasm opened up at her feet, and she was terrified that she was going to fall into the depths and never claw her way back to the top. Again and again she repeated his words in her head. *Everything is gone.*

It seemed impossible and at the same time terrifyingly real.

She clung to Kieran, unashamed. Nothing else made sense. Time lost all meaning.

When the tears ran out, she lay limp in his embrace, her breathing ragged. "Did they catch him?" For some reason, that was the first question that popped into her brain.

"Not yet. But they will. He knew you weren't at home. The police profiler doesn't think he really wants to hurt anyone. This was a bid for attention."

"What about my parents?"

"They're surrounded by a twenty-four-hour security detail. The authorities think you and Cammie need to stay where you are until the man is in custody."

The irony didn't escape her. Kieran was getting exactly what he wanted. More time with his daughter.

She jerked out of his arms, wiping her cheeks with the heels of her hands. "I have to see my house. If you won't take me, I'll go on my own."

"Of course I'll take you," he said, frustration replacing his solicitous tone. "But I think it's a bad idea. There's nothing there. You don't want to see it, believe me."

"I don't *want* to," she said bleakly. "I have to."

Kieran didn't know it was possible to hurt so badly for another human being. Standing beside Olivia a few hours later, giving her all the support he was able to in light of her mercurial mood, he watched as she surveyed what was left of her property. They'd made the trip via jet in record time, though sadly, there was no reason to hurry.

Yellow police tape cordoned off the area. Curious neighbors gawked, but kept a respectful distance. Olivia had already been questioned by police personnel as well as the chief fire marshal.

The house had literally burned to the ground, leaving nothing but a smoldering mass of debris. On a bright, sunny California afternoon, the evidence marking a violent act seemed even worse.

Olivia wrapped her arms around her waist, face paper-white, eyes haunted. "At least we weren't at home," she said.

"They think the man was watching the house…that he knew when you packed up and left."

Her bottom lip trembled. "Cammie was supposed to grow up here. I always felt so safe," she whispered. "Our little haven away from the world. But there's no hiding, is there?" She gasped on a hiccuping sob.

Kieran didn't bother to answer the rhetorical question. The difficult truth was one he'd learned at the tender age of four, a painful, vivid lesson that had marked the course of his subsequent life.

Rage filled him at the senseless destruction. Rage and an impotent guilt. A man was supposed to protect his family. Now, more than ever, he understood his father's actions. Though occasionally misguided, Victor Wolff and his brother, Vincent, had taken the necessary steps to protect what was theirs, to make sure their children were safe.

Losing their wives, having them murdered in cold blood, had been the catalyst for founding a sanctuary at Wolff Mountain. And now, thank God, Kieran would be able to keep Olivia and Cammie there, cocooned from further danger, until the dangerous fire-bomber was apprehended.

The thought that the man might track Olivia and Cammie to the mountain made Kieran's blood run cold.

Unexpectedly a uniformed investigator approached them, gingerly holding a small item that was apparently hot to the touch. He tipped his hat briefly in a polite salute and extended his hand toward Olivia. "I found this…thought you might want it. Be careful. It's still warm."

He ducked back under the tape and quickly returned to his job, perhaps not comfortable with tears. Kieran didn't think Olivia even realized she was crying. But slow, wet trickles made tracks down her cheeks.

She looked down at the silver object in her hand, and the shaking she'd finally brought under control began anew.

Kieran put his arm around her, holding her close.

When Olivia looked up at him, her wet lashes were spiky. "It's the baby rattle I bought for her when she was born. I had it engraved."

He glanced at the spot where she had rubbed away the soot to reveal a shiny patch. *To Cammie with love from Mommy and Daddy.* Throat tight, he shot her a questioning glance.

"I didn't want her to think that her father didn't care."

He should have been angry, faced anew with the proof that Olivia had hidden his existence. But he couldn't drum up any negative emotion, not with the mother of his child looking as if she might shatter into a million tiny pieces.

Not only that, but he ached from the certainty that his own mistakes had brought them to this tragic point. "Let's go," he said gruffly. "We need to get home to Cammie."

Even with the convenience of a private jet, crossing from the East Coast to the West Coast and back in one day was no easy feat. Jacob had called a pharmacy in Olivia's neighborhood and ordered a light sedative. Once on the plane, Kieran insisted she swallow it with a glass of milk and a handful of saltines.

So far he hadn't managed to persuade her to eat a morsel of food. Olivia was operating on nothing more than adrenaline and sheer will. He settled her in a seat and reclined it to the sleeping position. The steward furnished a pillow and blankets. Olivia was asleep before the wheels left the tarmac.

After takeoff, Kieran unfastened his seat belt and crouched beside her, brushing the hair from her face with a gentle touch. One of her hands was tucked under her cheek. Her eyelashes fanned in crescents over the dark smudges beneath her eyes.

As he watched the almost imperceptible rise and fall of her breasts, he felt a painful pressure in his own chest. *He loved her.* Body and soul. What he had tried to cut off at the root half a dozen years ago had regenerated in the warmth and sunshine of Olivia's return to his life.

And the knowledge that they shared a daughter….

He stood abruptly and strode up to the cockpit, unable to deal with the rush of emotion. It made him dizzy and sick and terrified. What if he lost one of them…or both? It didn't have to be some tragic circumstance. Olivia might simply take Cammie and walk away. After all, she had turned down his marriage proposal without so much a blink.

Kieran stepped through the curtain, legs weak. "Captain, how's the weather looking up ahead?" Idle chitchat wouldn't distract him for long from his dark thoughts, but sitting beside Olivia was torture.

Olivia fought the nightmares. At long last, her heart pounding and her skin clammy with sweat, she surfaced from a drugged sleep. It took several interminable seconds for her to identify her surroundings…and then to remember why she was on a plane.

A shaky sob worked its way up her throat, but she choked it back, sitting up to rub her eyes. Thousands of people around the world had lost their homes this year alone, during floods and tornados and hurricanes. Olivia had been knocked down. But the crying was over. She had Cammie. She had her health. And she had financial resources.

She would be fine. But in truth, the prospect of starting over was daunting.

Kieran appeared suddenly from the front of the plane. His shirt was rumpled. He hadn't shaved. And there were deep grooves etched into his forehead and at the sides of his mouth. Lines she could swear weren't there yesterday.

Exhaustion shrouded him, decimating his usual energy. Seeing Kieran made her wonder how bad she must look. He didn't give her the opportunity to find out. He took his seat and fastened the belt. "We're landing shortly."

She raised her seat and folded the blankets, handing them and the pillow to the steward with a murmured thanks. "How long was I out?"

He shrugged. "You slept across five states, give or take a few. But don't worry…you didn't miss much. It was mostly clouds."

For a wry attempt at humor, it wasn't bad, especially given the circumstances. She summoned a weak smile, her face aching with the effort. "Thank you, Kieran." She reached across the small space dividing them and took his hand in hers. "Thank you for going with me."

The sound of the flaps being deployed and the whine of the engines powering down made conversation difficult. Kieran stared down at their linked fingers. "You going to be okay?" He played with the small cameo ring on her right hand.

She nodded, unable to speak. Clinging to him and never letting go was very appealing. Either that or asking the pilot to fly them to Antarctica.

Thinking about what lay ahead scared her. How do you tell a five-year-old that the only home she has ever known is gone?

Kieran's grasp tightened on her hand. "What is it?" he asked. "What are you thinking?"

"Cammie," she said simply. "How am I ever going to tell Cammie?"

Thirteen

In the end, they did it together. Annalise had bathed Cammie and fed her and tucked her into clean pajamas. They were reading a book when Olivia and Kieran finally made their way upstairs to the bedroom that Kieran had so carefully picked out for his daughter.

The child's face lit up when she saw them. "Mommy! Kieran! I missed you. Did you bring me a present?"

Annalise excused herself quietly, pausing only to give Olivia a quick hug as she left the room. The gentle gesture of compassion tested Olivia's tear-free resolve.

Kieran scooped Cammie up in his arms and held her tight. On his face, Olivia saw her own sadness and thankfulness. Things could have been so much worse.

The three of them sat together on a cushioned window seat overlooking the mountainside in the gathering dusk. Kieran gazed at Olivia over the five-year-old's head, telegraphing a question. *You ready?*

She shook her head, putting her fist to her mouth. *You do it,* she signaled. If she tried to explain, she might burst into tears, and she didn't want to scare her child.

Kieran rested his chin on Cammie's head for a long moment, and then pulled back when she wiggled. "Something bad has happened, sweetheart. I need you to be brave when I tell you this."

Every ounce of childish glee melted away to be replaced by an oddly adult expression of anxiety. "What is it?"

Olivia saw the muscles in his throat work, and knew how unfair she was being to make him do her dirty work. He had to know the impending news would hurt their daughter. But like parents wincing in empathy for an uncomprehending infant about to get vaccinations, she and Kieran had no choice but to tell Cammie the awful truth.

"There was a fire at your house in California," he said slowly, choosing his words with care.

Cammie's eyes rounded. "Did Mommy leave the iron on?"

In spite of everything, Olivia wanted to giggle. "No, baby."

Kieran's sober expression softened. "A bad man made a fire and it got out of control."

"Is Princess Boots okay?"

At Kieran's baffled look, Olivia jumped in. "Kitty is still with Mrs. Capella. Remember?"

"Oh, yeah." She frowned, scrunching up her nose and eyes in concentration. "So we have to stay here for a while?"

Kieran nodded slowly. "If that's okay with your mom."

Olivia nodded, her eyes wet. Clearly Cammie didn't understand the import of what had happened...at least not yet. She was only five. Time enough for upsetting revelations as she asked questions in the coming weeks.

Cammie wiggled off Kieran's knee. "I'm glad Bun-Bun

was here with me." Bun-Bun was the much-loved stuffed animal without which Cammie couldn't sleep. Perhaps in Cammie's eyes, that was enough.

Kieran ruffled her hair. "I'm glad, too. Time for bed, big girl. Your mommy and I have been flying all day, and we're beat."

As they tucked her in, Cammie yawned and surveyed them sleepily. She studied Kieran's face. "Are you my mommy's boyfriend?"

Olivia choked. "Where did you hear about boyfriends?"

"Mrs. Capella says that her daughter is getting a dee-vors because she has a boyfriend *and* a husband. You don't have a husband, so I thought Kieran might be your boyfriend."

The two adults held back their laughter with heroic effort. Kieran's face was red when he said, "Your mommy and I are friends. And we both love you very much. Now go to sleep, and tomorrow, we'll all do something fun together."

Outside in the hall, they collapsed against the wall, laughing uncontrollably until at last they both wheezed and gasped and braced their hands against the Chinese silk wallpaper. Olivia knew the moment of hilarity was a cleansing response to the day's tragedy.

Trust a child to restore a sense of balance to life.

Olivia wiped her eyes. "Thank you," she said. "For telling her. You were perfect."

He put the back of his hand to her hot cheek. "Far from perfect. But I love that little girl."

What happened next was inevitable. In shared grief and exhaustion, they came together, heart to heart, breath mingling with breath. Kieran held her as if she might break, his embrace gentle, his body warm and solid and comforting.

They kissed carefully, as if for the first time. She came so close to blurting out her love, laying it at his feet in gratitude. It would be unfair to burden him with her feelings when he had done so much for her already.

Gradually tenderness heated to passion. She felt him tremble as her hands roved his back.

He sighed, hugging her so tightly her ribs protested. "I need to stay with you tonight, Olivia. To make sure you're okay. Please."

How could she deny what she wanted so badly? "Yes."

He kissed her again, covering her face with light, almost-not-there brushes of his lips. "But first I'm going to feed you."

Food? Her awakening arousal protested. She wrapped her arms around his neck and pressed closer. Sex offered oblivion. Forgetfulness. That was all she wanted and needed right now.

He broke free and stepped back, breathing heavily. "Go get cleaned up. Put on a nightgown. I'll consult with the chef and bring up a tray."

"I'm not hungry," she grumbled. The thought of food made nausea churn in her stomach.

"Doesn't matter." His mien was more drill sergeant than lover. "You have to eat."

She followed his initial direction and stepped into the shower. Beneath the hot, pelting spray, she had to admit that Kieran was right. The water was cleansing in more ways than one. If a few more tears were shed amidst the soapy rivulets swirling down the drain, no one was the wiser.

Though her body ached, her breasts felt heavy and full as she washed them. Imagining Kieran's hands on her sensitive flesh brought a different kind of healing. And she trembled anew with fear for the future. Not for lack of housing. That was minor in the grand scheme of things.

Saying goodbye to Kieran when she went home to start over would make today's events mere shadows of pain. How would she live without him in her life? She had been doing it for six long years. Cammie had filled her days with joy and purpose.

But now Olivia wanted more. She wanted and needed the man she'd fallen in love with during an idyllic semester in Oxford, England.

After drying off and dressing in her favorite silk peignoir of coffee satin and cream lace, she checked on Cammie. Her little girl was sleeping peacefully, but a forbidden thumb was in her mouth, a habit Olivia thought they had defeated a long time ago.

Was the childish comfort technique a sign that Cammie was more affected by the news of the fire than she had seemed?

Olivia removed the thumb without waking her and re-arranged the covers. "I love you," she whispered, kissing Cammie's cheek and inhaling the wonderful combined scents of shampoo and graham crackers from her bedtime snack.

When she returned to her bedroom via the connecting door, Kieran was already there…and in the process of setting a large silver tray on a low table in front of the settee. His eyes warmed as he turned and saw her. With heated regard he swept his gaze from her bare toes, up her body to her freshly washed hair. She'd shampooed it three times, convinced that the smell of smoke still lingered.

He held out a hand. "Come. Eat with me."

The massive fireplace normally sat empty in the summertime, hidden behind a large arrangement of fresh flowers. Kieran had removed the vase and stacked logs and kindling, which were now burning brightly.

She cocked her head, her gaze drawn to the warmth of the crackling blaze. "Isn't this extravagant?"

He shrugged, looking like a mischievous boy. "I had to

crank down the AC ten degrees, but I like the ambience. You deserve extravagance after the day you've had."

"The food looks amazing." She joined him on the small sofa, feeling oddly shy considering the activities they'd indulged in the past couple of days. Her stomach rumbled loudly. "I could get used to having a chef on call."

Kieran uncovered a silver salver. "Nothing too heavy... roasted chicken, lemon-infused rice and fresh kale from the garden." He waved at a smaller dish. "And a surprise for dessert if you clean your plate."

They ate in companionable silence, both of them starved. With the warmth from the fire and a full tummy, Olivia's lids grew heavy. At last she sat back, unable to eat another bite. "That was delicious," she said. "And I'm not just raving because I was so hungry."

Kieran poured two cups of fragrant coffee, handing her one. "I'm glad you enjoyed it." Leaning forward, he removed the top of the mystery dish and uncovered a bowl of sugared dates. "Now for your treat." He picked up one piece of fruit and held it to her lips. "Try this."

As she opened her mouth automatically, Kieran tucked the sugary sweet between her lips. She bit off a piece and without thinking, licked the crystals that clung to his fingertips. He froze, his eyes heating with arousal and his breathing growing harsh. "Have another."

The room was heavy with unspoken desire, hers... his. The fire played a mesmerizing symphony of pop and crackle. Three times he fed her, and three times she sucked his fingertips into her mouth to clean them.

Kieran cracked first. He stood up and strode to the window, throwing up the sash and letting in a rush of cool night air. "Bloody stupid idea having a fire," he muttered. He took off his shirt, exposing a chest that made Olivia's toes curl.

He was all hard planes and rippling muscle.

"I like it," she protested, removing the negligee that topped her barely there gown.

His eyes grew wide. "I am not going to have sex with you tonight. You don't need that."

"Don't tell me what I need."

She lowered the tiny straps of the satin garment and let it slither over her hips and fall to the carpet. "*You* haven't had dessert," she pointed out.

The front of his trousers lifted noticeably. His torso gleamed damp in the soft lamplight. Hooded eyes tracked her every movement. "I wanted to comfort you tonight…to hold you in case you had bad dreams."

"Perhaps if you *entertain* me, my dreams won't be bad at all."

He shoved his hands in the pockets of his pants, frowning. "I think you may still be in shock. You should get a good night's sleep."

Though his mouth spoke prosaic words, his body told a different story. His entire frame was rigid, the cloth of his trousers barely containing his thrusting shaft.

She walked right up to him, buck naked, her toes curling in the soft, luxurious carpet beneath their feet. Now the tips of her breasts brushed his bare rib cage.

"Stop." He inhaled sharply, groaning as she laid her cheek against his shoulder.

"We're just getting started," she murmured. Insinuating one of her thighs between his legs, she rubbed up against him like a cat.

Kieran was a strong man, but he was only a man. How in the hell could he cosset her when she was hell-bent on seducing him? He gave up the fight, because losing was better than anything he had planned. Cupping her firm butt in his palms, he pulled her closer still. "Did anyone ever tell you you're stubborn?"

She went up on tiptoe to kiss his chin. "All the time."

"The door?"

"I locked it. We'll hear her if she stirs…but she won't."

"I'll leave before morning." He wouldn't confuse Cammie, not with so much at stake.

"That's a whole seven hours from now," Olivia said, her nimble fingers attacking his belt buckle. "I can think of a few ways to fill the time."

The ornate mantel clock marked off the minutes and hours as Kieran devoted himself to entertaining Olivia. She tried rushing the game, but he was on to her tricks. With one hand, he manacled her wrists over her head, and at the same time trapped her legs with his thigh.

Her chest heaved, eyes flashing in annoyance. "I want to touch you."

The agitation of her breathing made her breasts quiver. The sight of those magnificent heaving bosoms mesmerized him for a split second. He cleared his throat. "Not yet."

"When?"

"After I've finished with you."

Eyes rounded, she gazed up at him. "That sounds ominous."

"I promise you'll enjoy every second."

Her eyes fluttered shut. A tiny sigh of anticipation slipped from her pursed lips and filled him with purpose. Tonight was for Olivia alone.

Flipping her to her stomach and sitting astride her thighs, he reached for a bottle of lotion on the nightstand and squeezed a generous amount into his hand. Warming the thick liquid between his palms, he gazed down at her. Those narrow shoulders had carried a heavy burden for the past six years, a burden that he should have been sharing.

The knowledge was a sharp pang in his belly. Deliberately he placed his hands on her upper back and began a deep massage. Olivia moaned and settled more deeply into the mattress, her body boneless and limp.

In his younger, wilder days, he'd once had the good fortune to spend a three-day vacation with a sexy Indonesian masseuse. She'd taught Kieran a thing or two about the human body and how to relax. Dredging up those pleasant memories, he applied himself to making Olivia feel pampered, hopefully draining away the stresses of their long, emotionally fraught day.

Touching her was a penance. If his hands shook, surely she didn't notice. He was tormented by the notion that Olivia and Cammie might have been in the house when it went up in a ball of flame. Nothing he could have done would have saved them if he had been on the other side of the world. Olivia could have died, and Kieran would not have known for weeks, months.

He'd been living without her for a long time. How was it that the possibility of her death, and his daughter's, as well, turned his stomach to stone?

He finished at last and brushed her cheek with a fingertip. "Olivia?" Though *her* muscles were warm and loose, he was strung tightly enough to snap. "Olivia?"

A gentle snore was his only answer.

Incredulous, frustrated, but oddly proud that he had lulled her into slumber, he slid down into the bed beside her, condemned to a painful night. Her nude body snuggled into his even in sleep, her bottom coming to rest against his rock-hard erection. He contemplated giving himself relief, but he didn't want to wake her.

He closed his eyes. The covers suffocated him. Willing himself to breathe slowly, he used the deep inhale and exhale technique he knew would eventually coax sleep.

Arms tight around Olivia, he yawned and pressed his cheek to her back.

As the moments passed, he gained control and a sense of perspective. Contentment washed over him with the unexpected advent of a gentle summer rain. This house had held nothing for him in the past but pain and duty. He'd never known real happiness here. All he ever wanted to do in the midst of his rare visits was to escape.

Even spending time with his family had not blunted the hurtful memories that in his mind hung over the massive house as a shroud.

Gareth had built a home here, as had Jacob. Why were they able to get past the tragedy when Kieran couldn't? Was he weaker than his brothers? Kieran and Annalise were the youngest of all six of the cousins when they lost their mothers. Did that make a difference? Annalise hadn't settled down on the mountain, either.

But unlike Kieran, she was filled with light and a happiness that was almost palpable. Her soul wasn't scarred by what had happened.

He allowed himself for one wary second to reach for the memories of his mother. A scent. A fleeting visual. The sound of her gentle laugh. She danced in his memory, hand in hand with her little son, twirling him around in a dizzying circle. Then the image faded. It was all he had...all he would ever have.

This was the point at which he usually surrendered to the urge to flee, a knee-jerk reaction to pain so strong it brought a toughened man to the brink of despair.

As he lay there in the darkness, dry-eyed, he realized with stunned certainty that the pain was gone. Obliterated. In the depth of the night, he heard his mother's whisper. *Be happy, Kieran. For me....*

Did she know about Olivia and Cammie? Was she somewhere up there in heaven, grieving because she couldn't meet her granddaughter?

He closed his eyes, throat tight with emotion, grateful that no one was around to see his weakness. Had his mother really counseled him to be happy? Was it even possible? Did he have it in him to let go and simply live again?

Existing from job to job, tent to tent, was the perfect camouflage for a man who was empty inside. He never stopped moving long enough for anyone to realize...to care.

Olivia murmured his name in her sleep. He stroked her hair, curling a mass of it around his hand and holding it in his fist as if by doing so, this unprecedented feeling of peace might last.

She felt perfect in his arms.

But he was an imperfect man.

Could he change for her? For his daughter?

Fourteen

When Olivia awoke, she was alone. The pillow beside hers bore the imprint of Kieran's head, but the bed was empty. She knew he had to leave her…it made sense. But her heart grieved.

Outside her window, dawn had barely arrived; the tree-tops no more than shadowy sentinels, though birdsong filled the early-morning air. She yawned and stretched, wondering how long it would be before Cammie bounded into the room with her usual burst of energy.

It was too soon to call Lolita and Javier. They were on Pacific Time, still the middle of the night in California.

Had the police made an arrest? Was her mother's stalker continuing to lurk in the shadows of their lives?

Itchy and restless, Olivia climbed out of bed, feeling the aches and pains of an old woman. The benefits of Kieran's selfless massage evaporated in a rush of uncertainty that tightened her neck muscles. It had been only a short time since the fire, but already, waiting for an end to the drama was unbearable. She longed to go home, but she had nowhere to call her own anymore.

The truth was ugly and inescapable.

By the time she finished her shower, Cammie was up and demanding breakfast. To Olivia's surprise, Victor awaited them in the formal dining room.

"Good morning, sir," she said, sitting stiffly in a chair and giving Cammie a visual warning to behave. Cammie needed little urging. She was too busy digging into a plateful of small pancakes shaped like bears and fir trees.

The old man had an empty plate in front of him, but it bore the evidence of bacon and eggs. He nursed coffee in a china cup that looked far too fragile for his big hands. Like his sons, he was a large man, but his hair had faded away to little tufts of white over his ears, and his florid skin spoke of unhealthy habits.

His portly figure and piercing eyes were intimidating to say the least.

Olivia ate without speaking, all the while making sure Cammie was not poised to launch into one of her stream of consciousness chattering sessions.

The meal was silent and uncomfortable.

When Olivia had swallowed as many bites as she could manage of an omelet and crisp toast, she shoved her plate aside. "We'll get out of your hair," she said, biting her lip when she realized that Cammie was still finishing up.

Victor Wolff raised one beetling eyebrow. "So soon? I've arranged for the sous chef to make cookies with Cammie so you and I can talk, Olivia. Is that okay with you, little one?"

Cammie looked up, a drizzle of sticky syrup coati_ side of her chin. Her mouth was too full for spe_ nodded enthusiastically.

Unease slithered down Olivia's spine. "Where is Kieran?" she asked, needing reinforcements before a confrontation with her host.

Victor shrugged. "He and Gareth and Jacob took off at first light for Charlottesville, something about buying a new Jeep."

"It takes three men to purchase a vehicle?"

"My boys are close. And they seldom have the opportunity to spend time together as a trio."

A pleasant young woman appeared from the direction of the kitchen, introducing herself as LeeAnn. Olivia watched, helpless, as Cammie's face lit up. She took her new friend's hand, and the two of them disappeared, leaving Olivia to face Victor alone.

He stood up. "We'll go to my study," he said, allowing Olivia no opportunity to refuse.

Trailing in his wake, she pondered his intent. There was little time to formulate a plan of rebuttal for whatever was about to transpire. Victor's private sanctum was on the main floor, as was the kitchen.

The room was like something out of a movie. Heavy hunter-green drapes flanked mullioned windows that sparkled as if they were cleaned every night by an army of elves…and perhaps they were. The thick folds of velvet picked up and accentuated the intricate design in an antique Persian rug that covered a large expanse of the hardwood floor.

Victor motioned to a wing chair opposite his dark mahogany desk. "Have a seat."

Feeling a bit too much like a wayward schoolchild, Olivia sat, hands in lap, and waited. She wasn't intentionally silent, but in truth, she could not think of a single subject, other than the weather, with which to counter Victor's liegelike summons.

He frowned at her. "When are you going to tell me I have a grandchild?"

Nothing like a direct attack to catch the unwary off guard. Olivia bit her lip, stalling for time. "Is that why you asked me to come in here? Did you wait for your son to leave so you could ambush me?"

Guilt landed briefly on his heavy features before disappearing. "You're impertinent."

"I mean no disrespect, but I won't be bullied."

They tiptoed around the subject that couldn't be broached. Not yet. Not without Kieran's participation.

Victor harrumphed and sat back in his chair, swiveling from side to side just enough to make Olivia dizzy. Despite his bluster, or maybe because of it, she suddenly saw that he was afraid. Of what? she wondered.

After tapping an empty pipe on the blotter, he put it to his lips and took a lengthy draw, perhaps using the scent of tobacco long past to satisfy an urge. "Ask him to stay," he commanded. "Ask Kieran to stay. He'll do it for you. I know he will. He's never before brought a woman to Wolff Mountain. You're special to him."

Her heart sank. "Sorry to burst your bubble, Mr. Wolff, but you're wrong."

"Call me Victor. And I'm seldom wrong. What makes you so sure that I am now?"

Time to bury her pride. Taking a deep, painful breath, she gave him the unvarnished truth. "He offered to marry me in order to give Cammie security. A family on paper. But he wasn't offering to stay. That wasn't part of the package. He's leaving for the Sudan in September. Nothing has changed."

Before her eyes, the old man aged a decade, his brown-spotted hands trembling before he gripped the arms of the chair to steady them. "Damn it. This is his home. He needs to settle down...."

His words trailed off in impotence. He wasn't the first parent to rue a son's choices, and he wouldn't be the last.

Olivia sighed. "I've never had any illusions about Kieran. He's a wonderful man, but more than anyone I've ever known, he needs to wander. It's a lifestyle well suited to a single man."

"And if he has a family?"

"If he has a family, it wasn't by choice." Her words were blunt. Said as much to remind herself of the truth as they were to make the truth clear to a desperate father. "He'll continue to come back from time to time if you don't harass him. That's probably the most you can hope for."

Victor glared at her. "In my day women knew how to use sex to get what they wanted from a man."

Olivia's face flamed. Aghast at his gall, she gaped at him. "Are you actually suggesting that I try to manipulate your son with intimacy?"

"Any fool, even an old one, can see the fireworks between you two. Make the boy crazy. Reel him in. Don't worry about being so damned politically correct."

"Forgive me if I don't want a man I have to coerce into loving me."

"Who said anything about love? Once he parks his boots, he'll figure out that you and Cammie are good for him."

"Like prunes and brussels sprouts? No, thank you. I deserve a man who will love me and my child and put us first."

"Then fight for the boy, damn it."

Olivia stood up, beyond finished with the circuitous conversation. "I appreciate your hospitality, Mr. Wolff, but my relationship with Kieran is none of your business. I wish I could give you what you want."

He waved a hand as if dismissing her stilted words. "Any

news about your house…or the stalker? I'm sorry about that, by the way. Must have been a damned shock."

"Nothing yet. I'll call my parents when it gets a little later." His compassion touched her in spite of their adversarial meeting.

"You're always welcome on Wolff Mountain. I give you my word." His rheumy eyes glittered with tears.

Her throat tightened. This magnificent house was part of Cammie's birthright. Whatever transpired between Kieran and Olivia, that relationship would never change. Victor Wolff was Cammie's grandfather.

"Thank you," she said softly. "I'll bring her to visit when I can."

He nodded, a single tear streaking down his leathery cheek. "See that you do, Olivia Delgado. See that you do."

She escaped Victor's study, and after checking on Cammie who was still elbow-deep in cookie dough, Olivia retrieved her cell phone from the bedroom and began making a necessary string of phone calls. The insurance adjuster, of course. And the neighbor to check on the cat.

That second call meant answering a host of questions. Mrs. Capella was a dear, but a notorious gossip. No doubt she'd be preening on the block since she had direct contact with Olivia.

Finally, when it was a decent hour to roust her night-owl parents out of bed, Olivia dialed their number.

Lolita's sleep-thickened voice answered. "You do realize that a woman my age needs her beauty sleep," she complained.

"You're gorgeous, Mother…with or without sleep." The implied request for flattery was received and acknowledged. "Are you and Daddy okay?"

Javier Delgado picked up the conversation. "She went

to make coffee. We're fine, baby. Are you and my grand-daughter staying put?"

"Yes." But not for long. She had another phone call to make that would set things in motion. Unfortunately every minute spent with Kieran made the inevitable parting that much harder. It was time to break free.

"Why didn't you tell us you were flying out here yester-day?"

Her father's pique made her feel guilty. "You said on the phone that Mom had gone to bed with a sedative. I didn't want her to see my house. Not yet. We both know she doesn't handle crises well."

"We'll get the bastard who did this."

Javier often spoke like a movie character. But his vehe-mence made Olivia smile. "I know. I just called to say I love you and to tell you to be very careful. This man is obsessed with Mother. No one knows what he'll try next."

"Not to worry, my love. The house is surrounded with so much firepower, I feel like we're hiding out at the Alamo."

"That standoff didn't end well, Daddy."

"No. But it was a hell of a role." Javier had played Davy Crockett once upon a time, and could still produce a cred-itable southern accent.

She wiped her cheek, surprised to realize she was crying. Her parents were eccentric and self-centered and prone to overdramatization in every situation, but she loved them dearly. "I'll call again soon," she promised. "Keep me posted."

When she hung up, she gnawed her lip, worried that her mother wouldn't take the threat seriously, despite the fire. Olivia was sure that a part of Lolita felt flattered that a fan cared enough to be irrational.

The three Wolff men were not back by lunchtime. Cam-mie pouted, missing Kieran's attentions. Olivia felt much the same, but without the luxury of acting like a five-year-old. For the next several hours, Cammie was fractious and inconsolable. Refusing to nap, she sulked around her wonderful bedroom until Olivia was at her wit's end. Was all this bad behavior a result of last night's news? Would it help if Olivia coaxed her daughter into talking about the fire? Or would that make things worse?

It was far too hot to play outside. Huge thunderclouds built on the western horizon, and the sticky, oppressive heat shimmered in waves, obscuring the usual, far flung vistas.

When Cammie finally succumbed to a fitful sleep, it was after four o'clock. Olivia fell into a chair exhausted. It was always a mistake to let her offspring nap this late in the day. It meant Cammie wouldn't want to go to bed at her normal bedtime, and battle would inevitably ensue.

But the child was clearly in need of rest. Olivia wasn't about to wake her up, even for dinner. They could always raid the kitchen later.

At six-thirty, Olivia dressed in a salmon voile sundress that she had not yet worn. The filmy layers were cool, and the color flattered her skin tones. No bra was required. Her breathing quickened as she pictured Kieran's reaction later when they were alone.

She owed him something for last night. After her insistence that they make love, she had flaked out on him in no time. Had he been terribly disappointed?

No matter. They had time for one last metaphorical dance. Then Olivia would go home. Kieran was who he was. He wouldn't change. And Olivia couldn't bruise her heart any longer hoping for a different outcome. After running a brush through her hair, she clipped it up in a loose chignon. Dangling crystal earrings added a note of formality to her appearance. If she had to play verbal badminton with Victor Wolff again, she needed all the armor she could muster.

Poor Cammie looked like an urchin when Olivia checked on her. She had shed her shorts and top and was wearing an old T-shirt Kieran had given her that said, Girls Rule, Boys Drool.

Grinning wryly, Olivia picked up the monitor and tucked it in the pocket of her full skirt. When Cammie awoke, it would be easy to hear her. The child usually demanded a snack before her eyes were open. More like her grandmother than her mother, she didn't waken easily.

Olivia descended the stairs to the main floor, stopping short when Kieran came striding toward her. Something was different about him, but she couldn't pinpoint it. There was almost a spring in his step.

He gave her a broad grin. "Hello, beautiful. Did you miss me?"

Fifteen

Kieran had thoroughly enjoyed the day with his brothers. Catching up on each others' lives, sharing stupid inside jokes from their adolescent years…all of it had been comfortable and familiar and pretty damned wonderful. There'd been nothing touchy feely or emotionally intrusive. But Gareth and Jacob, by their behavior and conversation, had made it clear how glad they were to have him home.

Even in the midst of a testosterone fest, though, Kieran had missed his girls. He hugged Olivia now, inhaling her scent with a deep, cleansing breath.

She pulled back and smiled at him. "Yes. We missed you. In fact, Cammie was a spoiled brat today. Not having you here to entertain her was not fun."

"Where is she now?"

"Taking a late nap." She pulled the monitor from her pocket. "I'll hear her when she wakes up."

"Do you think she was acting out because of what we told her last night?"

"I thought about that. But she never mentioned the fire."

"What have you heard from California?"

"Nothing much. The man is still on the loose. Mom and Dad are fine...holed up with a phalanx of security guards."

He squeezed her hand. "And how about you?"

"I'm fine."

Her words weren't all that convincing. The shadows smudged beneath her eyes accentuated her pallor. He had a feeling that she was running on nothing more than adrenaline and determination. Olivia was strong, very strong. But losing a home was a blow to anyone.

He put his arm around her as they walked to the dining room. "We'll do whatever needs to be done," he said quietly. "Try not to worry."

Gareth had lingered, and Gracie joined them for dinner. With Jacob and Annalise present, as well, it was a lively meal. Annalise's siblings and father were due back to the mountain in another week.

Surprisingly it was quiet Jacob who pressed Olivia for details. "When they catch the guy, what will you do?"

She took a sip of her wine and winced. "As soon as that happens, Cammie and I will head home.... I mean..."

Kieran's hand tightened on hers beneath the tablecloth.

She took a breath. "Cammie and I will stay with my parents, I suppose, until we decide what to do...whether to rebuild in the same place or closer to my mom and dad. I haven't really had time to think it through."

"Speaking of Cammie, I thought she'd be awake by now," Kieran said. He watched as she pulled the monitor from her pocket, listened a moment and shook it. He frowned. "What's wrong?"

"I think the batteries are dead."

Olivia's look of consternation mirrored his own gut feeling of trouble. "I'll go get her," he said. "Stay and eat your dinner."

But he'd barely had time to stand up when Cammie appeared in the doorway—sucking her thumb, wearing an old T-shirt. Her hair was sleep tousled. Relief flooded him, along with amusement. "Hi, sweetheart. You ready for some dinner?"

She surveyed the assemblage at the table, her small face solemn. "I forgot Bun-Bun. He wants to eat with us." Turning back, she ran out of the room.

"Put your clothes on," Olivia called after her.

Kieran sat back down. "Don't hassle her. As kids we showed up at meals in all varieties of threadbare shirts and jeans."

Victor chuckled. "Not for lack of trying on my part. Vincent and I did our best to impart rules of etiquette, but rarely did they stick. It was a household of hellions back in those days."

"Not me." Annalise's smile was smug. "Somebody had to have some couth around here."

The men hooted. Gareth grinned, his arm stretched out along the back of his wife's chair. "You were a goody two-shoes. But what Dad and Uncle Vincent didn't know was that you came home from playing in the woods just as nasty as the rest of us. Unfortunately you had this feminine knack for turning grubby Cinderella into an infuriating, sanctimonious princess in the blink of an eye. Made us mad as hell."

In the burst of laughter that followed, Kieran leaned toward Olivia. "Should I go get Cammie?"

She shook her head. "Not in the mood she's in. I'll deal with it. Just don't eat my dessert," she added as she went to retrieve her daughter.

Kieran had finished his meal and was having a second

glass of wine when Olivia rushed back into the room, panic written all over her face.

"She's not upstairs. I can't find her. She's gone."

He grabbed her shoulders, easing her into a chair before she fainted on him. Her skin had gone milk-white. "Don't jump to conclusions, honey. She probably got turned around and lost her way down a hall somewhere. You know how this house is."

"Cammie has a perfect sense of direction." Olivia gazed up at him, clutching his sleeve. "She never gets lost. Something's wrong."

Terror ripped at his chest, but he fought it back. There had to be a simple explanation.

Everyone at the table was on their feet in an instant, Victor included.

Kieran sucked in a breath and barked out orders. "Gareth, you and Gracie take the yard and your house. She loves the dog and the pool. Jacob, search this floor with Father. Olivia and I will start with the second floor and work our way up. Annalise, question the staff. When each of you finishes, come back. Does everyone have a cell phone? Call if you locate her."

The next half hour was a nightmare. They tore the house apart, from basement to attic. Cammie was nowhere to be found.

When the search parties met, empty-handed, Olivia broke down finally, sobbing so hard Kieran feared she would make herself ill. Holding her close, he breathed hope into her, shoring her up with only his will. Deep in his gut, her anguish was his own.

She sank onto a sofa, her eyes haunted. "That man has her. I know it. He said he was going to hurt the people my mother loves, and my mother adores Cammie."

Kieran's hands fisted. "How would he even know how to find you here?"

"The police said he's been watching my house. You came there. He must have figured out who you were."

"I was in a rental car."

"But you gave your real name?"

"Yes." Dear God in heaven…

Jacob spoke, his words carefully neutral. "We at least have to consider the possibility."

Olivia bowed her head. "There are no fences," she said dully. "Only the one at the front gate. Anyone could walk in."

Victor shook his head. "It would be a fool's mission. We have four hundred acres."

"Gracie made it up here," Gareth pointed out, his face troubled. His new wife had once upon a time sneaked onto the property to confront Gareth on her father's behalf.

"But Gracie didn't try to get into the main house, kidnap a child and leave again." Kieran's fierce shout cowed no one. In the faces of the people he loved, he saw compassion, concern and his own bubbling fear.

Olivia gathered her composure with a visible, superhuman effort, her chest heaving as tremors threatened to rattle her bones. "Do we call the police?"

A momentary silence fell over the room. The Wolff family had suffered terribly at the hands of the press over the years. Privacy was practically inscribed on the family crest. And for Lolita and Javier, this kind of publicity was not desirable, either. The tabloids would have a field day.

Kieran squatted in front of Olivia. "We'll do whatever you want. You're her mother." He took her hands in his, trying to warm the icy skin. She was close to being in shock, and he was damn glad Jacob was on hand.

"It will take them a long time to get here, won't it?" The words were barely a whisper, spoken through bloodless lips.

Everyone nodded. Victor's breathing was harsh and labored. "The nearest law enforcement is forty-five to fifty minutes away."

Olivia shook free of Kieran's solicitous grasp and stood up. "We'll give it an hour, then…before we make a call."

Gareth spoke up, pacing restlessly. "I scouted the perimeter of the house. No sign of forced entry, no footprints, nothing to indicate an intruder. But that doesn't mean anything. Psychopaths are often brilliant. He would try to cover his tracks."

A blinding flash of lightning lit up the room in which they all stood as a simultaneous crack of thunder roared across the mountaintop and rattled glass in the windows.

Kieran made a decision. "If he has her, he'll use one of the trails. It would be too hard to travel through the underbrush. I'm going to walk the closest sections to look for signs that anyone has passed by recently. I'll start with the north and the east since that portion of the property is nearest a road."

Jacob nodded. "Gareth and I will take the west and south quadrants."

"I'm going with you." Olivia in her dainty, feminine dress held her stance as aggressively as a bulldog.

"It's too dangerous," Kieran said through clenched teeth. "Trust me."

"I do trust you," she said. "But that's my baby out in the storm."

He eyed her low-heeled sandals. They were flimsy at best, but the clock was ticking. She was close to collapse, and the knowledge that he had not been able to protect her or his daughter flailed him like a whip. "Fine," he ground out, his anger self-directed. "Suit yourself. Let's move out."

Olivia stumbled behind Kieran, trying to keep up with his loping stride. She knew he was angry with her, but she couldn't stay inside the house and wait. She couldn't. Not when Cammie was terrified of storms.

Who had her? What was his intent? Ransom? Kieran's mother had been murdered in just such a situation. Was Kieran thinking of Laura Wolff right now? Did fear turn his limbs to jelly as it did Olivia's?

All around them lightning danced. Rain poured from the skies relentlessly, drenching Olivia to the skin and blinding her. Kieran called to Cammie again and again, until his voice was hoarse and exhausted.

There were at least a dozen trails crisscrossing the mountaintop. None of them showed a single sign that anyone had walked them recently. But the rain was rapidly turning everything to mud, so even if there had been shreds of cloth or remnants of footprints, they would soon be eradicated completely.

In a clearing, Kieran stopped abruptly. During a brief flash of illumination, Olivia saw anguish and grief on his face. But when she touched his arm, his expression morphed into determination.

Had she imagined his emotion?

He strode on, giving her no choice but to follow.

When they finally met up with Jacob and Gareth, the four adults looked for signs of hope in each others' faces. Huddled against the wind, they wordlessly acknowledged the truth. If an intruder had taken Cammie out in this storm, the chances of finding her were slim to none.

Stumbling back into the house with the others, Olivia struggled not to collapse in hysteria. Annalise and Gracie had prepared hot coffee. Olivia grasped a warm mug, trying to still the trembling that threatened to drag her under.

Annalise tugged her out of the foyer into a side chamber.

"I brought down dry clothes. You need to change immediately. It won't help Cammie if you make yourself sick."

With clumsy fingers, Olivia tried to do as she was asked. But her coordination was shot. Annalise took over, dealing with zippers and buttons. She stripped Olivia all the way down to her bare skin and then bundled her up quickly in dry underwear, a fleecy sweatshirt and jeans.

When they returned to the front of the house, the men were huddled together, their clothing still dripping onto the marble floor. Gareth turned his eyes to the ceiling, his body rigid with concentration.

Suddenly he swung around and pinned Annalise with a laserlike gaze. "Did you take Cammie to the secret tunnel?"

Annalise nodded. "I showed her where it was, but we didn't go in. The whole thing is probably full of spiders and mice. Ick. No child would want to get in there."

Kieran's expression was bleak. "I did. When I was just her age."

For a moment, the silence was stunned and uncomfortable. Olivia knew he was telling them that the secret tunnel was where he used to hide to grieve his mother.

En masse, they started up the stairs. Second floor, third floor, attic.

Olivia was confused. "But we've searched all this," she cried. "Several times."

"Over here," Kieran said, already crossing the attic to a portion of the wall where a frieze of carved flowers decorated a protruding section that looked like it was concealing ductwork. But it suddenly dawned on Olivia that the vents for the heat and air system were on the opposite side of the room.

Kieran pressed on a rose. Nothing happened. He glanced over his shoulder at Annalise. "Do you remember which one?"

She shrugged unhappily. "I never actually got it to open. All I did was tell Cammie how it worked in theory. I didn't think she paid attention to what I was saying."

Kieran pressed and punched until his knuckles were raw.

Annalise shoved him aside. "For Pete's sake. Move, you big lug."

Delicately, skimming her fingertips over the rough surface as if she were reading Braille, she searched for the mechanism. With a little click and a whir, the wheels engaged and the door swung open. It was only four feet high.

The seven adults gasped in unison. Annalise had not been wrong. The corners of the gaping opening were laced with spiderwebs. And the interior of the space was pitch-black, the single lightbulb long since burned out.

But lying curled up on the floor was Cammie, fast asleep. Her dirty face was streaked where tears had run through layers of dust. Her little fingernails were caked with grime from scratching at the inside of the door.

Kieran crouched and scooped her into his arms. "Wake up, baby. I'm here. Your daddy is here."

Olivia touched her daughter's soft cheek. "Wake up, Cammie. Please."

The child's lashes fluttered and lifted, causing her to blink against the sudden advent of bright light into her dark prison. "I got locked in," she complained, her arms around Kieran's neck. "Annalise never explained how to get out."

The indignant glare she shot Kieran's cousin might have made them all laugh had not each one been choking back emotion.

Olivia smoothed her daughter's rumpled hair, hoping it was spider free. "Why did you hide, sweetheart? We thought you were coming down for dinner, but when you went to get Bun-Bun you never came back."

Cammie's lower lip trembled. "When I woke up and went down to the dining room, I heard you say that when they catch the bad man you're gonna take me back to California. I want to stay here, Mommy. With Kieran. And you, too. I like it here."

"But, honey..."

Victor touched her arm in warning, silently pointing her attention to Kieran's face. Olivia's once incognito lover had nothing to hide now. His love and his pride were laid bare for all to see. He looked down at Cammie in his arms like a man who had finally found the treasure he'd spent a lifetime looking for.

Before Olivia could say another word, Kieran pulled her close, drawing the three of them into a tight hug. Saying a litany of thank-you prayers, she put her head on his shoulder and wept tears of gratitude.

When Cammie finally struggled to get down, demanding food, Olivia realized that the others had crept silently away, leaving this odd family of three to a reunion. Cammie faced off against her parents, arms akimbo. "You said you're my daddy," she accused, pointing at Kieran with an imperious finger. "I heard you."

Olivia saw him struggle for words. She knew he hadn't meant to betray her trust without her consent. The declaration had tumbled out, straight from his heart in the heat of the moment.

"Cammie, I..." He ran his hands through his hair, glancing in desperation at Olivia.

She stepped forward, squatting to look her daughter in the face. "He *is* your daddy, my sweet little jelly bean."

Cammie's eyes rounded. "Why didn't you tell me when we got here?"

It was a fair question. Cammie's hurt and confusion were exactly what Olivia had been hoping to avoid. Speaking slowly, choosing her words carefully, Olivia explained, "Kieran didn't know he was your daddy until I told him. When you were born, I didn't know where he was, because he works on the other side of the world."

"Did you look for him?"

Another zinger.

"I was busy taking care of you. I loved you very much and I was very happy to be your mommy."

Cammie stared at Kieran, Bun-Bun dangling from one fist, dragging the floor. "Do you want to be my daddy?"

Her innocence and vulnerability would have shredded a heart far more hardened than Kieran's. He blinked once. "I *am* your daddy," he said forcefully, crouching beside her. "But even if I weren't, I would want to be. Because I think you are the most special little girl in the whole wide world… and I love you."

Olivia knew the words were torn from his throat. He was not a man to say them lightly. When Cammie threw herself against his chest and his arms closed around her, Kieran's expression was painfully open, his raw and bleeding heart on display.

She had to look away, feeling anew the guilt of her decision to keep father and daughter apart.

The past couldn't be undone. Now all the three of them could do was move forward.

Kieran scooped Cammie up and stood with her, gazing at Olivia with an inscrutable expression. "Let's get our little chick some food," he said quietly.

Without ceremony, they made their way downstairs to Olivia's suite of rooms. One call to the kitchen netted them a child's feast of chicken fingers, peanut butter crackers, cooked apples and chocolate cake for dessert.

Olivia and Kieran sat side by side, not touching, as they watched their daughter devour an astounding amount of food given her small size. When she was satisfied, she wiped her mouth with her hand, yawning.

Suddenly her face brightened. "If our other house is gone, this can be my new bedroom. Forever."

Olivia felt Kieran tense. She gnawed her lip. "Kieran and I are going to talk about that," she said, wishing this conversation had been preceded by some kind of well-thought-out plan.

He had no such qualms. "It's your bedroom forever. Definitely. No matter what happens."

"You can stay here for the rest of the summer," Olivia conceded, knowing she had little choice at this point. "But Lolo and Jojo live in California…and you'll be starting kindergarten soon. We have lots to think about."

Kieran shot her a sharp glance, but didn't interrupt.

Puzzlement etched the features that already bore the stamp of the Wolff clan, emphasizing Cammie's resemblance to Annalise. "What does that mean?"

Kieran stood. "Grown-up stuff, poppet. Let's get you in a bath. You smell like a skunk."

With Cammie giggling in delight, the two of them disappeared into the bathroom, leaving Olivia to sit alone with her troubled thoughts.

Sixteen

Kieran brooded out on the terrace, reluctant to go back inside and face the inquisition from his family about why he'd had a daughter for five years and had never told them about her.

Cammie. His daughter. Even now the words sounded unfamiliar, and yet somehow right.

The storm had passed, and the summer sky was lit with scores of stars. The night was peaceful and serene in the aftermath of the tempest.

His own situation was not so calm. For his entire adult life, he'd had no one to worry about but himself. That thought drew him up short. It wasn't exactly true. He'd worried about his father plenty, especially after the heart attack that had brought Kieran home from university and caused him to leave Olivia behind.

Kieran had spent many a night praying for his father's recovery…wondering bleakly if Olivia had found some cocky English chap to pick up where Kieran had left off.

But as the months passed, once Kieran had made the choice to set out on the open road, he'd been remarkably self-centered. Okay, maybe not selfish exactly. He was kind, and his work was important to the people it benefited. But all in all, nothing had mattered to him but the next dot on the map and how soon he'd be on his way there.

Now, he stood at a new crossroads…one that a GPS couldn't locate on any grid. He had a daughter…and a lover…and a mountain that was calling him home. Normally he'd be chomping at the bit to pack his duffel bag and head out for parts unknown. Usually his passport was in his back pocket, ready for the next stamp.

But now, inexplicably, the thought of leaving at the end of the summer was unbearable.

He strode back into the house, eager to see Olivia, ready to make plans, to map out a course of action.

His father met him in the hallway. "There's a fellow at the front gate by the name of Jeremy Vargas. The guard wants to know whether to send him up or not."

Kieran frowned, wishing he could say no. "Let him in," he said.

Victor put a hand on his arm. "When you're ready, we'd all like to hear about you and Olivia and Cammie." He winced. "Olivia is the one you wanted to tell the truth to… back in Oxford."

It was a statement, not a question. "Yes."

"But I had a heart attack and you left her." His face twisted. "God, I'm sorry, son."

"It wasn't your fault."

"Why did she never let you know you had a daughter?"

"Because she thought my name was Kevin Wade, and when she found out I'd been lying to her…when she learned my true identity, she didn't think I deserved or needed to know."

Victor's head bowed. "Son of a bitch…" The expletive held little heat. The old man was defeated, worn down.

"Don't sweat it, Dad. It's all water under the bridge. We'll get through this."

The front door opened, and in walked Jeremy Vargas. Kieran introduced his father, then Victor excused himself. The two men faced off in the foyer.

"Why are you here?" Kieran asked bluntly, in no mood to play the welcoming host.

A lazy smile lifted the corners of a mouth that had kissed a variety of big name actresses. "Olivia called me after the fire. I'm to escort her home."

"The hell you say." Fury ignited deep in Kieran's belly. Caveman instincts kicked in. No one was leaving this house without his consent.

Olivia descended the stairs at that moment, wearing dark jeans and an emerald-green tank top. Her feet were bare. The smile she sent Jeremy's way was sweet, uncomplicated. Kieran had never received such a smile from her, and that pissed him off.

God, she was beautiful. Already it seemed like years since he had made love to her. He wanted to scoop her up and kiss her senseless. Or maybe kiss some sense into her.

He glared. "You never said anything about Vargas coming."

Her gaze was cool. "I wasn't sure how quickly he could get here. I didn't really expect him until tomorrow."

Jeremy stood in silence, allowing the two of them to duel with words and unspoken innuendo.

"I thought we agreed that you weren't leaving…not until your mother's stalker is in custody."

"Cammie will stay here. The two of you will have the

time you asked for to get to know each other better. I'll be able to deal with all the details about the fire and not have to worry about her."

Kieran ground his teeth. "May I speak with you in private?"

She shook her head. "We've said enough, I think. Once I've had some time to figure out my plans about what to do next, we can talk about custody arrangements."

She was shutting him out. Drawing a line in the sand. To hell with that. If she thought Kieran would agree to let her run the show, she was in for a big surprise.

"And when are you planning to leave?" He folded his arms across his chest.

"In the morning when I'm sure Cammie is okay." She turned to Jeremy. "I'll go check with Kieran's father and see if it's okay for you to spend the night. Thanks for coming, Jeremy."

In the wake of her departure, the silence lengthened. Jeremy stood, hands in his pockets, with an enigmatic smile on his handsome face.

Kieran wanted to punch him hard enough to rearrange those perfect features. He stared at the unwelcome intruder. "What's the deal with you and Olivia?"

Jeremy shrugged. "No comment."

"I don't like you, Vargas. Not one damn bit."

The smile deepened.

"You're in love with her."

Jeremy shrugged. "I *love* her. And I've known her long enough to realize you were the one who screwed over her life. I don't plan to let you do it again."

"Sanctimonious bastard." Kieran simmered, his fists itching for a brawl. But it had been years since he and his brothers had settled their differences with a fight. And

Victor would frown on bloodshed in his foyer. "You have no say in what goes on between Olivia and me."

"We'll see. But I'll be keeping an eye on you, Wolff. So watch your step."

The next morning, Olivia hugged Cammie so tightly the child finally wiggled free with a protest. Olivia brushed her daughter's wispy bangs with a fingertip. "You're sure you want to stay? You don't have to."

Cammie made a face. "I'll miss you, Mommy. Tell Lolo and Jojo I love them." Before Olivia could snag another kiss, Cammie was gone, running off to play with Gareth's dog.

Kieran stared at her, face impassive. She'd heard him knock on her door last night. But she had locked it. She was pretty sure he was going to propose marriage again, and that would have shattered her brittle heart. Everything was out in the open now. Cammie was Kieran's daughter…a Wolff who had been welcomed into the pack with open arms. His family loved her and had a lot of years to make up for.

This would be the longest time Olivia had ever been separated from her daughter. Leaving her this way was agony. But not even for Cammie's sake could Olivia linger. If Kieran continued to press for marriage as a practical solution, she might eventually cave to his persuasions. And that would be disastrous.

Olivia couldn't bear to play the dutiful wife, tucked away on Wolff Mountain like Rapunzel in her tower, waiting for her prince to come home. Not without love.

She handed her carry-on to Jeremy who was loading their belongings into his rental car. Turning back one last time, she went up on tiptoe and kissed Kieran's cheek. "Goodbye," she said quietly. "Look after our girl. I'll be in touch."

As Jeremy headed the car down the mountain, tears

trickled down Olivia's cheeks. He handed her a tissue. "Why don't you put him out of his misery? You love him."

"He doesn't love me. He's attracted to me, and he loves the fact that we share a daughter, but I can't live with that."

"So it's better to live without him?"

"Infinitely. I did it for five years and it wasn't so bad."

"But now you've been in his bed. You've shared things with him you've never shared with anyone else."

"How do you know?"

"Because I know *you*," he said simply, shooting her a sideways glance. "You've had maybe ten dates in the last five years, and a couple of those were premieres with me, which doesn't really count."

"It's hard being a single mom. A lot of men aren't interested in raising another man's child."

"That's not it. Most guys I know would fall all over themselves to be with you, even if you had a dozen rug rats. You're smart and funny and sweet and flat-out gorgeous."

She sniffled, wiping her nose and sighing loudly. "You're good for my ego, sweet Jeremy."

He waited for the massive front gate to slide open before steering the car through and aiming for the airport. "I call 'em as I see 'em, and I think you should decide what or who you want, and then fight for your future."

"That's funny. Victor Wolff gave me a variation of the same advice."

"Maybe you should take your head out of the sand and listen."

Olivia spent three weeks in California. The first seven days were filled with meetings and planning and insurance questions. Not only that, but she had to finish up her illustrations and overnight them to her publisher, a task that made her feel lighter once it was done. Fortunately she always carried her originals with her in a sturdy folio. Much had been destroyed in the fire, but not her latest work.

Week two brought the arrest of Lolita's stalker, a sad, lonely man with definite mental issues. After that came the really difficult decisions, such as Olivia giving the go-ahead to raze the remnants of her property in order to sell the lot.

Jeremy stood with her the day the bulldozers came. He held her hand, and she cried as the last of her "normal" life was lifted and dumped into rubbish bins.

She stared at the destruction, remembering Cammie's first Christmas…the marks on the kitchen wall that measured her height. The big, fuzzy leopard-print throw that they snuggled beneath together to watch cartoons on Saturday mornings.

"All I ever wanted was to have a regular family."

Jeremy's childhood and adolescence were as tumultuous as hers. He understood exactly what her dreams were and why. Which made the shock all the bigger when he turned on her.

"Quit being such a drama queen," he said, squeezing her shoulders. "Unless you're willing to admit you're more like your mother than you realize. You lost your house, and yeah, that's a bitch. But look what you've gained. A daddy for Cammie. Relatives who love you. And a new home if you're willing to think outside the box."

"Except for my time in school, I've never lived anywhere but California."

"Me, either. But it turns out, I love New York City. And I think you love Wolff Mountain. You've damn sure talked about it nonstop for the last two and a half weeks."

"What about my parents?"

"Your folks are a hell of a long way from needing a nursing home. They have their own life with all its crazy excitement. And we have these things called jets now that fly cross-country. Don't you think it's time for you to have everything you want?"

"I'm scared, Jeremy. He hurt me so badly the last time."

"You were a kid. Now you're a grown woman. And besides, he knows I'll kick his ass if he's mean to you."

They both laughed, arm in arm, feeling the warmth of a southern California sun. It was a long way to the Blue Ridge Mountains of Virginia.

Turning her back on what was but would never be again, Olivia walked back across the street, Jeremy at her side. As they paused, looking at each other over the top of the car, she grinned at him. "We've got to find you a nice woman, Jeremy Vargas."

He chuckled, sliding into the car and turning the ignition. "I like being single," he said. "Let's concentrate on you for now."

Seventeen

Olivia's return to Wolff Mountain was anticlimactic. The big house was virtually empty save for the staff who went about their work so unobtrusively that it seemed as if phantoms ran the place. The head housekeeper welcomed Olivia politely and was able to explain the whereabouts of almost everyone.

Annalise and Victor had taken Cammie to Charlottesville to buy her new clothes for school. Jacob was working in his lab. Gareth and Gracie were repainting a room at their house.

Only Kieran's activities were a mystery. Supposedly he was still on the mountain, but no one had seen him since breakfast.

Olivia freshened up in her suite and changed into casual clothes, glad to be alone for the moment. Her composure was in shreds. She had returned to Wolff Mountain for a brief visit because she missed her daughter terribly, and because she and Kieran needed to talk about custody arrangements. Cammie had been told her mother would stay a week. Olivia was not sure she could hold out that long. Returning to the mountain gave new life to her regrets.

She had pondered Jeremy's advice about fighting for what she wanted. And if she had believed it was possible to win, she would have. But she was a realist. The situation was beyond compromise. She and Kieran were too different. End of story.

All she needed now was closure. It would help if Kieran would go ahead and fly away. Then maybe her heart could finally accept that the two of them were never meant to be.

Olivia grimaced at the state of Cammie's room. Apparently without her mother around, she had forgotten every one of Olivia's lectures about keeping her toys and things tidy.

The housekeeper hovered in the doorway, bringing an armload of fresh towels. "Sorry about the mess, ma'am. But Mr. Kieran said that if I cleaned up after the little one, she'd never learn responsibility."

Surprised and impressed, Olivia nodded. "He's right. I'll have a chat with her at bedtime tonight."

"She's still a baby."

"Yes. But not too young to learn how to be neater."

The older woman smiled and excused herself, leaving Olivia to wander the halls, familiarizing herself once again with the sights and sounds and smells of the "castle." Kieran and his brothers called it that when they wanted to tease their father, but the description wasn't far off.

At last, she gave up on finding anyone to talk to and decided to take a walk. When Cammie came back, there would be little time for quiet reflection. It was a perfect summer afternoon, the moist air heavy with expectation. A day for dreaming…a day when time seemed to stand still.

Passing the turn to Gareth's house, Olivia wandered on, across the back of the property and deeper into the woods where the forest was cool and shady and the wind whispered secrets.

She needed to talk to Kieran about their future as a blended family. And it should be done in private. Which likely meant she'd have to wait until after dinner. Contact between the two of them had been virtually nonexistent since she left. Cammie got on the phone most evenings and Annalise always chatted when Olivia called. But Kieran was mysteriously unavailable whenever Olivia asked about him.

She had no clue as to his state of mind. And no idea what he expected of her.

Thinking about the intimacies they had shared made her face flame, even though she was alone. For three weeks she'd had trouble sleeping, tormented by memories of Kieran's lovemaking. In his arms, she'd felt complete…content.

As if she had conjured him out of thin air, he appeared suddenly, pushing aside a low-hanging branch of maple, ducking beneath it and stopping a few feet away. Hungrily she looked her fill. His shoulders were still as broad, his dark eyes as wary and unreadable as ever. Ripped, faded jeans covered the lower half of his body, but his torso was bare.

A faint sheen of sweat covered his chest.

He leaned against a tree, his indolent pose at odds with the intensity of his gaze. "You're back."

"Yes." She nodded, as if he might not have understood the word.

"Is Vargas with you?"

"Jeremy? No." Frowning, she wondered why he asked. "How are things with Cammie?"

His expression softened, making him look younger, happier. "She's great. We've been fishing, hiking… I taught her how to play checkers."

"Sounds fun."

"You've done a great job with her, Olivia. You should be proud."

His praise made her uncomfortable. "Thank you."

Straightening, he rubbed the back of his arm across his forehead. "I could use a drink. You ready to go back to the house?"

He held out a hand, but she couldn't bring herself to touch him, afraid that she might resort to begging. It was not a pose she wanted to assume.

Kieran's face darkened when she pretended not to notice his gesture. In silence, they made their way back.

He made a beeline for the kitchen, where a pitcher of fresh-squeezed lemonade sat ready on the granite counter-top, the sides of the glass container glistening with moisture.

As she watched, he poured two glasses, handing one to her. Their fingers brushed. A spark of electricity arced between them. Over the rim of his tumbler, his gaze tracked every move she made as she drank.

"I want to show you something," he said abruptly, draining his glass and putting hers in the sink, as well.

Puzzled, she followed him up the stairs all the way to the attic. One corner of the massive room had been partitioned off and a door added. Kieran ushered her inside.

She stopped, her progress halted by awe and amazement. A second enormous skylight had been cut into the roof, permitting rays of pure, brilliant sunlight to shine down on what appeared to be every art supply known to man. Brushes, canvases and easels. A top-of-the-line desk. Towels and turpentine. Palettes and paint.

Turning in a slow circle to take it all in, she said, "What is all this?"

He paced, not looking at her as he spoke. "A studio for you to use…when you're here."

Torn between confusion and despair, she touched him on the shoulder, halting his restless motion. "I don't understand."

They were so close she could see the muscles in his throat work as he swallowed. "I was hoping this could be your new home. Permanently."

Desperately she searched his face for clarification. "That's very kind of you, but I wouldn't want to impose on your family." And she needed distance to survive.

He brushed her cheek with the back of his hand. "Then marry me," he muttered. "And you'll *be* family."

Wincing, she pulled away, backing clumsily into a ladder-back chair that held an artist smock. "We've been through this," she said. "You're Cammie's father now. I've brought papers that give you shared custody. Fifty-fifty. Even if all three of us occasionally share the same roof, it isn't necessary for you and me to be married."

"It's necessary to me," he said quietly.

"I'll bring Cammie often. Every time you come home. You needn't worry that I'll try to keep her from you."

"Olivia," he said abruptly, running both hands through his hair. "For God's sake. You're not listening. I *love* you."

She bit her lip. "You want me," she corrected, not willing to be duped by her own wistful heart.

"Of course I want you. More than my next breath. These last few weeks have been hell. All I can think about is stripping you bare and sinking into you until we both die from pleasure. So yes, I do want you. But what I said was that I *love* you. Till death do us part. For eternity. Am I making myself clear?"

"You're shouting," she said, her teeth chattering with nerves. She wanted so badly for this scene they were playing out to be real, but caution held her back.

Cords stood out on his neck as he squeezed his eyes shut and pinched the bridge of his nose. "You weren't this much trouble at twenty-two."

"And you weren't Kieran Wolff. So I guess we're even." She picked up a small paintbrush and tested the sable bristles on the palm of her hand. "I'm not sure it would work."

"What?" he asked, confusion replacing annoyance.

"A long-distance relationship. Seeing each other only once or twice a year. Annalise told me your pattern. Father's Day, and sometimes Christmas. That's not much for Cammie and me to hang our hats on."

The string of curses he muttered beneath his breath was extraordinary for its variety and complexity. She was pretty sure the imprecations covered five or six languages.

He grabbed her by the shoulders and smashed his mouth to hers in a kiss that was not at all elegant, but that made her knees wobble. She tasted his desperation, her own dawning hope. Wrapping her arms around his neck, she moaned when his fingers plucked roughly at her tight nipples through the thin fabric of her blouse.

She wanted him so badly, she felt faint from need, weak with hunger.

Kieran came up for air at last, his chest heaving. She was pretty sure her fingernails had left scratch marks on his back. He stared down at her, telling her with his eyes the wild and wonderful truth. "I'm not going anywhere," he said.

"Today?" She tried to move back into her safety zone, but he had his hands at her hips, immobilizing her for the moment.

"Ever," he said flatly. "Do you believe me?"

"But what about your job?"

"I'll get someone to sub for me in September. Everything else can be passed off to other architects and engineers."

"What will you do?" This sudden about-face was mind-boggling.

He slid his hands up her waist until they landed beneath her breasts. Weighing each one with a gentle lift, he bent to kiss her again, this time with agonizing gentleness. "First of all," he said, his words slurred as he moved his mouth over the skin of her throat. "I'll build our house…and a swing set…and a corral for the pony…and—"

She put her hands over his lips. "You're serious?" It didn't seem possible. "You think you can give it up cold turkey? No more jetting round the globe? No more frequent flier miles? No more mosquito nets and hard hats?"

He bit her finger, enough to sting. "I have no reason to leave," he said simply. "Everything I want and need is here if you'll stay with me."

Tears stung her eyes. "Don't say it if you don't mean it," she begged. "I couldn't bear it if you changed your mind."

"God, Olivia. I know I kicked the shit out of your ability to trust me, but you have to believe me. If you give me another chance…if you'll make a family with me, you'll never regret it. I'm going to spend the rest of my life making you scream my name, night after night. It will be so loud, the neighbors will complain."

She laughed and hiccuped a sob at the same time. "There are no neighbors," she pointed out, caught by the image of Kieran making her cry out as she climaxed.

He scooped her up in his arms and crossed the room. "Did you notice I had the interior design team include a settee? All great artists have settees."

"Is that so people can pose for me?" She lifted her arms obediently as he undressed her with more urgency than care.

"It's so I can screw you," he panted, now working on his own clothing. His gaze was fixated on her chest. "Lie down."

She didn't have to be told twice. It was either that or melt into a puddle on the floor.

He came down between her legs, shifting her left foot to prop it on the back of their makeshift nest. His thumbs traced the folds of her sex, gathering moisture and spreading it on the head of his erection. The shaft was long and hard and throbbing with eagerness.

Kieran groaned, closing his eyes. "I love you, Olivia." Positioning himself at the mother lode, he plunged deep, wringing a cry from her and filling her so completely, she forgot to breathe. He stilled for a moment, allowing both of them to absorb the shattering pleasure.

Inside her, he flexed. She gripped handfuls of his hair as he bent to taste her breasts, one after the other, licking and suckling them until she sensed her first orgasm in the wings.

His hands moved, sliding under her bottom to lift her into his thrusts. She clung to him, dizzy and panting. "Kieran..." She didn't know what she wanted to say, what she needed him to hear.

"I'm here, honey. Always."

The vow... and the swivel of his hips that ground the base of his erection against her sweet spot sent her over the edge. The climax lasted forever, raking her body with shivers of sensation that rode the edge of pain and ecstasy.

Before she had fully recovered, he went rigid, his back arched in a rictus of release that lasted for long, shuddering seconds.

Minutes later, maybe hours, she recovered the ability to speak. "I love this settee," she muttered, licking a drop of sweat from her upper lip. The sun warmed them like a benediction. Kieran's weight was a delicious burden, his shaft still pulsing with aftershocks.

"Hell," he said, his body shaking with laughter. "I didn't wear a condom. I swear, woman. Around you I take leave of my senses."

She stroked his hair, staring up at a sky so blue it seemed to go on forever. Peace, utter and infinite, filled her heart, her mind, her soul. "I'd like to be pregnant again," she whispered, daring to dream of home and hearth with the man she loved.

Wolff Mountain was a wonderful place to grow up. And now that she'd experienced the fear generated by violence and danger, she decided that being tucked away from the world wasn't altogether a bad thing.

Kieran sat up, rubbing his eyes. "I haven't slept at all since you left. This wedding has to be soon. I want you in my bed. Every night."

"I want that, too." She bent down to rescue her bra and blouse. "Annalise strikes me as someone who would love to plan just such an occasion."

"We can set up a large tent…to keep the paparazzi at bay. Unless, of course, your parents don't mind being photographed."

She laughed. "You never know with them. My mother does love keeping count of how many times her face appears on the tabloids. She thinks they're sleazy gossip rags, but she hates being left out."

They managed to dress, but it was a slow process. Kieran kept interrupting her to nibble her rib cage, caress her bottom, bite her earlobe. Finally, completely clothed except for her shoes, she looked at him. "Do you think anyone is home yet?"

He zipped his fly. "Who knows? Why do you ask?"

She cupped him boldly, her fingers squeezing softly as

she found his sex tucked in the front of his jeans. "I'm still not sure I'm not dreaming. Maybe you could take another shot at convincing me."

By the time they ultimately made their way back downstairs, they were eager to share their news. Kieran used his cell phone to convene an audience for afternoon tea, and soon, in the large, formal living room, the entire clan was gathered, including Annalise's brothers and father.

Cammie spotted her mother and ran across the room, throwing herself into Olivia's arms. "You're back. You're back."

Olivia hugged her, feeling uneasy at being the cynosure of all eyes. "I surely am. Have you been a good girl while I was gone?"

"Yes, ma'am."

Victor stood up, his weathered face beaming. "I think some introductions are in order…and perhaps a formal announcement?" He looked inquiringly at his youngest son.

Kieran moved closer, putting his arms around Cammie and Olivia. "Six years ago, Olivia and I met each other at Oxford. But as you all know, we Wolffs attended college under false names. When I left suddenly to come home in the aftermath of Dad's heart attack, Olivia and I lost touch. But she had my baby."

Olivia wondered if she was the only one who noticed the crack in his voice.

He continued, scanning the room, his gaze landing one by one on the faces of the people who had shared tragedy with him in the past. "My traveling days are over," he said quietly. "Olivia has agreed to marry me. My next design project will be our new house here on Wolff Mountain."

The whoops and hollers that erupted rattled the rafters. Cammie and Olivia and Kieran were engulfed in a barrage of hugs and kisses and congratulations. Olivia enjoyed every moment of it. The Wolffs were not a normal family, but they were *her* family…from now on.

She managed to get their attention, and the room quieted. "Thank you all for welcoming me and for being so sweet to Cammie. This will be pretty close to a shotgun wedding as far as the time frame goes, but if Annalise is willing, I'm going to let her handle all the details."

Gracie piped up, eyes dancing. "I'll help, too. It's about time we had some girly stuff going on up on this mountain."

Everyone laughed.

Victor held out a hand, cradling a champagne flute as two young women passed around matching glasses to the crowd. Cammie's was filled with orange juice.

When everyone was served, Victor cleared his throat to quiet the rambunctious assemblage. "To Kieran…and his bride-to-be and daughter. May you always be as happy as you are today."

Glasses were raised and emptied. Kieran leaned down to kiss Cammie and then Olivia. "To my girls," he said softly. "I love you both."

Hours later, when the clock was about to strike midnight, Kieran and Olivia stood beside their daughter's bed. Olivia held his hand, her head on his shoulder. "You missed so much," she said. "I'll never be able to give that back to you."

He was quiet for long moments, his chest barely moving as he breathed. "We all walk our own road, Olivia. Yours and mine diverged at the worst possible time, but we won't ever have to worry about that again. Side by side. Day by day. We're marking a new path that will be ours alone."

"And you *do* want more children?"

He turned to face her. "Give me a dozen," he said, teeth

flashing white in the semidarkness. "We've got room to grow on this mountain. God willing, there will be plenty of cousins, too."

She went up on tiptoe and kissed him. "I knew the first day I saw you that you were the man I wanted to marry."

He scooped her into his arms, carrying her to the adjoining bedroom where half a dozen candles were lit. As he laid her on the bed, coming down beside her, he grimaced. "If I had handled things better back then, we wouldn't have wasted so much time."

She caressed his face, cupping his cheeks, rubbing her thumbs across his bottom lip. "I tried to convince myself that what we had was a fling, a college romance. But deep in my heart, I've always known you were the one. Which made it pretty difficult to go out with other guys."

"I don't want to hear about the other guys," he muttered. "Not now, anyway." He slid a hand along her thigh from her ankle to the place that readied itself for him with damp heat.

She stopped him, trapping his fingers by placing hers on top. "There were none," she said simply. "Only you."

Silence throbbed. His eyes widened, and something that was a combination of astonishment, relief, joy and humble gratitude flashed in their depths. "You're mine, Olivia. I'm yours."

As Kieran positioned himself for a thrust that would take him home, he heard a faint voice…words that faded as the one who spoke them moved into another realm. *I love you, my son. Be happy*….

Unexpected tears stung the backs of his eyes as he filled Olivia's tight passage with a surge of longing and the length of his passion.

He *was* home…and he was happy.

* * * * *

So you think you can write?

Mills & Boon® and Harlequin® have joined forces in a global search for new authors.

It's our biggest contest yet—with the prize of being published by the world's leader in romance fiction.

Look for more information on our website:
www.soyouthinkyoucanwrite.com

So you think you can write?
Show us!

A sneaky peek at next month...

Desire

PASSIONATE AND DRAMATIC LOVE STORIES

2 stories in each book - only £5.49!

My wish list for next month's titles...

In stores from 17th August 2012:

❑ The Temporary Mrs King — Maureen Child

& The Paternity Proposition — Merline Lovelace

❑ A Perfect Husband — Fiona Brand

& A Scandal So Sweet — Ann Major

❑ Relentless Pursuit — Sara Orwig

& Ready for Her Close-up — Katherine Garbera

❑ Unfinished Business — Cat Schield

& The Ties that Bind — Emilie Rose

Available at WHSmith, Tesco, Asda, Eason, Amazon and Apple

Just can't wait?

MILLS & BOON® *Book Club* 2 Free Stories!

Get your free stories now at
www.millsandboon.co.uk/freebookoffer

Or fill in the form below and post it back to us

THE MILLS & BOON® BOOK CLUB™—HERE'S HOW IT WORKS: Accepting your free stories places you under no obligation to buy anything. You may keep the stories and return the despatch note marked 'Cancel'. If we do not hear from you, about a month later we'll send you 2 Desire™ 2-in-1 books priced at £5.49* each. There is no extra charge for post and packaging. You may cancel at any time, otherwise we will send you 4 stories a month which you may purchase or return to us—the choice is yours. *Terms and prices subject to change without notice. Offer valid in UK only. Applicants must be 18 or over. Offer expires 31st January 2013. **For full terms and conditions, please go to www.millsandboon.co.uk/freebookoffer**

Mrs/Miss/Ms/Mr (please circle)

First Name

Surname

Address

Postcode

E-mail

Send this completed page to: Mills & Boon Book Club, Free Book Offer, FREEPOST NAT 10298, Richmond, Surrey, TW9 1BR

Find out more at
www.millsandboon.co.uk/freebookoffer

Visit us Online

0712/D2YEA

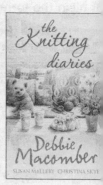

The World of Mills & Boon®

There's a Mills & Boon® series that's perfect for you. We publish ten series and, with new titles every month, you never have to wait long for your favourite to come along.

Blaze.
Scorching hot, sexy reads
4 new stories every month

By Request
Relive the romance with the best of the best
9 new stories every month

Cherish™
Romance to melt the heart every time
12 new stories every month

Desire™
Passionate and dramatic love stories
8 new stories every month